A LIFE *of* JOY

Also by Amy Clipston

A Gift of Grace
A Place of Peace
A Promise of Hope
A Plain and Simple Christmas
Naomi's Gift
Roadside Assistance (young adult)

A LIFE of JOY

Amy Clipston

BOOK FOUR

ZONDERVAN.com/
AUTHORTRACKER
follow your favorite authors

ZONDERVAN

A Life of Joy

This title is also available as a Zondervan ebook.
Visit www.zondervan.com/ebooks.

This title is also available in a Zondervan audio edition.
Visit www.zondervan.fm.

Requests for information should be addressed to:

Zondervan, *Grand Rapids, Michigan 49530*

Library of Congress Cataloging-in-Publication Data

Clipston, Amy.
A life of joy / Amy Clipston.
p. cm.—(Kauffman Amish bakery series ; bk. 4)
ISBN 978-0-310-31996-2 (softcover : alk. paper)
1. Amish—Fiction. 2. Amish Country (Pa.)—Fiction. I. Title.
PS3603.L58L54 2012
813'.6—dc23 2011029927

Cover design: Name goes here
Cover photography or illustration: Name goes here
Interior design: Christine Orejuela-Winkelman

Printed in the United States of America

In loving memory of my grandparents,
Emil and Emilie Goebelbecker

Glossary

Ach—oh
aenti—aunt
appeditlich—delicious
Ausbund—Amish hymnal
bedauerlich—sad
beh—leg
boppli—baby
bopplin—babies
bruder—brother
bruderskinner—nieces/nephews
bu—boy
buwe—boys
daadi—granddad
daed—dad
danki—thank you
dat—dad
Dietsch—Pennsylvania Dutch, the Amish language (a German dialect)
dochder—daughter
dochdern—daughters
Dummle!—hurry!
Englisher—a non-Amish person
fraa—wife
freind—friend
freinden—friends
freindschaft—relative
froh—happy
gegisch—silly
gern gschehne—you're welcome
grandkinner—grandchildren
grank—sick

grossdaddi—grandfather
grossdochdern—granddaughters
grossmammi—grandmother
Gude mariye—Good morning
gut—good
Gut nacht—Good night
haus—house
Ich liebe dich—I love you
Ich hap schmatza—I hurt myself
Kannscht du Pennsilfaanisch Dietsch schwetze—Can you speak Pennsylvania Dutch?
kapp—prayer covering or cap
kind—child
kinner—children
kumm—come
liewe—love, a term of endearment
mammi—grandma
maed—young women, girls
maedel—young woman
mamm—mom
mei—my
mutter—mother
naerfich—nervous
narrisch—crazy
onkel—uncle
Ordnung—the oral tradition of practices required and forbidden in the Amish faith
schee—pretty
schtupp—family room
schweschder—sister
Was iss letz?—What's wrong?
Wie geht's—How do you do? or Good day!
Willkumm heemet—welcome home
wunderbaar—wonderful
ya—yes
zwillingbopplin—twins

Kauffman Amish Bakery Family Trees

(boldface are parents)

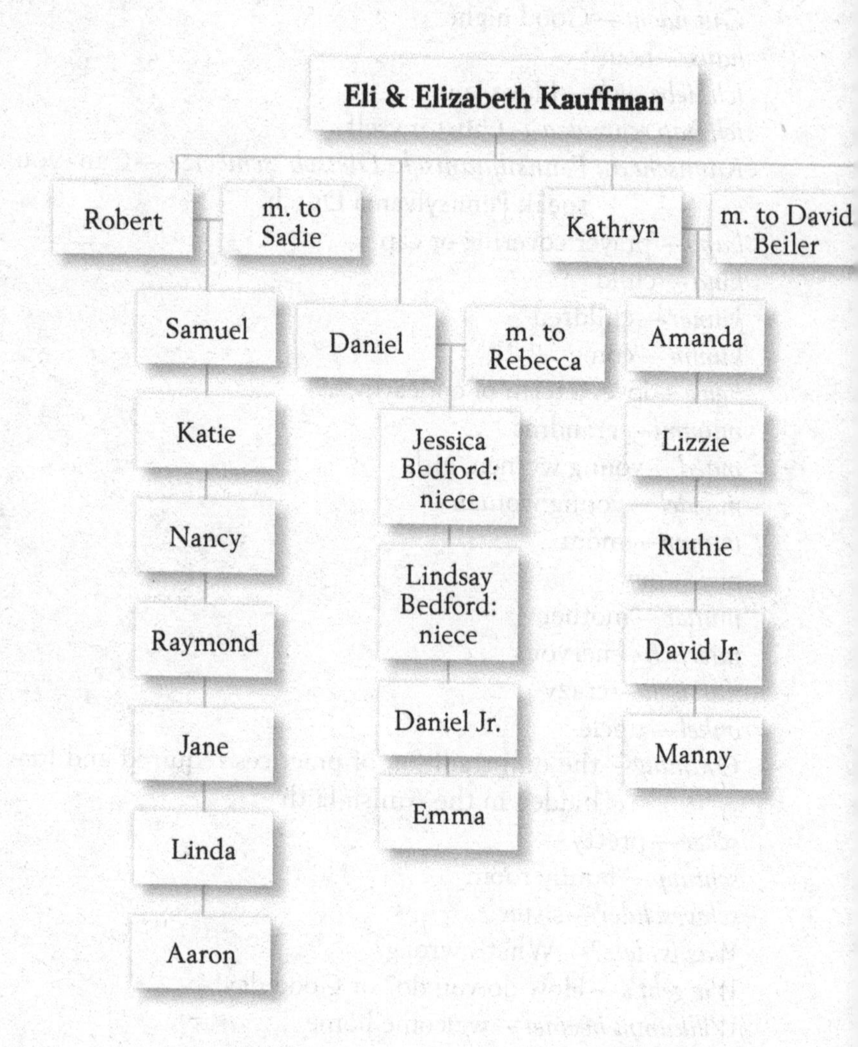

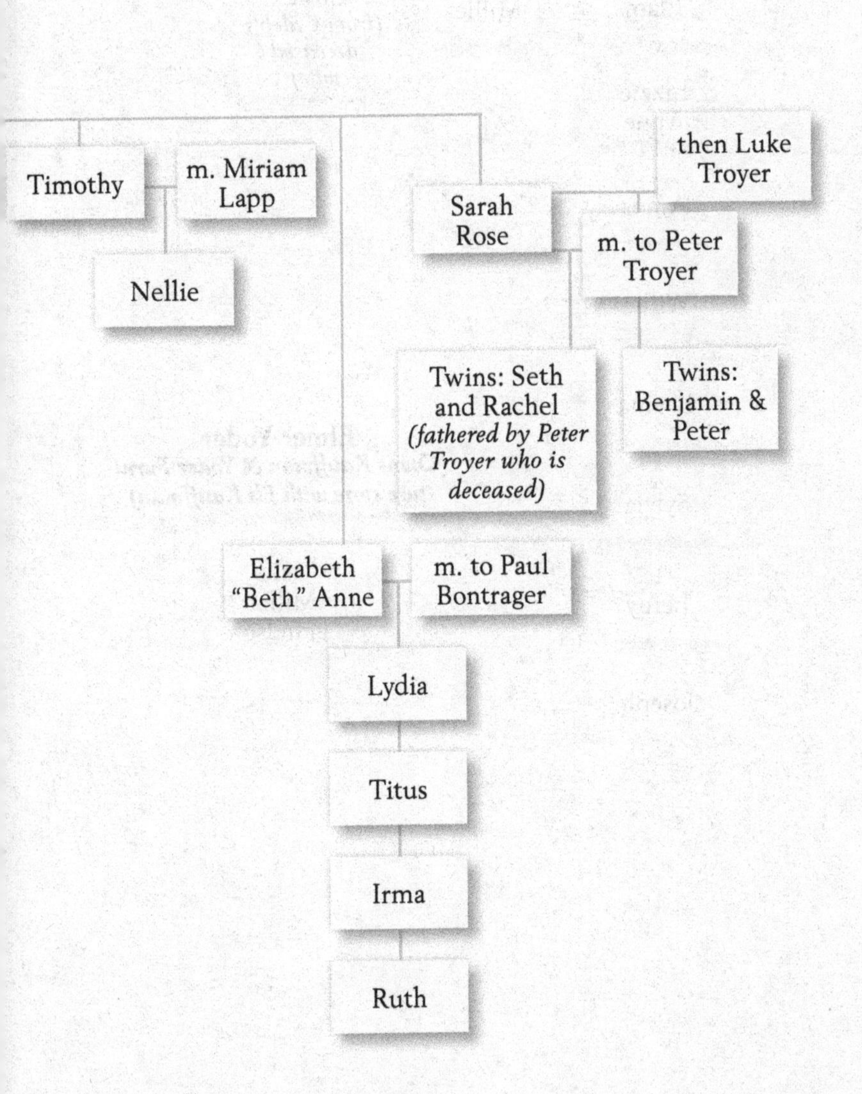
Timothy
m. Miriam Lapp
Nellie
Sarah Rose
then Luke Troyer
m. to Peter Troyer
Twins: Seth and Rachel (fathered by Peter Troyer who is deceased)
Twins: Benjamin & Peter
Elizabeth "Beth" Anne
m. to Paul Bontrager
Lydia
Titus
Irma
Ruth

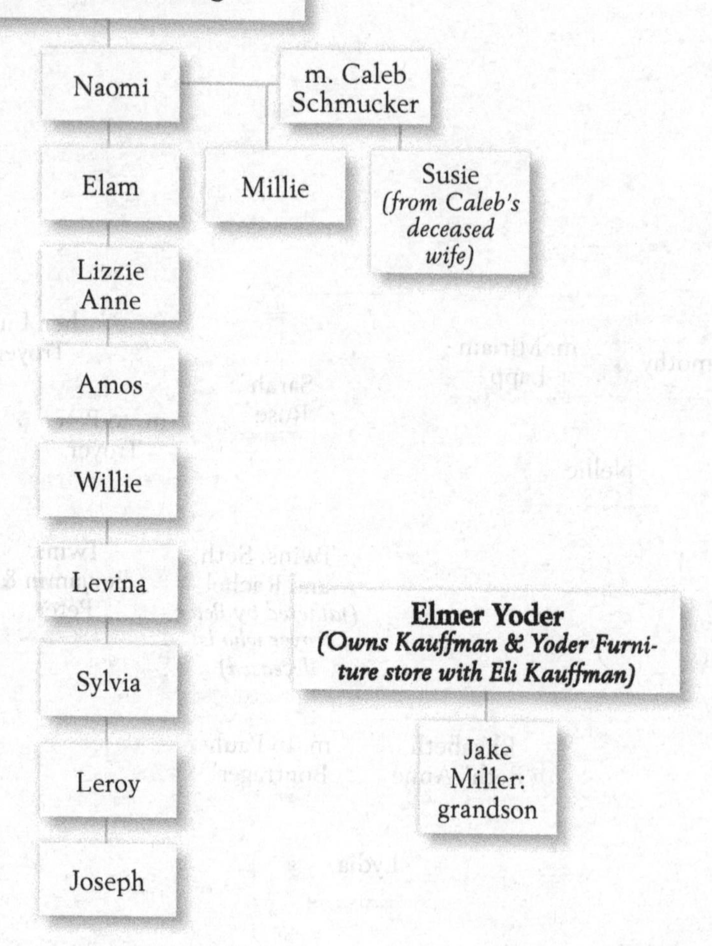
Titus & Irma King
Naomi
m. Caleb Schmucker
Elam
Millie
Susie (from Caleb's deceased wife)
Lizzie Anne
Amos
Willie
Levina
Sylvia
Leroy
Joseph
Elmer Yoder (Owns Kauffman & Yoder Furniture store with Eli Kauffman)
Jake Miller: grandson

Note to the Reader

While this novel is set against the real backdrop of Lancaster County, Pennsylvania, the characters are fictional. There is no intended resemblance between the characters in this book and any real members of the Amish and Mennonite communities. As with any work of fiction, I've taken license in some areas of research as a means of creating the necessary circumstances for my characters. My research was thorough; however, it would be impossible to be completely accurate in details and description, since each and every community differs. Therefore, any inaccuracies in the Amish and Mennonite lifestyles portrayed in this book are completely due to fictional license.

1

Lindsay Bedford smoothed the skirt of her purple frock as she sat on a hill with her best friends, Katie Kauffman and Lizzie Anne King. The gentle breeze blew back the ribbons of her prayer covering, and she watched a group of boys play volleyball in the pasture below them.

"It's hard to believe summer is almost here." Katie opened a folded napkin in her lap revealing a pile of chocolate chip cookies and handed a cookie to both Lizzie Anne and Lindsay.

"*Danki,*" Lizzie Anne said. "*Ya,* it's nice and warm today. I love May. Such a *schee* time of year."

"The bakery is already busy," Lindsay said, breaking the cookie in half. "The tourists are already descending on Lancaster County." She glanced at Katie. "Are you planning to work at the bakery during the summer?"

Katie grinned while lifting a cookie. "*Ya*. *Mammi* Elizabeth asked me just the other day, and my *mamm* gave me permission."

Lindsay squealed and squeezed Katie's hand with excitement. "We'll have so much fun! I've learned so much that I'm baking by myself now. I can't wait to show you. I made the best shoofly pie the other day that *Aenti* Kathryn said—" She stopped speaking when she spotted Lizzie Anne's frown out of the corner of her eye. She turned to her friend and touched her arm. "I'm sorry. I didn't mean to make you feel left out. I didn't mean to hurt your feelings."

Lizzie Anne shrugged and forced a smile. "It's okay. My sister Naomi asked me to work for her this summer. Millie is a handful, and she's expecting another *boppli* next year. I'll help her around the house and also do some quilting with Susie. I can't believe it's been more than one year since Naomi and Caleb were married. It seems like only yesterday that my sister met Caleb when he and Susie came to visit for Christmas."

"I'm certain we'll see each other plenty," Lindsay insisted, looking toward the volleyball game. "After all, we have plenty of youth functions coming up and we have our church services every other Sunday."

"And classes start in a few weeks," Katie chimed in.

"Classes?" Lindsay asked before biting into the cookie.

Katie laughed. "Don't be *gegisch,* Lindsay." She nudged Lindsay with her shoulder. "Instruction for baptism." Her smile faded into a concerned frown. "Aren't you going to come to class? I thought we would be baptized together."

"Oh," Lindsay said, her cheeks burning with embarrassment. She knew that this issue would come up at some point, but she hadn't realized it would be this soon.

"You're not going to be baptized this year?" Lizzie Anne asked.

Lindsay shrugged. "I didn't say that. I just didn't realize that the classes were starting so soon."

"You know that if you don't take classes with us this year," Lizzie Anne continued, "then you'll have to take classes and be baptized in another church district next year."

"I know," Lindsay whispered. She glanced toward the volleyball game in order to avoid their concerned stares. Her eyes fell on her friend Matthew Glick, a handsome young man who worked in the Kauffman & Yoder Amish Furniture store with her uncle, Daniel Kauffman. While Matthew served the volleyball to the opposing team with a powerful bump of the ball, Lindsay contemplated Lizzie Anne's and Katie's words.

In Lindsay's church district, baptisms were performed once every other year before the fall communion service in order to allow the newly baptized to commune with the rest of the church members. Communion was held twice per year—in October and April—as a special daylong service.

Most Amish youth were baptized between the ages of sixteen and twenty-one; although, sometimes community members chose to experience the English world before joining. The ministers held the instruction sessions during the first thirty minutes of church services over the summer months while the rest of the church members sang hymns. The ministers and bishop reviewed the eighteen articles of the *Dordrecht Confession of Faith* and emphasized aspects of the *Ordnung*.

Once Lindsay turned eighteen, there was more of an expectation for her to be baptized into the Amish community. However, she'd lived in the English world before coming to live with her Amish aunt four years ago. Although the Amish world felt like the right fit for her, something deep down in her heart was holding her back from making that final commitment.

"Lindsay?" Lizzie Anne asked, pulling Lindsay back to the present. "*Was iss letz?*"

"I know what's wrong with her," Katie said with a snicker. "She's staring at Matthew again."

Her friends giggled, and Lindsay rolled her eyes in response. "Stop it," she muttered. "Matthew is a friend."

"I've seen the way he looks at you," Katie said with a knowing smile. "He likes you."

"Please." Lindsay shook her head while looking at him. "We talk sometimes when I go to the furniture store or if he comes by the *haus* to see *Onkel* Daniel. And that's it—we're just friends."

Lindsay fiddled with the hem of her dress and grew serious. "How do you know you're ready to join the church?"

Katie shrugged. "I just am. My *mamm* was my age when she joined, so it just feels right."

"What about you, Lizzie Anne?" Lindsay asked. "How do you know you're ready?"

Lizzie Anne put her hand to her chest. "I can feel it in my heart. It's like God is telling me it's time."

Lindsay considered Lizzie Anne's words. She'd prayed about her faith nearly every night since coming to live with Rebecca and Daniel, and she thought God had wanted her to stay with the Amish. However, now her mind was assaulted with doubt, even though she had the opportunity to be baptized and join the church with the young members of her church district. She knew that once she joined the church, it was final and there was no going back to being a non-member. Her future as a member of the Amish community was sealed, and if she left, she'd be shunned.

"Matthew's a member of the church," Lizzie Anne said with a grin. "If you want to date him, then you need to join the church."

Lindsay glowered. "That's not a reason to become a member of the church, Lizzie Anne."

"I know," Lizzie Anne said. "I just meant that it was a ... perk for joining."

Lindsay shook her head and tossed a cookie crumb at Lizzie Anne while her friends laughed. "You two are *gegisch*."

As she joined in their laughter, Lindsay glanced back toward the volleyball game. Matthew met her gaze and waved, and her cheeks warmed as she returned the greeting. After turning to say something to Katie's older brother, Samuel, Matthew served the ball with a mixture of grace and masculine athletic ability while his dark brown curls danced in the warm spring breeze. While studying him, Lindsay wondered how Matthew knew when he was ready to be baptized.

Later that evening, Lindsay stood in the doorway of her little cousin Emma's room while her aunt Rebecca hugged Emma and said good night.

Lindsay smiled, and her thoughts turned to when she'd found out that Rebecca was going to have her second baby. The news was a miracle since Rebecca, who'd waited years to have a child, was blessed with two children in less than two years. Although Lindsay didn't know much about pregnancies, she'd learned from Elizabeth Kauffman, Rebecca's mother-in-law, that babies were always a blessing, especially when a woman was past the age of thirty-five.

Watching her aunt and cousin, Lindsay absently wondered if this was the future she was meant to have—a simple life with a family in Lancaster County. Did Lindsay want to join the church, marry an Amish man, and raise children in the faith?

Emma giggled, and Lindsay turned her attention back to her cousin.

After kissing Emma, Rebecca crossed to the doorway. "I believe she wants to say good night to you. I'll go check on Junior." She patted Lindsay's shoulder on her way to the bedroom across the hallway.

Lindsay stepped over to the crib and smiled down on her little cousin. At eighteen months of age, Emma had big brown eyes, rosy cheeks, and a smattering of light brown curls on her little head.

"*Gut nacht, mei liewe,*" Lindsay whispered. "*Ich liebe dich.*" She kissed Emma's cheek.

Emma smiled, and Lindsay's heart warmed.

Stepping out of the room, she gently closed Emma's door behind her before stepping into Daniel Junior's room, where she found her three-year-old cousin sitting up in his bed and smiling. While his younger sister had dark hair and eyes like

Rebecca's family, Junior had blond hair and blue eyes, resembling the Kauffman side.

Lindsay sat on the edge of the bed and touched his cheek. "*Gut nacht,*" she said. "I'll see you in the morning," she told him in Pennsylvania *Dietsch*.

"*Ich liebe dich,* Lindsay," he said.

"*Ich liebe dich,*" she echoed before kissing his head.

After tucking him in, Lindsay made her way down the stairs to the kitchen. Rebecca was sitting at the table, yawning and flipping through a cookbook.

Lindsay opened the refrigerator door and pulled out a pitcher of meadow tea. She loved to have the spearmint-flavored drink. "Would you like a drink?"

"*Ya, danki,*" Rebecca said, yawning again. "Excuse me. I can't stop yawning lately. I don't know what's wrong with me."

"I hope you're not getting *grank*." Lindsay poured two glasses before returning the pitcher to the refrigerator.

"I don't think it's that." Rebecca cupped her hand over her mouth to stifle another yawn. "I may go to bed early tonight."

Lindsay put a glass in front of Rebecca and then sat across from her. "That may be a *gut* idea." She took a sip of the tea and then pointed toward the cookbook. "What were you looking up?"

Rebecca took a drink and then placed her glass on the table. "I was trying to decide what to make for supper tomorrow night, but nothing appeals to me." She yawned again and took another drink of tea.

Lindsay studied her glass while the conversation she had with her friends earlier in the day rained down on her.

"What's on your mind, Lindsay?" Rebecca asked gently. "You look as if you're pondering something important."

Lindsay met her aunt's concerned stare. "Lizzie Anne and Katie told me that they're starting instruction for baptism in a few weeks."

"Oh?" Rebecca asked.

"They asked me if I was going to be in the class." Lindsay ran her finger across the cool wooden table.

"What did you tell them?"

Lindsay shrugged. "I didn't know what to tell them. The three of us had said that we would take the class and be baptized together. I sort of made a promise, but now I don't know if I can keep that promise."

Rebecca leaned forward, her eyes sympathetic. "Lindsay, do you want to join the church?"

"I don't know. I used to be so certain that I wanted to. But now I don't know." Lindsay shook her head. "I'm so confused."

"If you feel confused, then it isn't time," Rebecca said, reaching over and touching Lindsay's arm. "You'll know when you're ready."

"How did you know you were ready to join the church?"

Rebecca rubbed her chin. "I think I just knew in my heart that it was right for me."

"But my mom didn't ever feel that way, did she?" Lindsay asked.

Rebecca nodded. "She joined the church because our *daed* pressured her to, but she always knew that she longed for a different life. She wanted to go to college, and she felt as if she belonged in the English world instead of here."

"Like Jessica," Lindsay whispered.

"Yes and no," Rebecca said, folding her hands together on the table. "It was a little more complicated since we grew up here and our parents were raised in this community as well. Jessica has only ever known the English world. She's driven and determined to get her education, and there's nothing wrong with that. If you want more than this life, Lindsay, you're entitled to live it. Don't feel like you have to stay here."

The sadness in Rebecca's eyes betrayed her words.

Lindsay cleared her throat against the lump threatening to steal her voice.

"I know you'll make the right decision for you," Rebecca said, taking Lindsay's hands in hers. "God will lead you if you ask for His guidance."

Meeting her aunt's warm gaze, Lindsay's lip quivered. "I think I'm going to get ready for bed."

"*Gut nacht, mei liewe,*" Rebecca said. "Don't let this burden you. Let the answer come from God."

"*Ya. Gut nacht,*" Lindsay answered. She stepped into the doorway leading to the family room and spotted her uncle in his favorite easy chair reading his Bible. She leaned on the doorway. "*Gut nacht, Onkel* Daniel," she called.

Glancing up, he smiled. "See you in the morning, Lindsay."

Lindsay climbed the stairs and walked softly to her room at the end of the hall. While she undressed, she contemplated how much her life had changed during the past four years. Lindsay and Jessica had come to Bird-in-Hand, Pennsylvania, after their parents were killed in a car accident.

When Lindsay and her older sister first arrived, they both felt as if they'd entered another world, or perhaps another century, since Rebecca, Daniel, and the rest of the community lived simple, plain lives without modern clothes, television, electricity, or other up-to-date conveniences that Lindsay had taken for granted.

Lindsay had embraced life in the Bird-in-Hand community, quickly becoming a member of the Kauffman family. By contrast, Jessica protested and fought against the changes until she was permitted to move back to Virginia and live with their parents' friends, Frank and Trisha McCabe.

Lindsay stepped into the bathroom and climbed into the shower while she thought about her sister. Jessica was Lindsay's polar opposite, beginning with their appearances. Jessica had dark hair and eyes, and Lindsay had deep red hair and bright green eyes. Jessica had finished high school, graduating with honors, and then moved on to college, but Lindsay kept with

Amish tradition and didn't continue her education beyond eighth grade. Instead, she began working in the Kauffman Amish Bakery, owned by Elizabeth Kauffman, with Rebecca and her sisters-in-law.

Standing under the showerhead, Lindsay allowed the warm flowing water to rinse her wavy, long hair that fell to to the middle of her back. Suddenly a thought struck her: Although she loved living in Bird-in-Hand, she felt as if she were at a crossroads—she had to decide between her former English life and her new Amish life for good.

As she finished her shower, the same question echoed in her mind over and over again: Should she join the church with her friends this fall or should she wait and make sure this was the life God wanted her to live?

Closing her eyes, she held her breath and sent a fervent prayer for guidance up to God.

Rebecca crossed the family room and sank onto the sofa across from Daniel's chair. She smiled as she watched him read. In their twenty years of marriage, they'd faced many obstacles together, from seventeen years of infertility to the challenges of bringing her nieces to live with them. Yet, despite their ups and downs, she still cherished him now as much as she did the day they'd married.

He glanced up, his deep blue eyes meeting her stare. "How long have you been sitting there, Becky?"

"Just a few moments." She folded her hands in the lap of her plain blue frock. "I was wondering if we could talk for a minute before I head up to bed."

He closed his Bible and set it on the end table next to his chair. "Of course. What's on your mind?"

She yawned and covered her mouth with her hand. "Excuse me," she said. "I've been yawning nearly nonstop all day."

He tilted his head and studied her with concern. "Are you feeling well?"

"*Ya.*" She shrugged. "I guess I just need to go to bed earlier." She pushed the ties of her prayer covering back from her shoulders while she gathered her thoughts. "Lindsay told me that Katie and Lizzie Anne are beginning instruction classes soon."

Daniel nodded. "Robert mentioned to me that Katie and Nancy were going to be in the new class, along with a few of our other nieces and nephews. It may be a big class this year."

"I think Lindsay is considering taking the class, but she feels torn about making a final commitment to the Amish church."

"That's not something you can decide for her, Rebecca," he said with a gentle smile. "I know you want to be the best *mamm* you can for her in honor of your sister, but you have to let her think for herself. She's eighteen now."

"I know, but she seems very anxious about it, Daniel. I think it's eating her up inside."

He touched his beard, a mannerism he often practiced when he was deep in thought. "The decision to be baptized is a decision that is made between the candidate and God. You need to trust her to listen to her heart and to God."

Rebecca breathed out a deep sigh while she idly studied the clock on the wall. "I can't imagine losing her," she finally said. "I want her to decide to stay here permanently, but I know that's not my place."

"She's a very intuitive and special girl, but you have to remember that she lived among the English before she came here," he said. "Joining the church may not be what's right for her." He stood and took her hand, lifting her to her feet. "You look exhausted, Becky. I think you should head to bed."

"You're probably right," she said, squeezing his hand.

As he led her to the stairs, Rebecca sent up a silent prayer asking God to point Lindsay to a path that would lead to her happiness, preferably in Lancaster County.

2

"Have a *gut* day," Lindsay called to her uncle Daniel before hopping from the van and heading through the parking lot toward the front steps of the Kauffman Amish Bakery the next morning.

Daniel paid a driver to take him and Lindsay to work instead of using the horse and buggy. Every morning, the driver took Lindsay to the bakery before heading to the Kauffman & Yoder Amish Furniture store, where Daniel worked alongside his father, brother, brother-in-law, and friends.

While crossing the parking lot, Lindsay glanced toward the farm where a cluster of large houses sat back off the road surrounded by four barns, along with a beautiful lush, green pasture.

This area had become her home during the past four years. The property was owned by Elizabeth and Eli Kauffman, Daniel's parents. Daniel's younger brother, Timothy, and his wife, Miriam, lived in one of the houses. Nearby was the home Daniel's sister, Sarah Rose, shared with her husband, Luke, and their two sets of twins. The bakery was the fourth house, the one closest to the road. Daniel and his five siblings grew up in the biggest house, where his parents still lived.

Lindsay quickened her steps while approaching the white clapboard farmhouse with the sweeping wraparound porch.

Although it resembled a farmhouse, the building had served as the bakery for longer than Lindsay had been alive. A large sign with "Kauffman Amish Bakery" in old-fashioned letters hung above the door. Soon after the "Open" sign was turned over in the front window, the parking lot would be overflowing with cars as tourists came to sample a taste of the Amish way of life.

Out behind the building was a fenced-in play area, where Elizabeth Kauffman's grandchildren played during the day, and beyond that was an enclosed pasture. The three other large farmhouses and four barns were set back behind the pasture. The dirt road leading to the other homes was roped off with a sign declaring "Private Property—No Trespassing." A large paved parking lot sat adjacent to the bakery.

Lindsay cupped a hand to her mouth to curb a yawn. She'd spent most of the night praying—debating if she belonged in the Amish or English world and wishing her mother were alive to guide her. Of course, if her parents were alive, Lindsay would still be living in Virginia and finishing up her senior year in high school.

Pushing those thoughts away, Lindsay stepped through the back door of the bakery and inhaled the sweet smell of baking bread. A smile turned up her lips as she breathed in the aroma that had become so familiar and comforting since she began working in the bakery four years ago.

Elizabeth, her daughters Beth Anne and Kathryn, and Kathryn's daughters Amanda and Ruthie rushed around the kitchen preparing desserts for the day.

"*Gude mariye*, Lindsay! *Wie geht's?*" Beth Anne called while washing cookie sheets.

"Doing okay, *danki*." Lindsay stood at the sink and scrubbed her hands. "What should I start on?"

"Whoopie pies," Kathryn chimed in, stepping over to the sink with a smile. "They sold out, so we need some singles and some boxes of them. It's *gut* to see you." Her eyes turned suspicious. "You look tired. Did you sleep well last night?"

"*Ya*. I slept fine. *Danki*." Avoiding Kathryn's concerned stare, Lindsay greeted Ruthie and Amanda while gathering the ingredients and cooking supplies.

Lindsay fell deep into thought while she mixed together the ingredients for the cake shell that would encase the white filling.

Elizabeth placed a cake in the oven and then approached Lindsay. "You're awfully quiet this morning," she said, wiping her hands on her apron. "Is everything all right?"

"*Ya*. Everything is *gut*." Lindsay smiled at the Kauffman family matriarch. She loved Elizabeth like a surrogate grandmother and cherished the long talks they'd shared since she came to live with her aunt Rebecca.

Elizabeth gave a look of disbelief that mirrored Kathryn's expression earlier. "I know you like I know my other *grossdochdern*." She touched Lindsay's hand. "You know you can tell me anything, *ya*?"

Lindsay nodded. "*Ya*."

"If something is bothering you and you need to confide in someone, I'm happy to listen."

Lindsay glanced across the kitchen to where Amanda and Ruthie stood cutting out sugar cookies. She knew they would also take the baptism classes with their cousins, Katie and Nancy. Although Lindsay liked Amanda and Ruthie very much, she didn't want them to know that she was debating whether or not she'd join their class.

With a knowing smile, Elizabeth gestured toward the front door. "How about we take a walk out to the porch? We have a little over an hour before customers will begin arriving."

"Okay." Lindsay wiped her hands on a towel and then followed Elizabeth.

The two long counters would soon be filled with desserts

ready for sale. Beyond the counter was a sea of Lancaster County souvenirs, including carousel racks filled with books, maps, postcards, magnets, keychains, collectible spoons, and note cards. Shelves nearby overflowed with T-shirts, sweatshirts, hats, dolls, framed art, and figurines.

A cash register sat in the middle of the room, and the women would take turns operating it throughout the day, along with baking and caring for the younger Kauffman children.

Elizabeth and Lindsay stepped out onto the porch and sat at one of the little tables.

"*Was iss letz, mei liewe?*" Elizabeth asked with a warm smile.

Lindsay ran her finger over the cool aluminum table. "I'm confused about some things."

"I'd love to try to help lighten the load for you, Lindsay."

Sighing, Lindsay looked up. "Six months ago, I knew what I wanted. I was certain in my heart and in my mind that I belonged here. Now I'm not so sure."

Elizabeth raised her eyebrows. "I'm sorry, but I'm not sure what you mean. Are you leaving us?"

"No, no," Lindsay said quickly. "I'm not leaving. This is my home."

"Then why do you feel pressured to make a decision about your future?"

Lindsay nodded toward the door as if gesturing to Ruthie and Amanda. "The baptism class is beginning in a few weeks. I was certain a month ago that I wanted to be in it, but now I have doubts."

Elizabeth's warm smile was back. "No one is pressuring you, *mei liewe*. Everyone decides whether or not to join on his or her own time. In fact, if you're never absolutely certain, you don't have to join and, quite frankly, you shouldn't join. Whether or not you're baptized into the faith, you're still a part of our family, and we'll always love you."

"*Danki*." Overwhelmed by the sentiment of Elizabeth's

words, Lindsay's lip quivered and her eyes filled with tears. "How do I know where I belong? Jessica is so sure that she's supposed to be English, and she tells me all the time that I am too. I don't think I'm supposed to be English, but I also don't know if I'm really Amish either. When was the last time you saw a redhead with green eyes wearing a prayer *kapp*?"

Elizabeth chuckled while taking Lindsay's hands into hers. "Listen to God with your heart, and He will give you the answer. And I once saw a beautiful Amish girl with bright red hair and blue eyes in Ohio. We Amish are more diverse than you think."

"There are two of us redheads, *ya*?" Lindsay smiled and swiped the tears from her warm cheeks with the back of her hand. "I was up nearly all night trying to figure this out. I prayed until I ran out of words, and I'm just as confused this morning as I was last night, if not more so."

"You don't need to figure this out today, Lindsay. Nor do you need to decide tomorrow. Give yourself some time. You're only eighteen."

"But Katie and Lizzie Anne are very disappointed in me." Lindsay shook her head. "They can't understand why I'm not certain if I'm ready to take baptism class. Yesterday they asked me why I changed my mind, and I couldn't give them an answer."

Elizabeth patted Lindsay's arm. "You don't have to tell them anything. They won't judge you because the Bible tells us not to judge one another. Just say that you think you need to wait until the next class, and leave it at that. Did you tell Rebecca how you feel?"

Lindsay nodded.

"And she was supportive, *ya*?"

"She was."

"This decision is not one to be taken lightly," Elizabeth began, "and it doesn't need to be rushed. You'll know when and if the time is right for you to join the church. God will tell you loud and clear, so don't feel pressured to do it now simply because your friends are." She stood and motioned toward the door. "We best finish our baking. If last week is any indication of how this week is going to go, then we'll have empty counters before noon."

"Would it be okay if I sat out here for a few minutes?" Lindsay asked.

"Of course." Elizabeth touched Lindsay's shoulder. "Take all the time you need, but don't forget about those whoopie pies."

"*Danki*, Elizabeth." Lindsay watched Elizabeth slip back into the bakery and then turned toward the parking lot. Closing her eyes, she prayed for a clear head and strength, and then she stood and hurried toward the bakery to begin her day.

Later that evening, Lindsay set the last clean dish in the drying rack on the counter and then gazed out the kitchen window and spotted a horse and buggy clip-clopping up the long driveway toward the barn.

Giggles erupted from the bathroom where Rebecca bathed Daniel Jr. and Emma.

"*Aenti* Rebecca," Lindsay called. "Are you expecting company?"

"Not that I know of," Rebecca called over another chorus of giggles. "Is someone here?"

"*Ya*," Lindsay said, drying her hands on a towel. "A buggy just pulled up by the barn. I'm going to go see who it is."

She placed the towel on the counter and then made her way through the back door to the porch. Glancing toward the barn, she spotted Matthew Glick and Samuel Kauffman emerging from the buggy. Her hands immediately flew to her head, and she absently touched her prayer covering, making sure it was on straight.

She then silently chastised herself for worrying about her appearance. After all, Matthew was only a friend. Although he'd worked at the Kauffman & Yoder Furniture Store for the past two years and attended church in her district, Lindsay had never spoken to him for longer than a few minutes. He seemed very shy and standoffish, making conversation with him challenging at times.

Daniel emerged from the barn and shook hands with the young men. While Samuel followed his uncle into the barn, Matthew looked toward the house and a smile turned up the corners of his mouth as he waved to Lindsay.

Her heart fluttered as she waved back. "Hi."

"*Wie geht's*?" He sauntered over to the porch and rested his right foot on the bottom step.

"I'm doing fine, *danki*." She fingered the ribbons on her prayer covering. "What brings you and Samuel out here so late?"

He gestured toward the barn. "I'd stopped over to say hello to Sam earlier. He mentioned that his *dat* asked him to run over here and see if he could borrow a few tools from Daniel. So I offered to ride with him."

For a split second, Lindsay wondered if Matthew had wanted to ride over to see her, but she quickly dismissed that notion and motioned toward the porch swing. "Would you like to have a seat? I mixed some fresh tea earlier."

"That sounds *wunderbaar*." His smile was wide, and his golden brown eyes sparkled.

"Have a seat and I'll be right back." Lindsay rushed into the kitchen and gathered up a tray, a pitcher of tea, and a few glasses.

She was placing a plate of whoopie pies on the tray when Rebecca came to the doorway of the family room with Emma in her arms, her little face split with a wide grin. Daniel Junior stood beside his mother with his thumb in his mouth.

Rebecca's expression was curious. "What are you doing?"

"Samuel and Matthew stopped by," Lindsay said, wishing her cheeks would cool down. "Sam's in the barn talking to *Onkel* Daniel, but Matthew is sitting on the porch. I thought I'd bring him a snack."

Her aunt grinned, and Lindsay's cheeks burned hotter.

"Tell him I said hello," Rebecca said as she started toward the stairs. "I'm going to take the *kinner* upstairs and read their bedtime stories."

Lindsay kissed her cousins good night and then returned to the porch, balancing the tray in her hands.

"Oh," Matthew said, jumping up from the swing. "Let me help you with that."

"*Danki*," she said as he took the tray and placed it on the small table next to the swing.

He rubbed his hands together. "My favorite."

"What's that?" she asked, pouring the glasses of tea.

"Whoopie pies." He lifted one from the plate. "My *mamm* made the best whoopie pies I'd ever tasted before she got *grank*." He bit into the whoopie pie and groaned. "These are *appeditlich*. Just as *gut* if not better than hers."

Lindsay couldn't suppress the grin that overtook her lips. "*Ya?*"

"Mmmhmm." He continued to chew. "I don't think she even used a recipe. She seemed to make them from memory."

Lindsay lifted a glass of tea and contemplated his words. She knew that Matthew and his mother had moved to Bird-in-Hand to live with his sister so that his sister could help him nurse their mother during her last days. His mother had passed away last year. Although Lindsay had attended his mother's funeral, Matthew had never mentioned his mother to Lindsay until that moment. She hoped that this conversation was a bridge into a closer friendship. A strange excitement surged through her at the thought.

"I'm sorry that you lost your *mamm*. How are you doing?" she said. "I'm certain that was a rough time."

"It was, but I know you're experienced with that loss." He snatched a second whoopie pie. "Are you going to have one?"

She shook her head. "No, I sampled them earlier to make sure they were edible."

"Did you make these?"

She nodded, and he looked impressed.

"You're a talented baker," he said before biting into the second whoopie pie.

She shrugged and sipped her tea. "I learned all I know from Elizabeth Kauffman and the rest of the bakers at work."

He finished the whoopie pie and reached for a third.

"I'll have to remember that these are your favorite," she said. "You're going to finish the plate before Daniel and Samuel come out of the barn."

He frowned. "I have to share?"

She laughed. "No, I guess you don't. Just be certain you finish them all and sweep the crumbs onto the ground before they see."

"These are too *gut* to share anyway." He bit into the little cake.

"Rebecca told me to tell you hello. She's putting the *kinner* to bed." She gripped her glass in her hands and glanced across the pasture toward the setting sun.

"How are the *kinner*?" he asked.

"Doing well. How's your sister's family?"

"Fine." He lifted the glass of tea she'd poured for him. "Daniel mentioned today that the bakery has been very busy."

Lindsay snorted softly. "Busy is an understatement. It's as though we fill the counter with desserts to sell and it's immediately empty. We can't seem to bake fast enough. Elizabeth is talking about trying to find more bakers since we're so shorthanded. Rebecca, Miriam, and Sarah Rose are busy with their little ones, and they won't return until their *kinner* are older. We may need to train a few more of the Kauffman granddaughters." She decided to take a bite after all and snatched a whoopie pie from the plate before breaking it in half. "How is the furniture store?"

"It's steady. I have a few projects in my stall." He turned toward her. "I heard a baptism class is starting up in a few weeks."

She pursed her lips before responding to his statement. "I heard that too."

"Sam mentioned his sisters Katie and Nancy would be in that class," he continued. "He also thought his cousins Amanda and Ruthie would attend it."

Lindsay bit into half of the whoopie pie while studying the open barn door. She wanted to tell him that she wasn't sure if she belonged in the church or even if she belonged in the community, but worry stole her words. She didn't want to risk losing his friendship or his respect by sharing her self-doubt.

"The weather's nice tonight," he suddenly said. "There's a pleasant breeze in the air."

"Matthew, how did you know you were ready to join the church?" The question burst from her lips before she could stop the words from forming.

He shrugged. "I just knew."

She looked down at the half-eaten cookie in her hands. "You had no doubts at all?"

"Not really." He paused for a moment. "I guess part of it was that I wanted to prove I wasn't like my father."

She studied his handsome face. "What do you mean?"

His lips formed a thin line. "My father abandoned my mother and me when I was ten."

Lindsay gasped. "I had no idea," she whispered.

"He told her that the Amish life wasn't enough for him, and he wanted more." Matthew frowned, shaking his head. "He broke my mother's heart, and she never fully recovered. If it weren't for the generosity of her brothers, we wouldn't have made it financially. I saw what my mother went through, and I didn't want to let her down like he did. My sister joined the church when she was eighteen, and I followed in her footsteps when I was sixteen. I wanted to show my mother that I could keep my promises to her and to God."

Fascinated by his loyalty and faith, Lindsay nodded. "That makes sense."

He raised an eyebrow. "You have doubts?"

"*Ya*," she said. "I thought I was ready, but something is holding me back. That's why I won't be in the class. I'm just not certain I'm ready to join the church, if I join at all." She hoped Matthew would still consider her a friend despite her uncertainty about her place in the Amish community.

His expression was full of sympathy. "There's no need to feel rushed to join the church. Not everyone is ready at the same time. It's a lifetime commitment."

"I know." She turned back toward the barn. "I wish I was surer of myself." Her voice was a trembling whisper.

"God understands," Matthew said.

Samuel and Daniel emerged from the barn, and Lindsay wished she had more time alone with Matthew.

"If I stick these whoopie pies in my pocket, I won't have to share them," he said.

Lindsay wagged a finger at him. "Lying is a sin."

His grin was wide. "I'm not lying if I say that the whoopie pies are gone from the plate." He turned toward Samuel and Daniel, who were loading tools into the back of the buggy. "You get what you needed, Sam?"

"*Ya*," Samuel said, closing the back of the buggy. "Don't worry about getting up and helping. Daniel and I got it all loaded. You just continue to sit there and flirt with my cousin."

Lindsay's cheeks flamed and she studied her half-full glass of tea to avoid their eyes.

"She and I were having a very serious conversation about whoopie pies," Matthew said. "Right, Lindsay?"

Samuel gave a bark of laughter. "Is that what you call it?"

Clearing her throat, Lindsay stood and placed the glasses on the tray. "It was nice visiting with you, Matthew." As she stepped toward the door, she glanced at Samuel. "Have a *gut* night, Samuel. Tell Katie I said hello."

Lindsay balanced the tray in one hand while pushing the door open with the other. As she stepped through the doorway, Matthew called her name. She turned and found him standing close behind her.

"I'll see you soon," he said, his eyes intense.

"*Ya*," she said.

"*Gut nacht*," he said before loping down the porch steps toward Daniel and Samuel.

Lindsay placed the tray on the counter, put the pitcher into the refrigerator, and thought about Matthew. She remembered meeting him for the first time two years ago when Jake Miller, another carpenter at the furniture store, brought Matthew to a Kauffman Saturday night gathering. Back then, Matthew had hardly spoken a word and rarely smiled.

However, lately, he'd seemed to speak to Lindsay and smile more often. And tonight, he'd opened up to her and spoken about his parents for the first time.

What does this change in Matthew's demeanor mean?

"Did you have a nice time visiting?" Rebecca asked.

Startled, Lindsay jumped and placed her hand on her chest. She faced the kitchen table where Rebecca was sitting with a notepad and pencil in front of her.

"You scared me," Lindsay said as she sat across from her aunt.

"I'm sorry." Rebecca smiled. "I thought you saw me sitting here. Did you have a nice time?"

"*Ya*. I found out Matthew's a big fan of whoopie pies."

Rebecca chuckled. "That's *gut* to know."

"What are you doing?" Lindsay gestured toward the notepad.

"Making a list of things I need to do tomorrow." Rebecca

cupped her hand to shield a yawn. "I'm so exhausted that I didn't finish my list from today."

When her aunt yawned again, Lindsay studied her. Rebecca looked beyond exhausted; she seemed almost ill with her pale complexion and dark circles under her eyes.

"Are you okay?" Lindsay asked, worry gripping her. "Do you need to see a doctor?"

Rebecca waved off the question and gave a forced smile. "I'm just fine. I guess *mei kinner* are wearing me out."

"I should stay home from the bakery tomorrow. You need help around here."

Rebecca shook her head. "Don't be *gegisch*. You love the bakery, and I can make it just fine here. Besides, Elizabeth needs all the help she can get. But there is one thing you can do for me."

"Anything."

"I forgot to check the messages today. Would you mind walking out to the phone shanty?"

"Of course. I'll be right back." Grabbing a flashlight from a shelf by the door, Lindsay clicked it on, stepped onto the porch, and spotted the three men still talking by the buggy. She waved to them and then quickly crossed the driveway to the phone shanty, which was a small shed containing a phone, stool, and counter. She lifted the receiver and dialed the voicemail. After entering the code, a recorded voice told her that she had one message. She punched the button to activate her message, and her older sister's voice rang through the receiver.

"Hey Linds," Jessica called, her voice full of excitement. "Call me! I have amazing news. I wish you had a cell phone so I didn't have to wait for you to get this and call me back. Anyway, call me as soon as you get this! Bye!"

Lindsay deleted the message and then dialed her sister's cell phone. Curiosity surged through her while she awaited her sister's news.

Jessica answered on the third ring. "Hey! I've been waiting for you to call." Music blared in the background.

"Hi Jessica," Lindsay said, lowering herself onto the stool. "What's going on?"

"Hang on," Jessica said, nearly shouting over the noise. "I can't hear you. Let me move to another room." The music muted. "Okay. I'm in a bedroom now. Kim insisted on throwing a party since we're leaving."

"What?" Lindsay shook her head with confusion. "Where are you going?"

"Yeah. I've been dying to tell you." Her smile rang through the phone. "You remember when I told you that Kim's dad works for a big accounting firm in New York City?"

"Sure." Lindsay shrugged, even though she didn't remember ever hearing that.

"Her dad was able to get me an internship with his firm this summer." Jessica spoke quickly, her voice radiating with excitement. "It was totally unexpected. He had an intern back out at the last minute, so Kim and I are heading up there next week. We're going to stay with her parents, which means that all I need is spending money. It's so awesome because I'll get college credit, and I'll also be able to put this on my résumé. Can you imagine, Linds? I'll have job experience at a big accounting firm in New York City! I mean, that's like totally amazing, right?"

"Whoa." Lindsay held her hand up as if to shush her sister in person. Jessica's rapidly blurted-out words soaked through her mind while she tried to make sense of them. "Did you say you're going to New York City next week?"

"Yes! Trisha and Frank say it's a great opportunity. I mean, when will I have the opportunity to do something like this again? I'm so excited, Lindsay! I'm going to New York!"

"I thought you were going to spend the summer here, working for Uncle Daniel in the furniture store," Lindsay said.

"But this is the opportunity of a lifetime, Linds! How can I not jump on this?"

"I don't know," Lindsay said slowly.

"I have so much to do. I need to go shopping for some nice clothes. I can't wear jeans and T-shirts to a big-time accounting job, right?"

Jessica droned on about her to-do list, and Lindsay shook her head. She and her sister were polar opposites. While Lindsay was contemplating whether or not to join the Amish church, Jessica was packing up and heading to a big city for the internship of her dreams.

"So I was thinking," Jessica continued. "I want to see you before I go. I'm going to drive up there this weekend on my way to NYC."

"Oh." Lindsay sat up straight. "When will you arrive?"

"Friday," Jessica said. "Is that all right?"

"*Ya*," Lindsay replied. "Have you told Jake about this big adventure?"

"No," Jessica said quickly. "I want to surprise him. Please don't tell him, okay?"

"I won't. I'll leave that up to you." Lindsay frowned while imagining how Jake would take the news of Jessica's plans to go to New York.

Jessica had shared with Lindsay that Jake wasn't thrilled when Jessica accepted a scholarship to a college in Virginia instead of going to a school near Lancaster County. He would probably be even more disappointed to hear that she was traveling to New York City and not spending the summer working in the furniture store with him.

"I can't wait to see you!" Jessica said. "It's been too long. I bet Emma and Junior are big now, huh?"

"Yeah. They've grown like weeds."

"Give them a hug and kiss for me and tell them that their favorite cousin is coming to see them."

"I will," Lindsay said.

"Oh, hang on a minute," Jessica said.

Lindsay heard muffled voices and then Jessica spoke again.

"Hey, I gotta go, but I'll see you Friday, okay?" Jessica said. "Love you, sis."

"Love you too," Lindsay said before the dial tone sang in her ear. She stepped out of the phone shanty and found that darkness had descended on the farm.

With the flashlight in her hand, she started across the driveway. The buggy was gone, and she assumed Matthew and Samuel were on their way back to their homes, which were located a few miles away.

Lindsay climbed the porch steps while the conversation with her sister replayed in her mind. Jessica was going to break her promise to Lindsay, the rest of the Kauffman family, and Jake Miller and go to New York City for the summer. The idea seemed crazy and courageous all at the same time. Lindsay was disappointed in Jessica, but also a tiny bit jealous. And she knew the root of that jealousy—Lindsay would never be brave enough to leave home and travel to a big city. While she didn't understand her sister's priorities, she envied her confidence and bravery.

However, what bothered Lindsay most was that the news would most likely break Jake's heart. She absently wondered just how much longer Jake would wait for her older sister.

She entered the kitchen, and Rebecca and Daniel looked up from the table, each with a concerned expression.

"*Was iss letz?*" Daniel asked.

"I had a message from Jessica, so I called her back." Lindsay joined them at the table.

"Is she okay?" Rebecca asked.

"She's fine." Lindsay cleared her throat while choosing her words. "But she's not coming here for the summer."

"Oh?" Daniel looked confused. "Why not?"

"She's going to New York City next week to begin a summer internship with some big accounting firm."

"What?" Rebecca asked with a gasp before exchanging a shocked expression with Daniel.

"She's going to stop here on her way up to New York. She'll be here Friday night." Lindsay met Daniel's gaze. "She asked us to not tell Jake. She wants to share the news with him herself."

Daniel nodded. "I understand. It's best if he hears this news from Jessica."

Lindsay turned to Rebecca. "She and I are so different. I can't imagine picking up and moving to New York like that. I mean, she'll be staying with friends, but still. That's so ... brave."

Rebecca touched her hand. "You're very brave in other ways."

"God created us all differently, Lindsay," Daniel said. "Don't compare yourself to Jessica. What's right for her isn't necessarily right for you."

"You're right," Lindsay agreed.

Daniel stood. "Well, it's getting late. We better be off to bed."

Rebecca stayed in her seat and continued to write on her notepad. "I need to plan a big meal for Friday if Jessica is coming. And I'll have to do some extra cleaning."

"I'll stay home and help you," Lindsay said.

"No, no," Rebecca said. "I can handle it."

"Don't be *gegisch*, Becky," Daniel said. "I know you've been tired lately. We'll all pitch in."

"*Danki*," Rebecca said with a warm smile.

Daniel touched her shoulder, and Lindsay hoped that someday she would find a true love similar to the one her aunt and uncle shared.

3

Jessica drummed her fingers on the steering wheel of her dark blue Jeep Cherokee while driving up Route 340 in Bird-in-Hand Friday afternoon. After packing up everything she'd need for her summer in New York City, she'd set out from her apartment in Richmond, Virginia, and began her trek north to Pennsylvania.

Although she'd visited during spring break, it felt as if she hadn't been here in ages. It seemed as if so much had changed in her life since she'd come by the last time. Since that visit, Jessica had finished her sophomore year with a 3.8 grade-point average, she and her best friend Kim had moved into their own apartment off campus, and she had accepted an internship at one of the most prestigious accounting firms in New York City. She grinned at her last thought.

Mom and Dad would be so proud.

When she and Lindsay moved to Bird-in-Hand to live with their aunt Rebecca, Jessica was certain that things would never be normal for her again. While her younger sister had taken quickly to the Amish way of life, Jessica had felt as if she were suffocating.

Jessica had failed miserably when she struggled to fit in with Rebecca's community. Yet, she managed to rebuild her life again after moving back to Virginia to live with her parents' best friends, Frank and Trisha McCabe. She graduated from high school and then enrolled in college to pursue her dream of becoming an accountant. Jessica still missed her parents so much that her heart ached, but she truly believed that she was going to be okay.

However, she still worried about Lindsay.

Jessica's stomach tightened with anticipation as she slowed in front of a building displaying a sign that read "Kauffman & Yoder Amish Furniture," where her uncle and her good friend Jake worked. She'd spoken to Jake last Saturday when he called at their usual weekly time to check in with her. She suspected he would be very unhappy when he found out that she was going to spend the summer in New York City instead of working with him in the furniture store. She hoped he'd understand what this job could mean for her future.

Jessica parked her SUV next to the single-story white building. She then followed the stone path to the steps leading up to the store and wrenched open the front door. A bell rang, announcing her presence.

Large windows lined the front of the shop, and the walls were covered in crisp, fresh white paint. Memories of the previous summers she'd spent working in the store filled her mind as she glanced around the open area, taking in the sample pieces, including mirrored dressers, hope chests, entertainment centers, dining room sets, bed frames, end tables, and coffee tables. The familiar aroma of wood and stain permeated her nostrils.

A long counter covered with piles of papers and catalogs sat at the far end of the room, blocking a doorway beyond which hammers, saws, and nail guns blasted while voices boomed in Pennsylvania Dutch.

She crossed the room with her flip-flops slapping on the concrete floor, and a smile spread on her lips when she spotted Jake sitting at the desk and talking on the phone.

While she watched him, her hand flew to her neck and the

cross necklace Jake had given her as a gift two years ago. She cherished their close friendship. She knew that he dreamt of being more than friends, but she wasn't ready to make that kind of commitment. Being more than friends would be nothing short of complicated since he was Mennonite, and she wasn't. Their hopes and dreams were worlds apart: she wanted a career, and he was happy working in an Amish furniture store.

Yet, as different as they were, the attraction was still alive, just like the first time she'd met him. She'd met a lot of young men at college, but no one held a candle to Jake Miller.

He glanced up, and his Caribbean blue eyes rounded as they met hers. "Jessica?" His mouth gaped as he stood. "What in the world are you doing here?"

"Surprise," she said, opening her arms. "I'm here."

He started to hang up the phone and then stopped and put it to his ear. "I need to hang up, Bob. I'll call you back." He dropped the phone into the cradle and then rushed around the desk and swept Jessica into his arms. "How are you?"

She laughed and hugged him, taking in his musky scent of wood mixed with stain. "Fine. How are you?"

"Stunned, but happy." He grinned and leaned on the counter behind him. "I thought you weren't coming for a few more weeks."

"Well, plans have changed," she said, twisting a lock of her long dark hair around her finger. A saw blared in the workshop behind them. "Is there any way we can go for a walk or something?" she asked, raising her voice over the noise.

"Sure. Let me just go tell my grandfather that we're leaving." He started for the door leading to the shop and then faced her again. "Did you want to come with me and say hello to everyone?"

She shook her head. "Not just yet. I'd rather talk to you alone first."

He raised an eyebrow with suspicion and then shrugged.

"Suit yourself." He disappeared through the doorway and then reappeared a few moments later. After grabbing a baseball cap from the counter and shoving it on his head, he came around the corner, took her hand in his, and led her toward the front door.

Jessica's stomach fluttered as they started down the sidewalk toward the row of stores lining Route 340.

"Are you thirsty?" he asked, gesturing toward a little deli.

She shrugged. "Sure."

He steered her toward a little table outside of the building. "Have a seat. I'll be right back."

While sitting at the small table, Jessica studied the traffic roaring by on the highway and silently rehearsed how she was going to share her news with Jake. She wanted him to be happy for her, but her gut told her that he would be disappointed at the sudden change in her summer plans.

Jake appeared a few moments later carrying two plastic cups with lids and red straws. "Here you go." He set the beverages on the table.

"Thanks." Jessica bit her lower lip and gripped the cool cup.

"So, why are you back so early?" He adjusted his ball cap on his dark hair and then sipped his soda.

She smiled. "I have exciting news."

"Really?" His grin was wide. "You're transferring to a college here?"

Not this subject again. She bit back a groan. Ever since she'd started school in Virginia, Jake had suggested she transfer to a school closer to him. The subject came up at least once every few months.

She sipped her drink and shook her head. "No, I'm not transferring."

He leaned back in his chair and folded his arms across his wide chest. "You know I'll always keep trying to convince you that you belong here with me."

"I know you will," she said.

"It was worth a try anyway." He lifted his cup to his mouth. "I'm dying with anticipation. What's this exciting news? Spill it."

"I've accepted an internship with a very well-respected accounting firm."

His eyes were wide with excitement. "Congratulations! I'm so proud of you."

"Thank you." She paused for a moment. "There's one thing."

He raised his eyebrows while sipping his drink.

"It's in New York," she said softly.

He stopped drinking and set his cup on the table. "What did you say?"

"The internship is in New York." She cleared her throat and pushed her hair behind her ears.

"New York?" He said the words slowly as if trying to decode their meaning. "What do you mean by New York? It's a big state."

"I mean New York City."

He blinked. "You're going to New York City?"

She nodded.

"When?"

"Sunday."

"For how long?"

"Until classes start again in August. But you can come and see me," she added quickly. "Maybe you and Lindsay can visit. I'll be staying at my friend Kim's parents' house in New Jersey, and they have plenty of room. She said that—"

"Whoa." He held his hands up like a traffic cop and she stopped speaking. "So what you're not saying is that you're breaking your promise to me, your sister, my grandfather, Eli, and the rest of your family. You're going to work in New York instead of working here." He pointed toward the furniture store.

"Did you hear what I said, Jake?" Jessica snapped. "This is an internship at a big accounting firm. I'll get college credit and have the work experience on my résumé." She leaned forward, tapping the table for emphasis. "This is the opportunity of a lifetime for me."

"Really?" he muttered, looking unimpressed.

"Don't you get it?" She gestured widely. "I've been working so hard to prove that I can make it in this field. It's finally paying off. My professors wrote letters of recommendation for this job."

He shook his head and stood. "Unbelievable."

"What do you mean?"

"Jess, I've been waiting for you for four years now."

She frowned. "That's not fair, Jake. I never made any promises."

"Exactly." He started toward the furniture store, and she ran after him.

"Jake! Wait!" she called, her voice thick. "Don't walk away from me."

He stopped mid-stride and faced her, a wry grin on his face. "You're asking me to not walk away from you? What have you done to me repeatedly since the summer we met?"

She gasped, staring at him. "Is that what you think I'm doing—walking away from you?"

He threw his hands up in the air. "What else am I'm supposed to think? You could've had a scholarship to any college, and you chose to stay in Virginia."

She pinched the bridge of her nose where a migraine brewed. "We've been through this a thousand times, Jake."

"Have we?" He glowered. "I've been patient, Jessica. I've tolerated only seeing you every summer and for a few short weekend trips during the year. The only thing I've had to look forward to is summers, and now we're losing that."

"This isn't about you, Jake," she retorted.

"You're absolutely right. It's not at all about me," he said softly, his voice trembling with anger. "It's about you. It's *always* been about you, Jessica." Turning, he stalked back to the furniture store.

Her eyes filled with tears as she watched him walk away from her.

Lindsay finished setting the table and then opened the oven to check the pot roast. She glanced at the clock on the wall and found it was almost five.

"She'll be here," Rebecca said, while holding up another spoonful of applesauce to Emma.

"I thought she was going to leave early." Lindsay glanced out the kitchen window toward the driveway. "I wonder if she made a stop along the way." She fetched a pitcher from the cabinet. "I'll make some more iced tea." She fished the mix from the cabinet, poured the ingredients into the pitcher, and added the water. "I bet she went by the furniture store to see Jake."

"Daniel said he invited Jake to supper tonight, but Jake turned him down," Rebecca said.

"That's odd," Lindsay said, stirring the tea.

"He said that Jake seemed upset about something, but he wouldn't talk about it."

"Then she probably did stop to see him," Lindsay muttered.

The back door slammed open and Junior danced into the room. "She's here! She's here!"

Lindsay followed Junior out the door and down the porch steps to where Daniel stood with Jessica next to her Jeep.

"Hey, Big Sister!" Lindsay wrapped her arms around Jessica's neck. "It's so good to see you."

"You too," Jessica said, hugging her in return. She glanced toward the house. "Where are Emma and Aunt Rebecca?"

"*Aenti* Rebecca's giving Emma some applesauce. Emma's been really hungry all day and whined until *Aenti* Rebecca pulled out her favorite snack." Lindsay glanced toward the truck. "What can I carry?"

"Uncle Daniel has my bag." Jessica pointed toward the suitcase in his hand. "I don't need much since I'm leaving Sunday."

Lindsay bit back a frown at the thought of her sister's short visit. "Let's get you inside. I'm making a roast."

"Great." Jessica leaned down to Junior. "Would you show me the way to the kitchen?"

"*Ya*!" He took her hand and led her toward the porch.

Lindsay sat across from Jessica at the kitchen table. She bowed her head in silent prayer along with the rest of the family. She looked up when she heard Daniel shift in his seat, indicating that the prayer was over and the meal would begin. She took a piece of freshly baked bread from the basket and then passed the basket across to Jessica.

"So, how are you?" Lindsay asked.

"I'm okay," Jessica said. "I think I have everything ready for the trip. Kim left this morning and was driving straight through to her parents' place. I borrowed her GPS, so I should be fine on the road."

"How has school been, Jessica?" Rebecca asked from her seat beside her.

"Good," Jessica said while she chose a piece of bread and then buttered it.

While Jessica chattered away about classes and friends, Lindsay studied her. At twenty, Jessica was a striking beauty with her dark eyes and her dark brown hair falling to the middle of her back. She wore just enough makeup to accentuate her eyes and her high cheekbones.

However, her sister's eyes seemed to lack their usual brightness, and her voice wasn't as full of excitement as it had been on the phone. Jessica acted as if something was wrong, and Lindsay hoped she would share her worries in private later on in the evening.

During the rest of the meal, Jessica told stories about college and asked about the friends and family in the Bird-in-Hand district.

After supper, Daniel disappeared into the barn while Rebecca steered the children toward the family room. Lindsay began carrying dirty dishes to the sink.

"What can I do?" Jessica asked.

"Do you want to wash or dry?" Lindsay asked, filling the sink with soapy water.

Jessica moved to the sink. "I guess I can wash."

Lindsay placed the dirty dishes and utensils on the counter. "What time did you leave your apartment this morning?"

"I think it was about ten." Jessica scrubbed a pot. "I made pretty good time. Traffic wasn't too bad, and I only stopped twice."

"Huh," Lindsay said as she grabbed the basket of bread.

Jessica faced her. "What does that mean?"

"Well, you got here around five, and I know it doesn't take seven hours to drive to Bird-in-Hand from your place."

To her surprise, Jessica's face turned crimson before she spun back around to the sink.

Lindsay was silent for a moment while she waited for Jessica to elaborate. When she didn't speak, Lindsay racked her brain for something to say. "Haven't Junior and Emma gotten big? Emma spoke her first sentence yesterday. She spoke in *Dietsch* of course. When *Aenti* Rebecca asked her if she wanted a—"

"I went to see Jake before I came here." Jessica suddenly blurted out the words. "I couldn't wait to see him, and I thought maybe he'd be happy for me." Her voice trembled. "But he was really hurt. I don't think he'll ever speak to me again." She faced Lindsay, and tears streamed down her pink cheeks.

"It's okay." Lindsay rushed over to Jessica and handed her a napkin. "I'm sure he'll get over it." She rubbed Jessica's arm as she wiped her face.

"I doubt it." Jessica shook her head. "He said that everything is all about me and he's been waiting for me for years. Jake doesn't understand how this is the biggest and most exciting opportunity of my life. He pretty much told me off and left me standing on the sidewalk, so I drove around for a while and tried to figure out what to do." Jessica threw her hands up with defeat. "I don't think there's anything I can do except let it go. I mean, this internship isn't going to come around again, so if he really cares about me, he'll have to get over it."

Lindsay frowned. "Have you thought about apologizing to him?"

"Apologize for what?" Jessica frowned. "It's my life, Linds. I'm doing the best I can without Mom and Dad. I know that they would want me to work hard and be independent. If he can't understand that, then I guess he doesn't understand me."

Lindsay opened her mouth to speak but was interrupted by her little cousins running and shrieking their way around the kitchen table and then back out to the family room.

Rebecca followed slowly behind them with a smile on her face. "I wish I had just a tiny portion of their boundless energy." Her gaze met Jessica's and she gave a concerned look. "Are you okay?"

"Oh yeah." Jessica waved off the question. "I was just sharing a story with Lindsay." She turned back to the sink. "Supper was delicious, by the way."

"I did all of the cooking." Lindsay grabbed a towel and began drying the dishes in the rack.

"Wow," Jessica said while she scrubbed a pot. "You're little Miss Suzy Homemaker, huh?"

Lindsay glowered. Why did her sister always have to make sarcastic comments about her domestic skills? She glanced at Rebecca who gave her an expression that told her to let it go.

"I'll wipe off the table," Rebecca offered.

"No," Lindsay said with a shake of her head. "You go rest. You look exhausted."

Rebecca sighed. "I hate to admit you're right, but you are. I'll be in the *schtupp.*" She slowly moved from the kitchen toward the family room.

"Is she all right?" Jessica asked softly once Rebecca was gone.

"I don't know." Lindsay shook her head as worry filled her. "She's been really tired lately. But you remember what a hard worker she is. It's difficult to get her to slow down at all."

"I hope she's not coming down with something." Suddenly Jessica's expression brightened. "Tell me all about your life. How's the bakery? How's that handsome Matthew doing? Has he asked to give you a ride home yet?"

Lindsay swatted her sister with the towel. "Matthew is just a friend."

Jessica gave her a look of disbelief. "Yeah. Sure! And I'm the Queen of Sheba."

Lindsay laughed and couldn't help but think how good it was to have her sister back, even if it was only for a short weekend.

Rebecca stood in the doorway of Emma's room and watched while Jessica rocked Emma in the chair and quietly read her a story. Emma yawned and soon her eyes closed while the chair slowly moved back and forth and her older cousin's voice whispered the words to Emma's favorite book.

Rebecca's heart filled with warmth as she thought of her two nieces and how much they'd grown since they'd come to live with her and Daniel four years ago. Although it had broken Rebecca's heart when she'd allowed Jessica to move back to Virginia and live with friends, she'd known that it was God's will for the girl.

And now Jessica was all grown up. She was a beautiful young lady and about to embark on an exciting and challenging journey. Rebecca prayed that God would be with her and guide her this summer in the big city.

"You're asleep," Jessica whispered to Emma. "I guess I should put you in your bed, huh?" She glanced up at Rebecca and smiled.

Rebecca crossed the room and took Emma in her arms. After whispering good night in her ear, she placed her baby in her crib and covered her with a small quilt. "She's worn out from a busy day of play."

Jessica grinned. "I can see that." She followed Rebecca out of the room.

Rebecca closed the door behind them. "I think the children enjoyed having you read their stories tonight."

"Oh, it was fun." Jessica nodded toward Junior's room. "I can't get over how big he is. Emma too. They grow so fast."

"*Ya*, they do. Sometimes it seems like it's too fast." Rebecca motioned toward Lindsay's room across the hall. "Lindsay insisted that you take her room and she'll sleep in with Emma."

"She didn't have to do that, but I appreciate it." Jessica stepped into Lindsay's room and yawned. "I think I may turn in early. I'm worn out from the drive."

Rebecca leaned in the doorway and watched her niece fish through her duffel bag and pull out a pair of sweatpants and a T-shirt. "How are you, Jessica?"

"Fine." Jessica continued to dig, revealing a bottle of shampoo, a toothbrush, and toothpaste.

"Are you certain?" Rebecca stepped into the room and sank into a chair in front of the bed. "You seemed upset earlier. You know you can talk to me, *ya*?"

Jessica sat on the bed, hugging her sweatpants to her chest. "On my way here today, I stopped to see Jake at the store."

"Oh?" Rebecca smoothed the skirt of her dress. "How is he?"

Looking frustrated, Jessica shook her head. "Upset with me. He didn't take my news about going to New York well at all."

"He's hurt that you're going?"

"Yes, he is." Jessica sniffed and cleared her throat. "He said that it's always all about me, and he's been waiting for me for four years."

"It's not easy for him to let you go." Rebecca smiled. "Maybe he's afraid you'll stay in New York, and he'll lose you."

"I wish he could see that this isn't about trying to be independent or breaking away from something that's holding me back." Jessica shook her head. "Well, maybe I am trying to be independent. Anyway, this is an opportunity for me to earn college credit and build up my résumé, but he doesn't see that side of it. All he chooses to understand is that I'm abandoning him."

"Or breaking a promise."

Jessica's eyes widened. "Breaking a promise?" Her voice rose and shook with resentment. "I'm just spending a summer in New York City. Besides, we've never even officially declared ourselves a couple. We're just close friends. I've never promised him more than that."

Rebecca leaned over and patted Jessica's knee. "I know you don't mean to hurt him, but he was really looking forward to seeing you this summer. He asks about you all the time."

"He does?" Jessica looked surprised.

"Don't act so shocked, Jessica." Rebecca wagged a finger at her. "You know how he feels about you. It's written all over his face. You need to see beyond your own wants and needs and just consider how much this is hurting him. Come to a compromise."

Looking defeated, Jessica nodded. "I guess you're right."

Rebecca stood and cupped her hand to her mouth to stifle a yawn. "Excuse me. I think I'm going to go to bed."

"Are you feeling okay?"

"*Ya*, I'm fine. I'm just getting old." She started for the door. "You go ahead and take your shower. You remember where everything is."

"Thanks," Jessica said. As Rebecca moved out the door, Jessica called to her. "Aunt Rebecca. Wait."

Rebecca faced her.

"Do you think I should stay here and work for Yoder's this summer?" Her eyes implored Rebecca, as if begging Rebecca to give her blessing for Jessica's plans.

Rebecca paused, carefully choosing her words. "You're a very brave and driven young woman. I admire your courage, and I know that your mother would be very proud of you. I think you know what you want, and you're going after it with a tenacity that I never had."

"But you think I should forget my plans to go to New York and stay here instead," Jessica said simply.

"No, I didn't say that." Rebecca placed her hand on the doorknob as a wave of exhaustion overwhelmed her. "I think that you're making the right choice for you, given the circumstances. You have a place to stay and a friend who will help look after you. But I think you need to remember that your choices affect those who are close to you."

"Like Jake," Jessica whispered.

Mississippi Mud Pie

1 – 4 oz. pkg. ground pecans
3 reg. boxes instant butterscotch or chocolate pudding
1 large container whipped topping
1 – 8 oz. cream cheese
1 stick butter
1 cup flour
1 cup 10x sugar
1 can coconut

First layer:

½ pkg. ground pecans mixed with flour and butter. Press on bottom of 9x13 inch pan. Bake 350 for 20 minutes. Cool.

Second layer:

Mix cream cheese, 10x sugar, and 1/2 of whipped topping. Spread over crust. Then sprinkle with ½ can coconut and ½ chopped nuts.

Third layer:

Mix pudding with 5 cups cold milk. Spread over 2nd layer. Top with remaining topping. Sprinkle remaining coconut and nuts. Freeze. Remove 1 hour before serving. Cut while frozen.

4

Lindsay weaved through the knot of friends and family members milling about in Rebecca's family room the following evening. Saturday night was a night for the Kauffmans to visit, and Rebecca had suggested that they host the gathering and make it a party for Jessica.

Stepping into the kitchen, Lindsay surveyed the counter full of covered dishes and desserts, making certain there was enough food for the crowd. She felt a tap on her shoulder and turned to find Jessica standing behind her.

"Hey," Jessica said over the conversations circling around them.

"Hi," Lindsay said. "Having fun?"

Jessica shrugged. "Yeah. Sure. Listen, I wanted to talk to you. We haven't had a chance to really sit down and talk since I've been here. I fell asleep early last night, and we did nothing but cook and bake today."

Lindsay gestured toward the back door. "You want to go out on the back porch?"

"Sounds good," Jessica said.

Lindsay stepped out onto the porch and spotted the younger Kauffman children running in the pasture and playing tag. She searched the group of children for Katie and Nancy but didn't see them. Aunt Sadie said that they would be coming along shortly, and Lindsay hoped that they would. Lizzie Anne hadn't arrived yet either, and Lindsay wanted her best friends to see her sister before she headed to New York.

"I haven't been hugged so much in a long time," Jessica said as she dropped into the swing while holding a plate full of desserts. "It took me nearly twenty minutes just to cross the family room because I kept getting pulled into a hug or a handshake."

Jessica bit into a whoopie pie, causing Lindsay to think of her visit with Matthew a week ago. Lindsay idly wondered if Matthew would come to the party with Samuel and his sisters.

"You're awfully quiet," Jessica said between bites of the whoopie pie. "Mmmm. This is delicious. Can I pack some of these to go?"

"Sure," Lindsay said, swatting the ties of her prayer covering back behind her shoulders. "You can take any of the leftover food. I'll pack it up for you."

"Kim would love these." Jessica finished the little cake and licked her fingers. "So, where's your boyfriend?"

Lindsay glowered with exasperation. "He's not my boyfriend." She faced her sister. "You really should go see Jake before you leave. I don't think you left things very well with him."

Jessica opened her mouth to speak and then her expression softened. "You're right. I should."

Lindsay gave her a look of disbelief. "You're not going to argue with me?"

Jessica chuckled. "Am I really that bad?"

"Well . . ." Lindsay let her thought trail off, and Jessica shook her head in response.

"Rebecca said something similar to me last night, so I know you're right."

Stunned, Lindsay blinked. *Jessica's listening to* Aenti *Rebecca? How did this happen?*

"Don't look so surprised." Jessica glanced out toward the pasture and the children. "They look like they're having fun."

"*Ya,* they get along well."

"You don't have to talk Dutch to me." Jessica lifted a chocolate chip cookie from the plate. "You want anything?"

"No, thanks." Lindsay folded her arms across her chest. "I see the desserts all week, so they don't really tempt me anymore. What did you want to talk about?"

"New York," Jessica said. "I want to propose something to you."

Lindsay faced her sister. "This should be good."

"It is, actually." She smiled. "What if I made you a deal?"

"A deal?" Lindsay eyed her sister with cynicism.

"I know I drive you crazy when I tell you that you have to stop pretending to be Amish."

Lindsay bit back a groan.

"I'll promise to stop saying that if you do something for me."

"What?" Lindsay asked.

"Come with me to New York."

"What?" Lindsay stood. "Are you crazy?" Her voice transformed into a high-pitched squeak as resentment coursed through her.

"No, I'm not." She motioned for Lindsay to sit. "Calm down and hear me out."

Lindsay lowered herself into the chair next to the swing while still scowling. "I don't like the sound of this at all."

Jessica rolled her eyes. "Just listen," she huffed. "I know you think that this is all you'll ever want." She gestured around the porch. "But I don't think so."

"Jess—"

"Wait." Jessica held up a finger, silencing her. "I've asked you to hear me out."

Lindsay shook her head. Her sister would never understand her.

"I'm worried about you, Lindsay."

"Worried?" Lindsay gave a bark of laughter.

"Yes, worried." Jessica nodded with emphasis. "I'm afraid that in a few years you'll wish you'd made different choices.

You'll wish you'd finished high school and gone to college. You can't get these years back, Linds. You're only young once."

"We've been through this," Lindsay said, enunciating the words.

"I know, I know," Jessica said. "That's why I want you to come with me and spend the summer in New York. You can see if you still feel the same way about the farm and living here when you get back."

"I don't need a summer in a strange city to know that my purpose in life is here." Lindsay tapped the arm of the chair. "I belong *here,* Jessica."

"You know that for sure?" Jessica looked unconvinced.

"Yes, I do."

Jessica folded her arms across the front of her T-shirt. "How do you know?"

"I know here." Lindsay pointed to her chest. "In my heart."

"But you're worth more than this." Jessica touched Lindsay's hand, and Lindsay pulled it back. "You should be packing up and going to college somewhere and studying a subject that brings you joy, as Dad used to say."

"This life brings me joy," Lindsay said. "I love being a part of this family and working in the bakery. I have obligations here." She gestured toward the barn. "This is where I want to be. In fact, I'm considering joining the church."

"No, no, no." Jessica looked disappointed. "Don't say that." She took Lindsay's hand in hers. "Come with me to New York. I can get you a job at the firm where I'm working."

"No!" Lindsay pulled her hand back. "Why would I want to work in an accounting firm? I hate numbers, and I was never good at school."

"You sell yourself short. You can do anything that you set your mind to. I'll explain that you've been hiding away with the Amish as a way to deal with our parents' death, and they'll understand. They'll take pity on you and give you a job. I'm sure of it."

"What?" Lindsay stood in front of her sister and gestured widely. "Is that what you think of me? You think I've just been hiding away here and avoiding my grief for Mom and Dad? That is not true, Jessica! It's not true at all!"

Jessica glanced at something behind her. "Lindsay, just calm down, okay?"

"No, I will not calm down." Lindsay stomped her foot. "You're so wrong about so many things. You're all high and mighty because you graduated from high school and got a full scholarship to a great college. That's wonderful, and I'm proud of you. But that doesn't make you any better than me." Her voice and her body trembled with fury.

Jessica motioned for Lindsay to sit and compose herself. "Lindsay, come on. That's enough. You're making a scene."

"I'm not done! I had to hear you out," Lindsay said, her voice thick. "Now it's your turn to listen. I'm tired of your condescending attitude about how we live in this community. We live this way because—"

"Is everything okay?" a voice asked.

Lindsay spun and found Lizzie Anne, Katie, Samuel, and Matthew watching her with curious expressions. She hugged her arms to her chest in order to try to quell her body from shaking.

Katie climbed the steps and looked back and forth between Jessica and Lindsay. "You all right, Lindsay?"

"*Ya.*" Lindsay cleared her throat against threatening tears and started down the steps. "I need to take a walk."

"Wait!" Katie called.

"Hold on," Lizzie Anne chimed in.

Jessica swallowed a frustrated groan while her younger sister rushed across the driveway toward the barn with Katie and Lizzie

Anne in tow. Why did Lindsay have to get so defensive? Why couldn't her sister see that Jessica was only trying to help her?

Pushing her hair back behind her ears, Jessica glanced at Samuel and Matthew who were gazing at her from the bottom of the porch steps. *Can this possibly get any more awkward?*

"Hi," she said with a casual wave. "How are you?"

"Fine," they both mumbled in unison before heading toward the barn.

Blowing out a sigh, Jessica glanced toward the driveway, where a familiar four-door, dark blue Chevrolet pickup truck bounced toward the house.

"Jake," she whispered as she stood.

Jessica looked toward the barn, where Lindsay stood with her friends. For a split second, she considered running over and apologizing. She then cut her eyes back to the pickup rumbling forward. She knew in her heart she should make things right with her sister, but she didn't want to create more of a spectacle in front of the Kauffman family and friends.

Instead, she would work things out with Jake and then talk to Lindsay later after she'd taken some time to calm down.

Jessica set the plate of desserts on a small table next to the swing before hurrying down the stairs to the pickup truck, which came to a stop near the fence line. She loped over to the driver window and looked up at Jake.

"Hi," she said, jamming her hands in the pockets of her jeans.

"Hi." Jake's expression was hopeful.

"I didn't expect to see you here." She kicked a stone with the toe of her flip-flop.

He draped his arm over the steering wheel. "I couldn't let you leave for New York without saying good-bye."

She nodded. "That's very true."

He gestured toward the passenger seat. "Hop in. Let's go for a ride."

Jessica looked toward her sister one last time. Lindsay's eyes met hers for a brief moment before she angled her body toward her group of friends. For a split second, Jessica again considered approaching her sister.

Instead, she jogged around the front end of the truck and hopped in next to Jake. He backed out of the driveway and steered toward the road, keeping his eyes trained ahead while he drove. His usual informal, laid-back demeanor was replaced with an intense, erect stance.

For several minutes the only sound was the rumbling of the engine and the clicking of the key ring as it smacked the steering column. And the roar of the silence was eating her up inside.

"I know you're disappointed in me," Jessica began.

"Disappointed?" He snorted with sarcasm while keeping his focus on the road. "Disappointed doesn't begin to tell you how I feel, Jess."

She took a deep breath. "Look, I care about you, Jake, and I care about what you think. And I need you to trust me on this." She faced him. "I'm sorry that we won't be together this summer, but it's not forever."

"How long have you known about this internship?" he asked.

"I only found out on Monday that I was accepted into the program."

"And when did you apply?"

She paused as guilt swept over her. "A few months ago." She stared at her red toenails sticking out of her flip-flops.

He steered into the parking lot at the bakery and halted the truck. After killing the engine, he turned to her. "Do you know where I'm going with my questions or do I have to explain it?"

"You're upset that I never told you about the program."

"Exactly!"

The hurt in his eyes took her breath away for a moment. "I'm sorry that I didn't tell you sooner."

He lifted his ball cap and raked his hand through his dark

hair. "I don't ask for much from you, Jess. In fact, I've never asked for a commitment, but today you made me feel like a fool for sitting here waiting for you while you flitter off from college to New York City without looking back."

"Now wait a minute." She sat up straight and tapped her finger on the dashboard. "I don't flitter off here and there. I've made it perfectly clear that I wanted to get an education, and going on this internship is part of that plan."

His frown became sad. "I hold you back."

She winced at the change in his tone. "What are you saying?"

Looking defeated, he held his hands up in surrender. "I think it's obvious here. We're just too different. We're stuck in this holding pattern and there's no way out."

"Wait a minute," Jessica said slowly. "What do you mean exactly? How is this a holding pattern?"

"I don't know." He stared at the steering wheel while running his thumb over it. "I guess it means that I'll always be stuck here waiting for you, and I'm tired of it. I had hoped we could move beyond this point in our relationship, but we never will."

Jessica turned toward the windshield. "I thought you would be excited for me, which is why I waited to tell you in person. I wanted to call you and share my news the moment I found out about the internship, but I thought it would be really fun to tell you face to face. I guess I was wrong."

"No, you weren't." He touched her arm. "I am happy and excited for you, but I'm sad for me because this opportunity proves that you'll never be satisfied living here. You crave a life in a big city. We're just too different. As much as I love you, I know I have to let you go and let go of the hope of someday being more than your friend."

She gasped at his words. He'd never said them aloud until that moment, and the shock knocked the wind out of her and stole her ability to speak for a moment. A single tear trickled down her cheek, and she impatiently swiped it away. "This wasn't how I expected my weekend to go." She cleared her throat. "I've managed to upset both you and my sister in less than an hour."

"What do you mean?" he asked.

"Lindsay and I had a huge argument right before you came over tonight." She rubbed her hands on her jeans. "I had suggested that she come with me to New York to make sure she really wanted to stay in this community, and it upset her. I'm worried she's selling herself short by not finishing high school and going to college."

Jake shook his head while leaning back on the driver's-side door. "You know, Jessica, you really need to consider what other people want before you push your ideas on them."

She glowered. "I only have her best interests in mind. After all, she's my younger sister, and she's my responsibility now that our parents are gone. I don't want her to look back someday and regret her choices."

"They're her choices to make."

"You wouldn't understand." Jessica folded her arms across her chest and stared straight out the windshield. "I think we need to go back to the party."

"Jess." Leaning over, he touched her shoulder. "You need to stop being so defensive. I'm only suggesting that you take Lindsay's wishes into consideration. I know you mean well, but you're shutting people out by only thinking about what you want."

"This is about New York City, isn't it?"

He shrugged. "It's about a lot of things."

She studied his face, and her lip quivered. "I'm sorry I let you down this summer," she whispered.

"Me too." He turned toward the steering wheel and cranked over the engine.

As they motored down the road, Jessica wiped another tear. The hurt she'd seen on Jake's face and heard in his voice was breaking her heart. But she tried to convince herself that the internship was for the best.

After all, it was a once in a lifetime opportunity.

Lindsay was standing by the barn surrounded by her friends when she noticed the Chevy pickup rumbling down the rock driveway.

How typical that Jessica would start an argument and then take off before it was worked out!

She gritted her teeth as her sister's thoughtless words echoed through her mind. Anger swelled within her as she watched the truck bounce onto the road.

I wish she hadn't come to visit.

Closing her eyes, Lindsay pinched the bridge of her nose, willing herself not to cry. She wished she could stop the overwhelming mix of anger and frustration that was drowning her. Her eyes flooded with tears, and she sucked in a breath.

Don't cry. Not here. Not in front of your friends—especially Matthew.

"Lindsay?" Katie's voice was full of concern. "Are you okay?"

Lindsay opened her eyes and found Katie and Lizzie Anne studying her while Matthew and Samuel stood beyond them with uncomfortable expressions on their faces.

"*Ya*. I'm fine." Lindsay cleared her throat in an effort to stop her voice from trembling. "We just had a disagreement."

Lizzie Anne looked unconvinced. "It sounded like more than a disagreement. Do you want to talk about it?"

"No." The word came out as a mere whisper as her tears began streaming down her face. She groaned and swiped her hands across her hot cheeks. "I don't want to cry. Not here. Not now. This is so embarrassing."

Katie enveloped her in a hug. "It's okay."

"How about we go for that walk you wanted?" Lizzie Anne offered.

Unable to speak through her tears, Lindsay nodded.

Looping her arm around Lindsay's shoulder, Katie led Lindsay past the barn to the fence. They walked along the fence line while children screeched, laughed, and chased each other. Lindsay couldn't help but think back to her childhood and how simple things were back then. Of course, she and her sister would occasionally argue, as all siblings do. But those arguments were over things like borrowing a curling iron without asking, and their mom would always intervene and make things right again.

If only Mom were here now ...

Lindsay blew out a ragged breath.

"It's going to be okay," Katie said, rubbing Lindsay's arm. "I'm certain that whatever you and Jessica said to each other was only said in anger. You'll both cool down and apologize after a while. Nancy and I argue sometimes, and we always apologize and work it out after we've had some time to think it through and realize how wrong we were."

"It's not that simple." Lindsay stopped and leaned against the fence. "We said some pretty mean things."

"What happened?" Lizzie Anne asked, sidling up to Lindsay.

Glancing toward the barn, Lindsay spotted Samuel and Matthew watching her. She hoped Matthew didn't think she was a big baby for crying over the stupid argument. She turned back to her friends. "Jessica won't stop nagging me about leaving the community and going back to school in Virginia. She won't listen to me."

Frowning, Katie shook her head. "She thinks she knows what's best for you, and she won't respect your wishes."

"Exactly." Lindsay sniffed. "She tried to convince me to go to New York City with her."

Lizzie Anne looked surprised. "What did you say?"

"No, of course!" Lindsay exclaimed. "I don't want to go there. She even offered to explain to her new bosses that I've been hiding out with the Amish so that they would give me a job despite my lack of education. She said that once her bosses heard that our parents died, they'll pity me."

Katie scowled. "How did you respond to that?"

"I screamed and yelled and carried on." Lindsay glanced up at the sky and groaned. "My parents wouldn't have been very proud of me. Neither would *Aenti* Rebecca."

"It's okay." Lizzie Anne touched Lindsay's arm. "She upset you. We all say things we don't mean. Right, Katie?"

"*Ya*, we do." Katie's expression was full of empathy. "Don't let her get to you. I know it's easier said than done. Her heart is in the right place, but she doesn't respect you. Remember to believe in your choices. Only you know what you truly want. Follow your heart. What makes you happy?"

"Being here." Lindsay gestured toward the field in front of them. "This place gives me joy."

Katie smiled. "There's your answer."

Lindsay knew her friend was right, but she still had a sick feeling in the pit of her stomach. "I just don't understand why she had to pick a fight with me today. She's leaving tomorrow."

"That's right," Katie said. "She's leaving tomorrow. Just make the best of it. My *dat* always says that you can't make someone change. You have to accept people as they are."

Lindsay nodded. "My father told me that too."

"So then let's have some fun. It's a beautiful evening, and our family and friends are here." Katie pointed toward the house. "Should we go see what's going on inside?"

"Okay." Flanked by her best friends, Lindsay headed back toward the house. As they approached the porch, she spotted Samuel and Matthew sitting on the chairs next to the swing.

Samuel grinned over at them. "Did you ladies solve the problems of the world?"

"*Ya*, we did." Lizzie Anne's grin was wide, and for a brief second, Lindsay wondered if she liked Samuel.

"Oh?" Samuel's smile was equally bright. "And what problems did you solve?"

Lizzie Anne twisted her finger around the ribbon hanging from her prayer covering. "Wouldn't you like to know?"

Lindsay met Katie's gaze, and they both raised their eyebrows with curiosity.

Samuel folded his arms and looked unconvinced. "I would guess you were sharing baking secrets and nothing more important than that."

Lizzie Anne's eyes playfully challenged him. "Is that all you care about? Baking was important to you yesterday when you told me what your favorite cookies were."

Samuel stood and rubbed his hands together with anticipation. "Did you bring those chocolate chip cookies you promised?"

"I don't remember." Lizzie Anne touched a finger to her chin. "I may have to go check."

"I'll come with you." Samuel opened the door wide and gestured for Lizzie Anne to step through.

Giggling, Lizzie Anne moved through the door, followed by Katie.

Lindsay smiled. Watching the playful banter between her friends caused the sick feeling in her stomach to ease a bit. She was so thankful for her friends. She stepped toward the door but stopped when a hand brushed her shoulder.

"Lindsay," Matthew said. "Wait a minute."

She faced him and his intense eyes caused her pulse to skitter. "Yes?"

"Are you okay?" he asked.

She waved off the question and gave a forced laugh. "Oh, *ya*. My sister and I had a disagreement. You know how it is with siblings sometimes."

He continued to frown. "It looked like more than a simple disagreement. Is there anything you want to talk about?"

She hesitated, worried what he would think about the truth.

"It's none of my business." He reached out to touch her arm but then pulled his hand back. "I was concerned about you."

"*Danki*," Lindsay said. The genuine caring in his eyes caused her to want to share the truth with him. "It was just the same old issue with her. She doesn't understand why I want to live here. She thinks I belong with her at school. She's also convinced that in a few years I'll regret not finishing high school, going to college, and living among the English."

He shook his head. "I don't think she truly knows who you are."

Lindsay studied his expression, wondering what his comment meant. Did Matthew understand her? Did *he* know who Lindsay truly was on the inside?

"Matt!" Samuel called from the kitchen. "You're missing out. These cookies are *appeditlich*. Lizzie Anne outdid herself."

Lizzie Anne laughed. "Lindsay, you'd better hurry up before Samuel eats them all!"

"I guess we better get inside before they come for us," Lindsay said.

Matthew smiled. "They aren't very subtle."

Stepping through the door, Lindsay wondered why Jessica couldn't see how wonderful it was to be a part of the Kauffman extended family.

5

Rebecca stepped over to the sink where Lindsay was scrubbing the dishes. Her niece's hand moved back and forth with such force that she feared the dish would break in half.

"Lindsay?" she asked gently. "Are you okay?"

"I'm fine," Lindsay muttered without making eye contact. "You can go on up to bed. I'll finish cleaning this up."

Rebecca glanced over at her mother-in-law, who was placing the uneaten desserts in a large box. "Do you need any help, *Mamm*?"

"Oh no," Elizabeth said with a smile. "I'm just fine. I think Eli has the horse and buggy hitched. We're heading out." She looked toward the sink. "*Gut nacht,* Lindsay. It was a lovely party. *Danki* for inviting us."

"It would've been nice if my sister had stayed to enjoy her own party," Lindsay snapped as she faced them. She gestured around the room. "I invited everyone we know and many of us worked hard to make food. All of it was for her, and what did she do? She picked a fight with me and then took off. Why do I try to be nice to her? She's not nice to me."

Lindsay's eyes filled with tears, and Rebecca rushed over to her. "What happened, *mei liewe*?"

Shaking her head, Lindsay turned back to the sink.

"I'm sorry this wasn't a *froh* night for you." Elizabeth gave a sad smile and touched Lindsay's arm. "What did you and your sister fight about?"

Tears streamed down Lindsay's face. "It was awful. She wants me to go to New York with her, and I refused. She said some horrible things, and I did too. I didn't want to fight with her before she left for New York, but she argued with me and then took off with Jake in his truck."

Rebecca came up behind Lindsay and rubbed her back. "You mustn't let this come between you and your sister. I wish I had kept in closer contact with your mother all those years."

"I try, *Aenti* Rebecca." Wiping her eyes, Lindsay turned to Rebecca. "But she keeps pushing me. She's convinced I'm going to look back someday and regret not going to school. She says I'll think I've wasted my life, but I don't feel that way at all. This is my home now."

"Only you can decide where you belong." Rebecca touched Lindsay's shoulder. "And you don't have to stay here because you think it's what I want for you. You should only worry about what you want. Understand? You don't need to stay here for me."

"This is what I want." Lindsay faced Elizabeth. "I just don't understand why this has to be so hard. We lost our parents, but now she wants to argue about what I want for my life. Why does she have to make losing Mom and Dad even more difficult for me? Every time we argue, I feel like we're hurting Mom or disappointing her. Jessica makes the grief ache even more."

Elizabeth cupped a hand to Lindsay's cheek. "Unfortunately, life isn't easy, but we find comfort in the Lord. The Bible says, 'We also rejoice in our sufferings, because we know that suffering produces perseverance; perseverance, character; and character, hope.' "

Rebecca wished she could take away her niece's pain. "Elizabeth's right. You'll always miss your parents, but you have to hold strong to our faith. It will always get you through the rough times."

"*Ya*. You're right," Lindsay said.

Elizabeth kissed Lindsay's cheek. "I need to go. I'll see you soon." She turned to Rebecca. "You take it easy. You look exhausted."

Rebecca smiled. Elizabeth was thoughtful and loving, just like her own mother. "*Danki*. Be safe going home."

Elizabeth picked up the box of desserts and started toward the door. "*Gut nacht*. Sleep well." She disappeared through the door.

Lindsay continued washing the dishes while Rebecca cleaned the table and the counter. They worked in silence for a few minutes.

Once the counter was clean, Rebecca looked back toward her niece, who was working like a robot, washing the dishes, pans, and utensils with swift movements. A scowl twisted up her pretty face.

Rebecca wished she could read Lindsay's thoughts and comfort her grief. She sat at the kitchen table and tapped the chair next to her. "Lindsay. Sit with me."

Lindsay placed the last dish in the drain. "Do you want me to sweep the floor now or tomorrow?"

Rebecca tapped the chair again. "Forget the floor. Sit."

Lindsay lowered herself into the chair and rested her chin on the palm of her hand.

"Do you want to talk about your argument with Jessica?"

Lindsay shrugged. "There really isn't anything else to say. She'll never understand me or respect my decision. She'll always treat me like a child and talk to me as if I'm too uneducated or immature to know what's right for me."

"I know Jessica frustrates you," Rebecca began, "but you have to realize you can't change her. You're going to have to find a way to let her comments go before all of that anger eats you up inside."

Lindsay shook her head. "Funny. Katie said something similar."

"Katie is very wise." Rebecca glanced at the clock. "It's getting late. You should probably head to bed. It's been a long day."

Lindsay frowned. "I'm not ready for bed. I want to wait up for her and ask her why she walked out on her own party."

Rebecca shook her head. "I don't think that's a good idea to pick a fight with her. She's leaving tomorrow, so you should make peace with her. She's your only *schweschder,* and you love her, *ya?*"

Lindsay's green eyes were determined. "I'm tired of her stubbornness and self-centeredness. She owes me an apology."

"But she's your *schweschder,* Lindsay," Rebecca repeated. "The Lord wants us to love each other and live in peace. That's our way."

"I know. I'm just really frustrated." Lindsay popped up from the table and peeked through the kitchen window above the sink. "Here she comes. Jake's pickup just pulled up to the barn."

Rebecca said a silent prayer, asking God to change her nieces' hearts toward each other and help them work out their differences before Jessica left in the morning.

"Looks like they're having an intense conversation," Lindsay said, still staring out the window. "I wonder if she told him off too."

"Lindsay ..." Rebecca said. "That's not nice."

"I know, but she was on a roll today." Lindsay continued to gaze out the window.

Rebecca absently folded a stray napkin left on the table. "I saw you talking to Matthew Glick for quite a while in the kitchen. He's a nice young man, *ya?*"

Facing Rebecca, Lindsay's ivory cheeks flushed a bright pink. "He's nice. Very nice."

"It's *gut* how he spends time with Daniel," Rebecca continued.

"I think he sees Daniel sort of as a father figure since his own *daed* abandoned him."

"That makes sense," Lindsay said.

"He's a *gut* man, Lindsay." Rebecca smiled. What she wanted to say was that she also thought Matthew was sweet on Lindsay. However, she thought it best to keep that thought to herself for the time being.

"He is." Lindsay turned back to the window. "We're just friends."

The back door opened and then slammed shut, revealing Daniel, who had been taking care of the animals. He kicked off his boots and tossed his straw hat onto the peg by the back door. "Jessica is out back talking to Jake." He crossed the kitchen and kissed Rebecca's head. "You look worn out, Becky. Are you feeling all right?"

Cupping her hand to her mouth, she yawned and smiled. "I'm tired but doing fine, *danki*."

Daniel looked skeptical. "I think you need more rest. Come up to bed."

"I'll be up in a bit," she said, gazing up at him. "I want to speak to Jessica when she comes in. She's leaving tomorrow, and we haven't had much time to talk."

"If she'd stayed at the party ..." Lindsay began.

"Don't stay up too late," he warned. "I'll be down to get you if you're not up after my shower."

"Okay." Rebecca smiled at him before he headed toward the stairs. She glanced back at Lindsay, who was studying the scene out the window. Rebecca wanted to speak with Jessica, but she also wanted to be sure that the girls didn't get into another emotional argument. Her plan was to diffuse any bickering before it escalated, as her own mother had tried to do when she and Grace were young.

"Here she comes," Lindsay said from the window. "She's not smiling."

The back door opened and closed, and Jessica walked into the kitchen, her pretty face turned down in a frown and her eyes red and puffy.

Rebecca stood. "Are you all right, Jessica?"

"Where have you been?" Lindsay asked while standing hands on hips in front of her sister. "Didn't you remember that this party was for you? I can't believe you just took off and missed nearly the whole night. Do you realize how thoughtless that is?"

"Whoa!" Jessica held her hands up. "If I'd known I was going to get the third degree, then I would've found somewhere else to stay tonight."

"That's not necessary," Rebecca said. "You're family and always welcome here." She sat and pointed to the chair across from her. "Sit and tell us what happened, Jessica." She motioned for Lindsay to sit also.

"This better be good," Lindsay snapped, dropping into the chair next to Rebecca.

Rebecca shot her a warning glance, and Lindsay's expression softened. "Now, Jessica," Rebecca began, "please tell us why you're so upset."

"Jake and I had a terrible argument." Her voice was thick.

Rebecca reached over and took Jessica's hand in hers. "What happened?"

Jessica cleared her throat. "We talked, and Jake said that he feels like he holds me back. He said that we're from different worlds and want different things out of life. He said that he's tired of waiting for me and he thinks we're stuck in one place in our friendship. He said that we should remain friends but go our separate ways."

Tears spilled from Jessica's eyes, and Rebecca handed her the napkin she'd been folding and unfolding. "Oh, dear. I'm so sorry." She glanced at Lindsay who looked sympathetic. "Would you please get your *schweschder* a glass of water?"

Lindsay jumped up and rushed to the sink.

Rebecca patted Jessica's hand. "I know it hurts, Jessica, but maybe you can work things out when you get back from New York."

"I don't know," Jessica said while wiping her eyes. "He seems really hurt that I chose New York over him. He insists we'll never want the same thing. The truth is, I'm not sure what I want yet. I feel like I'm young and have a lot of living to do before I settle down."

Lindsay returned with a glass of water and set it in front of Jessica. "You say you don't know what you want, but you criticize those who do."

Jessica sipped the water and then turned to her sister. "I didn't criticize you, Lindsay. I merely suggested that you keep your options open."

"But that's not your decision," Lindsay countered, scowling. "It's up to me if I want to live here, just like it's up you if you want to go to New York."

"Can we not rehash this now?" Jessica snapped. "I think I've been through enough tonight."

"Have you?" Lindsay's voice rose. "I'm still reeling from what you said to me on the porch. Doesn't that count for something?"

"Girls! Girls!" Rebecca held her hands up. "You must lower your voices. You'll wake the *kinner*, and you'll upset Daniel." The groan of the water pressure above the kitchen sent relief flowing through Rebecca. She was glad Daniel was in the shower and out of earshot of the bickering. "Now, you two have argued enough for one day. You're family. Stop hurting each other and speak with respect."

Lindsay sighed. "Fine. Jessica, I'm sorry that you and Jake had a terrible argument. However, I want you to know that you hurt me when you took off after saying all of those hateful things to me."

Jessica wiped her eyes with the napkin. "I'm sorry that my words came across as hateful, but I was only trying to give you options."

"I don't want your options," Lindsay said simply. "I want your respect."

Rebecca was tickled by how mature Lindsay sounded. She bit her lower lip to stop a grin from forming.

Jessica sipped her drink. "I respect you, but I also want what's best for you."

"I'm not your child," Lindsay said. "And you were thoughtless to leave tonight. This party was for you."

"I didn't want a party," Jessica said. "I came here to see you, Rebecca, the family here in this house, and Jake. That was it."

Lindsay shook her head, looking frustrated. "How can you be so self-centered? Don't you realize that everyone loves you and wants to see you before you leave for New York? You're so into yourself that you can't see beyond your own world. It's not just about you. You think you're so grown up, but you're still the same selfish little girl you always were."

Jessica lips formed a wry smirk. "Really? Little Miss Baker is going to tell me what it's like to be an adult? What responsibilities do you have beyond making cookies for tourists?"

Rebecca's stomach twisted at the sting of their words for each other. She had to stop them before they permanently damaged their already fragile relationship. "Girls," she began with a frown. "You're getting out of hand again. Tone it down before you say something you'll regret."

"I want to answer that, *Aenti* Rebecca," Lindsay said. "I have quite a few responsibilities. I not only work for the bakery, but I do plenty around the house to help Rebecca and to care for our cousins. You may not see working in a bakery as a worthy job, but it is to me. I'm contributing to my community and my family—both my family in this house and the extended Kauffman family." She tapped the table for emphasis as she spoke. "I don't have to be a college student to be considered responsible. In fact, I'm more responsible than a college student because I'm thinking about more people than just myself."

Jessica rolled her eyes. "Lindsay, you've got it all wrong. I think of more than—"

"That's enough," Rebecca said, her voice louder than she expected.

Startled, her nieces jumped and stared at her.

"I'm not going to sit here and listen to you two try to destroy each other," Rebecca began. "I wish I could speak to *mei schweschder* one last time, but you two look as if you don't care if you ever see each other after tonight. You need to love each other, even if you don't agree on things. *Mei schweschder* and I were very different, as you two are." She pointed between them. "But I loved Grace, and she loved me. She chose a different path, just as you two seem to be choosing. That doesn't make one of you more mature or one of you smarter. That makes each of you different, and God loves all of us, no matter how different we are."

They both looked ashamed.

"Now, apologize and agree to disagree." Rebecca paused as the girls stared at each other. "Go on. It's getting late, and I'm tired."

"I'm sorry," Lindsay said softly. "I still feel that my choices are my business, but I didn't want to hurt you. You're my only sister, and I love you."

Rebecca smiled. *Lindsay is such a sweet and thoughtful girl, and she's growing up so quickly.*

"I'm sorry too, Linds." Jessica sighed. "I didn't mean to hurt you either. And of course I love you. You're my baby sister, and you mean a lot to me, which is why I care. But I didn't mean to hurt you."

Rebecca nodded. *She's grown up too.* She reached over and squeezed their hands. "I'm proud of you both. Now, it's bedtime. We can talk more in the morning, right, Jessica? You're not leaving at the crack of dawn?"

Jessica shook her head. "No, not at dawn. I'd like to get on the road before noon, though."

"*Gut.*" Rebecca squeezed Jessica's hand once more before she stood. "I want to get to bed. You two don't stay up too late now."

"We won't," Lindsay said.

"Good night," Rebecca said as she headed for the stairs. "See you in the morning." She climbed the stairs as the girls echoed her good-night wishes. As she started down the hallway toward her room, she hoped that her nieces would forget their differences and remember to always cherish each other.

Lindsay took Jessica's glass to the sink and began washing it. While the bubbles moved over the glass, she contemplated Rebecca's lecture. As usual, her aunt was right about things. It was more important for Lindsay to accept that Jessica had different ideas about her future than it was for her to continually fight with her sister about it. In the end, they would lose the argument along with losing each other.

"She has a way with words, huh?" Jessica said, leaning against the counter. "She gets right to the heart of things."

"*Ya,* she does." Lindsay placed the glass in the drain and wiped her hands on a towel. "I'm really sorry about how things went with Jake. I didn't expect that this weekend."

"Me either." Jessica hoisted her thin body into a sitting position on the counter. "I think he's right, though. I'm not sure what I want. I've never made any promises to him, and we never outwardly considered each other more than friends. He told me he loved me tonight, which sort of surprised me. But he also said we're too different." She frowned, looking defeated. "It's all so confusing."

"You can be together and be different." Lindsay tossed the towel onto the counter. "Mom and Dad were total opposites. I mean, she was a total neat freak, and he always threw his dirty socks onto the floor." She giggled. "I remember one day where they yelled at each other for hours because he walked across the kitchen in muddy boots."

Jessica guffawed. "I remember that!" She shook her head. "That was so funny. He couldn't understand what the big deal was until she made him mop."

Lindsay laughed and wiped her eyes with the back of her hands. "See? You and Jake can be different but still be more than friends."

Jessica shook her head, and her smile faded. "This is different. Mom and Dad wanted the same things. They wanted a family, and they wanted to live in Virginia. I don't know where I want to live."

"Only time will tell." Lindsay cupped her hand to her mouth as she yawned. "I think I'm ready for bed. It's been a long day."

Jessica hopped down from the counter and touched Lindsay's arm. "One thing. I know you and I will never agree on where you should live, but I have one request."

Lindsay squelched the urge to roll her eyes. "What now?"

"Please just consider getting your GED," Jessica began.

"Jess, we've been through this," Lindsay said, resentment bubbling inside her. "I don't want to—"

"Just hear me out." Jessica held her hands up as if to surrender. "I'm not saying that you need to go back to school, but getting your GED will give you more options if you decide to pursue employment outside of the bakery. It's not like going back to school full-time. From what I've found through research, you'd just have to study and take a test."

"You've researched this?"

"Yes."

Lindsay eyed her with suspicion. "Why?"

"For you." Jessica forced a smile. "Because I care."

Lindsay frowned, shook her head, and then hugged Jessica. "You make me crazy, but I still love you."

"I feel the same way about you." Jessica steered Lindsay

toward the stairs. "Let's hit the hay. I'm wiped out, and I have a long ride tomorrow."

"Hang on." Lindsay jogged back to the kitchen and made sure the back door was locked before snuffing out the lantern. She then followed Jessica up the stairs.

Standing outside her room, Lindsay smiled at Jessica. "Sleep well."

"You too," Jessica said through a yawn before disappearing into the room.

After changing into her nightshirt and shorts, Lindsay snuggled under the covers in the spare bed in Emma's room. She was careful not to wake her little cousin who was snoring softly. Lindsay closed her eyes and contemplated the whole emotional day. Two things haunted her mind—Matthew's intense eyes, and Jessica's insistence that Lindsay earn her GED.

Rebecca sat on the edge of the bed while running a brush through her waist-length hair. A hand on her shoulder caused her to jump with a start.

"You're not yourself lately, Becky," Daniel said, his voice warm and smooth. "Tell me what's wrong."

She faced him, and he placed the Bible he'd been reading on the nightstand next to the lantern. "I'm worried about the girls. They've been arguing, and I fear that they will get so frustrated that they'll stop speaking altogether. Grace would want them to remain close despite their differences. I know I have regrets in my relationship with Grace. I regret not visiting her more often."

Daniel reached over and pushed her hair back from her face. "You're very *gut* to those girls. Don't ever doubt Grace's faith in you."

Rebecca nodded. When a wave of pain stabbed her in the abdomen, she bit her lower lip and groaned.

Daniel scooted across the bed and pulled her to him.

"Becky?" His eyes widened with alarm. "Do you need a doctor? Should I go out to the phone shanty and call for a ride to the hospital?"

"No, no." She held onto his arm and breathed deeply as the pain lessened. "I'm okay. I think I just ate too much." She studied the pattern on his pajama pants until the pain evaporated.

He put a finger under her chin and pointed her eyes toward his. "You're not telling me the whole truth, Becky. I know it's more than just indigestion."

"I'm fine now. It was nothing." She touched his cheek, enjoying the roughness of his whiskers. "You worry too much. Let's go to bed."

He frowned. "I want you to see a doctor if this continues. I mean it. I'll drag you there myself if I have to."

"You worry too much," she repeated.

"Becky ..."

"Fine, fine." She said. "I promise I'll see a doctor if it continues."

"*Gut.*" He climbed over to his side of the bed.

Rebecca blew out the lantern and snuggled down beside Daniel. As she drifted off to sleep, she hoped that the strange pain in her abdomen truly was nothing, but she knew in her heart that something wasn't right.

6

"That should do it," Jessica said, slamming the tailgate of her Jeep Cherokee. "It's all packed."

Lindsay hugged her arms to her chest and wished her eyes wouldn't fill with tears. After all, she would see her sister in a few months. Lindsay glanced toward the porch. "You already kissed Emma and Junior, right?"

"Yes." Jessica lowered herself onto the bumper of her Jeep. "And I hugged Aunt Rebecca and shook Uncle Daniel's hand. I promised I'll call as soon as I get there."

Lindsay looked toward the end of the driveway. "I'm surprised Jake didn't come to say good-bye."

Jessica frowned. "I'm not."

"Are you going to call him?"

"Maybe in a couple of weeks." Jessica stood and stretched. "I better get going. I have a long drive ahead of me. I didn't get much sleep last night, so I don't want to be on the road too late."

Lindsay pulled her older sister into a hug and squeezed her tight. "You be safe. Don't go out alone, and stay away from clubs. Don't talk to strangers either. Remember what Mom and Dad told us about men who try to take advantage of young women."

Jessica laughed. "Now you sound like the overprotective one." She touched Lindsay's shoulder. "You know I'll be safe, and I'll keep in touch. You be sure to check that phone shanty every day."

"You can always write me a letter or call me at the bakery too," Lindsay said.

"Right." Jessica hugged her again. "You take care. Love you."

"Love you too." Lindsay stood by the porch steps while Jessica climbed into the SUV and brought the engine to life. She waved as Jessica motored down the driveway toward the main road.

Once the SUV was out of sight, Lindsay ascended the porch steps and sat on the swing. A gentle breeze moved over her as she pushed the swing back and forth. The door opened, and Rebecca appeared, sinking onto the swing next to her.

"She's gone," Lindsay said. "She blows in and out like the wind."

Rebecca smiled. "*Ya,* she does."

"Are Emma and Junior sleeping?"

"They are. They wanted to stay up and play, but I told them that it's nap time."

Lindsay crossed her arms over her chest and leaned back on the swing. "Do you think she'll stay in New York City?"

"No, I don't. I think she'll love her time there, but she'll go back to Virginia to finish college. Maybe she'll go back to New York after college, but she's determined to finish her schooling."

Lindsay stared across the pasture while contemplating her conversations with Jessica. "I didn't tell you what she said to me last night."

"What did she say?"

"She said that I should seriously consider getting my GED." Lindsay turned toward Rebecca to read her reaction to the words. "She said that if I ever decide to look for a job outside of the bakery, it will be easier for me if I have my GED. Do you think she's right?"

Rebecca touched Lindsay's hand. "I think that's up to you, Lindsay. I never saw the need to continue my schooling, and it wasn't an option after I joined the church. However, you haven't joined the church, so you're free to do as you like."

Disappointed, Lindsay sighed. She'd hoped Rebecca would give her the answer that would settle all of her anxiety. "That doesn't help me. That just makes me more confused."

"Don't try to figure everything out all at once. Open your heart to God and let Him guide you." Rebecca stood. "Would you like a glass of tea? I just mixed some."

"Yes, please." Lindsay smiled at her aunt.

Rebecca stopped at the door. "Are you going to Katie's this afternoon for the youth gathering?"

"*Ya*." "*Onkel* Daniel said he'd take me over there."

"*Gut*," Rebecca said. "You need a little fun to take your mind off everything that's bothering you. Tonight enjoy your friends and don't worry about the differences between you and your *schweschder*."

"Okay." Lindsay stared across the field and sent a silent prayer up to God, asking for His guidance on what path she should choose for her life.

Lindsay sat on a bench between Lizzie Anne and Katie in Katie's family's barn later that afternoon. Girls from the community surrounded them while the young men sat in groups on the other side of the barn. The young people had joined together to sing hymns from the *Ausbund*, and a table of snacks and drinks sat in the back corner.

"I can't believe Matthew came," Katie leaned over and whispered to Lindsay. "Samuel's been trying to get him to join in at the singings, and I guess Matthew finally gave in."

Lindsay cut her eyes to Matthew, sitting across the way, and she gasped when she found him watching her. She quickly averted her eyes and studied her hymnal.

"Maybe he'll offer to give you a ride home," Katie said.

Lindsay met her friend's grin with a questioning expression. "What are you saying?"

"Don't be *gegisch*." Katie bumped Lindsay's arm with her elbow. "It's obvious that he likes you."

Lindsay's cheeks heated. "We're just friends."

"So you say," Katie said with a laugh.

"What about you?" Lindsay said. "You're always so quick to tease me. Who do you like?"

Katie shrugged. "I don't know. No one strikes my fancy here. I think I need to look in other districts. I've known these *buwe* all my life."

Lizzie Anne leaned over. "What are you two whispering about? I feel left out."

"Matthew Glick," Katie said, gesturing in his direction.

"Stop!" Lindsay reached over and took Katie's arm. "He'll see you and know we're talking about him."

"What did I miss?" Lizzie Anne demanded. "What did you say about him?"

"I said that Samuel finally got him to come to a singing so he must be ready to date."

Lizzie Anne grinned. "*Ach*, you're right!"

Lindsay shook her head. "He might just want to get to know all of the youth in the community better."

"*Ya*," Katie said, elbowing Lindsay again. "Probably you." She stood. "I'm going to go see if we need more drinks."

"I'll come with you," Lindsay said.

"I will too," Lizzie Anne chimed in.

Lindsay followed Katie and Lizzie Anne to the snack tables, where they collected the empty pitchers of water and meadow tea and the empty food trays.

Balancing the trays and pitchers, they crossed the driveway to the house, passing groups of young people on the way to the kitchen.

After refilling the trays and pitchers, they headed back to

the barn. Lindsay bit her bottom lip while balancing two large trays in her hands, one full of whoopie pies and the other covered in an assortment of cookies. As she stepped over to a dip in the driveway, she started to stumble. A strong hand steadied her arm and grabbed a tray before she dropped it.

Lindsay glanced over and found Matthew smiling while holding the tray of whoopie pies. "*Danki*," she said. "You stopped me from looking *gegisch* and ruining our dessert."

"You brought these for me?" he teased with a smile. "How thoughtful of you. I'm *froh* I saved them before they hit the ground. *Danki*."

Lindsay chuckled. "*Gern gschehne*."

They fell into step, side by side on the way to the barn.

"I was surprised to see you here," she said. "You don't usually come to singings."

Matthew shrugged. "Samuel kept insisting I needed to get out more, so here I am."

She smiled. "I'm glad you were here to save the whoopie pies."

He laughed and gestured for her to step into the barn in front of him, where a chorus of voices continued singing hymns in High German.

Lindsay placed her tray on the table next to the whoopie pies that he'd carried. She then leaned over to him, taking in his musky scent. "Thanks, again," she said over the hymns. "That could've been a disaster."

"I'm glad I could help," he said. "Want to go for a walk?"

"That sounds nice." She absently smoothed her dress and touched her prayer covering.

He swiped two whoopie pies from the tray and then made a sweeping gesture toward the door. They stepped out onto the driveway and started slowly toward the pasture.

"It's nice out tonight," he said between bites. "Not too cool."

"*Ya*." She twirled her finger around the ribbon ties hanging from her prayer covering.

"Did your *schweschder* leave?" He finished the first whoopie pie while they walked.

"*Ya*. She left after lunch today. I would imagine she's arrived by now."

"Are you feeling better about her visit?"

Lindsay shrugged. "I guess everything is okay now. She upset me, but we sort of agreed to disagree last night before we went to bed. We're on speaking terms again."

"That's *wunderbaar*. It's not *gut* to harbor resentment. I know a lot about that." He walked over to a bench next to the fence. "Want to sit?"

"Sure." She dropped onto the seat next to him and pondered his words. What did Matthew Glick resent? Could it be his father?

He held the second whoopie pie. "Would you like half?"

She shook her head. "No, but *danki*."

He raised an eyebrow. "I don't think I've ever seen you eat."

She blanched. "I eat. In fact, I eat a lot."

He grinned. "I doubt that from the looks of you."

She placed her hand on her chest with feigned offense. "What's that supposed to mean?"

"I'm only teasing you." He bit into the whoopie pie. "You couldn't have made these. They're not nearly as *gut* as the ones I had at your house the other day."

"I didn't make them, but I won't tell the baker that they're not up to your standards." She studied him while contemplating his smiles and jokes. This was not the same Matthew Glick she'd met two years ago. "You're different. What made you change?"

His smile faded. "What do you mean?"

"When you first came here, you would hardly speak to me. Now you joke with me as if we're old friends." She held her breath, hoping she hadn't said too much to him. However, lately the truth seemed to flow easily from her lips when he was around.

"Aren't we friends?" He raised an eyebrow and then licked the remaining icing off his fingers.

"*Ya*." Her cheeks heated. "But I didn't think you liked me when I first met you. At least, it seemed like you didn't like anyone."

"I wasn't very friendly, was I?" He shifted his weight on the bench. "I had a lot of things to work out when I first came here. I was trying to figure out where I belonged in the community since I was living in my sister's house, but I wasn't the man of the house. I also had some issues with *mei daed* to work out."

"Was that the resentment you mentioned earlier?"

He nodded. "I'm glad you were able to talk to your *schweschder*. Family problems can wear on you."

"*Ya*, they can." Lindsay studied his eyes and wished he would open up more. However, she was thankful to have his friendship, no matter how little information he shared with her. "What do you want, Matthew?"

He looked surprised. "What do you mean?"

"What do you want for your life, for your future?"

He blew out a breath and stretched his arm out behind her on the back of the bench. "I guess I want what any one of us wants—a home, maybe even a family. I've been saving money so I can build my own place at the back of my sister's land." He pointed toward the adjacent farm. "She said I can build back there and have my own privacy. Daniel, Luke, and Timothy said they'd help me construct a little house when I'm ready. I may be close to starting it soon. My *mamm* left some money for mei *schweschder* and me. I'm anxious to be on my own for real."

"You're close to Daniel, *ya*?" she asked.

He nodded. "I guess the Kauffmans sort of adopted me. Daniel's easy to talk to."

"I know. I'm very thankful and feel very blessed to be a part of the family after losing my parents. The Kauffmans are wonderful people."

"And what about you, Lindsay?" he asked. "What do you want out of your life?"

She shrugged. "I don't know. I know I want to be near family and I want to be *froh*."

"Don't we all?"

"*Ya*." She leaned back on the bench and felt her body relax. For the first time since her sister's visit, Lindsay felt content. They sat in silence for several minutes while the sun began to set before them. Lindsay smiled, enjoying Matthew's company along with the golden hues of the setting sun.

"God paints with the most beautiful watercolors, *ya*?" Matthew asked.

"*Ya*," she agreed. "He does."

"Lindsay!" a voice called behind them. "Lindsay!"

"Yes?" Lindsay asked. Turning, she spotted Katie coming up the path toward the bench. She bit her lip, wishing Katie would keep walking so that she could continue her time alone with Matthew.

"Samuel said he'll take you home if you're ready to go," Katie said. "Lizzie Anne has to get home, so Sam told me to come and get you. He can drop you on the way."

"Oh." Lindsay glanced at Matthew, wishing that he would offer to take her home. However, she quickly pushed that thought aside, knowing the repercussions if he took her home. Getting a ride home from a boy would imply that they were dating. While Lindsay liked Matthew and wanted to get to know him better, she wasn't certain she wanted to date him or any other boy for that matter.

"I can take you home." Matthew gestured toward the neighboring farm. "I can go hitch up my buggy and get back here in a few minutes."

"That's okay. I'll just ride with Samuel and Lizzie Anne." Lindsay stood. "I enjoyed talking with you."

"Me too." He smiled. "I hope to see you again soon."

"*Ya*. You too." Her cheeks burned as she hurried up the path toward Katie. She thought of several things she should've said to Matthew that would've sounded more intelligent than "You too," but it was too late to say them now.

Katie grinned at her. "I guess I should've kept my mouth shut and told Samuel you had a ride."

"That's okay." Lindsay touched her friend's arm. "Matthew and I were only talking, and I wouldn't have wanted him to feel obligated to take me home and give people the impression that we're more than friends."

"Is that what you tell yourself?" Katie laughed while giving Lindsay a playful punch on her arm.

Lindsay smiled. She was so glad that she'd told Jessica she didn't want to go to New York City. She had all the joy she needed right here in Lancaster County.

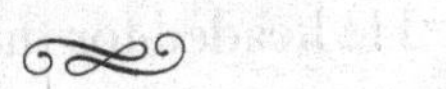

"Matthew offered to take you home?" Rebecca couldn't stop her smile as she cut up an apple for Emma's breakfast the following morning.

Lindsay gave a dramatic sigh and handed Junior a bowl of oatmeal. "We're just *freinden, Aenti.*"

"*Ya,*" Rebecca said. "For now you are."

While placing a slice of apple on Emma's tray, Rebecca remembered back to when she'd first met Daniel. They'd been friends for a long time, since they'd grown up in the same church district. However, one night at a singing he asked to take her home and something was different about him. She'd never noticed how blue his eyes were or how infectious his laugh was. It was as if she were seeing him with new eyes. She wondered if the same thing would happen to Lindsay someday—if Matthew was the one God intended for her niece to marry when the time was right.

A wave of painful exhaustion over took her, and Rebecca

placed the apple in front of Emma before she yawned. "Excuse me," she said. "I didn't sleep at all last night. I just tossed and turned. I couldn't seem to get comfortable."

"Oh," Lindsay said, looking concerned. "Do you think you need to see a doctor?"

Daniel stepped into the room. "*Was iss letz?* Becky?" His eyes mirrored Lindsay's concern.

"I'm okay," Rebecca told him. "I'm fine. I was just telling Lindsay that I didn't sleep last night. I couldn't get comfortable."

He frowned. "I'm going to call the doctor. This exhaustion has gone on too long. It's time to find out what's wrong." He turned to Lindsay. "Would you stay here with the *kinner* while I take Rebecca to the doctor?"

"*Ya.*" Lindsay gave a quick nod. "Of course."

"Our ride for work should be here soon, and I'll have him take us right way." He headed for the back door. "I'll go call the doctor and then let *mei mamm* know that Lindsay won't be at the bakery today."

"Daniel," Rebecca called after him. "It's not necessary."

The slam of the back door told Rebecca that there would be no further discussion. She turned toward Lindsay's worried expression. "I'm fine," she said. "There's no need to get upset."

Lindsay turned back to Junior. Speaking softly in Pennsylvania Dutch, she discussed his breakfast with him.

Rebecca sent up a silent prayer that she was okay and that God would comfort her family while she and Daniel were at the doctor's office.

Rebecca smoothed her hands over her dark purple dress while she sat on the examination table.

Across the small room, Daniel sat, turning his straw hat over and over again in his hands. It was a stance she'd seen many times during their marriage. Whenever Daniel was consumed by worry, he'd shut down, absently twiddling his hat and not answering Rebecca when she tried to speak to him. She learned soon after they were married to let him handle his worries his own way, even though it made her crazy when he didn't talk to her.

The door opened with a whoosh, and Dr. Moore stepped in, a clipboard in his hand and a pleasant expression on his face.

The doctor smiled, and instant relief flooded Rebecca. She released the breath she'd been holding for what felt like a long time.

"Mr. and Mrs. Kauffman," Dr. Moore began, "I have good news."

"I'm not sick?" Rebecca asked, clasping her hands together.

"No, ma'am. You're not." Dr. Moore took off his glasses and looked between them. "You are, however, expecting."

Rebecca gasped, cupping her hands to her mouth. "We're expecting?"

Daniel popped up from the chair and rushed over to her. "Another baby?" He gave a loud bark of laughter. "A third? God is so good!"

Tears filled Rebecca's eyes. "It's a miracle," she whispered. "Truly a miracle."

"When is she due?" Daniel asked.

The doctor looked down at the chart. "From my calculations, I would say early January—approximately January 11."

Rebecca smiled. "I can't believe it."

"I'm going to refer you to a specialist, since you're forty and considered a high risk," the doctor said. "The pain you experienced the other night is caused by your uterus expanding. You should take any pain like that as a warning sign that you need to take it easy."

Daniel stood beside her and rubbed her back while the doctor continued to talk.

Rebecca watched Dr. Moore's lips move, but his words were only background noise to her raging thoughts.

Another baby.

Three children.

Yes, God is good!

Maybe Rebecca and Daniel would finally have the large family they'd always dreamt of. However, the doctor said that this would be a high-risk pregnancy. She would have to pray often for the baby's health.

"Do you have any questions?" Dr. Moore asked, bringing Rebecca back to the present.

"No," she whispered, her voice trembling with emotion.

"All right then." Dr. Moore moved toward the door. "I'll have Libby make an appointment for you with a specialist. Congratulations."

Once the doctor disappeared through the door, Daniel pulled Rebecca to him, holding her tight. "Becky, can you believe it? Another baby? And we thought we'd never have one. Soon we'll have three."

"Three *kinner,*" she whispered. "It's a miracle." She let the news filter through her brain while she held onto Daniel.

Rebecca found Lindsay sitting on the family room floor with Emma and Junior. When Lindsay's eyes met Rebecca, they filled with concern.

"*Mamm*!" Junior ran over and wrapped his arms around Rebecca's leg.

Emma followed suit, and Rebecca scooped her up in her arms and hugged her tight.

Lindsay rose to her feet and watched Rebecca. Her eyes remained hesitant. "How'd it go?"

Rebecca dropped into a chair and held Emma close on her lap. "It went well." She held Emma's hands, and the baby giggled and swayed back and forth on her lap.

Lindsay held her palms up. "Are you going to tell me? The suspense is killing me."

"I'm not sick." Rebecca smiled at Emma and glanced at Junior, who played with homemade wooden blocks on the floor.

"What is it, *Aenti*?"

"It's a secret," Rebecca said. "It has to stay in this house."

Lindsay gasped. "You're having another baby!"

Nodding, Rebecca laughed.

Lindsay rushed over and hugged her, nearly knocking Emma off Rebecca's lap. Emma squealed and grabbed Rebecca's apron in response.

"Oh, sorry, Emmy," Lindsay said, hugging her. "Oh, this is such *wunderbaar* news! You and *Onkel* Daniel must be so happy."

"*Ya*, we are." Rebecca pushed one of Emma's light brown curls back from her face. "For many years we thought we'd never be blessed with a *boppli*, and now we'll have three."

"When are you due?" Lindsay asked.

"January 11."

"I'm so *froh* for you and *Onkel* Daniel! My mom used to always say that the Lord works in mysterious ways," Lindsay said, lowering herself into the chair next to Rebecca's. "She was right about that. We have to keep this a secret, right?"

"*Ya*." Rebecca smiled and touched Emma's curls. "That's our way. Having a baby is a very private miracle in our culture. We don't boast about it because it shows too much pride. As my *mammi* used to say, we celebrate it with a cautious joy and don't even tell our closest friends."

"May I tell Jessica? I was going to write a letter to her tonight."

"You may tell Jessica." Rebecca set Emma down, and she waddled over to Junior, dropped to the floor, and grabbed a block from the pile.

"Do you have to go back to the doctor?"

"Next week." Rebecca leaned back in the chair and rubbed

her abdomen. "I'm going to see a new doctor who is a specialist. I'm considered a high risk due to my age."

"Oh." Lindsay looked curious and then started for the door. "Would you like some meadow tea?"

"I think I'd rather just have water. *Danki.*" Rebecca watched her children play with blocks and wondered if she would have another boy or another girl. What would her next child look like? Would the baby be blond like Daniel or have dark hair like her? Closing her eyes, she sent up another prayer for a healthy baby. She opened her eyes and found Lindsay standing over her.

"You okay?" Lindsay asked, handing her a glass of water.

"*Ya.*" Rebecca sipped her drink. "*Danki.*"

"*Gern gschehne.*" Lindsay sat in the chair. "I'm so glad I didn't go to New York."

Rebecca studied her niece. "You considered going?"

Lindsay focused on the liquid in her glass as she spoke. "Last night I couldn't sleep and I was wondering what life would've been like if I'd gone with Jessica."

"Do you regret staying here?" Rebecca said the words slowly, hoping that the answer wouldn't break her heart.

"No." Lindsay met her gaze. "You need me here."

"But is this what you want?" Rebecca asked.

"I already told you, *Aenti*. My joy is here." She gestured around the room. "But sometimes I wonder if I should go see the world just to be sure before I join the church."

Rebecca sipped her water and watched her children while she considered Lindsay's words. Was her niece only staying here out of obligation or did she truly want to live here?

"I guess *Onkel* Daniel went back to work?" Lindsay asked.

"*Ya.*" Rebecca placed her glass on the end table. "He had a project he needed to finish up today."

"I bet he's excited, *ya?*" Lindsay said.

"He is." Rebecca chuckled, thinking back to their time in the examination room. "He nearly danced when he heard the news."

"I can see him doing that." She lifted her glass of tea. "Did the doctor give you any instructions? Are you supposed to take it easy, since you've been so tired?"

"He said to rest if I feel worn out." Not wanting to worry her niece, Rebecca was careful not to mention the pain she'd experienced.

"I should quit working at the bakery," Lindsay said. "I'm sure Elizabeth will understand I need to take care of you and the *kinner*." She finished her drink with one big gulp. "You need me here."

Rebecca studied Lindsay's face, searching for any regret but only finding genuine concern. "Lindsay, it's not your obligation to help me raise my *kinner*. You know that, *ya*?"

"Oh, I know. I'm here because I want to be." She stood and took their empty glasses. "You rest. I'm going to make lunch."

As Lindsay disappeared into the kitchen, Rebecca wondered if Lindsay felt trapped in Lancaster County while Jessica flew around New York City, free as a bird.

Rebecca hugged her cloak to her chest with one hand and held a lantern in her other as she stepped into the barn later that evening. The sweet aroma of stain filled her throat, and she cupped her hand to her mouth.

"Becky?" Daniel rushed over to her. "Are you all right?"

She moved to the rock path and blew out a deep breath and then gave a little chuckle. "I've never felt *grank* in your shop before."

"I guess this pregnancy will be different, *ya*?" he asked, while wiping his hands on a rag.

"I guess so." She studied his handsome face. "Did you tell anyone?"

"No, no." He shook his head. "I wanted to tell my *dat*, but I'm going to keep this one a secret, just like the rest." He touched her arm. "How are you feeling?"

"Fine."

"Lindsay seems excited about the baby," he said. "She'll keep it a secret, *ya*?"

"Of course she will. She kept Daniel Jr. and Emma a secret." Overwhelmed with emotion, she hugged him. "*Ich liebe dich.*"

"I love you too, Becky." He looked concerned. "*Was iss letz?* You look upset."

She looked up at him. "Do you think Lindsay feels trapped here?"

He looked surprised. "No. Why would you say that?"

Rebecca glanced toward the house, spotting a lantern burning in Lindsay's room. "She said today that she's glad she didn't go to New York with Jessica because she can help me with this pregnancy and with the *kinner*. She wants to quit working at the bakery and help me full-time."

"How could that be bad?" he asked. "She wants to help us. She's always been a sweet and thoughtful girl, so that shouldn't surprise you."

"But does she really love it here, or does she feel like she has to be here?"

He shook his head. "Becky, you're not making sense." He tossed the rag over his shoulder.

She rubbed her forehead while trying to sort through her swirling thoughts. "What I mean is—does Lindsay feel like she owes us because we took her in? Is she staying here and helping me because she thinks her mother would want her to?"

He touched her cheek. "Becky, you worry too much. Lindsay loves you and loves the *kinner*. What's keeping her here is that love, not obligation."

"Are you certain?" She gave him a hopeful expression.

"Why don't you go get ready for bed? Dr. Moore said you need your rest."

"Fine." She glowered. She hated it when Daniel dismissed her, but she knew he was right.

"I'll lock the barn and be up soon." He kissed the top of her head before he disappeared into the barn.

Her shoes crunching the rock, Rebecca walked toward the house. She breathed in the crisp spring air and hoped that Daniel was right about Lindsay.

Cherry Triangles

Filling:

¾ cup sugar
5 level T. cornstarch
¼ t. salt
1 qt. red cherries drained
1 cup cherry juice
1 T. butter
2 t. lemon juice
Few drops red food coloring

Mix sugar, cornstarch, and salt in saucepan. Add cherry juice and cook, stirring until thickened. Stir in lemon juice, cherries, and red food coloring. Cool.

Dough:

2/3 cup scalded milk
1 pkg. active dry yeast
1 cup butter
2 ½ cups sifted flour
4 egg yolks slightly beaten

Cool milk to lukewarm, add yeast, cut in butter into flour. Add liquid ingredients and egg yolks to dry ingredients. Mix thoroughly. Turn out onto floured surface and knead 10 times. Divide in half. Roll first half until large enough for greased 11 ½ x 17 ½ inch pan. Spread cooled cherry filling over dough. Roll out second portion of dough and fit over dough together. Allow to rise in warm place 15 minutes. Bake 350 degrees 45–55 minutes.

Frosting:

¼ cup butter
½ t. vanilla
¾ cup chopped nuts
2 T. cream
1 ½ cups 10x sugar

Cream together butter, vanilla, and cream. Add sugar, beating until mixture is well blended. Spread frosting over partially cooled cookies. Sprinkle with chopped nuts. When cool, cut into 3-inch squares and then cut again. Makes 48 triangles.

7

Lindsay fell in step with Matthew as they walked across the Esh family's pasture after the church service a few weeks later. She breathed in the warm spring air and smiled while a bird chirped in a tree nearby.

"I got a letter from *mei schweschder* yesterday," Lindsay said.

"How's she doing?" he asked, adjusting the straw hat and pushing back a brown curl that fell into his eyes.

"She said she loves her job and is also having fun with her friend Kim. They went to a club the other night and talked to some guys." Lindsay shook her head. "I hope she's not doing anything dangerous, you know? But I think she's very smart. She never went to wild parties or anything like that before."

"That's *gut*." Matthew looked toward a group of girls sitting on the grass. "Why aren't you over with your *freinden*?"

Lindsay shrugged. "I couldn't participate in the conversation."

He looked confused. "What do you mean?"

"They were talking about their class."

"What class?" He raised an eyebrow in question.

"You know. The baptism instruction class. They were going on and on about how much they couldn't wait to get started. I can't exactly add to that conversation." She frowned, wondering if she'd made a mistake by not joining the class. But if it didn't feel right in her heart, how could she consider making such a commitment? Yet somehow, she still regretted not doing it.

"Don't let them make you feel bad," he said. "I'm certain if they knew that they were hurting your feelings, they wouldn't discuss it."

"I know that," she began, "but I don't want them to feel like they have to censor themselves when I'm around. They have a right to talk about something that's important to them." She gestured toward the group of boys playing volleyball in the middle of the pasture. "Why aren't you with your *freinden?*"

He shrugged. "I didn't feel like playing volleyball today. Is that a crime?"

"No," she said with a smile. In all honesty, Lindsay was glad he was spending time with her and not playing volleyball. She enjoyed talking with him instead of listening to her friends discuss their excitement about being baptized.

She glanced at her feet and spotted a throng of dandelions peppering the lush green grass like bright yellow polka dots. Reaching down, she swiped a dandelion from the grass. "Jessica and I used to make necklaces out of these when we were kids."

He smiled, and his eyes seemed to sparkle in the bright June afternoon sun. "My nieces like making them sometimes."

"Do they?" she asked. "Funny how all little girls do that, no matter if they are English or Amish."

Leaning down, he began plucking the dandelions from around his feet.

"What are you doing?" she asked.

"You'll see." He continued gathering the yellow flowers until he had a small bouquet. He then sank onto the ground and began tying the flowers together.

Laughing, Lindsay lowered herself down next to him and watched him create a long chain of dandelions. "It's a lovely necklace, but I don't think yellow is your color."

"No, but it's yours," he said without looking up. He tied the rest of the dandelions together and then glanced over at the one in her hands. "Are you going to use that?"

"No." She held out the flower. His hand brushed hers when he took it, and warmth ran up her arm. Overwhelmed by the feelings he conjured in her, she bit her bottom lip and hugged her arms to her chest.

"*Danki.*" He tied in the last dandelion and then held up the chain. "What do you think?"

"It's *schee,*" she said with a grin. "You'd be a *wunderbaar* jeweler. Perhaps you missed your calling."

He gave a bark of laughter as he leaned over and dropped the chain over her head. "You think so? Maybe I should quit my job at the furniture store and go to jeweler's school."

"Do you think the bishop would approve?" She stifled a chuckle while playing along with the banter.

"Hmm." He tapped a finger to his chin. "Possibly not."

She glanced down and touched the necklace. "It's beautiful. I'll be the envy of the girls at the singing tonight."

"And you thought your sister was having fun going to bars in New York. She'll never get a dandelion chain there."

"You're absolutely right," Lindsay said, her smile fading at the truth in his words. "No, she won't."

He stood and then held out his hand. "Hungry?"

She took his hand, and he lifted her as if she were weightless. "Starved," she said.

While they strolled side by side back toward the house, Lindsay kept her hand on her necklace. She glanced up at his smile and contemplated his thoughtful words. No, Jessica wouldn't ever spend an afternoon like this, nor would she have a handsome young man like Matthew create a dandelion chain just for her.

Thursday evening, Lindsay washed the dishes while Rebecca bathed the children. She'd offered to do both the dishes and the bathing, but Rebecca insisted she would handle the children, even though she looked exhausted. Lindsay worried that Rebecca was doing too much, but her aunt refused to slow down.

"Lindsay!" Rebecca called from the bathroom.

Lindsay dropped the dish she'd been scrubbing and rushed to the bathroom, where she found Rebecca sitting on the cover of the commode while the children splashed and laughed in the tub. "Are you okay?"

"I'm sorry for startling you." Rebecca yawned, covering her mouth with her hand. "I'm fine. Would you mind checking the messages for me? I forgot to do it earlier, and I'm too tired to walk out there."

"Of course." Lindsay grinned at the children and then headed through the kitchen and out the back door toward the phone shanty. She pushed the door open and sat on the stool while dialing.

After hearing that there were four messages, she began listening to a message that had arrived earlier in the day. She sat up straight when a vaguely familiar voice rang through the receiver.

"Um, this message is for Lindsay Bedford," the masculine voice said. "This is Frank McCabe in Virginia."

Lindsay's eyes widened with surprise—it was her father's best friend! She hadn't spoken to him or his wife, Trisha, in a few months. Normally Trisha called, so it was unusual to hear Frank's voice on the message.

"Lindsay, would you please call my cell phone as soon as you can," he said.

She scrambled for the pen and paper sitting on the little desk and wrote quickly while he rattled off the number.

"Thank you," he said. "Bye."

Wondering what Frank could want, she deleted the message and then played the next one.

"Linds," Jessica's voice was rushed. "It's an emergency. Something's happened to Aunt Trisha. Call me as soon as you can."

"Oh no," Lindsay groaned. She hit the keypad, and Jessica's voice rang through the phone again. "Lindsay? Please call me, okay. It's important. Bye."

The last message was from Dr. Fitzgerald's office, reminding Rebecca of an appointment next Monday.

With concern filling her, Lindsay dialed her sister's number.

Jessica answered on the second ring. "Linds!" she yelled into the phone. "I've been waiting for you to call. I tried to reach you at the bakery, but you'd already left for the day."

"What's going on?" Lindsay asked.

"Uncle Frank called me earlier," she said. "Aunt Trisha had an accident."

"What?" Lindsay bit her bottom lip. "What happened?"

"She fell and broke her leg," Jessica continued. "It's pretty bad."

"But she's going to be okay, right?" Lindsay confirmed.

"Yeah, she will. Eventually."

"What do you mean by 'eventually'?"

"She was in surgery last I heard. She has to have a rod put in her leg or something and won't be able to walk for a couple of months." Jessica blew out a sigh. "I feel so bad because I'm so far away. She'll be incapacitated, and Uncle Frank has to work. His construction firm has really taken off lately. They're building condos on the Outer Banks, and he's working long hours."

Lindsay grimaced while thinking of how much pain Trisha must be in. "How long will she be in surgery?"

"I don't know. Hang on one sec. Someone's in my office." She put her hand over the receiver, and muffled voices reverberated through the line. "Okay. Right. I'll be right there. Sorry, Linds. It's crazy here. Anyway, her surgery is probably over. I told Uncle Frank I would call him later."

"You're still at work?" Lindsay glanced at the battery-powered clock on the little counter in the shanty and found it was after six.

"Yeah," Jessica said with a sigh. "It's crazy busy."

"But you're an intern, Jess," Lindsay continued. "Should you be working that much?"

"If they need me, I work. Anyway, back to Aunt Trisha. I'm really busy here, and I can't get away. If I walk out of this place, I'll probably lose my internship and not get a letter of recommendation. Do you think you can go to Virginia and help Aunt Trisha and Uncle Frank until she's back on her feet?"

"What?" Lindsay asked with surprise. "What did you say?"

"You heard me," Jessica said, annoyance ringing in her voice. "I can't get away, but you can."

"Wait." Lindsay gestured with her hand, even though Jessica couldn't see her through the phone. "I told you already that I have responsibilities here. Aunt Rebecca's expecting a baby and needs extra help at home."

"I understand that, but Aunt Rebecca has a big family, so someone else can help her in your place. Uncle Frank and Aunt Trisha need us. Remember all the times they helped when Mom and Dad were alive? Remember when Dad lost his job, and Uncle Frank hired him? Or when we had the flood after that hurricane, and Uncle Frank and his crew came and dried out the carpets? And how about after Mom and Dad were gone? They took us in and helped us. And they've always been there when we—"

"Okay, okay! I get it. You can stop lecturing me now." Lindsay blew out a deep sigh. "I'll call Uncle Frank and see what he needs."

"Cool. Oh, I gotta go. Call me later."

"Yeah. Sure."

"Bye!"

"Bye." Lindsay hung up the phone and stared at the wood grain in the desk. The weight of the situation caused her shoulders to hunch. Taking a deep breath, she lifted the receiver again and dialed Frank's cell phone number.

"Hello?" Frank's voice asked.

"Uncle Frank," Lindsay said, her voice sounding small and strange to her ears. "It's Lindsay."

"Lindsay!" he said. "It's good to hear your voice. I'm so glad you called me back." She was almost certain she heard road noise in the background, and she imagined him driving his Chevrolet Suburban down the winding streets of Virginia Beach toward their house at Sandbridge Beach.

"I just got your message," she said, winding the phone cord around her finger. "I talked to Jessica and she said that Aunt Trisha had an accident. How is she?"

"She's doing okay," he said. "She broke her leg pretty badly, and she needed surgery. But she's awake and feeling pretty embarrassed about it now. She admitted she never should've stood on the railing to try to water that plant." He snickered a little.

"What did she do?"

"She was trying to water one of her plants on the back deck, and she decided not to use a stepladder."

"Oh no." Lindsay shook her head, imagining Trisha standing on the railing while balancing a watering can. She cringed, remembering just how high that deck was on their oceanfront home. It teetered close to two stories. "What was she thinking?"

"I've been wondering that myself all day," he said.

"Can I possibly talk to her?" Lindsay asked.

"Oh, not right now, sweetie," he said. "I'm on my way home to pick up a few of her things. But how about you call me sometime tomorrow afternoon? I'm sure I'll be up at the hospital. Just call my cell, and I'll hand it over to her. She would love to hear from you."

"I will." Lindsay cleared her throat. "Jessica mentioned that Aunt Trisha is going to be laid up for a while."

"Oh yeah," he said. "She will be for sure."

"Will you and Aunt Trisha need help?"

"Yes, we're trying to figure out what to do. I can't stay home and take care of her because I have a big condo job down at the Outer Banks. She won't be able to get around on her own." He paused for a moment. "Do you think you could come and help her? I know you're busy with your aunt and family, but we could really use the help. What do you think?"

Lindsay bit her bottom lip and took a deep breath. She knew Trisha and Frank needed her more than ever, and her heart ached for their predicament. She thought about Rebecca and her pregnancy and remembered that her aunt had made it through her previous pregnancies without any problems. Surely Rebecca would be fine without Lindsay's help. Trisha and Frank's problems were much more serious.

"I'll talk to my aunt Rebecca about coming down to help you," Lindsay said. "I'm certain she'll be supportive."

"Thank you so much," he said, sounding relieved. "I really appreciate it. I called Trisha's older sister in Boise, but she's really busy baby-sitting for her grandkids. She said it would be a hardship to try to find someone to help her daughter. I'm so glad you offered to come. I just don't know how we'd manage. All of our friends are busy working during the day, and I can't let this job in the Outer Banks go. I'm the boss, you know, and unfortunately, I have to be on the job site every day. You don't know how much this means to us. Trisha will be thrilled when I tell her that you're going to try to come."

"I'll talk to Rebecca tonight and get back to you as soon as I can," Lindsay said. "Give Aunt Trisha my love."

"I will, sweetie," Frank said. "Thank you again for offering to try to help us. Take care."

"You too. Bye." Lindsay hung up the phone and rested her face in her hands while the reality of the situation soaked through her. A knock on the shanty door caused her to jump.

Glancing over, she found Daniel peering in at her. "Rebecca asked me to come find you. She said you've been in here for quite a while, and she's worried." His expression became concerned. "*Was iss letz?*"

"I just talked to Jessica and also to Frank McCabe, my parents' friend."

"*Ya?*" He leaned on the door frame. "Is everything okay?"

"Aunt Trisha fell and broke her *beh*."

"*Ach*." He rubbed his beard. "I'm sorry to hear that."

"She had to have surgery, and she'll be unable to walk for quite a while."

"That's *bedauerlich*. Must be very painful."

"*Ya*." Lindsay ran her finger over the small desk. "She'll need some help at the house since Uncle Frank works a lot. His construction business has been very busy lately."

"I see." Daniel continued to rub his beard. "Do they have family nearby who can help?"

Lindsay shook her head. "No."

"Do they want you to come and help?"

"Yes."

"Do you want to go?"

"Jessica thinks I should."

He gave a knowing smile. "Jessica likes to tell you what to do and likes to make your decisions, but you're a young lady now, Lindsay. You're eighteen and should make decisions that feel right for you."

"I know," she said.

"And what do *you* think is right for you?"

Lindsay gestured in the direction of the house. "On one hand, I feel like *Aenti* Rebecca needs me since she's expecting a baby and she's been so tired lately. I worry that she'll overdo it and not get the rest she needs. However, on the other hand, Aunt Trisha and Uncle Frank need me more. Aunt Trisha is going to need someone to take care of her, and in my heart, I feel like it should be me."

He nodded slowly. "You're a very thoughtful and caring *maedel*. I agree that my Becky does work too hard, and I know for certain that she's stubborn. But if you feel that you need to go stay with Trisha and Frank for a while, we can make do. One of our nieces will come and help us if we need them. And I agree with you—it does sound like Trisha is going to be in bad shape and needs someone to take care of her. You would be a *wunderbaar* help to her."

"I feel bad leaving our family, but I know it's the right thing to do," Lindsay said.

He leaned down, meeting her at eye level. "Look at me, Lindsay."

She sat up straighter on the stool. "*Ya?*"

"We know that you love us, but you have to remember that Trisha and Frank are family too. God and family are the most important things in our lives."

She nodded.

"Rebecca will understand if you feel God calling you to go help Trisha for a while," he said. "Just talk to her."

"I will."

He stood and motioned for her to follow him. "She's concerned about you. Why don't you go tell her what's going on? I'm certain she can help you sort this out."

They walked to the house together. Lindsay found Rebecca sitting at the kitchen table.

"Lindsay!" Rebecca stood. "You look upset. Are you okay?"

"*Ya.*" Lindsay sank into the chair across from her. "I'm okay."

Daniel kissed Rebecca on her head. "I'll go check on the *kinner*. You two go ahead and talk." He nodded at Lindsay, giving her a sympathetic expression before heading toward the stairs.

Sitting down in the chair, Rebecca eyed Lindsay with concern. "*Was iss letz?*"

Lindsay took a deep breath and then explained the conversations she'd had with both Jessica and Frank. She couldn't stop the lump that swelled in her throat, and her voice sounded thick by the time she finished her story.

"Oh, Lindsay." Rebecca took her hands in hers. "If you want to go help Trisha, you can." She squeezed Lindsay's hands. "You do what feels right to you."

"But I don't know what's right," Lindsay said. "I feel like I belong here, but I also feel that I'm needed back in Virginia. Jessica lectured me, reminding me of all Aunt Trisha and Uncle Frank have done for us and our parents over the years. She said it's only right for me to go help them too."

Rebecca nodded. "She's right."

Lindsay gestured toward Rebecca. "But you need me too. You're my family, my real, blood family."

"I'll be just fine if you want to go to Virginia," Rebecca said.

"What about the bakery? Elizabeth depends on me."

With a grin, Rebecca reached for Lindsay's hands again. "I'm sure we will make do until you come back."

Lindsay held her breath, attempting to curb more tears.

Rebecca patted Lindsay's hands. "You need to pray about it and let God show you the answer."

"Okay," Lindsay said.

"And I'm doing fine. The doctor said that everything looks good." She stood. "You go get some sleep. Pray about it and let God lead you. You'll know the answer when you feel it. Once you feel comfortable with your decision, you can call Frank back and tell him what you've decided to do."

"Oh," Lindsay said. "The doctor's office called to remind you of your appointment on Monday."

"*Danki,*" Rebecca said.

Lindsay followed her to the stairs. She said good night and then retreated into her room, where she changed into her nightclothes and climbed into bed. Her mind raced with thoughts while she attempted to pray.

Finally, after what felt like hours, Lindsay's thoughts settled down, and she opened her heart and mind to God as she fell asleep.

8

Lindsay awoke the following morning with a Bible verse floating around in her head:

Thank You Lord that You will sustain them upon their sickbed. In their illness You will restore them to health. In the name of Jesus Christ.

Sitting up straight, she rubbed her eyes and then looked up at the ceiling. "You want me to go to Virginia and take care of Aunt Trisha," she whispered. "That's my answer."

The Scripture continued swirling through her head during breakfast and throughout the ride to the bakery. She was relieved that neither Rebecca nor Daniel asked her why she was so quiet.

When she arrived at the bakery, she greeted her aunts and cousins and then busied herself with straightening the shelves of T-shirts for sale in the front part of the bakery. Lindsay was deep in thought about Frank and Trisha when she heard footsteps approaching behind her. She turned and smiled at Elizabeth. "Good morning."

"Good morning." Elizabeth smiled. "How are you today, Lindsay?"

"*Gut,*" Lindsay said while she folded the shirts. "How are you?"

"*Gut.*" Elizabeth stood beside her. "May I help you with those shirts?"

"No, *danki*." Lindsay nodded toward a table with chairs nearby. "I'm almost done, but you can keep me company while I work."

"That sounds like a *gut* plan." Elizabeth lowered herself into one of the chairs. "How was your evening last night?"

"*Gut*," Lindsay said, placing another folded shirt into the cubby hole with matching shirts of different sizes. "How was yours?"

"It was *gut*." Elizabeth smiled. "Sarah Rose and Luke stopped by with the *kinner*. Seth and Rachel are talking up a storm and Benjamin and Peter are running around, toddling all on their own."

Lindsay smiled and nodded while Elizabeth discussed Sarah Rose and Luke's twins, but her mind was focused on her decision to go to Virginia Beach. A glimmer of anxiety surged through her at the thought of leaving her family that she'd grown to love during the past four years. How would she manage without them?

"It's fun watching them learn new things," Lindsay said without looking up from the shirt she was straightening. She finished folding the last shirt and then examined the cubby holes, which were all tidy and presentable for the tourists who would stop by throughout the day for baked goods and souvenirs.

"Lindsay?" Elizabeth asked, breaking through Lindsay's thoughts. "Are you okay, *mei liewe*? You seem a bit distracted."

Lindsay glanced up. "I do?"

Elizabeth gestured toward the chair across the small table from her. "How about we talk for a few minutes?"

Lindsay sat on the chair. "Okay."

Elizabeth leaned forward and folded her hands. "Now, I know something is wrong. You look as if you're going to explode if you don't let it out."

Lindsay yanked a napkin from the metal holder in the middle

of the table and began to absently shred it. "Last night I received some bad news."

Elizabeth listened with a sympathetic expression while Lindsay explained the phone calls regarding Trisha's accident.

"I need to go and help Aunt Trisha and Uncle Frank," Lindsay began while pushing the pieces of napkin around on the table. "But the idea of leaving the family is a little scary. I've been living here for four years, and now I'll have to go back to my old way of life." She looked at Elizabeth. "Does that make sense? I feel like it's the right thing to do, but I'm really jittery."

"*Ya*, it makes sense," Elizabeth said with a gentle smile. "You sound like you doubt yourself. What's your heart telling you to do?"

Lindsay swiped the pile of napkin bits into her hand, and dropped them into the pocket of her apron. "I think God wants me to go to Virginia. I prayed about it all night, and I woke up thinking of a verse that I'd heard a few weeks ago in church service."

Elizabeth's eyes widened. "What verse is it?"

"Psalm 41, verse 3," Lindsay whispered.

Elizabeth recited it from memory. "I remember when the minister read that. It touched my heart." She smoothed her apron and paused, as if contemplating the Scripture. "And you think God is telling you to go?"

"*Ya*, I do, but I'm nervous about going." Lindsay gestured around the bakery with her hands. "This is my life now. Going back to the English way feels uncomfortable."

"But you know Trisha and Frank," Elizabeth said. "They're family to you. It will be like living here, only you'll be with different family members."

"You're right." Lindsay nodded with emphasis. "I keep wondering if maybe God is sending me to Virginia to help me figure out which world I truly belong in, this world or the English world."

"That's a *gut* possibility." Reaching over, Elizabeth gently squeezed Lindsay's hand. "You may decide that you belong with the English. And if you do, you know that you'll always be welcome here. In the meantime, I will find another helper for the summer."

"*Danki*," Lindsay said. She suddenly felt the knot in her stomach loosen as a small glimmer of confidence ignited within her.

Elizabeth stood. "I guess I better get back to work. Are you coming to the kitchen or are you going to work out here?"

Lindsay pointed toward the carousel of keychains and magnets nearby. "I think I'll organize those since the personalized keychains look to be out of order. I spotted a 'Zach' keychain by a 'Joe.' "

"*Danki* for doing that. I'll see you in a bit," Elizabeth said before heading behind the counter toward the kitchen.

Lindsay leaned back in the chair, closed her eyes, and sent up a prayer, begging God to give her more confidence in her decision to go to Virginia Beach and care for Trisha.

Rebecca stepped onto the porch later that evening and found Lindsay sitting in the swing. Swishing back and forth slowly, Lindsay held a glass of tea in her hands while she stared across the dark pasture.

"May I join you?" Rebecca asked.

"Of course." Lindsay moved over and patted the seat next to her. "How are you feeling?"

"*Gut*," Rebecca said, sinking down next to her. "How about you? You've been awfully quiet."

Lindsay bit her bottom lip, and Rebecca dreaded her response. She'd spent all day worrying about Lindsay and what she would decide. While Rebecca knew it was selfish to want to keep Lindsay with her, she also knew she would miss her if she went to Virginia.

"I've made my decision," Lindsay began. "I've prayed about it and I talked to Elizabeth today." With a determined expression, she faced Rebecca. "I'm going to Virginia Beach."

Rebecca nodded with understanding. She'd known in her heart that her niece would go since she was such a caring and loving girl.

"I feel like God is telling me to go there," Lindsay continued. "I woke up this morning with Psalm 41, verse 3, echoing in my head, and I know that would only have come from God."

"*Ya*, you're absolutely right." Rebecca silently marveled at how much her niece had matured since coming to live with her four years ago. "God is speaking to you."

"It breaks my heart to consider leaving you and the rest of the family, especially the *kinner*, but I think this is what I'm supposed to do."

Rebecca took a deep, cleansing breath, hoping to hold back the tears brewing in her eyes. "How soon do you think you'll leave?"

Lindsay shrugged. "I guess early next week? I need to tell my friends. I thought I would break the news tomorrow night at the Kauffman gathering at Elizabeth's house."

"That's a *gut* idea," Rebecca said, trying to keep her tone positive, despite her breaking heart. "They would want to hear it from you."

They were silent for a moment, and Rebecca wondered how her children would take the news of Lindsay's leaving. She imagined they would be just as sad as she was since Lindsay was almost like their other mother.

"Have you called Frank and discussed this with him?" Rebecca asked, breaking the heavy silence.

Lindsay shook her head. "Not yet. I needed to really think about it and be certain before I told him. I'll go call him now. I think he's probably still up. It's not quite nine yet."

"While you're there, can you check the messages? I forgot to earlier."

"Sure. I'll go check the machine and then call Jessica and Uncle Frank." Lindsay stood and lifted the lantern from the small table next to the swing. "I'll be back soon."

"Take your time."

As Lindsay hopped down the steps and headed for the phone shanty, Rebecca glanced toward the barn, wondering if Daniel was finishing up his work in his shop.

After a few moments, the door to the barn opened, and Daniel sauntered out, locking the door behind him. He crossed to the porch and took the steps two at a time before lowering his tall body onto the swing next to her. He placed his hand on her back and rubbed it gently.

"Are the *kinner* asleep?" he asked.

"*Ya*." Rebecca's voice was thick.

"*Was iss letz?*"

"Lindsay's leaving." She met his gaze and tears pooled in her eyes. "She's going to Virginia to help Trisha."

Daniel pulled her into his arms. "She'll be fine. She's a smart *maedel*. She'll take good care of Trisha."

Rebecca sniffed. "I don't know why I'm so emotional. It must be the hormones. I know she'll come back to us once Trisha is better. Don't you agree?"

"I believe so. We've become her family." He rested his chin on her head. "But you must remember that she'll follow whatever God puts in her heart, and we have to leave that up to Him. It's not our place to decide what's best for her."

Rebecca wiped the tears seeping from her eyes. "I'm being silly and overly emotional, but I feel like I'm losing a child. I'm going to miss her so much."

He continued rubbing her back. "I'll miss her too, and so will Emma and Junior. But we have to let her go and trust that she'll come back to us soon."

They sat in silence for several minutes, and Rebecca managed to stop her tears. She knew she had to let Lindsay go, but it was painful—just like when she let Jessica go to live with Trisha and Frank four years ago.

Breaking the silence, Daniel patted her back. "I'm going to head in. Are you going to stay out here?"

She nodded. "Lindsay went to the phone shanty. I want to wait for her to come back."

He kissed her cheek. "I'll see you upstairs." He disappeared into the house.

Rebecca hugged her arms to her chest and rocked back and forth in the swing while she waited for Lindsay. The gentle evening breeze kissed her cheeks. She looked up at the bright stars in the sky, contemplating God's beautiful creation. The night was quiet, except for the occasional hum of a car passing by on the main road and the bark of a dog in the distance.

The shanty door squeaked, and Lindsay crossed to the porch with the lantern glowing in her hand. She gave Rebecca a surprised look while climbing the steps. "I thought you would've gone up to bed."

Rebecca tried to force a smile but couldn't form it on her lips. "I wanted to wait for you and see how your phone calls went."

"They went fine." Lindsay dropped into the chair next to the swing. "Jessica is thrilled that I'm going. Uncle Frank and Aunt Trisha can't wait to see me."

"How's Trisha doing?"

"She sounded okay on the phone. She said she was feeling a little woozy from the painkillers, but she's happy to be going back to her own home on Monday."

"Did you make any plans for when you'll travel?"

Lindsay placed the lantern on the table next to her. "I said I'd check the bus schedule and see about traveling on Tuesday. That way I'll be there soon after Trisha comes home. Would that be okay?"

Rebecca patted Lindsay's arm, silently marveling at how thoughtful her niece was. "That sounds like a *wunderbaar* idea."

Lindsay bit her lower lip. "I guess I need to start making a list of what I need to take. I'll have to get a ride to the bus station to pick up a ticket."

"Daniel can call the driver for you in the morning," Rebecca said.

"Okay." Lindsay stood, yawned, and stretched. "I think I need to call it a night. Are you coming in now?"

"*Ya.*" Rebecca stood.

As Rebecca followed Lindsay into the house, she hoped that someday soon she would sit out on the porch, welcoming Lindsay back home and listening as she shared stories from her trip.

"I have something to tell you," Lindsay began, her hands trembling as she fingered the ribbons of her prayer covering. She faced her friends while they stood in Elizabeth Kauffman's pasture the following evening.

Samuel and Matthew looked curious, while Lizzie Anne's and Katie's expressions were filled with worry.

"I'm leaving Tuesday," Lindsay said. "I'll be gone for a while."

"Where are you going?" Katie asked, her eyes wide.

"Virginia," Lindsay said.

"Why?" Lizzie Anne asked.

"My aunt Trisha needs help. She was in an accident and broke her *beh*. I'm going to help out until she can walk again." Lindsay lowered herself onto a tree stump. "I feel like God needs me to do this. I prayed about it, and I feel His answer speaking to my heart."

"It sounds serious." Katie sat on the grass across from her, and Lizzie Anne sank down beside her. "When did she get hurt?"

"She fell Wednesday morning. She stood on the railing of her deck and slipped while trying to water a hanging plant.

She's coming home from the hospital on Monday. It was a really bad break and she had to have surgery." Lindsay glanced up at Samuel and Matthew, who were standing behind the girls. She wished she knew what Matthew was thinking. All she could read was disappointment, or perhaps sadness, in his eyes.

"That's dangerous," Lizzie Anne said. "She's lucky she only broke her *beh*. My *onkel* fell off a ladder several years ago, and he broke his back. He's still in bad shape."

"I remember that," Samuel said, lowering his lanky body onto the grass beside her. "He's lucky to be alive."

Matthew leaned against the tree next to them. His expression was unreadable as he pushed his hat up higher on his head and squinted in the sun.

"We'll miss you," Lizzie Anne said. "It won't be the same without you at services and singings."

"*Mammi* will miss you at the bakery," Katie added. "I've heard they've been very busy."

"I won't be gone too long," Lindsay continued. "I just need to help out Aunt Trisha and Uncle Frank for a while and then I'll be back."

"When are you leaving?" Matthew asked.

"Tuesday afternoon." Lindsay smoothed the skirt of her purple dress.

Matthew glanced down and fingered the bark on the tree.

"You'll have to write us letters and tell us everything that you're doing," Katie said. "Trisha lives on the beach, right? Isn't her house right on the sand?"

"*Ya*," Lindsay said. "You can hear the waves inside the house."

"I bet that's nice for sleeping at night," Lizzie Anne said. "That will be different than waking up to the sound of a rooster."

Samuel laughed. "That's for certain."

"I bet you miss Virginia sometimes," Lizzie Anne continued. "You'll get to see your old *freinden* from school too."

"I suppose." Lindsay shrugged and then stood. "I really don't keep in touch with anyone anymore. Besides, they're all graduating this month, and I bet they're getting ready to leave for college. I don't think I'd have much in common with them anymore."

Katie stood and wiped the grass off the back of her dress. "We'll miss you." She hugged Lindsay.

Lizzie Anne hopped up and hugged Lindsay too. "You better come back soon. Don't forget about us while you're living at the beach and listening to the waves."

"How could she forget about us?" Samuel grinned as he stood. "We have these *wunderbaar* bugs here." He held up a worm and jiggled it in front of Lizzie Anne, who shrieked and ran. He chased her toward the house while she continued to giggle.

"They act like *kinner*," Katie said with the shake of her head. "My brother flirts like he's still on the playground, and Lizzie Anne seems to enjoy the attention."

Heading back to the house, Lindsay fell in step between Matthew and Katie. They passed a group of younger Kauffman children playing tag. One of the little boys fell, and when he began to cry, Katie took off running.

Lindsay started after her but stopped when Matthew touched her arm.

His expression was intense as he studied her face. "Don't be gone too long."

He turned and headed toward the barn before she could respond.

9

"I guess that's my ride." Lindsay pointed toward the large bus parked outside the station. "I have to go." She looked between Rebecca and Katie, and tears filled her eyes.

Rebecca wrapped her arms around Lindsay's neck and squeezed her tight. "Call me and write me. I'll worry about you every day."

Lindsay wiped her eyes. "Take good care of yourself and the *kinner.* Don't overdo it." She then hugged Katie. "Please watch out for *Aenti* Rebecca. Be sure she takes care of herself."

"I will," Katie said. "And you'd better write me."

"I'll definitely write." Taking a deep breath, Lindsay hefted her duffel bag over her arm. "Good-bye."

She hugged each of them one last time and then hurried off to the bus. After checking her luggage, she climbed on and chose a seat near the back. Once she was settled in her seat, she closed her eyes and let her tears flow.

"Do you think she'll come back, *Aenti* Rebecca?" Katie asked while they sat in the back of Nina Janitz's van on their way home from the bus station.

Rebecca turned from the window and studied her niece's pretty face. "You have doubts that she will?"

Katie was silent for a moment, pondering the issue. "I believe in my heart that she will, but my *mamm* says that sometimes young people experience the English way of life and don't want to come back. There are so many temptations out there, and they can be overpowering. Plus, my *mamm* says that since Lindsay grew up in the English world, she may become like her sister and want to run off and live in a big city, where there is even more temptation."

Rebecca resisted the urge to glower. It was so typical of Sadie, Katie's mother, to think the worst of Lindsay and Jessica. After all, Sadie had contributed to the rumors that had painted Jessica as a detriment to the community.

"I understand your mother's point about temptation, but I don't think we need to worry about Lindsay falling into something bad," Rebecca said. "As for Jessica, she didn't run off, as your mother said. She's working in New York City and getting experience for college. She's a smart girl too."

Katie nodded. "I'm going to miss Lindsay so much. She and Lizzie Anne are my best friends. It won't feel right for Lizzie Anne and me to be without her."

Rebecca touched her niece's arm. "I know. My *kinner* and I are going to miss her very much. But we'll have a lot to celebrate when she returns."

"*Ya*, we will," Katie said with a tentative smile.

Lindsay's stomach fluttered as the bus weaved through traffic in Virginia Beach. Familiar sights whizzed by—favorite stores, the car dealership where her mother got her last SUV, the main library—and Lindsay felt transported to an alternate universe. Traffic was dense, and there were no horses or buggies in sight. Although she'd grown up in this city, she felt as if she didn't belong here.

A strange excitement gripped her as the bus steered into the parking lot at the station. Sitting up straight, she gathered her purse and small tote bag, which held her Bible and a notepad. While she'd spent some time reading the Bible last night, she hadn't felt inspired to write a letter during her fourteen-hour trip. She'd slept little in the bus seats in between her stops and bus connections.

When the bus came to a stop, Lindsay waited her turn before following the crowd out to the station. She felt eyes watching her as she exited the bus, and her hand flew to the ribbons dangling from her prayer covering. Her cheeks flushed with heat as she passed two girls about her age, who stared at her, wide-eyed. Both were dressed in denim shorts and tank tops, with their long, bleached hair falling in waves past their shoulders.

With her eyes focused on the toes of her black sneakers, Lindsay kept moving, almost walking straight into Frank McCabe.

"Uncle Frank," she said. "Hi."

"Lindsay!" Frank opened his big arms and swept her into a tight hug. "It's so good to see you. Thank you so much for coming to help us out."

"It's really good to see you too." Lindsay hiked her tote bag and purse up on her shoulder. "How's Aunt Trisha?"

"She's doing all right. The doc gave her some good painkillers, and she's feeling okay." He nodded toward the baggage claim area. "Do you have any luggage?"

"Just one duffel bag."

"Let's find it and get on the road. I left Trisha home alone." He started toward the baggage area. "She was snoozing in the recliner, so she should be okay for a little while."

Lindsay located her bag and tried in vain to ignore the curious stares while walking with Frank to his Suburban parked in the back of the lot.

During the ride to his house, Frank prattled on about the humid weather. Lindsay gazed out the window, oblivious to what he was saying. Instead, she took in the scenery, feeling as if she'd been transported back to a former life. Yet, it didn't exactly feel like her former life. She didn't look the same or feel like the same person she was four years ago.

"I really appreciate you coming here to help Trisha out," Frank said as he steered onto Sandbridge Road. "I've been working long hours these days. We've got a big condo project going up down on the Outer Banks in Duck. Construction is finally moving again. We were dead for a long time." He glanced over at her, his brown eyes full of concern. "You okay, Lindsay?"

She forced a smile. "Yeah, I'm fine."

The truth was, she was drowning in memories of the thousands of times she'd driven out to Sandbridge Beach with her parents and Jessica to visit Frank and Trisha. They'd been her parents' best friends since before Jessica and Lindsay were born. Since Frank and Trisha never had children of their own, they attended every birthday celebration, school function, and holiday gathering that Lindsay could remember. They were more like an aunt and uncle than family friends.

"Must seem strange to be back here, huh?" Frank asked while motoring through the twists and turns of the winding Sandbridge Road. "You're used to the countryside now and not as much traffic as we have here."

She cracked open the window, breathing in the humid ocean air. "It's sort of surreal. It's home, but it's not home. I can't explain it."

The SUV negotiated onto Sandfiddler Road, and Lindsay took in the view of the ocean. She'd almost forgotten how much she loved to watch the waves crash onto the beach and feel the warm sand between her toes.

"Trisha is excited to see you," Frank said. "She said it's been too long since we came to visit you last summer."

Lindsay nodded while studying the beachfront homes whizzing by. "It has been too long."

Frank steered into the driveway of the three-story wooden

home facing the oceanfront and Lindsay's stomach fluttered. The last time she'd been in this house was four years ago when Jessica had run away and Lindsay, Jake, and Rebecca had rushed to Virginia to make sure she was okay. The house still looked the same with its two-car garage on the bottom floor and two stories of living space above.

Slowing to a stop in front of the garage door, Frank poked the button on the controller attached to the visor above his head, and the garage door lifted. "Here we are."

Lindsay gathered her tote bag and purse and then climbed from the truck. She met Frank by the garage entrance and followed him into the house and up the stairs to the main level. Glancing around, she found the house looked the same. A large, open family room flowed into a spacious kitchen. Past the kitchen were a laundry room and two bedrooms. Upstairs were two more bedrooms and another den area.

Trisha was lounging in the recliner with her eyes closed while the television played a movie softly across the room. She was pale, her brown hair looking darker than usual against her ivory skin.

Frank crossed the room and stopped at the recliner. Leaning down, he kissed Trisha's forehead. "Hey, sleepy head. Lindsay's here."

Opening her dark brown eyes, Trisha glanced over at Lindsay, and a smile exploded across her tired face. "Lindsay!" she said, her voice gravelly. "How are you?"

Frank smiled at her. "I'm going to take Lindsay's bag to her room and check my voicemail. You two catch up." He then disappeared through the kitchen toward the master bedroom.

Trisha motioned for Lindsay to come over. "Get over here. Let me get a good look at you, sweetie. I'm so glad you're here."

"Aunt Trisha." Lindsay dropped her tote bag and purse and crossed the room. She cupped Trisha's hands in hers. "How are you feeling?"

Trisha smiled. "Oh, I'm okay. Groggy." Reaching up, she

touched the ribbon hanging from Lindsay's prayer covering. "You're such a beautiful young lady. You've grown up since we saw you last year." She shook her head and gave a little laugh. "We never expected this to happen. Thank you so much for coming to help us out. I feel like such a fool for falling like I did, but like the doctor said, it could've been much worse."

"I'm happy to come and help you, Aunt Trisha." Lindsay lowered herself into the chair beside her. "I'm glad that it wasn't worse. That deck is really high from what I remember." She folded her hands in her lap and smiled. "So, how are you feeling? How did your surgery go?"

"Oh, it went fine." Trisha motioned toward her cast. "I have to wear this thing for eight weeks. Can't wait until I get it off."

"How does your leg feel?"

"It throbs." She lifted a glass that looked as if it was filled with iced tea. She took a sip and then placed it back on the table. "I'm so glad you're here. You're all grown up. I can't believe you're eighteen and Jessica is going to be turning twenty next month. Where has the time gone, Lindsay-girl?"

Lindsay smoothed her hands across the skirt of her purple frock and fought the lump in her throat. The only people who called her "Lindsay-girl" were her parents and Trisha and Frank. Hearing the nickname caused something deep in her soul to melt. "Yeah, time passes quickly. My little cousins are getting so big. It seems like yesterday they were just born."

"We have to visit more often," Trisha said with a yawn.

"I agree," Lindsay said. "Can I get you anything? Are you hungry?" She glanced toward the kitchen and wondered if she could throw something together for Trisha to eat. "I could make you some breakfast. Have you eaten?"

"I'm fine, but you should make yourself something. When was the last time you ate?"

"Last night." Lindsay covered her mouth to shield a yawn

as the exhaustion of the trip suddenly drowned her. "I don't remember what time it was when I ate."

Trisha gave her a stern expression. "You should make yourself a snack and then go take a nap. You look wiped out."

Lindsay wagged a finger at her. "You look like you need a nap too."

"I think you both need a nap." Frank stood grinning in the doorway. "Lindsay, I put your bag in your room. How about I make you something to eat and then you go rest for a while?"

Lindsay got to her feet. "I can make myself something to eat. I don't expect you to wait on me."

"Okay." He crossed the room and came to a stop behind Trisha. "But I want you both to rest. No more talking until noon."

Trisha grinned up at him. "Yes, sir."

He touched her nose. "You're very smart to listen to your husband." Leaning down, he kissed her forehead and then touched her shoulder. "Do you need anything? You haven't eaten much."

"I'm fine." Trisha glanced at Lindsay and held out her hand, taking Lindsay's in it. "Thank you again for coming. I'm so glad you're here, Lindsay-girl." She squeezed Lindsay's hand.

"Me too," Lindsay whispered. "It's good to see you again." After kissing Trisha's cheek, she headed into the kitchen and made two pieces of cinnamon toast, which she ate at the table while flipping through the paper.

Once she was finished eating, she cleaned up the kitchen and then headed to the guest bedroom. Moving through the den area, she found Trisha asleep in the recliner. She smiled, hoping Trisha was getting the rest she needed and having pleasant dreams.

Lindsay stepped into the guest room and felt as if she'd been taken back in time to four years ago, when she and Rebecca had stayed in the room when they came looking for Jessica after she'd run away. The room looked exactly the same with its peach walls, white wicker furniture, and lighthouse and beach paintings. The colorful decor was a stark contrast to the plain white walls in Rebecca's simple home.

She found her duffel bag on the bed and unpacked, hanging her frocks and aprons in the closet and placing her pajamas and underclothes in the wicker dresser. She pulled out a cookbook that she'd borrowed from Rebecca and placed it on the dresser. She opened the side pocket of her bag and found her favorite photo of her parents and Jessica, taken during their last family vacation at Disney World, and placed it on her nightstand next to a digital alarm clock.

She moved to the window and pushed back the shade, taking in the beautiful scene of the waves crashing on the golden sand. When she was a child, Lindsay loved to come to this house and spend hours on the beach, building sand castles and body surfing in the salty water. Tears filled her eyes as she remembered those long hot days on the beach with Jessica, their parents, and the McCabes. Somehow it felt like another lifetime, and maybe it was since her life had changed so drastically after her parents died.

Lindsay yawned, and a wave of exhaustion crashed down on her. She glanced at the queen-sized bed and felt the urge to take a nap. She carefully removed her prayer covering and placed it on the dresser next to her comb and brush before she climbed onto the plush comforter displaying a beach scene and snuggled down into the pillow. Her mind raced with thoughts of her family back in Lancaster. She wondered how Rebecca was feeling. Her thoughts moved to the cadence of the waves crashing outside her window, and soon she fell asleep.

Lindsay's eyes flew open and she glanced around the room, unsure of where she was for a moment. Memories of the past twenty-four hours flooded her, much like the surf pounding the beach below. Sitting up, she stretched and then turned to the digital clock, which read 5:30. With a gasp, she popped out of bed, grabbed her cookbook, and rushed toward the kitchen. She passed through the den and found Trisha lounging in the recliner, staring at an evening news commentator talking about a robbery at a convenience store in Norfolk.

"Hey, Lindsay-girl," Trisha said with a weak smile. "Did you nap well?"

"*Ya,*" Lindsay said. She shook her head. "I mean, yes, I did sleep well. Thank you."

Trisha's eyes moved to the cookbook in Lindsay's hands. "What do you have there?"

Lindsay held it up. "This is one of my aunt Rebecca's favorite cookbooks. I thought I could pick out something nice for you and Frank, depending on what you have in the kitchen."

Trisha gave an expression that was a mixture of surprise and amusement. "You were planning on cooking tonight?"

Lindsay nodded. "Of course I was. I didn't expect you to cook in your condition."

"I obviously can't cook, but Frank went out to get us a pizza from your favorite place." Trisha gestured toward the sofa next to her. "Have a seat. We haven't had much time to talk yet."

Lindsay lowered herself onto the sofa and placed the book on the coffee table. "You didn't need to spend the money on pizza. I love to cook. Aunt Rebecca and my other aunts have taught me how to make some delicious meals, and eating out really is a waste of your hard-earned money. I'd be happy to cook every night."

Trisha's expression turned to surprise. "It isn't necessary for you to cook every night, Lindsay. We're used to getting takeout every now and again."

Lindsay nodded, but she didn't feel right letting Frank and Trisha spend the money at a restaurant when she could cook something healthier and less expensive at home. She wasn't used to eating out much anymore, even though her parents also enjoyed eating out frequently.

"I'll plan to cook tomorrow," Lindsay finally said. "But I'll have to see what you have in the kitchen first."

"You do that." Trisha yawned, cupping her hand to her mouth. "These painkillers are taking a lot out of me, and I can't seem to get comfortable." Biting her lip, she gingerly shifted her weight in the chair, wincing as she moved her injured leg.

Lindsay stood. "Do you need anything? A drink maybe? Or do you need help getting to the bathroom?"

Trisha shook her head. "Will you please sit down? I'm fine. Tell me what's been going on with you."

Lindsay dropped back onto the sofa. "What did you want to know?"

"How are things in Pennsylvania?" Trisha asked.

"Things are really good. Emma just started talking," Lindsay said. "Rebecca just found out that she's expecting another baby in January, so we're really excited." She reached up and touched her head. She bit back a gasp when she found it uncovered. She started to stand and then stopped. She knew Trisha wouldn't understand why it was so important to her to wear it.

"Something wrong?" Trisha asked.

"I forgot to put my covering back on after my nap. I should go grab it or get a kerchief to wear."

Trisha raised her eyebrows. "You can't take it off in the house?"

"I'm not supposed to."

"Oh, well, you don't need to worry about it here, but if you're uncomfortable, you can go get it." Trisha smiled.

"It feels strange and almost uncomfortable not to wear it," Lindsay said. "But I'll be okay." She'd become accustomed to keeping her head covered at all times. Therefore, it felt as if something was missing to not wear her covering.

"Do you have summer clothes to wear while you're here?"

Trisha asked. "I'm sure you remember that it gets really hot and humid here. We'd all melt without central air conditioning."

"Dresses like this are all I own." Lindsay glanced down at her lap. "I gave all of my other clothes to Jessica."

"It's so much warmer here than Pennsylvania," Trisha said. "I know you don't have English clothes anymore, but you may feel more comfortable in something lighter. Why don't you let me buy you some clothes to wear just while you're here?"

"There's no need to waste your money," Lindsay said. "I'm comfortable in these clothes."

"I don't see it as wasting money, Lindsay. I want to do this for you as sort of a thank-you. You're making such a sacrifice to be here with me, and I want you to be happy while you are here," Trisha said. "I'll have Frank take you out shopping. He has tomorrow off, so you two can go out for a little bit. I can make it on my own for an hour or two, as long as I visit the bathroom before you leave."

"Are you sure?" Lindsay asked.

"Of course I am, sweetie. I want you to be comfortable while you're here helping us out." Trisha reached over and picked up her glass from the table beside her. "Oh, it's empty. Would you get me some more ice water?"

"Of course." Lindsay jumped up and carried the glass into the kitchen, where she flipped on the faucet.

"Honey, we use the water from the fridge," Trisha called.

"Oh." Lindsay turned toward the refrigerator, opened the door, and searched the shelf for a pitcher of water. She pushed aside a carton of milk and a container of orange juice but didn't spot any water. Further down on the shelf, she found cans of soda, but no bottled water. "I'm sorry, Aunt Trisha, but I don't see any water in the refrigerator."

"I'm sorry, sweetie," Trisha called. "I didn't mean a bottle of water. I meant from the tap on the front of the refrigerator—on the door."

"Oh, that's right." The big, stainless steel refrigerator was a far cry from the propane refrigerator at home. Lindsay stared at the buttons and pushed one for water. She then placed the glass under the tap and pushed it back, causing water to squirt down, filling the glass. She grinned, wondering how excited Emma and Daniel Junior would be to see the water shoot out from the front of the refrigerator. For a brief moment, she contemplated how Daniel would feel about having a luxury like this, but she quickly shooed away the thought, knowing the bishop would never approve it.

"You okay?" Trisha asked.

"Yes," Lindsay said with a little laugh, heading back to the den area. "I forgot."

Trisha smiled as Lindsay handed her the glass. "Thank you."

"Would it be okay if I set the table?" Lindsay asked.

Trisha sipped her drink and then waved off the question. "That's not necessary. We'll eat in here on paper plates."

"Okay." Lindsay glanced around the den area, remembering all of the times she'd eaten casually there with her parents, Jessica, and the McCabes.

Trisha sighed. "It will be more comfortable for me in the recliner. We still keep the snack trays in the closet." She pointed across the room. "Would you mind getting them out?"

Lindsay crossed to the closet and found a set of wooden snack trays jammed behind a curtain of bulky coats. She pulled three out, one at a time, and set them up in front of the sofa. She knew that Rebecca and Daniel would never consider eating in the den, except after church services when they had the benches set up and it was necessary in order to feed everyone. A grin formed on her lips when she thought about Frank's arrival. She hadn't had pizza in a long time.

After setting up the snack trays, Lindsay grabbed paper plates, forks, knives, and napkins from the kitchen and placed them on each of the little tables.

"Thank you," Trisha said between sips of water. "Frank should be back any moment now."

"What do you think he'll want to drink?" Lindsay asked.

"Probably a soda," Trisha said. "He loves his Coke and pizza."

Lindsay went back into the kitchen and returned with a Coke for Frank and a can for herself.

The door opened, and Frank appeared, carrying a large pizza box. "Dinner is served!" He grinned at Lindsay. "I got your old favorite."

"Sal's Pizza?" Lindsay asked, and her stomach growled in response.

He tipped the box and she read the familiar logo. Sal's was her father's favorite place to eat on Friday nights. Memories washed over her, and she bit her bottom lip.

"Let's eat!" He placed the box on the coffee table and opened the lid. Steam wafted up from the large pie dotted with pepperoni.

Lindsay's stomach growled again from the delicious smell. She moved a wooden tray next to Trisha's chair and then sat on the sofa. Bowing her head, she began to silently pray, thanking God for the delicious meal and asking for His healing hand to touch Trisha.

"Would it be okay if I offered a prayer?" Frank asked from across the room.

"Oh." Lindsay glanced up and found Frank settling in a wing chair across the room.

"That would be nice," Lindsay said with a smile. "Please do."

"Okay." Frank bowed his head, and Lindsay and Trisha followed suit. "We thank You, Lord, for bringing Lindsay to us. We also thank You for this delicious food and our time together again as a family. Please bless Trisha with a quick and easy recovery and watch over us, our family, and our friends. In Jesus' name we pray. Amen."

"Amen," Lindsay whispered.

"All right," Frank said, lifting his piece of pizza from his plate. "Grab a piece while it's hot, Lindsay-girl." He lifted the remote and flipped the channels, settling on the news, turning it down so that it was low enough to carry on a conversation.

"This pizza is heavenly," Trisha said while leaning back in her chair and holding the pizza in one hand and her plate in the other. "Good choice, Frank." She turned to Lindsay. "Go on and grab a piece before Frank and I eat it all."

Lindsay slapped a large piece of pizza onto her paper plate and then sank into the sofa. She stared at the television and bit into the pizza, which was hot and delicious. She wondered if Matthew and Katie had ever had pizza this good.

"Thank you for getting Sal's," Lindsay said. "It's wonderful. I wish my friends were here to have some."

"You need to bring them here sometime to visit," Frank said. "Then we can take them to Sal's."

"That's a great idea," Lindsay said with a grin. "I'll have to tell them."

"So, Frank," Trisha began, "I was thinking you and Lindsay could go shopping tomorrow. I'll be okay if you go for a quick trip."

"Shopping?" Frank placed his Coke on the table. "Do we need groceries?"

"I think we're okay for a few days with groceries," Trisha said, wiping her mouth. "I think Lindsay needs some lighter clothes to wear. It gets awfully hot here, and I thought she might feel better in summer clothes."

Lindsay nodded. "She's right. I gave all of my casual clothes to my sister awhile ago."

"I thought that if Lindsay goes for a walk on the beach, she might feel better in shorts and sandals than a heavy dress." Trisha turned to Lindsay. "Also, you might feel more comfortable walking on the beach in English clothes since people might stare at you. You know how some people can be. But it's only if you're okay with dressing more casually. It's up to you, Lindsay. You do what feels right for you, okay?"

"I see what you're saying," Lindsay said. She was thankful that Trisha was so understanding.

Frank nodded. "That makes sense." He looked at Lindsay. I'd be happy to take you out."

"Maybe you can run to Lynnhaven Mall real quick tomorrow," Trisha said. "Just be sure to help me to the bathroom before you leave." She wagged her finger.

"Of course," Frank said with a smile. He turned back to Lindsay. "Does that sound good?"

Lindsay shrugged. "Sure." As she lifted her can of soda, she hoped she could find something decent to wear that was more appropriate for the hot weather. However, she also didn't want to feel as if she were disappointing Rebecca.

Blueberry Muffins

1/2 cup butter
1 cup sugar
1 egg, beaten
1 cup milk
2 cups flour
4 tsp baking powder
1/2 tsp salt
1 cup blueberries

Cream butter and sugar. Add blueberries and egg, then milk and flour sifted with baking powder and salt. Bake in muffin tins at 350 degrees for 25 minutes.

10

Lindsay carried a large shopping bag from the Suburban into the beach house late the following morning. Frank followed close behind her with another couple bags. She had spent nearly two hours at the mall with Frank, searching for new clothes.

Walking into Lynnhaven Mall was almost surreal. Lindsay felt as if she'd stepped into a time machine and entered an alternate lifetime. In order to remain a little less conspicuous while shopping, she'd left her prayer covering home but still worn her hair in a tight bun. While she shopped, she'd felt eyes studying her, and she frequently spotted strangers staring at her.

As much as she hated to admit it, she realized Trisha had been right about getting clothes that looked more English. Yet, the shopping wasn't as easy as Lindsay had hoped it would be. Picking out clothes had been a tedious chore.

Frank held open the door, and Lindsay stepped into the large family room. Sunlight flooded in from the large windows facing the beach, and the waves pounded the sand with a loud cadence that Lindsay was starting to get used to. The noise had lulled her to sleep last night, like a warm lullaby from her childhood. She decided that she needed to make time to go for a long walk on the beach when Trisha was settled and she could get away.

"You're back," Trisha called from the recliner. "Just in time to help me to the bathroom."

"I'll help you." Frank moved past Lindsay and lifted Trisha from the chair with ease. "How are you feeling?" he asked, while carrying her toward the hallway. Instead of using the wheelchair as Lindsay did, Frank seemed to like carrying Trisha to the bathroom.

Lindsay flopped onto the sofa. Spreading her bags out beside her, she shook her head. While fashion was never her thing, she knew Jessica would've loved the opportunity to traipse through the mall in search of a new wardrobe. She heaved out a sigh while wondering how her sister was doing in New York City. She made a mental note to call her later.

She glanced toward the mantel across the room, opposite the large flat-screen television. Her eyes focused on a familiar family photo that she hadn't noticed last night. She crossed the room, lifted the photograph, and studied it—the events of that evening coming back to her as if it had been only yesterday. The picture had been taken nearly five years ago at Frank's company Christmas party. Posed with genuine smiles, her parents sat with Frank and Trisha while Lindsay and Jessica stood behind them, their hands on their parents' shoulders.

Lindsay studied the photograph, memorizing her parents' faces. She wished she could go back to that night and hear her mother's laugh and touch her father's hand just one more time.

"So, what did you buy?" Trisha asked, breaking Lindsay's trance.

"Oh," Lindsay said, placing the frame back onto the mantel. She found Trisha leaning back in the recliner, a curious expression on her face. Lindsay wondered how long Trisha had been back in the room. She crossed to the sofa and lifted one of the bags. "I'm sorry. I hadn't noticed that photo last night."

"I've had that photo there for quite a while," Trisha said. "If it upsets you, I can put it in my bedroom."

"No, no." Lindsay sank onto the sofa. "It doesn't bother me."

"I'm dying of curiosity," Trisha said. "Frank told me that you picked out quite a bit at Penney's."

Lindsay pulled a stack of clothes from the bag. "I did find a few things, but it wasn't easy."

"What do you mean?" Trisha looked surprised.

"Clothes just aren't my thing, I guess." Lindsay held up a plain white blouse and then a dark blue jumper. "I would look out of place here wearing my Amish clothes, but I also didn't feel comfortable buying typical English summer clothes either."

"Oh." Trisha smiled. "That jumper is cute. What else did you get?"

Lindsay held up two more jumpers, three plain blouses, and a plain skirt.

"Very nice." Trisha nodded with approval. "It's going to be very hot soon, so you might want to get something lighter too for those really humid days. Did you get any shorts or a bathing suit?"

Lindsay shook her head. "I haven't worn pants or shorts outside of the house in so long that I don't know if I'd feel comfortable wearing them. I only sleep in shorts sometimes, but I never wear them in public."

"Oh. And a bathing suit?"

"I have one," Lindsay said. "I brought my one-piece that I wear when I go up to the lake with the family or with the youth."

"That's good. That's neat that you go to the lake with your family." Trisha gestured toward the door. "You may want to go for a swim while you're here."

"That would be fun," Lindsay said. "I went to the lake with Rebecca and some of the other girls and women in the community last summer. Everyone had a really nice time."

"I remember you and your sister having a blast in the waves, when you were— " Trisha stopped speaking, winced, and settled back in the chair.

"Are you okay?" Lindsay popped up and headed over to the chair. "Can I get you anything?"

"Yeah." Trisha's voice was hoarse. "I think my painkiller wore off. Would you check the kitchen counter for my pills and bring me a pill and a drink?"

"Sure." Lindsay rushed to the kitchen. After locating the pills, she retrieved a glass of ice water and brought them both back to Trisha. "Do you need anything else?" she asked after Trisha had taken the pill.

Trisha shook her head and sighed. "I think I need to rest."

"You okay?" Frank looked alarmed as he approached, clad in khakis and a collared shirt with his company logo where the breast pocket would be. He held a briefcase in his hand.

"Yeah." Trisha closed her eyes. "I just took another pain pill. I'm going to rest now."

He leaned over and kissed her forehead. "You take it easy. I'm going to head into work. Bob just called, and he needs me to help out with an issue with the electricians." Frank then moved over to the kitchen and gestured for Lindsay to follow. "I need to go to the office and job site. Will you be okay?"

"I can handle it," Lindsay said.

He pointed to a piece of paper pinned to a little bulletin board above the cordless phone. "There's my cell number and also the office number in case I'm out of range if you get my voicemail. Don't hesitate to call me if you have any questions or you're concerned about something." He pointed to a business card below his number. "That's Trisha's doctor. You can call his office if something comes up too."

Lindsay nodded. "Okay. When will you be home?"

He frowned. "Traffic is pretty bad around here these days. I'll call you when I'm on my way home." He started for the door, and Lindsay trailed behind him. "Call me if you need anything." He disappeared through the door.

Lindsay glanced around the family room and smiled when

she heard a soft snore coming from Trisha's chair. She quietly gathered up her clothes from the sofa and carried them to her room, where she hung them in the closet. Lindsay moved to the laundry room, located off of the large master bathroom, and found a laundry basket.

While humming a hymn she'd often heard Elizabeth humming in the bakery, Lindsay gathered up the dirty laundry from the bathroom hampers and then stood in front of the washing machine. She bit her lower lip and tried to remember seeing her mother do laundry in their old house. Her mother had often threatened to stop doing Lindsay's and her sister's laundry because they would wear their clothes for only a short time and then toss them into the hamper.

A smile turned up the corners of Lindsay's lips while she recalled one of her mother's rants, accusing Jessica and Lindsay of being princesses who thought that new clothes and water were inexpensive. Only a week before her mother died, she'd promised to teach the girls to use the machine in order to lighten her housekeeping load, but she never got the chance to give the girls the lesson.

Lindsay had mastered Rebecca's wringer washer and actually enjoyed doing the laundry for Rebecca on Mondays. She frowned, wondering how Rebecca was faring without Lindsay's help in the house. She hoped someone would step up and help her aunt, and she assumed Katie would be the one to take her place.

She leaned over and opened the door to the front-loading machine. Lindsay remembered helping her mother separate clothes, and she understood that dark colors and whites were always washed with like shades. She pushed the dark-colored shirts and trousers into the machine until the drum was close to being full.

Standing, she examined the bottles and boxes of detergent, stain lifter, and softener sitting on top of the white metal work area above the expensive looking machines.

"This can't be too hard," she whispered. Standing in front of the washer, she stared at it, wondering where the detergent was supposed to go. She stepped back, examining the machine, taking in the complicated-looking control panel and the large, circular glass door, but nothing looked like a place for detergent.

"I can do this," she muttered. "After all, I conquered a wringer washer."

Lindsay stood up on her tiptoes and peered over the counter and looked behind the machine, spotting only hoses. She then opened the door and pushed back the clothes, peeking around inside the drum for a compartment.

Finding nothing, she closed the door and stepped back to study the machine. She spotted a compartment at the bottom and crouched down to examine it. She pulled it open and found a round top and instructions for cleaning out the filter bimonthly.

"This is ridiculous!" She smacked the door closed and stood, contemplating if she should wake Trisha to ask how to load the detergent. However, she knew that Trisha needed her sleep, and Lindsay was too embarrassed to admit that she'd been fooled by a washing machine.

While studying the control panel, she spotted an indentation to the left of the control panel, under the machine's name. Placing her hand on the indentation, she pulled open a small drawer and spotted small compartments designed for bleach, laundry soap, and softener. A laugh escaped her lips as she shook her head, marveling at how obvious the drawer had been. She examined the box of detergent and then scooped the prescribed amount before dropping it into the drawer. She then added half a capful of softener.

Lindsay then studied the control panel, wondering how she would start the washer. She bit her lower lip, reading the buttons for the water level, spin, and temperature. Placing her hand on the large dial, she turned it, and the control panel lit up with a series of beeps.

While the lights seemed to indicate a normal wash cycle, she pushed the start button and hoped that the machine wouldn't ruin the clothes or flood the laundry room.

The washer beeped, clicked, and then was silent for a moment. Lindsay sucked in a breath and hoped she hadn't broken the machine by pushing the wrong button. Soon the water began to pour into the drum, and Lindsay blew out a sigh of relief.

Moving back into her bedroom, Lindsay found an apron and slipped it on over her purple frock. She then tiptoed to the kitchen, careful not to wake Trisha, who was sleeping in her chair, as she passed through the family room.

She decided to clean for Trisha and went to the kitchen to find the vinegar, a bucket, and rags, which was how Rebecca had taught her to clean. She found a bottle of vinegar, which was almost empty. She paused, wondering what to do. She'd seen Elizabeth clean with just plain water when they ran out of vinegar at her house, but she wasn't sure Trisha would be comfortable with that since she tended to worry about germs when Lindsay and Jessica were little.

Lindsay searched the cabinets and pantry and found a bottle marked "bathroom cleaner." She grabbed a sponge and small bucket from under the sink and headed to the bathroom. When she sprayed the tub, she did her best not to gag. She wondered how Trisha could stand the strong, unappealing smell of the cleaner.

While working, she thought about her life back in Lancaster and wondered how her friends and family members were doing without her. Did they miss her? Did Matthew think of her?

After the bathrooms were clean, Lindsay moved on to the other rooms. Keeping with the method of cleaning that she'd learned from Rebecca, she wiped down the walls, floors, and drawers. She worked swiftly and quietly, stopping only to move the clothes to the dryer and then throw a load of whites into the washer.

While folding the dark load, Lindsay held a pair of Trisha's jeans up to her nose, breathed in the synthetic, flowery scent of laundry detergent, and grimaced. The clothes smelled much fresher back home after hanging them on the line. She filled the laundry basket with the dark load and then carried it out to the deck, careful not to wake Trisha, who was still snoozing in the chair.

She'd spotted some twine and old clothespins in the pantry in the kitchen while she was searching for cleaning supplies. After grabbing the twine and slipping the clothespins in her apron pocket, she created a makeshift clothesline by carefully standing on a chair, stringing the line across the deck, and tying the twine to empty hooks that she assumed used to hold the hanging plants that now lined the deck railing. She hung out each piece of laundry while humming to herself and then returned to cleaning the main level of the house.

Since it took quite a bit of time to thoroughly clean the main level in the Amish method she'd learn from her aunt, Lindsay decided to clean the guest rooms and den on the third level the following day. After putting the cleaning supplies away, she searched the pantry and refrigerator for supplies for supper.

"Lindsay?" Trisha's voice croaked from the family room while Lindsay was flipping through her cookbook.

Lindsay dropped the book onto the counter and rushed out to the den. "Yes?"

"Could you help me get up?" Trisha asked.

"Of course." Lindsay fetched Trisha's wheelchair from the corner and helped her climb into it. "Do you need more pain medicine?" she asked, while pushing Trisha toward the bathroom.

"No," Trisha said. "I can't stand the foggy feeling I get when I take them. Could you grab me some new pajamas? I think I want to wash up."

"Absolutely." Lindsay took Trisha's arm and guided her while she hopped from the wheelchair to the commode. She then slipped into the master bedroom and fished through Trisha's dresser until she found fresh pajamas and undergarments. On her way back to the master bathroom, she snatched a washcloth and a couple of towels from the linen closet. She entered the bathroom and found Trisha scowling while staring at the bathtub.

"Do you need help?" Lindsay asked, placing the clothing on the counter.

Frowning, Trisha shook her head. "No, I can do this. Just stay within earshot in case I fall and can't get up."

"Okay," Lindsay said, moving to the doorway. "Would you like meatloaf for supper? I found most of the supplies to make my aunt's recipe. I just need to improvise some of it, but I'm sure it will come out okay. Even my fussy uncle likes when I customize my meals."

Trisha grinned. "Sounds delicious."

"Thanks." Lindsay felt her cheeks heat at Trisha's wide smile. "Why are you smiling like that?"

"I'm proud of how much you've matured," Trisha said, pushing her messy brown hair back behind her ears. "Your mom and dad would be proud of you too."

Lindsay backed out of the bathroom. "I better get cooking. Call me if you need any help. I won't have the television on or anything, so I'll be able to hear you."

Lindsay contemplated Trisha's words while she mixed the meatloaf. Would her parents be proud of her? She shook her head while adding spices to the meatloaf mix.

It seemed to Lindsay that Jessica would be the daughter who made her parents proud. Jessica was the one who was driven and knew what she wanted. She was off in a big city, learning how to survive at a powerful company. Jessica would probably graduate from college with honors and go on to make a lot of money doing what she loved.

Lindsay, on the other hand, would be able to run a household and make a good wife and mother someday. She might know how to cook, clean, and baby-sit, but she didn't know who she was or where she belonged. But she loved to bake and try new recipes. Didn't it matter that she excelled in what she loved more than finding a powerful, high-paying career?

She blew out a deep sigh while pouring the meat mixture into a loaf pan. It didn't make any sense to her that Trisha was proud of her, but she hoped that Trisha was right about her parents. Perhaps her parents were looking down from heaven and smiling on their daughter. Whether Trisha was right or wrong, Lindsay just wished for one thing: to figure out where she belonged.

Once the meatloaf was in the oven, she stepped out to the deck and pulled a pair of jeans off the clothesline. Inhaling the fresh air, she smiled.

"Much better than the smell of laundry soap," she whispered while folding them. After folding each garment and placing it in the basket, she retrieved the other load from the washer and hung the items on the line to dry so that they would also smell fresh.

Won't Aunt Trisha and Uncle Frank be surprised when they smell their clean clothes? She grinned while heading back into the kitchen.

"Lindsay-girl," Frank began between bites of meatloaf, "this is fantastic! Your aunt has taught you well."

Lindsay patted her mouth with a paper napkin. "Thank you, Uncle Frank. I've learned quite a bit from my aunt Rebecca and also my aunts at the bakery."

"I bet they like it when you cook for them," Trisha added, lifting her glass of ice water.

Lindsay shrugged. "I don't get many complaints."

Trisha and Frank laughed and the phone began to ring.

"Should I get it or let it ring?" Lindsay looked between them, not knowing what to do. Nothing interrupted meals in Daniel's home.

"It's up to you," Trisha said. "We're not formal here. Check the caller ID."

Lindsay hurried to the phone and spotted Jessica's number. "It's my sister."

"Take it in your room," Frank said. "I'll clean up the kitchen if you girls are long-winded."

"Thanks!" Lindsay grabbed the phone and rushed toward her room while pushing the button. "Hello?"

"Linds!" Jessica nearly yelled into the phone. "How are you?"

"I'm doing okay." Lindsay dropped onto her bed. "How are you?"

"Doing well," Jessica said. "Tired. I've been working nearly twelve hours every day this week. We have a big project due next Tuesday."

"I hope they're paying you well." Lindsay crossed her legs under her and cradled the phone between her shoulder and cheek while removing the pins that held up her tight bun. Although she wasn't wearing her prayer covering, she felt more comfortable wearing her hair up like the other Amish women back home.

"They are, but I'm still tired." Jessica sighed. "So, how's Aunt Trisha doing?"

"Okay, I guess." Lindsay rubbed her scalp in an effort to stop it from throbbing. Her hair fell in waves to the middle of her back. "She had some pain today and had to take her pain pills. I also helped her to the bathroom so she could wash up. I think she felt better after that."

"That's good."

"Uncle Frank went back to work this afternoon, so I took care of the laundry, did some cleaning, and made a meatloaf for dinner. They both thought it was delicious. I used Aunt Rebecca's recipe, and it turned out pretty well. Not as good as hers, of course."

Jessica snorted.

"What?" Lindsay asked.

"You're so domestic, Linds."

Lindsay rolled her eyes. "Please don't start. You're just jealous because you would starve if you had to live without drive-through meals or frozen dinners."

"I resent that," Jessica quipped. "I made dinner the other night."

"Oh? And what did you make?" Lindsay asked, finger combing her long, red hair.

"I made spaghetti and meatballs," Jessica said, sounding proud.

"Oh really?" Lindsay grinned. "Mom's recipe?"

Jessica paused, and Lindsay laughed.

"Sort of," Jessica said. "At least, it was almost as good."

Lindsay's smiled faded a little as she thought of her sister, parents, and their nights gathered around the table eating their mom's delicious dinners. "I miss you."

"I miss you too," Jessica said. "Maybe you can come visit after Trisha's better. We have plenty of room here in Kim's house. You could bunk in with me, and I could give you a tour of the city."

Lindsay shook her head. Jessica would never give up her dream of taking Lindsay to experience the big city. "Maybe," she said. "Have you heard from Jake?"

"No," Jessica said, and Lindsay could hear the disappointment in her sister's voice.

"Have you tried calling him?"

"No," Jessica said.

"Why not?" Lindsay flopped back onto her pillow. "You should be the better person and make the first move. I know you're never shy, so what's the problem?"

"I don't know what to say," Jessica said.

"You shouldn't give up. He told you that he loves you."

"Let's change the subject," Jessica countered. "What about you? Have you done anything else besides cooking and cleaning?"

"I went shopping with Uncle Frank earlier today."

"Oh? Where'd you go?"

"Lynnhaven Mall." Lindsay studied the white ceiling while she talked. "It looks so different now. They've added some new restaurants out front. You'd love it."

"Cool," Jessica said. "What'd you get?"

"Some clothes." Lindsay hoped she wouldn't ask for details. "Nothing exciting, but it's functional."

"To get you out of your Amish garb?"

"Please don't start," Lindsay warned. "I don't feel like arguing."

"Have you called any of your old friends? Like maybe Vicki or Heather?" Jessica asked.

"No." Lindsay glanced across the room at her pink address book sitting on her dresser. "I've been here less than forty-eight hours, so I haven't even thought about calling anyone."

"You should call Vicki and Heather," Jessica continued. "I'm sure they'd be thrilled to hear from you."

"I'll call them once Aunt Trisha is doing a little better," Lindsay said, sitting up and leaning against the wooden headboard. "I bet they're busy shopping and packing for college."

"Well, maybe they'll inspire you to pursue higher education."

"Jessica, we've been through this," Lindsay snapped through clenched teeth.

"I know, but it's my job to look out for you. I still think you should get your GED while you're there," Jessica said. "You should check out the city schools' website and see if you can—"

"Can you please drop this?"

"I think you should do it, Linds," Jessica continued. "You're so smart, and you could be anything. You should get that GED so you can get a job outside of the bakery if you decide you want to. Education leads to choices. Remember, Dad used to say that all the time?"

"Yeah," Lindsay said, defeated. "I do remember that."

"You should seriously think about it," Jessica said. "I don't think it costs much, and I can send you money if you need it. I'd be happy to help you pay for it. I know that there's money put away for us, but I always have at least some money. I mean, I've been working overtime for weeks now."

"Fine," Lindsay said, cupping her hand to her temple. "I'll look into it."

"Awesome!" Jessica said. "Oh, hang on a minute." Muffled noises sounded in the background, and Lindsay imagined her sister sitting in a plush office while talking to an important man wearing an expensive suit. "Listen, I gotta go. Would you please give Aunt Trisha and Uncle Frank my love and tell them that I'll call soon? I want to talk to Aunt Trisha, but I have to run for a meeting."

Lindsay glanced at the clock. "Jess, it's after six. What on earth are you still doing at work?"

"I told you," Jessica began, "I'm working on an important project. Look, I gotta run. Talk to you soon. Love you!"

"Love you," Lindsay said. "Bye."

She pushed the button to end the call and then stared at the receiver, wondering when her sister would stop trying to run her life. She grabbed a rubber band from her dresser and pulled her hair back into a loose ponytail while she contemplated her sister. Would Jessica ever stop focusing on Lindsay and just worry about herself? Or was it Jessica's intent to fill in for their mother and give Lindsay unsolicited advice for the rest of her life?

The question was still floating through Lindsay's mind when she stepped into the kitchen, where Frank and Trisha sat finishing their meatloaf. Trying in vain to stop the scowl on her lips, Lindsay sank into her chair.

"We had a visit from one of our neighbors while you were on the phone," Trisha said with a smile.

"Oh?" Lindsay asked as she grabbed the bowl of mixed vegetables and scooped a small pile onto her plate. "Which neighbor?"

"Mrs. Morton," Frank said, rolling his eyes. "She's the busybody on our street."

Trisha shook a finger at him. "That's not nice." She then looked at Lindsay. "Did you make a clothesline and hang out our laundry today?"

"Yes," Lindsay said. "I love the smell of the clothes after they dry outside, so I did it as a surprise for you. I wasn't going to tell you. I was hoping you would notice when you wore your clean clothes." She looked between Trisha and Frank, wondering why they were smiling. "Did I do something wrong?"

"No, no." Trisha touched Lindsay's hand. "We think it's wonderful that you did that for us, but our neighbors, well, they don't exactly agree with some of our ideas."

Lindsay studied their expressions. "I don't understand."

"Lindsay," Frank began, "I don't know how else to explain it except to say that Mrs. Morton is a snob. She didn't like the clothesline. She said it, well, brought down the view."

"Brought down the view?" Lindsay asked. "You mean like it somehow cheapened the pretty houses out here?"

"Exactly," Frank said with a nod.

"We don't agree with her," Trisha quickly chimed in. "I told her that. I also said that it doesn't make sense since she hangs her towels over her deck. She insisted that towels are acceptable, but other laundry isn't."

"It's ridiculous," Frank said. "But we have to agree with her in order to keep the peace. We don't need any problems with the housing association."

"Oh," Lindsay said. "I won't hang the laundry outside anymore."

"But thank you for your efforts," Trisha added as she cut up a piece of meatloaf on her plate. "The house looks beautiful. You've worked so hard for us. Thank you."

"We want to pay you an allowance," Frank said after wiping his mouth. "You've been working so hard already, and we appreciate it so much. You need some spending money so you can have some fun while you're here."

"That's not necessary," Lindsay said, scooping up the vegetables with her spoon.

"Yes, it is," Trisha said between bites of meatloaf. "I insist."

"So, how was your phone call?" Frank asked. "How's your sister?"

"The same as usual," Lindsay muttered.

"Your tone makes it sound as if it didn't go well," Trisha said. "What happened?"

"My sister is determined to run my life," Lindsay said while shaking her head with frustration. "Every time I talk to her, she lectures me on what I should be doing and makes little sarcastic comments about my domestic skills and plain clothes. She thinks I'm wasting my life."

Trisha glanced at Frank. "Do you have something important that you need to do in another room? Like maybe go for a run on the beach or something?"

"Yes, I do need to go for a run since I haven't had a chance to run since your accident." Frank pushed his chair back and took his dish and utensils to the counter. He then stepped over to the table and touched Lindsay's shoulder. "I'm going to leave you two ladies to talk. Lindsay, you shouldn't let your sister upset you. What's right for her isn't necessarily right for you. You're both wonderful young ladies with bright futures." He gave her shoulder a light squeeze and then kissed Trisha's head before disappearing into the den.

"He's right," Trisha said with a gentle smile. "Don't let Jessica make you feel bad about your decisions."

Lindsay dabbed her mouth with a napkin. "Earlier you said that my mom would be proud of me. Did you mean that?"

Reaching across the table, Trisha took Lindsay's hands in hers. "Of course I did. Why wouldn't she be?"

"Because I didn't finish high school or move to a big city. I've chosen to stay in the Amish community."

Trisha shook her head. "Honey, your mom and dad wanted you and Jessica to live with your aunt Rebecca. Doesn't that give you the answer you need? If your mom didn't want you to be in that community, why would she have chosen your aunt to be your guardian?"

Lindsay paused as the words soaked through her mind. "That makes sense. Jessica keeps bugging me about getting my GED. Do you think I should look into that while I'm staying here with you?"

Trisha shrugged. "That's not a bad idea, but it should be *your* choice."

"I know, but I'm not sure what I want," Lindsay said.

Trisha patted Lindsay's hands. "You should give yourself time. You don't have to make a choice right now, and you don't have to do what Jessica says. She means well, but you are the only one who can decide what's best for you." She gestured toward Lindsay's plate. "You need to eat your delicious meal."

Lifting her fork, Lindsay glanced down at her plate and her half-eaten piece of meatloaf. She suddenly wasn't hungry, and she instead moved the food around on the plate.

"I think Jessica feels like she has to take care of me since Mom and Dad are gone," Lindsay said. "I miss our parents too, but they are the only ones who have the right to tell me what to do. Of course, I guess Aunt Rebecca and Uncle Daniel do too, since I live in their house."

"Yes, I agree that Rebecca and Daniel can have input into your life, but you're a young lady now. I can't imagine Rebecca giving you orders or telling you how to live your life. She doesn't seem like that type of person." Trisha tapped the table for emphasis. "You're putting too much pressure on yourself. Give it some time and think about how you see yourself in five years. Follow that plan and see where it takes you."

Lindsay speared a piece of carrot with her fork. "That makes sense. But I can't stop thinking that maybe getting my GED is a good idea. I could study while I'm not helping you."

"You could, but would it create problems for you if you return to the Amish community with a GED?" Trisha asked.

Lindsay shook her head. "No. I haven't joined the church yet, so I can get my GED without upsetting the bishop."

Trisha shrugged. "Then maybe you should think about it."

Swallowing the carrot, Lindsay nodded. "Okay."

"You should call your aunt too," Trisha said. "I bet she's thinking of you."

"I will," Lindsay said, lifting the phone from the table. "I left her a message yesterday telling her that I arrived safely, but I bet she is thinking of me. I'll call her again."

Rebecca hugged her arms to her chest as she crossed the rock driveway and headed toward the phone shanty. She'd been thinking of Lindsay all day long. She hoped Lindsay was doing well and enjoying her time with Trisha and Frank. However, she also hoped that Lindsay wasn't enjoying it too much. Although she knew it was selfish, she wanted Lindsay to miss Lancaster County enough to want to come back, join the church, and stay for good.

However, Rebecca knew that wasn't her decision to make; it was between Lindsay and God.

Stepping into the phone shanty, Rebecca sank into the chair in front of the small desk, picked up the receiver, and smiled when she heard the beeping dial tone, indicating that there was at least one message waiting for her. She dialed the voicemail and punched in the code, and a computer voice told her that she had two messages.

The first was from Elizabeth, asking how Rebecca was doing and offering to come by to visit over the weekend to give Rebecca a hand with the children. Rebecca smiled. She was so blessed to have Elizabeth for a mother-in-law. She would tell Elizabeth their exciting news about the new baby in person the next time she had the opportunity to talk to Elizabeth alone. She couldn't bear to keep it a secret from her any longer. She deleted the message and then held her breath, hoping the next one would be from Lindsay.

When Lindsay's sweet voice rang through the phone, Rebecca blew out a deep sigh. She hung on every word while her niece's voice spoke.

"*Aenti* Rebecca," Lindsay began. "*Wie geht's?* I hope you, *Onkel* Daniel, Emma, and Junior are doing well. I think of you all constantly. I'm doing fine here. Today I did some cleaning and laundry." She snickered a little. "I wish you could've seen me trying to figure out the washing machine. It's quite different from the wringer washer at home, but I conquered it without a mess."

Rebecca smiled when she heard Lindsay say "home." She was thankful Lindsay still considered Lancaster County her home.

"Tonight I made your famous meatloaf for supper," Lindsay continued, "and Uncle Frank and Aunt Trisha loved it. I had to improvise a little bit, but it turned out well. Aunt Trisha and Uncle Frank were both impressed. You taught me well." Lindsay gave a little laugh again. "Aunt Trisha is doing okay. She has some discomfort, but it seems manageable with the pain pills."

Lindsay paused, and Rebecca fiddled with the phone cord, absently wrapping it around her finger while she waited for her to continue.

"I miss you," Lindsay said. "I'm praying that you're feeling well. You can give me a call anytime. We have a phone in the house, of course. If I'm not here, please leave me a message and I'll call you right back." She rattled off the phone number, and Rebecca wrote it down on the notepad she kept by the phone. "I love you," Lindsay said. "Bye."

The line went dead and Rebecca sucked in a breath, hoping she wouldn't cry. Her eyes welled with tears, and she felt silly. She knew her niece was doing well and was safe. Rebecca also realized that she was overly emotional these days due to the pregnancy. She ripped off the piece of paper with Trisha's phone number and stuck it in her apron pocket.

The clip clop of approaching hooves drew her attention to the rock driveway. Rebecca sniffed and touched her prayer covering, making sure she was presentable before stepping out into the setting sun.

A buggy stopped in front of the barn, and the door opened, revealing Katie climbing from the driver seat and Lizzie Anne exiting the passenger side.

"*Wie geht's*," Katie called with a wave. "We thought we'd stop by to see you."

"It's so *gut* to see you." Rebecca gestured for them to follow her into the kitchen. "*Kumm*. We'll sit and talk."

The girls followed Rebecca into the kitchen, where she brought out a plate of cookies, a pitcher of meadow tea, and three glasses.

"Where are my little cousins?" Katie asked as she poured a glass of tea.

"They were cranky and went to bed early," Rebecca said, sinking down into a chair across from her. "What are you two doing out so late?"

Lizzie Anne and Katie exchanged looks.

"The truth is," Lizzie Anne began with a frown, "we've been worried about Lindsay. I was so upset that she didn't come by and say good-bye to me, and I've been wondering how she is."

"Have you heard from her?" Katie interjected.

Rebecca poured herself a glass of tea. "She's left me a couple of messages ..."

"And ... ?" Lizzie Anne asked.

"She said she's doing fine, but she misses home." Rebecca suppressed a smile as she said the word out loud. "She left her phone number and asked that I call her."

Lizzie Anne's expression brightened. "Can we call her?"

"Now?" Rebecca asked.

"*Ya*," Lizzie Anne said with a nod. "I'd love to tell her that I missed saying goodbye to her."

Rebecca shook her head. "I wanted to give her a few days to get settled in. I'd hate for her to cry because she's homesick, you know?"

Katie's lips formed a thin line. "I agree. She seemed sad about leaving, and it would be terrible to make her feel worse."

Lizzie Anne sighed. "You're right, but I miss her so much."

"I do too." Rebecca pushed back her chair and crossed to the counter, where she pulled her address book from a drawer. "I don't see any problem with writing letters to her." She returned to the table with her address book, a notepad, and a pen. "I'll give you her address and phone number, and you can contact her. I don't think we should call her for a few days, though. No need to upset her." She wrote out the address and phone number twice and then handed the pieces of paper to the girls.

"*Danki*," Lizzie Anne said, looking at the address.

Katie seemed to study Rebecca. "Are you doing all right?"

Rebecca sipped her tea and then lifted a cookie from the plate. "I'm doing pretty well. The *kinner* and I miss her, but we're getting by."

"If you ever need any help," Katie began, "I can always come over and lend a hand."

"You're sweet," Rebecca said. "But I know your *mammi* needs you at the bakery. I wouldn't want to steal you away."

"Then I'll just stop by every so often to check on you," Katie said between bites of a cookie.

"I'll come too," Lizzie Anne chimed in.

"*Danki*." Rebecca smiled, thankful for her niece and her friend. They discussed the warm weather and then the girls talked about their families. Soon it was starting to get dark out, and Rebecca encouraged them to get on the road before it became too dangerous to travel on the roads in the dark.

Standing outside in the driveway, Rebecca hugged the girls and then waved as the buggy started down the driveway. As they drove off, Rebecca thought again of Lindsay and decided that she couldn't wait a few days to call her. She would give her a call tomorrow afternoon while the children were napping.

11

Lindsay sat at the kitchen table clad in a new jumper and made a shopping list while a stew cooking in the crockpot on the counter filled the kitchen with a delicious aroma the following afternoon. She'd scrounged around the kitchen to pull together something for supper, and the only idea she had was making a stew. Although she'd considered using an old-fashioned pot, Trisha suggested a crockpot. The concept of the crockpot seemed a little odd, but she decided to try it and made a mental note to tell Rebecca about it. Since the cabinets and freezer were bare, despite snack foods and a few frozen dinners, she didn't have any ideas for what she could prepare tomorrow.

Flipping through Rebecca's cookbook, she chewed on the end of her pencil and wondered how things were back in Lancaster County. She hoped Rebecca had remembered to check the voicemail last night and had received her message.

When the phone began to ring, she jumped up and grabbed it from the wall on the second ring without checking the caller ID, in hopes of not waking Trisha, who napped in the den.

"Hello?" Lindsay asked.

"Lindsay?" Rebecca's voice asked. "Is that you?"

"*Aenti* Rebecca!" Lindsay nearly shouted. She then cupped her hand over her mouth, realizing she was too loud. "How are you?"

"*Gut,*" Rebecca said. "How are you?"

"Fine," Lindsay twirled the pencil in her hand as she spoke. "How are the *kinner?*"

"*Gut, gut,*" Rebecca said. "They miss you. Junior says you're better at reading the nighttime story to him than I am."

Lindsay smiled while thinking of her two little cousins. "I miss reading to him, but I don't think I'm a better reader than you."

"He thinks so," Rebecca said. "Lizzie Anne and Katie came to visit me last night."

"Oh?" Lindsay asked. "How are they?"

"Doing fine," Rebecca said. "They wanted to know how you're doing. Lizzie Anne was disappointed that you didn't say good-bye to her in person."

Lindsay grimaced. "I should've invited her to come to the bus station, but I didn't think she could've come."

"It's okay," Rebecca said. "I didn't mean to make you feel bad. They just miss you. I gave them your address and phone number, so don't be surprised if you hear from them."

"*Danki,*" Lindsay said. "It would be nice to hear from them. How's *Onkel* Daniel?"

"*Gut,*" Rebecca said.

"Has he talked to Matthew?" Lindsay asked before she could stop the words from leaving her lips.

"He didn't tell me if he did," Rebecca began. The smile in her voice emanated through the phone. "But you know how reticent your *onkel* can be. I'm certain Matthew asked about you, and Daniel probably said he'd heard you were fine."

Lindsay felt her cheeks heat at the thought of Matthew talking about her with her uncle. She changed the subject to the weather, and they talked about the long warm days and how much the children loved playing outside in the pasture.

"Are you making supper now?" Rebecca asked.

"*Ya,* I threw together a stew." Lindsay crossed the kitchen and stood by the crockpot, inhaling the aroma. "I'm using a crockpot."

"I've heard that they're really *gut* for stews," Rebecca said.

"I don't know how it will taste, but it smells awfully good."

Rebecca chuckled. "I'm certain it will be *appeditlich*. You're a good cook."

"How about you? What are you making tonight?"

"I made a chicken pot pie," Rebecca said.

"Oh." Lindsay licked her lips. "That's my favorite."

"I know," Rebecca said.

They were both silent for a moment, and Lindsay longed to tell Rebecca how homesick she was and how much she wanted to come back home. Instead, she bit her bottom lip to stop the words that she feared would upset her aunt.

"How are you feeling?" Lindsay asked. "Are you getting enough rest?"

"Oh, I'm just fine," Rebecca said. "But I can never get enough sleep."

"Maybe someone can come over and help you so that you don't work too hard," Lindsay said, moving to the windows and gazing out over the beach below. "Nancy or Katie could come and stay with you so you don't overdo it. I know you. You won't slow down even though the doctor tells you to."

"I'll ask for help if I need it," Rebecca said. "Well, I need to see if the *kinner* are still asleep. I better go."

"It was good hearing your voice," Lindsay said.

"*Ya*, it was *gut* hearing yours too," Rebecca said.

"I'll call you soon," Lindsay promised.

Hanging up the phone, Lindsay sucked in a deep breath and willed herself not to get emotional. Yes, she missed her family back in Lancaster County, but she had to be strong and mature. She wasn't a kid anymore, and Trisha needed her.

She set the table and checked the stew before stepping into the den where Trisha was staring at the television.

"Who was on the phone?" Trisha asked as she turned down the volume on the evening news.

"Aunt Rebecca," Lindsay said, sitting on the arm of the sofa. "She wanted to see how everything was going here."

"I bet she misses you."

Lindsay nodded. "I'm sure she does, but the family will take good care of her."

Trisha adjusted herself in the chair, wincing as she moved her leg.

"Do you need some medicine?" Lindsay asked, moving over to her chair.

"No, no." Trisha waved off Lindsay's outstretched arm. "I'm fine. That stew smells so good. I'm glad you used the crockpot."

"Yeah," Lindsay said, leaning back on the sofa arm. "We're out of meat now. I really need to go to the grocery store. Do you think Frank could take me tonight after supper if you're feeling okay?"

"I'm sure he will. He should be home any moment." Trisha gestured toward the sofa. "Take a load off and sit with me while we wait for him. I heard you cleaning the upstairs earlier. You work too hard."

Lindsay sank into the sofa and stared at the television, wondering how Rebecca's potpie tasted.

"You want me to take half of the list?" Frank asked Lindsay while they crossed the parking lot of the Bloom grocery store later that evening. "Grocery shopping isn't my thing, but I can handle finding the easy stuff."

Lindsay examined her list. "How about you get the milk, bread, and eggs, and I'll meet you at the checkout?"

He gave a mock salute. "Sounds like a plan, Lindsay-girl."

The entrance doors opened with a whoosh, and they each grabbed a shopping cart and took off in opposite directions. Lindsay marched through the aisles on a mission, filling the cart with meat, poultry, spices, vegetables, pasta, and produce. She steered toward the checkout and scanned the knot of customers for Frank.

Voices swirled around her, and for a brief moment, Lindsay thought she heard her name ring out among the chatter. She scanned the sea of faces, searching for Frank and wondering how long it could possibly take him to find milk, bread, and eggs while she'd nearly filled her cart with a variety of items.

"Lindsay Bedford?" a feminine voice called. "Lindsay Bedford? Is that you?"

Lindsay spun and nearly knocked over a young woman. Lindsay studied the girl, trying to place her face. The woman was clad in short denim shorts and a gray tank top with bright pink bathing suit straps tied in a bow at the nape of her neck beneath her platinum blonde ponytail.

"Lindsay?" the woman asked again. Her smile transformed to a frown. "Don't tell me you don't remember me. We survived crazy Mr. Richardson's English class together."

Lindsay gasped. "Vicki?"

"Yeah!" Vicki opened her arms. "It's so good to see you."

Lindsay stepped into her old friend's hug and laughed. "You look so different."

Vicki snickered. "You like the platinum blonde?" She pointed to her scalp. "I need to get my sister to take care of the roots. It's been about a month since my last touch up." Her gaze raked over Lindsay. "You look so different. Isn't it a bit hot for a denim jumper? Besides, you're at the beach. You should be in shorts and tank tops."

Lindsay glanced down at her dress. "Oh. Right."

Vicki pointed to Lindsay's head. "Why do you have that gorgeous hair up in that tight bun? Your hair was always the envy of the school." She laughed again. "Remember when I tried to dye my hair your color? I looked like a Muppet! The color was all wrong and the towel ended up redder than my head."

Lindsay joined in the laughter as the memories of their fun sleepovers returned to her. "That was funny. My mom never got the stain out of the towel."

Vicki's smile faded. "How are you doing since ...?"

"Fine." Lindsay folded her arms across her chest. "I've been living with my aunt in Pennsylvania and I really love it there."

"And Jessica?" Vicki asked, leaning against her cart. "How's she doing?"

"She's great. She's a sophomore in college and in the middle of an internship in New York City with a big accounting firm."

Vicki looked impressed. "Wow. She was always brilliant. I'm not surprised."

"How about you?" Lindsay asked.

"Oh, I'm doing fine," Vicki said, a grin spreading on her face. "I'm leaving for Oregon in less than a month. I can't wait!"

"Wow! Oregon." Lindsay smiled. "That's really awesome."

"Thanks. It's always been my dream to go to the Pacific Northwest." Vicki held up her hand, where a tiny heart shaped diamond sparkled in the fluorescent lights. "Do you remember Brandon Walsh?"

Lindsay tried to think back to any of the boys from school but couldn't remember any of them. She shook her head. "Sorry, but I don't."

"We've been dating for, like, forever," Vicki said with a grin. "Brandon's going too. He gave me a promise ring last week. We're going to get married after we graduate and live out in Oregon together."

Lindsay examined the ring. "That's really pretty, Vicki. You must be so happy."

"Oh yeah." Vicki examined her ring and then grimaced. "My parents aren't happy. They say that I'm too young to be tied down, and I should concentrate on my studies. I guess they don't remember what it's like to be young and in love." She met Lindsay's stare. "What about you?"

"What do you mean?"

"What are your plans? Do you have a boyfriend?"

"Well, I work—" Lindsay began.

"Lindsay!" Frank sidled up to her. "There you are."

Lindsay glanced down into his cart full of packs of Coke, frozen pizzas, boxes of microwave popcorn, and bags of chips and pretzels. "I thought you were getting milk, bread, and eggs."

"We need to load up on some fun stuff too." He held out his hand to Vicki. "I'm Frank McCabe."

"Vicki Swan." She shook his hand. "I think we met a few years back when Lindsay was still living here."

"That's right." Frank smiled. "I believe I remember you. It's good to see you. I'm glad you two caught up. Trisha and I were just discussing that Lindsay needs to get out and have some fun while she's staying with us this summer."

Vicki's eyes lit up. "You're staying here all summer?"

"Yeah," Lindsay said. "My aunt Trisha broke her leg, so I'm going to be here for a while to help take care of her."

"Oh." Vicki frowned for a brief moment. "I'm sorry to hear about her accident, but I'm glad you're going to be in town. I'm having a pool party at my parents' house tomorrow night. You should come."

Lindsay paused, wondering what to say in response. A strange excitement filled her at the thought of seeing her old friends. She then felt a little guilty—wondering how Rebecca would feel if she went to a party. However, going to a party wasn't breaking any rules, as long as there wasn't alcohol or inappropriate behavior. She glanced at Frank. "Will Aunt Trisha need me tomorrow night?"

"Of course not. I'll be home to take care of her. You should go." Frank tapped Lindsay on the shoulder. "Find out Vicki's address and I can drop you off and pick you up."

"You don't have your license?" Vicki looked surprised.

Lindsay felt her cheeks heat. "No, I don't."

Vicki fished a pen and a small piece of paper from her purse and scribbled out her address. "The party starts at six. We'll have hot dogs and hamburgers."

"Do you need me to bring anything?" Lindsay asked. "Maybe a dessert?"

"Oh, no," Vicki said, shaking her head. "We'll have plenty. Just bring your bathing suit and a towel."

"Okay. Sounds good." Lindsay glanced at the address, and memories of fun times spent at Vicki's house rained down on her. "Thank you for the invitation."

"Well, we better get back," Frank said. "I don't want to leave Trisha alone too long." He smiled at Vicki. "Nice seeing you."

"I'm so excited that you're here," Vicki said to Lindsay. "I can't wait to tell Heather that I ran into you. She'll be so psyched to see you tomorrow too."

"Great," Lindsay said. "Have a good night." She followed Frank to a short line, where he paid for the groceries.

During the ride home, Frank prattled on about his condo project in the Outer Banks and about the weather. Lindsay only half listened while she contemplated her conversation with Vicki. It was both fun and a little nerve-racking to see friends from her past. Memories of school and time with her parents floated through her mind like bubbles.

When they arrived back at the beach house, Frank helped Trisha take a shower while Lindsay put away the groceries. While she filled the pantry, she was still silently analyzing her conversation with Vicki. While Lindsay was drifting without a map between two worlds, the English and the Amish, Vicki was brazenly heading to Oregon with her confident head held high and a promise ring on her finger. Vicki knew exactly what she wanted and whom she wanted to marry.

Lindsay wondered why she couldn't be that confident or sure of her future. Was something wrong with her? Wasn't she smart enough to figure out her own destiny like Jessica and Vicki?

The questions tumbled through her mind as she stepped into the den and found Frank sitting in his favorite chair and typing on a laptop with the Weather Channel droning quietly in the background.

Lindsay sank into the sofa across from him. "How's Trisha?"

"Fine." He picked up the remote and muted the sound on the flat-screen television. "She took a shower and then I helped her to bed. She's watching a movie now."

"That's good," Lindsay said, crossing her legs. "I put all of the groceries away. We should be set for a while."

"Thank you. I'm so grateful for all you're doing for us." He closed the top of his laptop. "That's really great that you ran into an old friend at Bloom."

"I didn't recognize her at first," Lindsay said. "The last time I saw her was at my parents' memorial service."

"I told Trisha about how you saw Vicki, and she's happy that you're going to the party." He tapped the top of the laptop. "It'll be good for you to get out of the house for a while tomorrow night and spend some time with old friends. I'm sure you've missed them, and they've missed you."

Lindsay nodded while she thought about the party. What would Lindsay and her old friends possibly have in common? Her friends would leave for college soon and Lindsay would return to Pennsylvania to work in a bakery and help her aunt raise her young children.

Her eyes flickered to the laptop and she remembered her conversation with Trisha about the GED. She wondered if she should look into the GED program by surfing the internet.

Frank raised an eyebrow. "Something on your mind?"

"Your laptop," she said. "Could I possibly borrow it when you're not using it?"

"Sure." He held it out. "Can I help you search for something?"

She placed the warm computer on her lap. "I was wondering about how you go about getting your GED." She hoped her cheeks wouldn't reveal how much the statement embarrassed her.

"Oh," Frank said. "I had a guy on my crew get his GED last year. He went through a program at the Adult Learning Center in Virginia Beach."

Lindsay bit her bottom lip. "Was it difficult?"

He shrugged. "I don't think it was too bad. He studied and took a test. Did you want me to help you find the website for the Adult Learning Center?"

"Maybe later." She gave the computer back to him. "Thanks."

"You're welcome." He flipped open the laptop and began clicking away.

She watched him, wondering about his employee who got his GED. "How old was he?"

Frank looked up. "What's that?"

"Your employee," she said. "How old was he when he got his GED?"

He raked his hand through his thinning brown hair. "I guess he was about twenty-two. Why do you ask?"

"I was just wondering." She cleared her throat and glanced at the television, wishing she had the confidence to ask the questions that were heavy on her mind and heart.

"Lindsay?" he asked gently. "Is there something you want to talk about?"

She took a deep breath, gathering up her confidence. "Jessica says I should get my GED while I'm here. Do you think it's a good idea?"

"Sure." He shrugged. "It's a great idea."

"What did it do for your employee?" She paused. "What I mean is—did it really make a difference for him to have his GED?"

"Yes, it did." He nodded with emphasis. "Although it's not

a college degree, it showed that he had skills, and it makes him more employable."

Lindsay shook her head. "I just don't know if I want to do it. I'm sort of scared."

"I understand that. You've been out of school for four years now, but I definitely think that you're smart and motivated enough to go after it. You should look into it, and if you decide you want to pursue it, then I'll help you find the information you need."

"Thank you, Uncle Frank." Lindsay glanced toward the door leading to the outside stairs. "I think I'm going to go for a walk on the beach. Would that be okay?"

He grinned. "Of course it would. Go right ahead."

Lindsay trotted back to her room and slipped off her sandals. She grabbed a notepad and pen from her dresser and then ran out the door and down the stairs toward the beach.

When her feet sank into the sand, she smiled and blew out a sigh. The sand felt so warm and natural as it squeezed between her toes while she walked to the waves, which crashed and retreated with a gentle cadence that took her back to time with her family. She stepped into the edge of the cool water and closed her eyes while remembering times she and her sister played in the water while her parents and the McCabes sat on the deck drinking lemonade, talking, and watching them swim.

Turning back toward the deck, she imagined her parents still sitting there, her father leaning back in a chair and laughing at Frank's jokes while her mother sat at the table watching Trisha with interest while they discussed the latest news about their friends.

Lindsay walked slowly up the beach, enjoying the feel of the sand in her toes as she approached the deck. She climbed the steps to the second story and sat at the table under the lights. Opening her notebook, she began to write:

Dear Katie,

Wie geht's! How's your family? I'm doing well here in Virginia Beach. Aunt Trisha is doing pretty well. She has some pain, but it seems to ease more every day.

How are the rest of the Kauffmans? Is the bakery staying busy? How is Aenti Rebecca doing?

The beach is so pretty. I'm sitting outside on the deck listening to the waves while I write this. I wish you were here with me to see and hear the sights.

This evening I went to the store with Uncle Frank, and we ran into one of my friends from school. She invited me over tomorrow night, so I'm going to go see her and some more old friends. It should be fun.

Well, I'm going to close for now. It's getting late, and I'm tired.

Please tell everyone hello for me.

With love,
Lindsay

Lindsay wrote a similar letter to Lizzie Anne and then folded both of them up. Cupping her hand to her mouth to stifle a yawn, Lindsay climbed the deck stairs and then entered the house through the sliding glass door. She stepped into the family room and found Frank still working on his computer in front of the television.

Glancing up, he smiled. "Did you have a nice time out on the beach?"

"I did," Lindsay said. "It's beautiful out." She held up her notepad. "I wrote a couple of letters to my friends." She yawned. "It's getting late. I think I need to shower and get to bed."

"You do that," he said with a nod. "You worked hard today."

"Good night. I'll see you in the morning."

"Good night," he said. "Thank you for all you're doing to help us."

"You're welcome." Heading down the hall, Lindsay yawned again. She would sleep well tonight after all the excitement of the evening. After placing her letters in envelopes, she sealed and addressed them. She then grabbed her pajamas and undergarments and headed down the hall toward the shower.

12

The following evening, Lindsay gnawed on her bottom lip and stared at the familiar brick colonial while sitting in Frank's Suburban parked out front. A herd of sedans and SUVs clogged the long driveway in front of the two-story house.

Loud music blared from the backyard as young women in string bikinis and young men in swim trunks paraded past the fence. Some were laughing and others were dancing. Anxiety surged through her, and her heart pounded in her chest.

"Lindsay?" He touched her arm. "You okay?"

"I'm not like them," she said. "Our youth gatherings back home are very different. We sing hymns and never listen to music or dance. We talk about our families and work, and we don't ever get rowdy."

He pointed toward the fence. "I'm certain those young people in there are talking about their families and work. They may sing a different kind of music, but inside we're all the same, right?"

She nodded.

"Now go on." He gestured toward the house. "Get on in there before I push you out the door," he joked with a grin.

She gave a little nervous laugh. "Okay."

"Call me when you're ready for me to pick you up." He leaned on the steering wheel. "I'll be up late working on my computer, so don't feel like you have to leave before eleven. I'm a night owl, and any time is fine with me."

She gripped the door handle. "Wish me luck."

"Honey, you don't need luck," he told her. "You'll do just fine. Go have some fun. You deserve it after working so hard at our place. It's time for a little R&R."

"Thanks." Lindsay wrenched the door open and climbed from the truck. Her heart thumped in her chest as she gripped her soft beach towel and weaved through the knot of cars toward the back gate.

Behind her, the Suburban motored down the street, the horn tooting before it disappeared around the corner.

She closed her eyes and sucked in a breath.

Great. Now I'm trapped here.

With a shaky hand, she approached the gate and peered over at the throng of young men and women talking, dancing, eating, and swimming. A concrete patio spilled out from a large deck and surrounded a vast in-ground pool that included a deep and shallow end, along with a diving board. Several lounging chairs, and a couple of chairs with umbrellas dotted the pristine concrete. A small pool house sat at the back corner of the yard.

The smell of cooking hamburgers filled Lindsay's senses, and she smiled, remembering the barbecues she'd enjoyed with her parents over the years. Turning toward the deck, she spotted three young men standing around a grill while smoke poured out from under it, indicating that burgers were cooking. A long table covered with platters of food, bowls of chips, beverages, plates, and cups stood nearby.

The music continued to blare, and she wondered if any of them could even hear anyone else talking. She glanced across the concrete and found Vicki standing with a group of bikini-clad girls. Vicki wore a short yellow sundress with her blonde hair falling in curls past her bare shoulders. Lindsay spotted the same bright pink bathing suit straps poking out from under Vicki's dress that she'd noticed the previous day at the grocery store.

Vicki's gaze met Lindsay's and she ran toward the fence. "Lindsay!" she cried, pulling her into a quick hug. "You made it. I was beginning to think you flaked out on me."

"Well, I—" Lindsay began.

Taking Lindsay's arm, Vicki yanked her toward the other party guests, causing Lindsay to stumble without finishing her sentence.

"Follow me," Vicki instructed, dragging Lindsay past a group of young people standing near the pool drinking from plastic cups. A few of the curious faces looked familiar, but the names escaped Lindsay.

"Heather is so excited to see you! I told her all about how we ran into each other in Bloom." She pulled Lindsay toward a group of young women at the far end of the pool. "How wild was that, right? I mean, I haven't seen you in four years, and I run into you while I'm picking up chips and dip for my party. Such a crazy coincidence."

They came to stop in front of a group of girls sitting at a round table with an umbrella in the middle. Lindsay immediately recognized her old friend, Heather Fernandez.

"Lindsay! How are you?" Heather said, leaping up from her chair and rushing toward her. She was dressed in short shorts that came to her mid thigh and a blue bikini top with her dark brown hair cut short. Makeup accentuated her deep brown eyes, high cheekbones, and red lips.

Lindsay briefly wondered if she was breaking dress code by wearing a one-piece plain black bathing suit under her denim jumper since she was the only female not wearing a bikini.

"I'm fine, thank you," Lindsay said. "You look fantastic."

"You do too," Heather said, her curious gaze sweeping over Lindsay's attire.

Vicki touched Lindsay's arm. "Would you like a drink? I'm going to go check on Brandon at the grill. I can pick up a drink for you while I'm over by the food."

"Sure." Lindsay folded her arms across her chest.

"We have punch," Vicki said as she started toward the deck. "Or Coke."

"Oh," Lindsay said. "How about a Coke?"

Heather held up her plastic cup as if to toast Lindsay. "The punch is good." She grinned, angling her cup closer to Lindsay. "Want to try it?"

"No, thanks," Lindsay said quickly. "A Coke would be great, though."

"Be right back!" Vicki called, heading toward the deck.

Lindsay felt as if her security had evaporated as soon as Vicki stepped away. She glanced between the three women at the table, giving them an unsure smile while shifting her weight on her sneakers.

"Lindsay, this is Robin and Marci," Heather said.

Lindsay gave them each a half wave. "Nice to meet you."

The girls nodded and then sipped their drinks.

Heather motioned toward a chair across from her. "Have a seat. I want to hear all about what you've been doing for the last four years."

Lindsay sank into the chair, feeling as if she were on trial. Now the tough questions would be hurled at her.

"So, what are you up to these days?" Heather asked, lifting her cup to her mouth.

"Oh, not too much." Lindsay fingered the armrests of the cool metal chair. "I'm still living with my aunt in Pennsylvania. I love it there."

"Great." Heather smiled. "I guess you're leaving for college soon, right?"

Lindsay shook her head. "No."

"Oh. So you're going to college nearby?"

"No." Lindsay absently touched her ponytail, which fell past her shoulders. She needed to take the focus off herself. "How about you? Where are you going to school?"

Heather smiled with pride. "UVA."

"That's fantastic." Lindsay glanced toward Robin and Marci, who looked bored. "How about you two?"

"I'm going to Longwood," Robin said, pointing to herself. She then gestured toward Marci. "She's going to William & Mary."

"That's so exciting." Lindsay plastered a smile on her face.

Heather looked curious. "You're not going to college?"

Lindsay shook her head.

"How come?" Marci asked, looking equally intrigued.

"I'm working for the family business," Lindsay said, crossing her legs.

"Which is ...?" Marci prodded.

"A bakery."

"Bakery?" Heather asked.

Vicki reappeared and handed Lindsay a can of Coke before sitting next to her. "Brandon's still on the deck cooking and talking with his buddies. I wanted to be sure he didn't take off without telling me where he's going."

"You need to stop being his baby-sitter," Heather warned with a sharp expression. "You're going to smother him before you even leave for Oregon."

Vicki glared at her friend. "And you need to mind your own business."

Lindsay sipped from her can. Although the disagreement made her uncomfortable, it was less painful than the cross-examination she'd endured in Vicki's absence.

"You're working in a bakery?" Marci asked, steering the conversation back to Lindsay.

Lindsay swallowed a groan. "Yes, that's right." She sipped her drink.

"Is it like a specialty bakery or something?" Marci asked,

looking as if she were trying to figure out why Lindsay would work there.

"Yes," Lindsay said. "It's Amish."

"Amish?" Heather asked. "Why do you work at an Amish bakery?"

"Wait." Robin held up a hand like a traffic cop. "You said it's a family business. So, is your family, like, Amish?"

Lindsay nodded.

"That explains the clothes," Robin muttered.

Lindsay felt her cheeks heat, and she considered leaving the table and slipping out the gate.

"That's rude," Vicki snapped.

"I didn't mean it like that," Robin said, holding up her cup for emphasis. "I just meant that she's dressed very conservatively, and I was wondering why. I mean, it's like almost one hundred degrees out, and she's wearing a denim jumper with a short-sleeved blouse."

"I have my bathing suit on under my blouse and jumper," Lindsay said before sipping her Coke.

"Did you see Jason Klein is here?" Vicki asked Robin. "I saw him come in with Ray Smith."

"No!" Robin said. "I should go ask him if he misses me yet."

Marci looked alarmed. "Don't do that! Then you'll look desperate."

"So?" Robin pushed her dark hair off her shoulder with a dramatic toss. "He'll realize what he lost when he broke up with me for that loser Shannon Wright."

The girls laughed, and Lindsay ran her fingers over the cold can. She was glad that the focus of the conversation was off her, but she felt out of place. They were talking about people she didn't know.

A cell phone sang out in the melody of a rock song, and Robin pulled the phone from the pocket of her shorts. She answered it and then walked across the yard toward an empty corner of the fence while motioning for Marci to follow.

"Nice to meet you," Marci said to Lindsay before she left the table.

Vicki blew out a frustrated sigh as she dropped onto a chair next to Heather. "I'm sorry Robin is so thoughtless and rude. Sometimes I wonder if she was raised by wolves."

Lindsay chuckled. "It's okay. I know I look different, to say the very least."

Heather shook her head. "Still, that's no reason to be rude. I think your jumper's kinda cute."

"Thanks," Lindsay said, placing the can on the end table beside her. "You must be excited about leaving for college."

Heather shrugged. "Yeah. I still have a ton of things to do." She looked at Vicki. "We need to go shopping. Are you free tomorrow?"

"Yeah." Vicki looked at Lindsay. "You could come too."

"Oh yeah," Heather agreed.

"Thanks. I'll have to see what Uncle Frank is doing," Lindsay said. "I'm here to take care of Aunt Trisha, so I can't just take off."

"Your aunt and uncle live in Virginia Beach?" Heather asked.

Lindsay explained her connection to Frank and Trisha and told them about Trisha's accident. They listened intently and seemed interested. Lindsay felt more at ease with her old friends.

"I hope she feels better soon," Heather said. "My little brother broke his leg last year, and he was in a lot of pain. I wouldn't wish that on anyone."

"Right," Vicki said. "So, tell us about the bakery where you work."

"Yeah," Heather chimed in. "What kind of food do you make? I bet it's delicious."

Lindsay found herself prattling on about the treats in the bakery and the wonderfully warm Kauffman family. While she talked, Heather and Vicki smiled and nodded, and Lindsay began to relax.

Heather asked questions about the Amish beliefs and clothing, and Vicki wanted her to tell them about the members of the Kauffman family. Lindsay smiled as she shared how much she loved being a part of the family and then told them about her friends. She also explained that the Amish didn't believe in education beyond the eighth grade.

"So, the Amish don't go to college?" Heather asked.

Lindsay shook her head. "No, they don't. They graduate from an Amish one-room schoolhouse when they're fourteen."

Heather looked fascinated. "And they really live without electricity?"

"That's right," Lindsay explained.

"How do you dry your hair?" Vicki asked.

"I wash it and let it air dry." Lindsay shrugged. "It doesn't matter because we always wear it up in a tight bun under our prayer covering."

"Prayer covering?" Heather asked.

"You know," Vicki said, smacking Heather on the arm. "We've seen the Mennonites at Walmart before. They wear those little white bonnets on top of their heads."

"Prayer covering," Lindsay corrected. "It's the Amish culture to always have our head covered. The Bible says that women should have their heads covered when they pray, so we're always ready to pray at any time."

"Interesting," Heather said. "Do you like wearing it?"

Lindsay nodded. "Yes, I do. I actually sort of miss wearing it since I've been here. It sort of gives me security."

"That's interesting," Heather said.

"So you always wear your hair up?" Vicki asked.

"Yes, and we never cut it." Lindsay pulled her long ponytail over her shoulder.

"And you never cut it," Vicki repeated. "Wow. I bet your aunt's hair is super long, huh?"

"It is," Lindsay said. "It's almost to her waist."

"Do Amish kids date?" Heather asked.

Vicki laughed. "Of course they do. How else would they get married, dummy? They have to date first!"

Lindsay snickered as Heather glared at Vicki.

Vicki turned back to Lindsay. "How do Amish kids hook up?"

"What do you mean?" Lindsay asked, lifting her Coke can.

"They obviously can't go to concerts or the movies," Heather quipped. "How do you meet?"

"We have youth gatherings on weekends," Lindsay said.

"What are those like?" Vicki asked, placing her cup on the outdoor coffee table.

"We go to someone's farm on a Sunday night, and we have what we call a singing," Lindsay said. "We all bring food to share, and we sing hymns and visit."

"No rock or any other instrumental music, right?" Heather asked. "And no dancing, like that old movie with Kevin Bacon?"

Lindsay nodded.

"But you date, right?" Heather asked. "There's some form of getting to know the opposite sex."

"If a boy wants to court you," Lindsay began, "he'll ask to give you a ride home in his buggy. But you have to join the church before you can date. And if you date, it's assumed that you'll marry, so it's taken very seriously."

"They use buggies?" Heather asked.

"Right," Lindsay said. "It's a horse-drawn buggy. The courting buggy is open air, meaning that it doesn't have sides or a roof."

Vicki raised an eyebrow. "Wow. So he asks to give you a ride home in order to confess his love for you, huh? Has anyone ever asked you?"

Lindsay felt her cheeks heat. "I was asked once, but I turned him down."

Vicki and Heather gasped in unison.

"You turned him down?" Heather asked. "Why would you do that?"

"Was he unattractive?" Vicki chimed in.

Lindsay smiled as she thought of Matthew. "He's very handsome, and he's smart and talented. He works with my uncle at the furniture shop."

"What's his name?"

"Matthew," Lindsay said. "He moved to our community four years ago. He's really nice and sweet. We're really good friends."

Vicki and Heather exchanged knowing glances.

"What?" Lindsay asked.

"You like him," Vicki said.

"And it sounds like he likes you," Heather added. "But you're hesitating. Why?"

"I would have to join the church before we could date," Lindsay explained. "I'm not sure I'm ready to do that."

"What does joining the church mean?" Vicki asked.

Lindsay finished her soda and placed the empty can on the table. "It means that you commit yourself to God and the church, and you can't change your mind. If you do, then you're shunned."

Heather grimaced. "That's kind of harsh, don't you think?"

Vicki shook her head. "That's their culture."

Lindsay nodded.

"Are you going to join the church?" Vicki asked.

"That's what I'm trying to figure out," Lindsay said. "I'm not sure where I belong."

"That's heavy," Heather said. "You're definitely not going to college, right?"

Vicki rolled her eyes. "Did you hear what she said? They don't believe in education past the eighth grade."

Heather rolled her eyes. "Duh! I know that. But she just said that she's not sure if she's going to join the church. I assume she can go to college if she doesn't join the church, right?"

"That's correct," Lindsay said.

"Oh," Vicki said, looking surprised. "You mean you can go to college if you want?"

Lindsay shrugged. "I could."

"Let's go get something to eat," Vicki said. "I'm starved."

Lindsay followed Vicki and Heather to the deck, where they loaded up their plates with burgers, chips, and potato salad. They then crossed the concrete back to the table and sat in the same chairs.

Lindsay took a bite of her burger and savored the juicy patty. It was just as good as the ones her father made on their grill at the house where she grew up. She glanced toward the pool and found a group of swimmers laughing and splashing.

"Do you want to swim?" Vicki asked between bites of her burger.

Lindsay shrugged. "I'm having a good time talking."

"I am too," Heather chimed in while lifting a chip from her plate.

"I agree." Vicki smiled. "I don't feel like swimming either."

Heather turned back to Lindsay. "How's your sister?"

Lindsay told them about Jessica's adventure in New York. While they talked, a few more acquaintances came over to say hello and welcome Lindsay back to Virginia. She chatted with them, telling stories about Lancaster County and listening to their exciting plans for college in the fall.

The conversation stretched over the hours, and soon it was dark. The music was only quiet background noise, due to a noise ordinance, according to Vicki. Outdoor lights and tiki torches illuminated the backyard and gave the pool a shimmering blue hue.

Lindsay glanced at a clock on the side of the pool house and found it was close to eleven. "Oh no," she said to Vicki. "I can't believe how late it is."

Vicki waved off the comment. "Oh, that's nothing. We usually stay up until about three or four some nights. My parents are at the Outer Banks for the weekend. They go down there quite a bit during the summer, and they're totally fine with me having some friends over."

"I need to be up early tomorrow," Lindsay said, standing and grabbing her towel from the back of the chair. "Uncle Frank may have to go to the office, and I have to be ready to take care of Aunt Trisha."

"Oh, okay." Vicki sidled up to her. "I'm glad you came."

"Thanks." She smiled at Heather. "It was good seeing you again."

Heather looked disappointed. "I wish you could stay later."

"Yeah, I have to get back to my aunt Trisha's house. I need to be up early to take care of her." Lindsay followed them toward the gate leading to the front of the house.

The crowd had dissipated. Only a few couples sat scattered throughout the backyard; two were talking and one was kissing. Lindsay quickly looked away, silently thinking how appalled her Amish friends and relatives would be at the public display of affection.

Pushing those thoughts away, Lindsay turned to Vicki. "Can I borrow your phone to call Frank?"

"Sure." Vicki pulled her phone from her pocket. She shook her head as she handed it over. "I don't know how you live without cell phones."

"Totally," Heather chimed in. "I'd, like, die without mine!"

Lindsay laughed. "You'd be surprised what you can live without, and how much you'd like living without it. It's nice not having to be tied to a phone."

Lindsay called Frank and he said he'd head right over. She disconnected the call, handed the phone back to Vicki, and then glanced toward the fence. "How about we wait outside for Frank? We can sit and talk on the porch."

"Sounds good," Vicki said while Heather nodded.

They walked around the house to the porch and sank into the chairs. Lindsay found it ironic that she was sitting on Vicki's porch, just as she liked to do back in Lancaster County. And then a thought hit her—maybe Frank was right, and everyone was the same on the inside, despite whether they were Amish or English.

The front door opened with a whoosh, revealing a handsome young man with dark hair, clad in flip-flops, a T-shirt, and swim trunks.

"There you are," he said to Vicki, plopping onto the swing next to her. "I was looking all over for you." He wrapped his arm around her waist and kissed her cheek.

"Lindsay," Vicki began, "this is Brandon. Brandon, this is my old friend Lindsay from eighth grade. She's visiting from Pennsylvania this summer."

"Nice to meet you," Lindsay said.

"You too," Brandon said before kissing Vicki on the lips.

Lindsay looked away, staring at the traffic whizzing by the house and wondering how Matthew was doing back home. Was he at a youth gathering? If so, was he thinking of her?

"We have to get together again before I leave for school," Heather said, breaking through Lindsay's thoughts. She pulled out her phone. "What's your number? I'll give you a call."

Lindsay rattled off Trisha's number, and Heather pushed the buttons on her cell phone.

"Cool," Heather said. "I'm working at Lynnhaven Mall until I leave for UVA."

"Really?" Lindsay asked.

They made small talk about Heather's job until Lindsay spotted the Suburban at the curb.

"That's my uncle," she said, standing. "It was good seeing you."

Vicki pried herself away from Brandon and gave Lindsay a hug. "Thanks for coming. I'll call you."

Heather stepped in and hugged her too. "Keep in touch."

Lindsay waved to her friends and then rushed down the steps to the Suburban. She climbed into the passenger seat and buckled her seat belt.

"How was it?" Frank asked as he put the truck in gear.

"Not as bad as I thought it would be." Lindsay waved to her friends again as the Suburban pulled away.

Lindsay tossed and turned in bed later that night. Thoughts of her family and friends back in Lancaster mixed with memories of the party and swirled through her mind, keeping her awake past one in the morning. She couldn't stop her mind from mulling over her conversations with Jessica, Heather, and Vicki about college, and then her discussions with Frank and Trisha about looking into achieving a GED certification. Their words seemed to beckon to her, telling her that she needed more than the bakery and life as a member of the Amish community.

Frustrated with her haunting thoughts, she climbed from the bed and walked to the den, where she spotted Frank's laptop on the coffee table in the middle of the room.

She sank onto the floor in front of the coffee table and pulled the laptop to the edge. Flipping it open, the screen came to life, glowing like a beacon in the dark.

Lindsay searched for GED courses in Virginia Beach and found her way to the Adult Learning Center. She skimmed the pages and wished she could print them out and read them later with a clearer head. She spotted a printer across the room and hoped that it was somehow connected to the laptop. She'd once heard Jessica mention her wireless setup at college, which allowed her to print out her term papers from across the room.

She hit the print button and quietly cheered when the

printer across the room woke up and hummed while spitting out pages. After she was finished printing all of the pages she wanted to research later, she closed up the laptop and retrieved the pages from the printer.

Lindsay went back to her room and placed the stack of paper on her dresser. Climbing back into bed, she closed her eyes and listened to the sound of waves crashing on the beach outside her window.

She rolled onto her side and sent up a silent prayer, asking God to guide her in her journey toward figuring out which path she was supposed to follow.

The next morning, Lindsay sat the breakfast table with Frank and Trisha. The aroma of sausage, bacon, eggs, and toast filled her senses as she loaded her plate.

"You really outdid yourself, Lindsay," Trisha said. "This is delicious."

"Thank you," Lindsay said. "I was in the mood for eggs, bacon, and sausage. So, I decided to make them all."

Frank chuckled while buttering his toast. "And you eat like a bird."

Lindsay smiled, remembering when Matthew said something similar to her. She swiped a piece of bacon from the plate in the center of the table. "Are we going to church today?"

Frank and Trisha exchanged surprised expressions.

"That would be wonderful," Trisha said. "Frank and I were discussing that last night and wondering if you'd want to go with us."

Frank held his hand up. "We don't want you to feel pressured to go, Lindsay, since we know you worship differently now that you're living with the Amish."

"I would love to go with you," Lindsay said. "It would be almost like old times. You both always went every Sunday when my mom and dad were alive. I don't remember many Sundays when you weren't beside my parents, Jessica, and me in the pew."

Trisha touched Lindsay's hand. "You're right."

"So, we'll go?" Lindsay asked. "I would love to see the pastor and my old friends, if they're still there."

Frank glanced toward the clock. "I don't think we have enough time to make it today. How about we go next week?"

"I'm sorry that I didn't have Frank get you up earlier," Trisha said. "I wasn't sure if you'd want to go. I should've asked you last night."

"It's okay." Lindsay shrugged. "We'll make a plan to go next week." While she finished her breakfast, she wondered how it would feel to step back into her former church after four years.

Crullers

2 eggs
3/4 cup cream
1/2 cup milk
1 – 1/4 tsp baking soda
3/4 tsp salt
1/4 cup sugar
4 cups flour

Beat eggs; add cream and milk. Sift dry ingredients and combine with liquid, using enough flour to make dough that can be rolled but remain soft. Mix well and let stand for 2 hours. Turn out on floured board and roll to 1/4-inch thick. Cut into strips and fry in deep fat at 350 degrees until brown on both sides. Drain on absorbent paper and dust with powdered sugar.

13

Rebecca brought the homemade bread and butter to the table the following Thursday morning. It had been more than a week since Lindsay had left, but it felt like a month. She found herself glancing toward the stairs in the morning, waiting for Lindsay to come down, and then watching the back door, expecting her to come home after work in the evenings.

Aside from the heartache of missing her niece, Rebecca also was exhausted. The pain in her abdomen was becoming constant, and the children wore her out every day. She wished she had some help, and she knew she needed to ask one of her nieces to come over and fill Lindsay's role. However, she hadn't had a chance to discuss it with Daniel, since he was preoccupied with a project at work, and she didn't want to add to his stress.

Emma squealed, and Rebecca handed her a piece of bread before kissing her head. The pitter-patter of little feet on the stairs announced Junior coming into the kitchen.

"*Bruder* is awake," Rebecca said with a smile.

Emma laughed and clapped her hands as Junior bounced toward his chair.

"*Gude mariye*," Rebecca told him, handing him a piece of bread. "I made your favorite—sausage." She placed the patties in front of her son, and he frowned.

"What's wrong?" she asked with surprise.

Hesitating, he frowned.

"It's okay." She sank into the chair next to him. "You can tell me anything."

He rested his chin on his hand and stared at the plate of sausage. "Your sausage is *gut,* but I like Lindsay's better."

Rebecca touched his hand. "I do too."

"When is she coming back?" he asked.

"Soon," Rebecca said with a sigh. "Very soon."

Daniel's boots clomped down the stairs, and Rebecca touched Junior's hair before popping up from the chair. She brought his usual breakfast of oatmeal to the table and then greeted him with a kiss when he stepped into the kitchen.

Daniel kissed each of the children on the head before sitting at the head of the table. Rebecca sat across from him and bowed her head in silent prayer before buttering her bread.

He gave one-word answers and nodded frequently while she prattled on about the weather and upcoming church service. Soon she heard the crunch of tires in the driveway, and Daniel jumped up from the table.

"Mike is early," he said, wiping his beard. He stood and kissed Emma's cheek. "Be *gut* for your *mamm* today."

Emma giggled in response.

He then patted Junior on his head. "You too."

Junior smiled up at him. "Have a *gut* day, *Dat.*"

Rebecca crossed to the counter, grabbed Daniel's lunch pail, and handed it to him as he headed for the door. "I hope you have a *gut* day."

"*Danki.*" He kissed her cheek, his whiskers tickling her skin.

"*Ich liebe dich.*" She wrapped her arms around his neck and held him close.

He looked concerned. "*Was iss letz, mei lieb?*"

Rebecca glanced back toward the children and found them eating breakfast and making faces at each other across the table.

Emma squealed while Junior crossed his eyes and stuck out his tongue.

"I miss Lindsay, and I worry about her all the time," she whispered. "I keep thinking that she's going to come through the door or down the stairs from her bedroom. She's on my mind all the time, Daniel. I hope she comes back to us soon."

"I know you're worried about her, and I think of her too," he said, his expression softening. "But you have to trust her to make the right decision about her future. You also have to trust God. He knows what's best for her, and He'll help her make the right choice."

"I know," she said, straightening his shirt. "But I can't stop my thoughts, and I can't shake the feeling that she belongs here with us."

"All you can do is let go and let God guide her," he said. "You can be her strength when she calls and writes, but you have to leave it to God."

A horn tooted out in the driveway, and Daniel touched her cheek. "I have to go. We'll talk later, *ya*?"

"I'll see you tonight," she said as he disappeared out the door.

Rebecca hugged her arms to her stomach as a wave of nausea gripped her. Instead of finishing her breakfast, she cleaned up the dishes while the children ate the rest of their meal. She talked with the children about their upcoming day in order to steer her thoughts away from her sick stomach.

Once breakfast was finished, she took the children into the family room and brought out their toys, and then she returned to the kitchen. While keeping an eye on the children, she swept the floor and straightened the counters. When a wave of nausea overtook her, she ran to the bathroom.

Stepping back into the kitchen, she ran cold water over a paper towel, sat at the kitchen table, and dabbed her forehead. She broke out into a cold sweat, and she breathed deeply to stop her racing heart. She prayed that this horrible sick feeling would dissipate soon. However, after nearly twenty minutes, she still felt ill.

The clip-clop of a horse drew Rebecca's attention to the back door. She wondered who was coming to visit. She wasn't expecting anyone today.

Slowly, Rebecca rose and started for the back door, trying in vain to ignore the dizzy feeling washing over her. Pulling the door open, she found Elizabeth and Katie standing on the porch, studying her with concerned eyes.

"Elizabeth," Rebecca said, leaning on the door. "Katie. What are you doing here?"

"How are you?" Elizabeth asked.

Rebecca swiped her hand over her clammy forehead. "I'm fine, *danki*."

Reaching out, Katie touched Rebecca's arm. "You don't look okay, *Aenti*."

Elizabeth gestured toward the kitchen. "Why don't we go sit down and talk?"

Rebecca led them into the kitchen and moved toward the refrigerator. "Would you like a drink?"

Katie appeared behind her. "Sit. I'll get the drinks."

Rebecca gave a sigh of defeat and moved to the table.

Squealing sounded from the doorway as Emma and Junior appeared and climbed onto each of Elizabeth's knees. The children hugged and kissed Elizabeth while she laughed.

Rebecca smiled as she watched her mother-in-law talk to the children and then listen intently while they responded to her questions.

Katie brought three glasses of tea to the table for the adults and then two plastic cups of water for the children.

"*Kinner*, why don't you draw me a picture?" Elizabeth suggested, glancing at Katie. "You could draw while I talk to your *mamm*."

The children became excited at the suggestion, and Katie

brought them paper and crayons from the drawer at the end of the counter. Katie lifted Emma into her high chair and gave her paper and one crayon. Junior hopped into his chair and began scribbling on the paper.

"*Danki*," Rebecca told her niece.

Katie sat next to Rebecca. "*Gern gschehne*."

Rebecca sipped her drink. Her stomach sickness eased and she felt her shoulders relax. She glanced at her children and smiled and then looked at her mother-in-law. "Did Daniel send you to check on me?"

Elizabeth gave a knowing smile since Rebecca had shared her secret in confidence when they visited last Saturday. Elizabeth was elated but promised to keep it a secret. "He called me at the bakery and mentioned that you seemed out of sorts this morning."

Rebecca raised an eyebrow at the statement. "Out of sorts?"

"Are you feeling okay?" Katie asked. "You look as if you're sick to your stomach."

Rebecca was always impressed by how observant her niece was. "I think I may have a bit of a stomach bug, but I'm feeling better now."

"You look a little green," Katie added. "Did you eat something unusual last night?"

Rebecca shook her head. "I'm certain it was just a fluke." She hoped the Lord would forgive her white lie to her niece, but it was Amish tradition to keep pregnancies a secret in order to surprise family members and friends, and also to avoid heartache and disappointment if something went wrong early.

"Have you heard from Lindsay?" Katie asked, her eyes hopeful.

Rebecca nodded. "I did get a letter from her yesterday, but I haven't talked to her on the phone in a few days. I was planning to call her later today. I'm sure she's just busy."

"Please tell her I said hello when you talk to her," Katie said.

"I got a short letter from her, and she sounded like she was having a good time."

"That's *gut*," Rebecca said. "How is the bakery? Very busy, *ya*?"

"*Ya*." Elizabeth gripped her glass. "It's very busy with nonstop customers, but we've hired some more help."

"Oh?" Rebecca asked with surprise.

"*Ya*, a few more women from the community have joined us for the season," Elizabeth explained. "Kathryn and Beth Anne are enjoying training them."

"That's *wunderbaar*," Rebecca said.

They discussed recipes and the most popular dishes at the bakery and then Elizabeth asked the children to tell her about their drawings. Rebecca glanced at the clock and noticed that Katie and Elizabeth had visited for more than an hour.

"I guess you need to get back?" Rebecca asked. "I'm sure the ladies at the bakery miss you."

Katie stood and gathered up the glasses. "We have a little bit of time." She moved to the sink and washed the glasses.

"Katie," Rebecca said. "I can take care of those."

"Don't be *gegisch*, *Aenti*," Katie said without turning around. "I'm taking care of it for you."

Rebecca glanced at Elizabeth who shrugged.

"She's just like her *dat*, I guess," Elizabeth said with a chuckle.

Rebecca laughed. "I guess so. Stubbornness runs in the Kauffman family."

Katie placed the clean glasses on the drain and faced them. "Do you know when Lindsay will be back?"

Rebecca shook her head. "No, but I assume it will be a few weeks. Trisha has a bad break and won't be able to get around for a while."

"How are you going to cope without her?" Katie folded her arms across her chest.

"I'll be just fine, *danki*." Rebecca leaned down and picked up a crayon that Emma had dropped onto the floor. "We miss Lindsay, but we'll get by."

"I think I should come help you," Katie said, stepping over to the table. "Since *Mammi* has the bakery under control, I can fill in for Lindsay here."

Rebecca shook her head. "That's not necessary. I don't want to take you away from the business. Besides, Lindsay worked at the bakery and didn't stay home and help me. Why should you leave your job to help me when I've never had help before?"

Elizabeth touched Rebecca's shoulder. "Because you seem like you have your hands full here. Daniel is concerned about you."

Rebecca was surprised to hear that Daniel had shared his feelings with his mother, since he wasn't one to open up very often, and rarely to anyone other than Rebecca. "He said that?"

Elizabeth shook her head. "He didn't say it with words, but he said it with his tone. You know your husband—he isn't good at expressing his feelings. But I'm his mother, and I can tell by his voice when he's upset or concerned."

Katie's eyes pleaded with Rebecca. "I would love to come and help you, *Aenti*. Please say that I can."

Rebecca considered it for a moment, weighing the options. "What would your mother think of this arrangement?"

Katie shrugged. "I think she'd be okay with it."

Rebecca patted her hand. "Why don't you discuss it with your parents, and I'll talk to Daniel tonight."

"Okay." Katie smiled. "I'll call you tomorrow."

Rebecca nodded. "*Gut*."

Elizabeth stood. "We'd better get going now." She kissed each of the children and then gave Rebecca a gentle hug. "You take *gut* care of yourself."

"Of course I will," Rebecca said.

Katie hugged and kissed the children and then followed Elizabeth to the door. "Good-bye. I'll talk to you soon."

"*Danki* for checking on me," Rebecca called after them.

As the kitchen door clicked shut behind them, Rebecca smiled. She was thankful for her wonderful family.

Later that evening, Katie dried the dishes while her sister Nancy washed, and her mother swept the floor.

"*Mamm*," Katie began, "would it be okay if I went over to help Rebecca during the day instead of working at the bakery? I think she needs help while Lindsay's in Virginia. *Mammi* and I talked about it, and she thinks it's a *gut* idea."

Sadie stopped sweeping and looked surprised. "Doesn't your *grossmammi* need help in the bakery?"

Katie wiped her hands on a towel. "*Mammi* hired a few more bakers, and we're all set for the summer. She suggested I start helping Rebecca right away."

Nancy placed a pot on the towel lying on the counter. "Like Monday?"

"*Ya*," Katie said.

Sadie looked curious. "Lindsay worked in the bakery when she was here. Why does Rebecca suddenly need help?"

"She hasn't been feeling very well." Katie shrugged. "Maybe it's because she and the *kinner* miss Lindsay so much. I can watch after them while she gets rest."

"Lindsay's coming back, *ya*?" Nancy asked. "She's not staying in Virginia forever, no?"

"She's coming back," Katie said. "At least, I hope so." She glanced at her mother. "What do you think, *Mamm*? May I work for Rebecca since *Mammi* says it's okay? It would be fun to care for little ones for a while."

Sadie paused and tapped the broom handle while considering the question. "I think you should ask your *dat*. He should agree to it, but you know how your *dat* can be. Go on out to the barn and ask him. Nancy and I can finish up the kitchen."

"*Danki.*" Katie rushed out the back door and found her father, Robert, and her oldest brother, Samuel, sitting in the barn with the cows. "*Dat,*" she said as she approached. "*Mamm* told me to ask your permission about something."

Samuel looked on with interest while adjusting his straw hat on his head.

Robert leaned against the wall. "What is it?"

Katie explained that she wanted to work for Rebecca, detailing the reasons why it was so important to her.

Robert rubbed his beard and frowned. "If it's okay with your *mammi,* then it's okay with me."

"*Danki*!" She hugged her father and then started toward the house.

"Wait up," Samuel called after her. He fell into step with her as they approached the porch. "What's wrong with Rebecca?"

"I'm not certain," Katie said. "I think she has a stomach flu. *Onkel* Daniel and *Mammi* are worried about her."

"Have you heard from Lindsay?" he asked.

Katie sat on the porch steps and shook her head. "I got a short letter from her. I'm going to write her back tonight."

He glanced toward the pasture, and Katie thought about their mutual friends.

"Has Matthew mentioned her?" she asked.

"No, not to me." Sam gave her a suspicious expression. "Why do you ask?"

"I don't know," she said quickly. "No reason."

"How's Lizzie Anne?" he asked, leaning on the railing.

"I don't know." She grinned. "Why do you ask?"

He smirked. "No reason."

She laughed, thinking that her brother should ask Lizzie Anne directly how she was. "You need to be braver with Lizzie Anne. You might surprise yourself."

He crossed his arms over his chest. "What's that supposed to mean?"

"I don't know." She stood and started toward the house. "I need to go finish up the kitchen."

He walked in the direction of the barn. "See you later."

Finding the kitchen empty, Katie headed upstairs to the room she shared with Nancy. Voices echoed down the hall, and Katie assumed Nancy was helping the younger siblings with their baths.

Katie opened her nightstand drawer and pulled out a pad of stationery and a pen. Propping herself up on her pillows, she began to write a letter to her best friend. As she wrote, she hoped Lindsay would find the letter an inspiration to come home to Lancaster County soon.

Rebecca climbed into bed next to Daniel, who was reading his Bible. "What are you reading?"

"Proverbs," he said without glancing up. "Trust in the Lord with all your heart and lean not on your own understanding; in all your ways acknowledge Him, and He will make your paths straight."

She listened to his words, thinking of Lindsay and how much she missed her. She felt eyes studying her and looked up into his smile.

"That verse touched you, *ya*?" He closed the Bible and placed it on the nightstand beside him.

"The Word has a way of speaking to us," she said, placing her hand on his arm. "Did you send Elizabeth and Katie over to check on me?"

"*Ya*, I did," he said. "I didn't actually send them over, but I called my *mamm* and told her I was concerned about you."

"Katie wants to come and help me. Elizabeth gave her permission to stop working at the bakery since she hired more help. Do you think I should let Katie come work for me?"

"I think that's a very *gut* idea," he said, moving his hand over hers. "You look like you could use some help. You're so tired all the time. I worry about you. This pregnancy seems to be much harder on you."

She blew out a defeated sigh. "*Ya,* I think you're right, and I think I do need the help. I'll call Sadie tomorrow and ask her if Katie can start Monday."

"*Gut.*" Daniel gave her a suspicious expression. "Did you tell my *mamm* about the baby?"

"*Ya,*" Rebecca answered. "I felt that she needed to know. Are you angry?"

He smiled and shook his head. "No, I'm not. I had a feeling that you told her since she seemed to understand my concern very quickly today." He leaned down and kissed the top of her head. "*Gut nacht.*"

"*Gut nacht,*" she said, snuggling under the sheet. As she fell asleep, the verse echoed through her mind, like a gentle reminder of God's love and protection.

14

"We're still going to church, right?" Lindsay asked with a smile while standing in the doorway to Trisha's room Sunday morning.

Trisha looked up from the magazine she was perusing while sitting on the bed. "Yes, I want to go, but I was just trying to get motivated. I'm not very excited about trying to hobble around in public."

"You'll be fine." Lindsay grinned. "We can bring your wheelchair, so it's easier for you to get around. I'll even push you gently and not send you racing down a steep hill into oncoming traffic," she added, hoping the humor would lighten the mood.

Trisha laughed. "That's a deal." She placed the magazine next to her on the bed and glanced toward her closet. "I'll have to figure out something to wear."

Lindsay moved to the closet and opened the door. Fishing through, she pulled out a light purple sundress and held it up. "How about this? It will be easy for you to get into."

Trisha nodded. "That works. You're welcome to borrow anything in my closet if it strikes your fancy."

"Oh, no thank you," Lindsay said, glancing down at her denim jumper. "I'm comfortable in this."

"That's fine." Trisha smiled. "I just want you to be comfortable. I don't mean to force anything on you."

"Do you want me to help you get dressed?" Lindsay offered.

"Sure." Trisha frowned. "I'm so tired of being waited on."

The bathroom door opened, revealing Frank dressed in jeans and a white T-shirt. His dark hair was still wet from his shower. He looked between the two women. "What's going on here?"

"Church," Trisha said.

"Oh good," Frank said. "I was hoping you'd still want to go."

Lindsay smiled. "Let's get ready. It's almost time to leave."

Forty-five minutes later, Frank steered the Suburban into the parking lot at the Beach Community Church. Lindsay gripped the door handle and stared at the sprawling brick building. The tall steeple and large wooden doors brought back memories of the Sundays spent there with her parents and sister. She glanced around at the sea of cars and wondered if any of her old friends would be there and if they would recognize her.

"Well, Lindsay-girl," Frank began, "I'll get the wheelchair, and you help the cripple out."

"Hey!" Trisha protested. "That's not nice."

Lindsay snickered to herself. Frank and Trisha's banter reminded her of her parents, who often teased and laughed together.

Lindsay hopped out of the backseat and opened Trisha's door. She then took Trisha's hand and helped her turn her body toward the door.

"I can't wait to start physical therapy," Trisha muttered while grimacing. "I'm so over this."

Lindsay smiled. "I'm sure you are."

"Even crutches would be nice," Trisha said. "I'd like to give the crutches a try."

"Why don't we try them this coming week?" Lindsay asked.

"Okay," Trisha said. "Why not?"

The tailgate slammed, and Frank appeared with the wheelchair.

"Enough gabbing, ladies. All right, Princess Trisha, let's get you into your royal chair."

Lindsay stepped away from the truck, and Frank lifted Trisha with ease and deposited her into the wheelchair. After adjusting the height of the leg supports, he pushed the chair forward. Lindsay fell into step with him as they started toward the front door. She held the door open, and Frank pushed Trisha into the foyer, where they were greeted by a couple who recognized Trisha and Frank. The woman looked familiar, but Lindsay couldn't remember her name. However, she remembered her mother frequently talked with the woman at services, and Lindsay had also seen the woman in the Sunday school rooms.

Lindsay stood by and was happy to be anonymous for the time being while they discussed Frank's business, the economy, and Trisha's broken leg.

The familiar woman, who looked about forty with graying brown hair, studied Lindsay, and her eyes widened. "I can't believe it," she said, covering her mouth. "You're Grace Bedford's daughter."

Trisha took Lindsay's hand and squeezed it. "Yes. This is Lindsay. She's visiting for the summer from Pennsylvania to help me with my predicament. We're so happy to have her here."

"I can't believe it," the woman repeated. She then pulled Lindsay into a tight hug, causing her to gasp for breath.

"I think of your parents all the time," the woman continued. "I enjoyed talking with your mom at services, and I've wondered how you and your sister are." She then turned toward a crowd behind her. "Wanda! Luann!" she called across the foyer. "Come here and see Lindsay Bedford, Grace's daughter. She's visiting for the summer."

Lindsay forced a smile onto her face while a group of women gathered around her and discussed how much she looked like her mother, how much they missed her parents, and how wonderful it was to see her. She breathed a sigh of relief when Frank interrupted the group.

"Let's go find a seat," Frank said. "We can visit after the service." He then addressed the crowd of curious women. "It was nice seeing you again."

Lindsay followed Frank into the sanctuary where they took a seat in the back row, pushing the wheelchair to the end of the aisle.

Lindsay sat next to Frank. "Thank you for saving me."

He grinned while opening his bulletin. "You're welcome. People are happy you're back, so be prepared for a mob after the service. Next week should be easier after they get over the surprise of seeing you here with us again."

Lindsay glanced around the sanctuary while memories emerged in her mind. She had spent the first fourteen years of her life worshiping with this congregation, including the weekly services, the Christmases, the Easters, and the most devastating event of her life—her parents' memorial service.

The images of that day assaulted her mind, and Lindsay turned her gaze to the bulletin in her hand and studied it in an effort to block out those horrible memories.

How strange it felt to use a bulletin for a service again. She'd become accustomed to the Amish way of worshiping, during which services were held in the home or barn of a member every other week. There was neither an altar nor flowers in the Amish church tradition. No instruments were played during the hymns. Lindsay looked up at the large stained glass cross hanging over the pulpit and felt as if she'd stepped back into her former life attending a service in a church.

The organ sounded, and the voices swirling around Lindsay faded to a murmur as if on cue. The knot of people loitering in the aisle filed into pews, and Lindsay glanced up as vaguely familiar faces stopped to greet Frank and Trisha.

When the music stopped and the pastor took his place in the

pulpit, Lindsay lost herself in thoughts of Lancaster County. She missed hearing the Pennsylvania *Dietsch* and German during the services at home.

The congregation stood and sang a hymn, and Lindsay stood silently while the rest of the congregation sang.

Once the hymn was over, the congregation sat and a reader approached the pulpit and read aloud the lessons for the day. Lindsay held her breath in order to hold back her threatening tears and concentrated instead on taking in God's Word. One verse in Psalm 62 struck a chord in her: "Trust in him at all times, O people; pour out your hearts to him, for God is our refuge."

The verse echoed through her mind while the reader finished the lessons, and it continued to float through her thoughts during Pastor Lane's sermon. She had always enjoyed listening to the pastor for as long as she could remember. He was a friendly man, whom she guessed was in his mid-forties, and he had a kind face and warm brown eyes. He and his wife had a son, Taylor, who was the same age as Lindsay. Taylor had always been friendly to Lindsay, going out of his way to talk to her during Sunday school and youth events.

Lindsay went through the motions for the remainder of the service, singing the hymns, partaking in Communion, and reciting the prayers.

When the service ended, Lindsay found herself blocked in the pew by a crowd of people who were hugging her and talking with Trisha and Frank.

Lindsay smiled and shook the hands that were extended to her, doing her best to remember the familiar faces. When she heard someone call her name, she searched the sea of faces surrounding her until she spotted Taylor, waving and grinning.

She waved back and then excused herself and moved through the knot of people until she reached him. Taylor looked just as she remembered. He resembled his father with his kind face and big brown eyes, but he had grown, towering over her mere five-foot-five height by at least six inches.

"Lindsay Bedford," Taylor said. "It's been like a million years."

She held out her hand. "It's so good to see you."

He shook his head and opened his arms. "Don't I get a hug from my old friend?"

She gave him a quick hug, feeling a little uncomfortable with the embrace since it wasn't customary for men and women who weren't married to touch in the Amish culture, except to shake hands.

"How've you been?" he asked.

"Good," she said. "How about you?"

"Good." He stuffed his hands into the pockets of his Dockers. "Are you back for good?"

"No. Just visiting for part of the summer." She pointed toward Trisha. "My aunt Trisha is injured as you can see, so I came down to help her out until she's back on her feet."

"You live in Pennsylvania now, right?" he asked.

"Yeah," she said. "You remembered."

"Of course I did," he said. "I paid attention." He gestured toward the doors leading to the hallway. "Are you going to youth group?"

"Oh." She hesitated. "I don't know if they want to stay."

"With the crowd they have gathered around them, I think they may be stuck here for a while." Taylor started toward the door and motioned for her to follow. "I think there are some folks who would be happy to see you."

"Okay." Lindsay followed him toward the door, stopping to tell Frank that she would be in the young adult class.

"How's Pennsylvania?" Taylor asked as they headed down the hallway toward the classrooms.

"It's good," she said. "I'm living with my aunt, uncle, and cousins, and I work in a bakery owned by my uncle's mother. I really enjoy it."

"Cool," Taylor said.

"What about you?" she asked.

"I just graduated from Kellam High and I'm working at Best Buy right now," he said.

"Are you going to college?" she asked as they approached a classroom at the end of the hallway.

He seemed to hesitate. "Yeah, but I decided not to go away to school. I'm going to go to Tidewater Community College for a couple of years until I figure out what I want to do."

"That sounds like a good plan to me," she said as they stood by the doorway. Glancing in the room, she spotted a half dozen young people sitting in chairs set up in a semicircle and talking.

"And you?" he asked. "Going to college?"

She shook her head. "No."

"Oh." He smiled and made a sweeping gesture toward the room. "Ladies first."

"But I don't know anyone," Lindsay began.

He nudged her arm. "Just go."

Lindsay stepped into the room. The young men and women smiled, and a few said hello. A couple of the faces were familiar, but she couldn't remember the names. She took a seat next to a pleasant-looking blonde girl while Taylor stood near the front of the room.

"Good morning, everyone," Taylor said. "We have a new friend with us today." He gestured toward Lindsay. "This is Lindsay Bedford, who grew up in our church and then moved to Pennsylvania four years ago. Let's go around the room and introduce ourselves."

The members of the class told Lindsay their names, and she recognized a few of them. She smiled and thanked them for welcoming her.

Taylor turned a chair around and straddled it backward. "I'll bring Lindsay up to speed on what we've been discussing. We started talking about how much things have changed now that some of us are considered adults and about to embark on a new journey in our lives. Most of us are graduating from high school and some are leaving for college. That led to a discussion of how we can stay focused on our Christian values while we make our way in the world."

He gestured toward the pretty blonde next to Lindsay. "Bonnie had a great idea about how we can still put God before ourselves instead of getting caught up in the mundane and stressful parts of being on our own. Why don't you explain it, Bonnie?"

"Sure," Bonnie said, turning toward Lindsay. "I'm leaving for college in western Virginia at the end of the summer, and I wanted to make an impact on my community before I go. I was trying to think of ways that I could give back since so many people helped me throughout my childhood, and I thought of volunteering at the children's hospital. It's been really rewarding. I shared my story with the class, and now everyone is volunteering and giving back in their own way."

"Wow," Lindsay said. "That's wonderful."

They took turns around the room sharing their volunteering stories. One young man shared that he helped out at a food bank weekly, and another young man talked about providing dialysis patients rides to their appointments.

Lindsay listened with her hands clasped in her lap. While she felt like an outsider returning to this church, hearing her peers share their stories of volunteerism gave her a link to them. Much like her Amish family and friends, these young people wanted to give back to the community and help others. This was her connection to her former church.

"I'm helping out at a nursing home," a pretty brunette named Andrea said. "I've been visiting the patients, reading to them, and helping them write letters to family members."

Lindsay's eyes widened. "I've always wanted to do that."

The other members of the class turned to her.

"Really?" Taylor asked. "What makes you want to volunteer at a nursing home?"

Lindsay thought back to her childhood. "My grandfather Bedford lived in one located in Williamsburg before he passed away when I was small. Once or twice a month, I used to go with my father to visit him, and I felt sorry for the people who didn't have anyone come to visit them. It really made an impression on me, even though I was only about seven or so."

"Would you like to participate in our volunteering project?" Taylor asked.

Lindsay looked at Andrea, who nodded. "Maybe I can volunteer on Saturday when Uncle Frank is home to take care of Aunt Trisha."

"I think you could," Andrea said. "I help out on Tuesdays. I can give you information about the nursing home where I'm working. It's not far from here."

Lindsay smiled while excitement surged through her. "That would be great."

"How was Sunday school?" Trisha asked from her recliner as they sat in the den and ate subs for lunch.

Lindsay nodded while chewing her turkey and cheese. "It was good. Taylor leads the class, which sort of surprised me. I didn't know he was the leader type."

"He seems like a nice young man," Frank said while sitting on the sofa. "His father is very friendly."

"What did you talk about in class?" Trisha asked.

"We talked about volunteer projects," Lindsay said. "The local kids plan to start their volunteer projects and continue in the fall. The kids who are leaving for college will find an organization to help after they get to school."

Trisha looked impressed. "That's really generous and admirable."

"One guy volunteers at a food bank and another drives dialysis patients to their appointments," Lindsay explained, placing her sandwich on a wooden snack tray in front of her. "There's a girl who helps out at the children's hospital and another one who volunteers at a nursing home."

"Oh?" Trisha asked. "That's very nice. I bet they can use a lot of volunteers at nursing homes."

"I remember when my grandpa was in one," Lindsay said. "I always felt so sorry for the people who didn't have any visitors."

"I can understand that." Trisha looked at Frank. "Remember that nursing home your aunt was in? It was such a sad place. All of those people sitting in the hallways in their wheelchairs."

"I remember," Frank said, swiping a napkin over his chin. "I hated going there."

Lindsay turned to him. "I never minded going to see my grandpa. In fact, I actually looked forward to going with my dad after church on Sundays."

"Really?" Frank looked surprised. "You were a little thing. I remember your dad telling me that Jessica never wanted to go."

"Jessica was afraid, I think," Lindsay said. "I enjoyed talking to the nurses and some of them knew me by name. I remember one nurse who always gave me a lollipop. I can't remember her name. She called me Raggedy Ann because of my red braids."

"That's sweet," Trisha said, leaning back in the chair. "I would imagine you brought some life into the place."

Lindsay wondered if she could bring life into a nursing home again as a young adult. "Aunt Trisha, do you think it would be okay if I volunteered at a nursing home while I'm here? I could go on Saturdays so Uncle Frank is here for you." She glanced at Frank. "What do you think? There's one close by so you could run me out there in the morning, if it doesn't interfere with what you have planned for the day."

Frank shrugged. "I don't see why not. What do you think, Trish?"

"If that's what you want to do, Lindsay," Trisha began, "then I think you should do it."

"Great," Lindsay said. "Thank you!" The phone rang and she jumped up from the sofa. "I'll get it." She rushed into the kitchen and grabbed the phone from the cradle on the wall. "Hello?"

"Linds!" Jessica's voice nearly yelled into the phone. "How are you?"

"Fine." Lindsay leaned against the counter. "How are you?"

"Great. I tried to call you this morning."

"We were at church."

"Really?" Jessica sounded surprised. "Aunt Trisha and Uncle Frank made you go to church?"

"No, I wanted to go," Lindsay said. "What's the big deal?"

"Oh wow," Jessica said. "I'm surprised you'd go to a service that wasn't Amish. Was that pastor's son there? What was his name?"

"Taylor," Lindsay said. "Yes, he was there."

"He's cute," Jessica said. "Did you talk to him?"

"Yes. I went to his Sunday school class."

"Cool," Jessica said. "Maybe you can have yourself a little summer romance."

Lindsay rolled her eyes. "Please."

"What else have you been doing besides going to church?"

"Not much. I've been taking care of things here at the house and I went to a party at Vicki's house last weekend." Lindsay glanced out the window at the waves crashing against the golden sand. A young couple walked hand and hand along the water, and she absently thought of Matthew.

"Oh?" Jessica's voice was full of curiosity. "How was that?"

"Good. I saw Vicki, Heather, and a few other people from school. Everyone is doing well."

"What are their plans? College?"

"Yes." Lindsay braced herself for the lecture.

"Did you sign up to get your GED?"

"Not yet." Lindsay sank into a kitchen chair. "I looked up the information and I know where to register."

"Well?" Jessica was impatient. "What are you waiting for?"

I'm waiting for you to stop nagging me. She scowled with frustration. "I don't know." She had to change the subject fast. "How are things going for you?"

"Great!" Jessica launched into a long discussion of her work, her coworkers, and her nightlife. She spent a good amount of time talking about her friend Kim's new boyfriend, Eddie, a graduate student who worked at a nearby law firm.

"Sounds like you're having a good time," Lindsay said. "But I hope you're not having too good of a time."

"What does that mean?" Jessica snapped, sounding offended.

"You're not considering staying there, are you?"

"Are you kidding me?" Jessica exclaimed. "I have to finish college, you know. I mean, New York City is great, but I would never consider moving here until after I graduate with my degree, Lindsay."

"Good." Lindsay was glad that Rebecca had been right about Jessica planning to finish college before considering a move to New York City. "Have you talked to Jake?"

Jessica was quiet for a moment. "No."

"Are you going to call him?"

"I don't know what to say."

"How about you just call him up and say that you've been thinking of him and you hate how things were left between you?" Lindsay shook her head in disbelief. While her older sister was overly confident and driven when it came to school and her career, she was timid and hesitant when it came to relationships.

"Maybe I will," Jessica said. "Is Aunt Trisha around? Can I talk to her?"

Lindsay nearly laughed out loud at her sister's obvious change in the subject. "Sure. She's awake and resting in her recliner. Hang on one sec." Lindsay stepped into the den, where Frank and Trisha were watching a movie. She held out the phone to Trisha. "It's your other favorite niece."

Trisha's expression brightened as she took the phone. "Jessie! How are you?"

Lindsay gathered up the dirty paper plates from lunch and took them into the kitchen. She glanced out the door leading to the deck and felt an invisible magnet pulling her toward the beach. She needed to go walk and try to sort through all of the emotions swirling inside her.

Standing in the doorway leading to the family room, she caught Frank's eye as he sat on the sofa, and she motioned toward the beach to alert him that she was going for a walk. He smiled and waved, telling her to go and enjoy herself. Lindsay kicked off her shoes and then stepped out onto the deck.

While she made her way down to the sand, she wondered if Jessica's goals and aspirations were ones she should have. The sand provided comfort and solace as she pondered all of the questions echoing in her mind and made her way down the beach. Was Lindsay wrong to not want to pursue a college education and degree like her friends at church and her old friends who were at Vicki's party?

Was Lindsay destined to float through life without a purpose, or was she headed for greater things? She stopped and let the water roll over her toes while she wondered when she would figure out what God's plan was for her. How would she know when He presented it to her?

She didn't know what God had in store for her, but she knew one thing—she wanted to volunteer in the nursing home in memory of her grandfather. Lindsay smiled as another wave crashed in front of her. She was so thankful for the clarity that the smell of the salty ocean, the warmth of the sand, and the cleansing of the water brought to her.

15

Tuesday morning, Lindsay looked up just as Frank stepped into the kitchen. Clad in shorts and a T-shirt, he smiled at Trisha.

"Today is doctor's appointment day," he announced with enthusiasm. "Are you ready, Trish?"

Trisha looked at Lindsay across the breakfast table and rolled her eyes. "I can't wait."

"Maybe you'll get good news," Lindsay said, touching Trisha's hand. "You said you can't wait to start physical therapy so you can walk again."

Trisha sighed. "I'm just so tired. Why is it that I sleep all the time, but I'm still tired?"

"Because you need to get up and go. You said you wanted to try crutches, so let's do it." Frank grabbed the crutches leaning against the wall by the doorway and brought them over to Trisha. "Your chariot, my lady."

Trisha rolled her eyes again, and Lindsay swallowed a snort. While Frank helped Trisha up from her chair, Lindsay took the dirty dishes to the counter and began to fill the dishwasher.

"Okay," Trisha said, thumping her way to the doorway. "Let's go."

"Have fun," Lindsay said with a smile. "I'll run the vacuum and clean the bathrooms while you're gone."

Trisha gave Lindsay a confused expression. "You're not coming with us?"

"Oh." Lindsay looked between them. "You want me to come?"

"You're not Cinderella or Rapunzel," Trisha quipped. "You're allowed to leave the house occasionally and visit civilization."

Lindsay bit her bottom lip. She'd been up late last night surfing the internet on Frank's laptop and considering whether or not she wanted to register to get her GED. She longed to go to a bookstore to buy a study guide before she signed up to take the test.

"Would it be possible for me to run a couple of errands while we're out?" Lindsay asked.

"Sure," Frank said with a shrug. "I may even buy you two ladies lunch while we're out too."

Lindsay placed the last glass into the dishwasher and closed the door. "Let me just get my purse. I want to get a study guide book for the GED test."

Frank smiled. "Good for you."

"That's wonderful, Lindsay. I'm glad that you're going to do it," Trisha said. "All right. I'm ready to do this. Let's go get in the truck."

Lindsay flipped through a magazine in Trisha's orthopedist's waiting room. She glanced at the clock on the wall and found that it had been forty-five minutes since Trisha had been called back to the examination room.

Out of her peripheral vision, Lindsay spotted a young woman about her age staring at her. Lindsay assumed it was due to her attire, and she absently smoothed the skirt of her jumper over her legs. The young woman wore shorts and a tank top while her leg was encased in a calf-high cast.

The door leading to the examination rooms opened, and Trisha hobbled out, her crutches thumping on the tan carpet.

Frank held the door for Trisha and then moved to the counter, where he spoke to the receptionist.

With her face twisted in a grimace, Trisha slowly made her way to Lindsay.

Lindsay stood and met Trisha halfway across the waiting room. She touched Trisha's arm. "Are you okay?"

Trisha sighed. "Two more weeks."

"Until what?" Lindsay asked.

"Until I find out if I can get a walking cast and start really walking." Trisha balanced her crutches in one hand and scratched her nose with the other. "Why is it that every time I try to walk with crutches my nose gets itchy? Is it Murphy's Law?" She put her crutches back under her arms. "But the good news is that a physical therapist is going to come to the house beginning tomorrow and start teaching me exercises that will help strengthen my leg."

"That is good news, Trisha," Lindsay said with a smile. "You're getting better."

"Yeah, I am." Trisha forced a smile. "But it's not happening soon enough."

"Okay, ladies," Frank said as he approached. "Where to next?"

"The bookstore is right up the street," Trisha said, starting her trek toward the door. "How about we go there and then go to lunch?"

"Sounds like a plan," Frank said, holding the door open for Trisha.

Lindsay munched on a chip covered in salsa while they sat in Frank's favorite Mexican restaurant. "It's been so long since I've had Mexican food. It's so delicious."

Frank grinned. "I guess you don't cook tacos for your aunt and uncle, huh?"

Lindsay chuckled. "No, I don't think *Onkel* Daniel would like tacos or even chips and salsa." She placed the GED Study Guide, which was more like a catalog than a book, on the table and flipped through it, her stomach twisting at the thought of trying to learn and memorize all of the information contained in it.

"You'll do fine," Trisha said as if reading her mind.

Lindsay looked up at her. "You think so?"

"I know so." Trisha touched Lindsay's shoulder. "We're so proud of you for taking this on."

Frank nodded while munching chips. "Yes, we are."

The waitress appeared with their lunch and placed the chicken fajita special in front of Lindsay. She bowed her head in silent prayer, thanking God for all of her blessings, and then began filling a tortilla with the chicken strips and vegetables.

Frank dug into his grande beef burrito, and Trisha picked at her taco salad.

"The doctor said that your physical therapy starts tomorrow?" Lindsay asked between bites of her fajita.

Trisha nodded. "The therapist will be at the house around ten."

"Are you excited?" Lindsay asked.

Trisha shrugged. "I guess so. It's going to be a lot of work, and I'm already exhausted from schlepping around with the crutches."

"You'll do great and quickly regain your strength," Frank told her as he lifted his glass of Coke. "You worry too much, but you've been strong throughout this whole ordeal."

Trisha stabbed at her taco salad. "So, Lindsay. You've been stuck in the house with me too long. Where do you want to go next?"

"Where do you guys want to go?" Lindsay asked.

"I asked you, Lindsay," Trisha said.

Lindsay fiddled with her napkin on her lap. "I would really like to go by the nursing home and ask about volunteering on

Saturdays. Aunt Trisha is getting better, and I'd love to do more while I'm here. I'm used to always being busy and working a lot back home in Pennsylvania. Would that be okay?"

Trisha smiled. "Of course it's okay. We'll go there next."

"Great." Lindsay made another fajita.

Lindsay's stomach fluttered as she stepped through the front door of the Sandbridge Beach Rehabilitation and Nursing Center. She cleared her throat and then touched her hair, making sure her ponytail was still neat and tidy.

Crossing to a long reception desk, she smiled at a nurse who was talking on the phone.

The nurse hung up and gave Lindsay a curious expression. "May I help you?"

"Yes." Lindsay clasped her hands together in order to try to stop them from trembling. "I wanted to talk to someone about volunteer opportunities."

"Oh." The nurse stood and came around the desk. "Come with me. I'll introduce you to the social worker."

Lindsay followed the nurse around the corner from the front desk to an office where a young woman sat at a desk, typing on a computer.

"Janice," the nurse said. "This young lady would like to discuss volunteering."

Janice looked up. "Come in." She gestured toward a chair in front of the desk. "Have a seat."

While the nurse disappeared from the office, Lindsay sank into the chair and forced a smile, despite her frayed nerves. "Hi," she said.

"Hello." Janice leaned across the desk and shook Lindsay's hand. "What's your name?"

"Lindsay Bedford."

Janice sat back in her chair. "Tell me why you'd like to volunteer here."

"Andrea Clark is in my Sunday school class, and she said she volunteers here on Tuesdays," Lindsay said.

"I know Andrea," Janice said. "She's a nice girl."

"Yes, she is. I've always wanted to help out in a nursing home because my grandfather was in one in Williamsburg when I was little, and I felt sorry for the people who didn't have anyone come visit them." Lindsay absently played with the hem of her jumper. "I would like to visit the people who don't have family members or help someone read a letter or even write a letter."

Steepling her fingers, Janice nodded and smiled. "That's very admirable of you."

"Thank you," Lindsay said with a modest smile. "It's just something I've always wanted to do. I grew up here, but I've been living with my aunt in Pennsylvania since my parents died four years ago."

Frowning with sympathy, Janice shook her head. "I'm so sorry for all you've been through. You're a very mature young lady."

"Thank you," Lindsay said.

"Are you back in town visiting friends?" Janice asked.

"Actually, I'm helping my aunt Trisha recover from an accident," Lindsay explained. "She broke her leg after a bad fall, but she's been doing a lot better now."

"That's good to hear," Janice said, folding her hands on the desk. "What else have you been doing while you're in town?"

"I've been having fun walking on the beach since I don't get to see the beach anymore in Pennsylvania," Lindsay said, while absently smoothing the skirt of her jumper. "I've also visited some old school friends. I'm planning on getting my GED too. In fact, I just picked up my study guide today."

"That sounds like a wonderful idea." Janice stood. "Let me show you around."

Janice showed Lindsay the facility and introduced her to

a few of the nurses. Lindsay couldn't stop smiling while she thought of how much good she could do if she were able to help the patients. She couldn't wait to tell Rebecca about this opportunity. She hoped that Rebecca would be proud to hear that Lindsay was going to volunteer her time in order to help others.

While moving down a long hallway, she glanced into a room and thought she spotted a woman wearing a prayer covering. She stopped and considered stepping in to see the woman, but Janice called to a nurse who came over to meet Lindsay.

After the tour, they moved back to Janice's office, where Janice explained that she would have to do a background check before allowing Lindsay to volunteer. Lindsay filled out the paperwork and then shook Janice's hand.

"You seem like a very nice young lady," Janice said. "I'll get in touch with you as soon as I get this paperwork back."

"Wonderful," Lindsay said as they walked to the doorway together.

"Did you have a particular schedule in mind to work?" Janice asked.

"I think Saturdays would work best for me," Lindsay explained. "My uncle Frank is home on Saturdays and can take care of my aunt Trisha, so I can come here and help out."

"That sounds good," Janice said.

"Great," Lindsay said with a wide smile. "I hope to see you soon."

"Me too." Janice patted Lindsay's shoulder.

Later that evening, Lindsay sat on the sofa and powered up Frank's laptop. With her heart thumping in her chest, she found her way to the website and registered for the GED test.

"I did it," she said. "There's no turning back now."

"What's that?" Frank said while flipping channels.

"I just signed up for the test." Lindsay closed the laptop and blew out a deep sigh. "Let's hope I pass it."

"You will." He nodded toward the kitchen. "I forgot to tell you that a letter came for you today. It's on the counter."

Lindsay hurried into the kitchen, wondering if she would find a letter from Matthew. She picked up the envelope and found that the return address was from Katie.

She grabbed a can of Coke and then headed to her room. Sitting on her bed, she opened Katie's letter. She immediately recognized Katie's neat script writing:

Dear Lindsay,

Wie geht's! How are you? I hope you're having fun in Virginia, but not too much fun.

How's Trisha doing? I pray she's continuing to heal well as you mentioned in your last letter. How's Frank?

Are you still enjoying the beach? I can't imagine what it's like to live in a house that is on the beach! I would assume that the waves sing you to sleep at night. I hope I can see the ocean someday. I've always dreamt of walking barefoot in the sand and watching the sun set.

Have you heard from your sister? I hope she is doing well and being safe in New York City.

How was your visit with your old school friends?

I suppose I have asked you enough questions. Things are the same as usual here. However, things don't seem as fun without you. Lizzie Anne and I miss you very much, but of course we wish you well.

I've been working in the bakery every day, and it's very busy with nonstop tourists. We can't seem to bake fast enough for them! Mammi Elizabeth is happy that we're busy, and she never gets excited or stressed out. She hired two women from our district to help with the baking. They're very nice and they're good bakers, but it's not the same without you. Kathryn said she misses talking with you and Beth Anne misses your laugh. Don't forget us at the bakery, ya?

We had a couple of youth events since you left. Matthew looked like he was moping at the singing. I asked Samuel if Matthew has asked about you, and he said he hasn't. But that doesn't mean Matthew doesn't miss you! You know how buwe are—they aren't very good at expressing their feelings.

Mammi and I visited Rebecca, and she seemed very tired. She said she was fine, but I don't believe she was telling the whole truth. I offered to come and help her since we have new bakers working at the bakery to help carry the summer load. Since my parents gave me permission, I'm going to start helping her this coming week. I'll let you know how she is.

I just heard my mamm calling me to come and share devotions with my siblings before we go to bed. Write me soon! I miss you.

Love,
Katie

Lindsay reread the letter and tears filled her eyes. She missed her family back in Lancaster. Worry filled her as she thought of Rebecca. She prayed that Rebecca was tired from the pregnancy and not experiencing complications. She also hoped that Rebecca or Katie would tell her if Rebecca needed Lindsay to come home sooner than planned.

She stared at the news about Matthew and how he behaved at the last singing. Did he miss her or did something else make him melancholy?

Yanking her pad from her nightstand, she turned to a new page, grabbed a pen, and began to write.

Dear Katie,

Wie geht's! How are you doing? Thank you for your letter. I'm glad to hear that everyone is well.

Please keep me posted on Aenti Rebecca and how she's

feeling. I'm so happy that you're going to help her. Give her a hug for me.

That's interesting that Matthew wasn't himself at the last singing. Tell him that I said hello.

How wonderful that Mammi Elizabeth hired a couple of new bakers to help keep up with the tourists. I miss everyone too. Again, tell them hello!

I'm doing well and staying busy. Trisha is still progressing well with her healing and will start physical therapy at home this week. She's anxious to get off the crutches and into a walking cast, but it may be a few weeks before she does.

We attended my former church on Sunday and I participated in the young adult Sunday school class. The class has taken on volunteer projects in the community, and I've signed up to help out at a nursing home near the house. I'm excited because my grandpa was in a nursing facility until he died, and I feel like I'm honoring his memory by helping others in the same situation.

Lindsay glanced over at the GED Study Guide on her dresser and considered telling Katie that she was going to take the test. Would Katie approve of Lindsay's decision to pursue an educational certification? Lindsay loved her best friend and knew that Katie had an open mind. After all, Katie accepted Lindsay as a family member even though she wasn't a true Kauffman. But would Katie understand why Lindsay wanted to prove to her sister that she could get her GED?

Lindsay pondered that question for a moment. Was she only trying to get her GED to prove something to her sister or was she doing it for herself? She flopped back onto the bed and stared at the ceiling while the crash of the waves echoed from beyond her window.

Her gaze moved back to the book on the dresser and she sighed. She knew she wanted to prove that she could get her

GED. However, she didn't expect Katie to understand why she was doing it.

Lindsay wished she could share the news with Katie, but she thought it best to keep it to herself for the time being. Katie had grown up in a traditional Amish household, and education beyond eighth grade wasn't expected, nor was it encouraged or approved by the church. If Lindsay shared that she was pursuing her GED, Katie might feel awkward, akin to how Lindsay felt when she was with her friends at the pool party and they discussed their college plans. Lindsay decided it was best to keep that information to herself for now.

Sitting up, Lindsay crossed her legs and continued her letter. I walk on the beach every day, and I love hearing the waves and feeling the sand between my toes. It helps me think and relax. Maybe someday you and I can visit Frank and Trisha together, and you can live your dream of walking barefoot on the beach at sunset. It would be so fun if we could get a group together and come and visit for a week. Maybe we'll discuss that when I get home. Do you think your parents would let you go on a trip to Virginia Beach?

My sister and I talk about once a week, and she's doing well in New York City. From the stories she's shared, I believe she's only working and not spending much time having fun. She reported that her friend Kim has a new boyfriend who is a graduate student working for a law firm. I think Jessica misses Jake, but she hasn't admitted it to me. Have you seen or talked to him? Would you ask Matthew how Jake is doing? Jessica is too stubborn to give him a call herself, but I can give her a report.

I had fun visiting my school friends. I'm hoping to see them again soon. Even though they're getting ready to go to college and our lives are different, we had a nice time talking and getting caught up again.

Lindsay chewed the end of her pen as her eyes moved back to the study guide. She needed to start studying if she was going to pass that test in about a month.

I should close for now. It's late and I need to get up early tomorrow. Please give *Aenti* Rebecca, Junior, and Emma a kiss for me and tell *Aenti* Rebecca to take good care of herself. Tell Lizzie Anne I miss her too!

I look forward to seeing you all again.
Write soon.

Love,
Lindsay

She addressed and stamped the envelope and then slipped the folded letter inside. She wrote similar letters to Rebecca and Lizzie Anne and also addressed their envelopes. After changing into her pajamas, Lindsay curled up on the bed with the book and began studying.

Crumb Cake

1/2 cup sugar
3/4 tsp cinnamon
1/2 cup chopped nuts
3/4 cup flour
3 Tbsp melted butter

Combine dry ingredients. Work in melted butter until crumbs form. Add nuts. Sprinkle over top of coffee cake dough.

16

Katie hugged her arms to her chest and glanced around the barn where her friends were singing and talking together Saturday. She touched her pocket where the letter from Lindsay was folded up and hidden. She'd been carrying the letter around since she'd received it this afternoon, and she'd read it several times. She'd been relieved and excited to receive news from Lindsay.

What she read hinted that Lindsay missed Lancaster County, but Katie also worried that Lindsay was enjoying herself too much. She hoped Lindsay would still return to Bird-in-Hand as planned.

Lizzie Anne dropped onto the bench next to Katie. "You've been quiet."

Katie patted the pocket of her apron. "I got a letter from Lindsay today."

"Oh?" Lizzie Anne asked. "I did too. What did yours say?"

Katie handed the letter to Lizzie Anne and watched the crowd around her while she read it.

"It sounds very similar to what my letter said," Lizzie Anne said. "I think she's having a good time."

Katie nodded. "*Ya*. Do you think she'll come back?"

Lizzie Anne gave a surprised expression as she handed over the letter. "Of course I do. Don't you?"

Katie folded the letter and put it back in her apron pocket. "I hope she does."

"Didn't you read the letter?" Lizzie Anne pointed toward Katie's pocket. "She's very concerned about Rebecca and she misses us and her cousins. Of course she's coming back. Her heart is here." Lizzie Anne's expression turned sly. "Besides, we all know who likes her." She nodded in the direction of Samuel and Matthew who were across the room with a group of young men. "I think she likes him too. Remember the dandelion chain?"

"*Ya*, I do," Katie said. "But she didn't grow up Amish. If her old friends are going off to college, she may feel like she's missing something."

Lizzie Anne grimaced. "You sound like your mother when she was talking about Jessica."

Katie frowned. "I don't sound like her."

"*Ya*," Lizzie Anne said. "You do. Don't you remember how upset Lindsay gets when Jessica lectures her about going to school and making something of herself? Remember that disagreement they had when Jessica came to visit before she left for New York City?"

"I do." Katie stared across the barn as she talked. "But maybe Lindsay went back to Virginia and decided Jessica was right."

"You're *gegisch*," Lizzie Anne said, waving off the thought.

"I hope you're right," Katie said with a sigh. "Because I miss her."

"I miss her too." Lizzie Anne sat up straighter while she stared at something across the room.

Katie witnessed Lizzie Anne touching her prayer covering and then smoothing the skirt of her dark blue frock. She then followed Lizzie Anne's gaze to her older brother who was talking to a few friends across the barn.

"You like Samuel," Katie said before she could stop the observation from leaving her lips.

"No, I don't." Lizzie Anne's expression defied her words as her cheeks flushed a bright pink.

Katie grinned. "You're blushing."

"I am not," Lizzie Anne insisted. "Don't tease me."

"You like my brother," Katie repeated. "I thought something was blooming between you two, and now I see it. It's as obvious as that blush on your cheeks."

"Stop it," Lizzie Anne said, swatting Katie's arm.

"I knew it," Katie said. "You and Samuel. That's so cute."

"Shush!" Lizzie Anne hissed.

"Hello, ladies," Samuel said as he approached with Matthew beside him. "What are you two scheming?"

"Nothing," Lizzie Anne said, shooting Katie a sideways warning glance. "We were just discussing Lindsay."

Matthew's eyebrows shot to his hairline. "Have you heard from her?"

Katie nodded. "I received a letter from her today."

Matthew lowered himself to the ground next to her. "How is she doing?"

"She's doing well," Katie said. "She's volunteering at a nursing home along with taking care of her aunt Trisha. I think she misses us, but I think she's also having a good time in Virginia Beach." She glanced at Lizzie Anne and found her friend engrossed in a conversation with her brother.

"Volunteering at a nursing home?" Matthew looked confused. "What made her decide to do that?"

"Her Sunday school class at her former church," Katie said. "They're taking on volunteer projects to help their community."

"Oh." Matthew frowned and looked away.

"I hope she comes back," Katie said.

He met her gaze. "You think she's considering staying there?"

Katie shrugged. "I don't know. She didn't say that in her letter, but there's a part of me that wonders if she'll want to be English."

Glowering, he shook his head. "I hope not."

"I can't imagine not having her around," Katie said.

"Daniel told me that you're working for Rebecca now," Matthew said.

Katie absently picked at some hay. "I started there on Monday. *Aenti* Rebecca hasn't been feeling well, so I'm helping her with the *kinner*. She's been resting more."

"Is she *grank*?"

Katie shook her head. "I think she has a lingering stomach flu. She seems very tired all the time, and I get the feeling that her stomach hurts."

"Has she seen a doctor?"

"I think she has an appointment next week, so maybe we'll know more."

He looked concerned. "I'll have to ask Daniel how she is."

"How are things at the furniture store?" Katie asked.

"Busy. I heard that the bakery is very busy too."

"*Ya*, but my *mammi* hired more bakers to help with the load. She insisted I go work for *Aenti* Rebecca. She said that they would be fine with the new bakers."

"That's *gut*." He stood and brushed some hay off his trousers. "Would you like a drink and some cookies?"

"*Ya, danki*." Katie smiled.

Matthew smacked Samuel's shoulder. "Let's go get these ladies a drink and a snack."

Samuel agreed and they walked off together.

"He's so nice," Katie told Lizzie Anne after the men had left. "I can see why Lindsay likes him, even though she says she doesn't."

Lizzie Anne laughed. "*Ya*, he is. And Samuel is too."

Katie smiled. "It's pretty obvious that my brother likes you."

"You think so?" Lizzie Anne looked hopeful.

I know so. "*Ya*, I think so." Katie smiled at her friend. A romance was budding right in front of her, and while she was happy for them both, she missed Lindsay. Soon Katie would be the fifth wheel at youth gatherings. While her brother and Lizzie Anne would go off to visit together, Katie would be left alone.

By the time the sun began setting, Katie was ready to go home. Although she'd enjoyed spending time talking with Matthew, she was tired and ready to take a bath and head to bed. She and Matthew followed Lizzie Anne and Samuel out to the pasture filled with buggies.

Samuel suddenly stopped mid stride and his smile faded when he faced Lizzie Anne. "Would you like a ride home?" Hope and anxiety glittered in his eyes.

Lizzie Anne's eyes widened, and her mouth gaped. She nodded without speaking.

Katie swallowed a groan. It was now official—Samuel and Lizzie Anne were courting.

And Katie was stranded without a ride home.

She glanced toward the youths behind them and scanned the crowd for someone who wouldn't mind her tagging along.

"I can give you a ride home," Matthew said.

Katie glanced at him, hoping to conceal her shock at the suggestion. She prayed Matthew didn't think that she liked him because she had spoken with him earlier in the evening. After all, her best friend was interested in him. She would surely lose Lindsay's trust if Lindsay returned to find Katie dating Matthew.

But Katie didn't see Matthew as more than a friend!

Her stomach twisted. *Could this evening get any worse?*

Matthew's eyes suddenly widened. "Wait a minute. I didn't mean that I wanted to give you a ride home, in order to, well—" he stammered. "I just meant that since Samuel finally asked Lizzie Anne if she wanted a ride home, then I would give you a lift back to your house. Just as a friendly favor since I live next door to you."

"Oh!" Katie blew out a sigh of relief. "Good. I didn't want it to imply more than that."

He laughed. "*Gut.*"

Katie turned to Lizzie Anne who looked as if she were glowing in the low light. Joy shone brightly in her brown eyes. "Enjoy your ride home," she whispered in her ear while squeezing her arm.

Lizzie Anne blushed.

Katie then slapped her brother's back. "I'll see you at the house. Don't be too late."

"You got a ride?" he asked.

"I'll be fine," she said. "Matthew took pity on me since I was abandoned and all alone. You behave yourself with my best friend."

He snickered and then said good night to Matthew.

Once the horse was hitched to the buggy, Katie climbed in. As Matthew hopped in, Katie wondered if rumors would be flying about her and Matthew. If so, she hoped they wouldn't reach Lindsay before she could write a letter to tell her about the crazy evening that had led to Samuel and Lizzie Anne's official courtship. She thought it would be best to tell Lindsay everything as soon as possible in order to quell any rumors that might hurt Lindsay's feelings.

She hoped that Samuel and Lizzie Anne would be happy together, but she also prayed that she would find someone soon. While Katie wasn't ready to court and get married, she did dream of having a family someday.

"Samuel finally did it," Matthew said, breaking the silence as he steered down the rock driveway leading to the main road. "He told me he planned to ask Lizzie Anne if he could give her a ride home, but he's chickened out at the last two youth gatherings."

"Really?" Katie asked. "He'd been planning it, but he hadn't told me. In fact, in a roundabout way, I asked him if he liked her, and he denied it."

Matthew snorted. "Wasn't it obvious to you, Katie?"

She laughed. "*Ya,* it was. And she has worn her feelings on her sleeve for a long time too."

"*Ya,* she has." Matthew stared out at the road. "When do you think Lindsay will be back?"

Katie swallowed her smile. Matthew definitely liked Lindsay if he was thinking about her while he was discussing Samuel and Lizzie Anne's new courtship.

"I'm not certain," Katie said. "She said in her letter that it'll be awhile before Trisha can use a walking cast. Maybe she won't be home before August."

He looked disappointed. He was silent for a moment, and Katie turned her attention to the road in front of them. She wondered what he was thinking, but she didn't want to pry.

"May I ask you a question?" he finally said, breaking through the silence again.

"*Ya,*" she said.

"Do you think Lindsay wants to be here with us? I know that you believe she'll come home this summer, but do you think she wants to be here permanently?"

Katie considered his words. "Are you asking if I think she wants to be Amish and join the church?"

He kept his eyes on the road. "Yeah, I guess so."

"I've wondered that for a long time," Katie said. "In fact, Lizzie Anne and I were discussing it earlier. In my heart, I think she does, but I have some doubts that haunt me at times. She gets upset when her sister tells her that she needs to do more with her life and go to school, but at the same time, she backed out of the baptism class with Lizzie Anne and me."

Matthew glanced at her, and his expression was concern mixed with worry.

"I do think she wants to be Amish," Katie continued, "but sometimes it feels like something is holding her back. It seems as if her sister has planted doubt in her mind."

He nodded as they approached Katie's house. "I see what you mean."

"I think she'll come back to the community," Katie said. "I just hope that she decides to stay and join the church. I can't imagine going to church services and not sitting with her."

"I feel the same way." He guided the horse up to the barn.

"Oh," Katie began, remembering a question Lindsay had asked in the letter. "Have you talked to Jake Miller lately?"

"*Ya*." He shrugged. "I usually talk to him at least once a day."

"Has he said anything about Lindsay's sister, Jessica?"

He shook his head. "Not really. Why do you ask?"

"Lindsay asked about him in her letter. I think she's hoping Jessica and Jake will talk because they had an argument when she was here."

"Oh." He shook his head. "I don't know anything about their argument. He hasn't mentioned her to me at all." He halted the horse. "Here we are. It was nice talking to you tonight."

She gripped the door handle. "*Ya*, it was. I'll see you at service tomorrow."

"*Gut nacht*," he said.

"*Gut nacht*," she echoed before hopping out of the buggy and heading up the steps to the back door.

Rebecca lowered herself onto the rocker on the porch Sunday evening. She felt wretched both physically and emotionally. She'd planned to go to church services this morning, as they always did every other Sunday. However, her body wouldn't allow it. She was so physically ill that she spent the morning between her room and the bathroom. To make matters even worse, she had a pounding headache that made her dizzy.

She'd told Daniel to go and take the children to services, but he was too worried and concerned to leave her alone.

This pregnancy was so different from her other two that

she was beginning to worry about the baby. She was glad that a routine appointment was scheduled for tomorrow. She prayed that the doctor could shed some light on what was wrong. Her sisters-in-law had experienced difficult pregnancies, but she'd never heard that they were as ill as she was. She hoped that the doctor would put her at ease tomorrow.

The clip-clop of a horse and the crunch of wheels on the driveway drew her gaze to a buggy making its way toward the barn. Rebecca wanted to stand up and see who was approaching, but her body was too weak to move. Instead, she lifted her glass of water to her lips and took a long drink.

The buggy came to a stop in front of the barn and a tall, lean man climbed out. Rebecca expected the man to be one of her nephews. However, she was surprised when Matthew waved as he crossed to the porch.

"*Wie geht's?*" he said, climbing the steps.

"I'm doing okay," she said. "How are you today?"

"I'm well." He nodded toward the chair beside her rocker. "May I have a seat?"

"Of course." She gestured in the direction of the chair. "Would you like me to go find Daniel for you?"

"No, *danki.*" He folded his tall body into the chair. "I actually came to speak with you."

"Oh," she said with surprise. "How may I help you?"

He removed his straw hat from his head and began to fiddle with it in his hands. "I was surprised when I didn't see you, Daniel, and your family in church today."

"I wasn't feeling well. I really wanted to come, but I couldn't make it. Daniel was worried about me, so he didn't want to leave me."

"Oh." His eyes were full of concern. "I'm sorry to hear you're ill. Katie mentioned you haven't been feeling well, and that she's been helping you out. Are you going to be okay?"

"*Danki* for asking. I'm certain I'll be just fine."

"It's not my business, but are you seeing a doctor?"

"*Ya,* I am. In fact, I have an appointment tomorrow."

"I hope that you're feeling better soon."

"*Danki.*" Rebecca couldn't help but think Matthew was a nice young man. She hoped his friendship with Lindsay lasted a long time.

He studied his hat, and she wondered what he was hesitant to say.

"Would you like a drink?" she asked in order to break the awkward silence.

"No, *danki.*" He looked up and cleared his throat. "I was wondering if you knew how Lindsay was doing."

She smiled. His adoration for her niece was written all over his young face.

"I spoke to her a few days ago and also received a letter. She said that she was doing quite well," Rebecca said.

"I've been hoping she was doing well," he said, leaning back on the wooden chair. "Katie mentioned that she received a letter from Lindsay yesterday, and she was enjoying her time in Virginia. I just hope she isn't getting too accustomed to the English life again."

"I've had the same thought, but I have a feeling that her heart is here."

"I hope so." He glanced off toward the pasture.

Rebecca studied his expression, trying to figure out what he was thinking about her niece. "You know, Matthew, I think Lindsay would be delighted to hear from you."

He met her gaze and raised his eyebrows. "What do you mean?"

"I mean that she gets lonely sometimes and would be very happy to hear from her friends back home." She slowly pushed herself up from the swing, trying in vain to ignore the aches and pains radiating through her abdomen and legs. "I'll go get her address and phone number for you."

"Oh no." He shook his head. "I don't want to cause you any trouble."

"Don't be *gegisch*." She made her way to the back door. "I'll be right back."

Rebecca found Lindsay's address and phone number on the counter and copied it onto a blank page in a little notepad she kept handy for shopping lists. She then poured him a glass of tea and brought them both out to Matthew.

"*Danki*," he said, taking the paper and the drink. "You really didn't have to get this for me."

"It was no trouble at all," she said, gingerly sinking back into the swing.

He grimaced. "The truth is, I wouldn't know what to say if I called her or wrote her."

Rebecca smiled. "Tell her what's happening at singings and at work. You could tell her how you feel. Tell her you miss her or that you want her to come back soon."

She could've sworn his cheeks blushed a light pink.

He folded up the piece of paper and stuck it into the pocket of his trousers. "I'll think about it. *Danki* for the information."

"*Gern gschehne*. How's your sister doing?" she asked.

They talked about his sister and her family for a few minutes. While they were talking, the back door opened, and Daniel stepped out onto the porch.

"Matthew," Daniel said. "What brings you out here today?"

"I was concerned when I didn't see you at service today," Matthew said. "Rebecca was telling me she wasn't feeling well."

Daniel rubbed his chin. "*Ya*, she had a rough morning." He turned to her. "I think you should head up to bed. You need your rest."

"*Ya*, you should go rest," Matthew echoed. "I can visit with Daniel for a while."

"That's a *gut* idea," Daniel said, holding out his hand to her.

Rebecca took his hand, and he helped her stand. "*Danki*," she said. She faced Matthew. "It was *gut* seeing you. Please give my regards to your sister and her family."

"I will," Matthew said. "You take care of yourself."

Stepping into the kitchen, Rebecca hoped that Matthew would write or call Lindsay and remind her of what awaited her back in Lancaster County.

17

Dr. Fitzgerald frowned, and Rebecca held her breath. The hand on her shoulder gave little comfort. She glanced up and found Daniel staring down at her, his eyes full of the worry she felt in her heart.

"Mrs. Kauffman," Dr. Fitzgerald began, removing his glasses. "I'm very concerned about your blood pressure. The aches and pains are normal, but the rise in blood pressure gives me pause."

"Is the baby going to be all right?" Rebecca's voice was a trembling whisper.

"The ultrasound shows that the baby is growing as it should, but the swelling in your legs and feet and the blood pressure could lead to serious complications," Dr. Fitzgerald said. "I would like you to rest more. You need to stay off your feet as much as possible. Can you possibly find someone to help you with the children during the day?"

Daniel cleared his throat. "My niece has been helping Rebecca during the past week."

"Good. She needs to come over every day and do as much around the house as possible. I want Mrs. Kauffman to stay in bed or even on the sofa with her feet up." He wrote in the medical chart. "I would like to see you back here in two weeks. If there is any change at all that concerns you, please call as soon as possible. You can't ever be too cautious."

Daniel squeezed Rebecca's shoulder. "I'll keep a good eye on her, Doctor. I'll be sure to call if we have any worries."

"Good." The doctor shook Daniel's hand. "I'll see you back here in two weeks." He met Rebecca's stare. "Take good care of yourself, Mrs. Kauffman."

Rebecca stared out the window during the ride home. Her mind raced with questions about the pregnancy. The worry she saw in the doctor's and Daniel's eyes filled her with dread. She prayed that the baby would continue to develop normally and that she wouldn't be sentenced to bed rest for the next several months. However, she was willing to follow the doctor's orders if it meant the baby's health.

When the van steered into the driveway at the house, Rebecca stared at the back door. She knew she would have to tell Katie why she was resting, and she hoped that her niece would honor their wishes and keep the secret to herself. Rebecca worried that if Katie's mother, Sadie, found out, then the news would spread quickly through their church district.

The van stopped at the back door and Daniel turned to Mike, the driver. "I'll just be a moment," he said before jumping from the van and opening the back door for Rebecca. He took her hand and helped her out of the van and then guided her up the porch steps.

When they reached the back door, she stopped him by gently nudging his arm.

"*Was iss letz?*" His eyes were full of worry again.

"Do you think the *boppli* is going to be okay?" she asked, praying his answer would be positive.

He touched her cheek. "*Ya,* I do, but you're going to have to follow the doctor's orders. I don't want anything to happen to you or the *boppli*."

She squeezed his arm. "I promise I will, but we're going to

have to trust Katie with the secret. It won't make sense to her if I have to remain on bed rest for a stomach flu."

He touched his beard, considering her suggestion. "That's true. I think she can keep a secret. She's a *gut* girl." He squeezed her hand. "I have to get to work. Do you need me to walk in with you?"

Rebecca shook her head. "I'm fine. You have a *gut* day."

"You too. Take it easy, just like the doctor ordered." He jogged down the steps and climbed into the van.

Rebecca opened the back door as the van sped down the driveway toward the main road. The sweet smell of baking cookies filled Rebecca's senses, causing her to smile. She spotted a batch of chocolate chip cooling on a rack on the counter. Her niece was so thoughtful to mix up some cookies for the children.

She found Katie in the family room reading to the children.

Katie looked up at Rebecca as Emma and Junior rushed toward her.

Rebecca sat on the sofa and hugged the children. They returned to the floor, playing with a set of blocks in the middle of the room.

"What did the doctor say?" Katie asked.

"I have to rest as much as possible." Rebecca lifted her feet onto the sofa and leaned back against the arm. "My blood pressure is up, causing my legs and feet to swell."

Katie's eyes rounded. "Are you going to be all right?"

"*Ya,* I am, but I have to be very careful."

Katie crossed the room and stood over Rebecca, her eyes flashing with concern. "*Was iss letz?* Is it serious?"

Rebecca glanced at the children and then back at Katie.

"Oh," Katie whispered. "You don't want the *kinner* to hear. Do you want me to ask them to go to the kitchen for a cookie and then I'll come back and talk to you?"

Rebecca shook her head. "No, I'll tell you, but you have to keep it to yourself."

"Of course." Katie nodded, her expression grave.

She motioned for Katie to come in closer and then she leaned up to Katie's ear. "I'm expecting a *boppli*."

Katie gasped, cupping her hand to her mouth.

Engrossed in their playtime, the children never looked up.

"Now, you can't tell anyone."

Katie grinned, her head bobbing excitement. "I won't. I promise, *Aenti* Rebecca." She leaned down and hugged her. "I'm so *froh* for you. When are you due?"

"January eleventh."

"That's *wunderbaar*." She stood up. "Why do you have to be on bed rest? You said your blood pressure is up high?"

Frowning, Rebecca nodded. "*Ya*. The doctor is concerned about my blood pressure and the swelling in my legs and feet. He said I must call him if something changes or I start feeling worse."

Katie took Rebecca's hand in hers. "I promise I'll run like the wind to the phone shanty if you need me to." She bit her lower lip. "I think my *mamm* had problems with her blood pressure when she was pregnant with my brother Aaron and everything turned out fine. I'm certain the doctor will take *gut* care of you."

Rebecca gave a sad smile. "I hope so, Katie."

"Does Lindsay know about the *boppli*?"

"*Ya*, but you mustn't tell Lindsay that I need to rest all the time. I don't want her to be so worried that she changes her plans and rushes back here. I want her to enjoy Virginia without any guilt about my condition. Understand?"

Katie gave a serious expression. "*Ya*, I promise I won't tell her anything, but you have to promise to follow the doctor's orders and let me take *gut* care of you."

Rebecca couldn't stop her smile. "You're a *gut maedel*, Katie."

"*Danki*." Katie grinned. "You're a *gut aenti*."

As Katie hugged her again, Rebecca closed her eyes and silently thanked God for her family, and also prayed that Katie was right about the pregnancy being healthy despite the worrisome complications.

Later that evening, Katie climbed the stairs toward her bedroom. All day long she'd been thinking of Rebecca and worrying about her condition. While she'd been following the doctor's orders, Katie couldn't stop herself from worrying that Rebecca was more ill than she'd ever seen her mother. She was concerned that Lindsay would be upset if she didn't know just how sick their aunt was, and she needed someone's advice on what to do.

Although she longed to tell her mother, she also was aware that her mother was known for having a loose tongue. Her mother had a good heart, but she didn't always use caution when sharing information. Katie had once confided in her mother about a girl at school who had kissed a boy behind the outhouse. Instead of keeping the information to herself, Sadie told the girl's mother, and the girl never spoke to Katie again.

Katie knew that if she told her mother about Rebecca and the news was shared, Rebecca would never trust Katie again.

However, Katie needed someone to listen to her worries. Glancing down the hallway, she spotted a lamp burning in Samuel's room. She believed that Samuel was capable of keeping a secret. He'd proven that time and again when Katie had asked his advice on how to handle a sticky situation with friends at school. As far as Katie knew, Samuel never once repeated her questions about boys. She believed she could trust him with this too.

She walked down the hallway and peeked in his doorway, finding her older brother propped up on his bed, reading the Bible. She tapped on the door frame, and he glanced up.

"*Ya?*" he asked, closing his Bible and placing it on the nightstand. "Didn't Raymond take out the trash?"

"I'm not here to ask about the trash." She gestured toward the chair near his bed. "Do you have a minute?"

He looked suspicious. "This sounds serious."

She pursed her lips. "Sort of."

He motioned toward the chair. "Have a seat."

She stepped into the room, closing the door behind her, and then sat on the chair across from his bed.

"*Was iss letz?*" he asked. "*Bu* trouble?"

"*Bu* trouble?" she muttered. "What *buwe?*"

"What was that?" He raised an eyebrow with curiosity.

"Never mind," she said, sitting up straighter in the chair. "Listen, I have something that's bothering me, but I'm supposed to keep it a secret. You're a very *gut* secret keeper, and I need someone to listen. Would you please listen in confidence?"

He grimaced. "I don't know. This sounds awfully serious, and I don't want to get in the middle of something that would potentially get me into trouble with *daed*."

"Samuel, you won't get in trouble." She held her hands up for emphasis. "I promise. The only way we could get in trouble is if this leaks out before it's supposed to."

"We?" He shook his head. "Don't put me in the middle of your schemes. I know how *maed* can be."

Frustration built within her, and she glowered at him. "I thought I could trust you to help me, but I was wrong." She stood. "Forget I even came in here." She stomped toward the door and wrenched it open with as much force as she could muster.

"Wait," he said with defeat in his voice. "Don't get all angry and storm out of the room as if I just insulted you."

She faced him, crossing her arms in front of her chest with defiance. "You did insult me. You said you didn't want to get involved when I asked you for help."

"Fine, fine," he said, gesturing widely. "I'll help. Close the door, sit down, and tell me what's wrong."

"*Danki*." She pulled the door closed with a soft click and then returned to the seat. "I'm very concerned about *Aenti* Rebecca."

"I know she hasn't been feeling well."

"It's more than that." Katie leaned forward and lowered her volume. "She's pregnant and having complications. Her blood pressure is very high, and she has swelling in her legs and feet. The doctor said that she has to rest as much as possible, and I need to do all I can to help her around the *haus*."

He shook his head. "I'm sorry to hear that. I'll pray that her pregnancy goes well and that she's feeling better soon."

"I can't share this with anyone," Katie continued. "But I think *Aenti* Rebecca is wrong to keep this from Lindsay. If Lindsay knew that she was having these problems, she would come home and help her. She would be very upset to find out that *Aenti* Rebecca needs her, but *Aenti* Rebecca didn't want her to know."

"That's *Aenti* Rebecca's choice," Samuel said. "It's her business."

"I disagree," Katie said with a shake of her head. "It's more than that. Lindsay is like a *dochder* to her. If *Mamm* was sick and needed me, I would be devastated if she didn't tell me. Besides, Lindsay already knows that *Aenti* Rebecca is pregnant. She needs to know that she's having these problems."

He shrugged. "You're right, but it's *Aenti* Rebecca's choice."

"But if something happened to *Aenti* Rebecca or the *boppli* and Lindsay wasn't here to help," Katie began, "Lindsay would be very upset."

"We're supposed to respect and honor our elders," Samuel said. "I understand what you're saying. But if you go against *Aenti* Rebecca, you'll be in trouble with *Aenti* Rebecca and possibly *Mamm* and *Dat*. Do you want that? You could jeopardize your relationship with *Aenti* Rebecca."

"You're right," Katie said. "I'm just worried about *Aenti* Rebecca, and I'm worried about what Lindsay will say when she finds out."

"I think Lindsay will be home soon enough, and she can help *Aenti* Rebecca too." He pushed back a lock of blond hair that fell over his forehead. "Maybe by the time Lindsay gets home, she'll be doing just fine, and Lindsay won't have to feel guilty for leaving."

"I hope so," Katie said, swatting the ties from her prayer covering back from her shoulders. "That would be a miracle."

"Is there anything else you want to talk about?"

She grinned. "How about you and Lizzie Anne?" She thought she might've caught a glimpse of a blush, but his cheeks were their normal ivory almost instantly.

"What about Lizzie Anne?"

"You're courting?" she asked.

"Not officially until after she's baptized. We have fun just being together and talking. Nothing serious." He looked nonchalant. "What's wrong with that?"

"Nothing, but I hope you don't break her heart. She really likes you."

"She does?" His smile was wide.

She shook her head. "You two are so *gegisch*." Standing, she smiled. "*Danki*. I'll let you get back to your devotions. *Gut nacht*."

"*Gut nacht*," he repeated. "Don't forget what I said about keeping the news to yourself."

"I won't," she said, heading to the door. "And don't forget that everything I told you was a secret that you have to keep to yourself. And more importantly, don't forget what I said about treating Lizzie Anne right."

"I heard you, Katie," he said with a chuckle. "It's late. Get on to bed. You need to take *gut* care of *Aenti* Rebecca tomorrow."

"I will." She slipped out the door and crossed the hallway to her room. Sitting at her small desk, she pulled out her stationery and a pen.

Pulling the letter she'd received from Lindsay from her pocket, she stared at the words and silently debated how to begin her reply. While she longed to tell Lindsay everything about Rebecca, she knew her brother was right. Sharing a secret that was supposed to be private would only result in hard feelings and possibly punishment. She still believed that Lindsay had a right to know about their aunt's health struggles, but it wasn't Katie's place to tell Lindsay the news.

She poised the pen in her right hand and began to write.

Dear Lindsay,

Wie geht's! Thank you for your letter. I'm glad to hear that you're doing well and that Trisha is healing.

That's wunderbaar that you saw some old friends and you're attending services and Sunday school at your former church. Please tell me all about your volunteering experience at the nursing home. I would imagine that you'll do a great job and take gut care of the people who need your help.

Saturday night I went to a singing at the Esh farm, and I wish you'd been there. You'll never believe what finally happened—Samuel gave Lizzie Anne a ride home! We all knew it was coming, and he finally did it. Lizzie Anne was grinning when she climbed into his courting buggy.

She was hyper and even more talkative than usual at service yesterday too. I'm very happy for her, but I have to admit it's going to be difficult being the fifth wheel with her and Samuel at youth gatherings. I may have to spend time with Nancy and her friends instead of feeling like I'm interfering between my brother and Lizzie Anne. I'm certain she and I will remain close friends, but it will be different. She'll be the one with a boyfriend, while I'm the one who is all alone.

When I was left without a ride Saturday night, Matthew was gracious enough to offer to take me home. Please don't be upset or jealous—we spent the ride talking about you. In fact, we spent nearly all evening talking about you. It's very apparent that he likes you, Lindsay. I'm certain he's concerned that you won't come back to Lancaster County. And when you do come back, I'm certain he'll be anxious for you to join the church so that he can court you.

A tap on the door frame drew Katie's attention to her mother watching her.

"It's getting late, Katie," Sadie said with a frown. "What are you doing?"

"I'm writing a letter to Lindsay," Katie said. "I'll only be a few minutes longer."

"Finish up," Sadie said, pointing to the battery-operated clock on Katie's dresser. "You have to be up early tomorrow so you can get a ride to Rebecca's."

"Yes, *Mamm*," Katie said. "I'll be finished very soon, and I'll change and get into bed."

Sadie nodded. "*Gut nacht*. See you bright and early. Nancy is finishing up in the shower."

"*Gut nacht*," Katie echoed. As soon as her mother disappeared from the doorway, she turned back to her letter. She stared at the page, again considering whether or not she should tell Lindsay about Rebecca.

With a heavy sigh, she continued writing.

I'm enjoying helping *Aenti* Rebecca with the *kinner* during the day. They all miss you, and Emma and Junior ask about you all the time. I tell them that you will be back soon and will give them plenty of hugs and kisses to make up for the time that you've been gone.

My mamm just told me that it's time to snuff out the lantern because it's late. I pray that you are doing well. Keep in touch and write very soon.

Love,
Katie

18

Humming one of her favorite hymns from the Amish services back in Lancaster, Lindsay walked through the halls of the Sandbridge Beach Rehabilitation and Nursing Center. She smiled at the residents sitting in the corridor in their wheelchairs and waved to a nurse at the end of the hallway. Although it was only her second time volunteering at the home, she felt like she knew everyone as old friends.

The past two weeks had flown by at near lightning speed. She spent her days taking care of Trisha, cooking, cleaning, writing letters to friends and family back home, and walking and swimming at the beach. Whenever Trisha was working with her physical therapist or resting, Lindsay pored over the GED Study Guide, memorizing information and taking practice exams. She studied late into the night, sometimes even dreaming about the book and the tests.

When Lindsay spoke to Jessica a few days ago, Lindsay finally admitted that she was planning to take the test, and Jessica was thrilled. Lindsay immediately regretted telling her about the test because it would be painful to admit if she'd failed. However, she refused to let that worry haunt her. She pushed that thought from her mind and continued to study, putting her heart and soul into every page of the study guide.

On Sundays, she stopped studying long enough to go to

church and Sunday school, and she planned to attend church and Sunday school every week until she returned to Lancaster County. While she enjoyed going back to her childhood church, she missed the Amish way of worshiping. Being among the Amish had become her home and her security, much like the prayer covering she missed wearing.

During her journey down one of the main hallways in the nursing facility, Lindsay stopped and peeked into the room of Mrs. Warren, an elderly lady who'd asked Lindsay to read the Bible out loud to her last Saturday. The older woman was completely bedridden and also hard of hearing, but she'd smiled while Lindsay read from the book of John when they sat together previously.

The stark white walls in Mrs. Warren's private room were dotted with family photos, showing smiling faces of people Lindsay assumed were adult children, grandchildren, and possibly even great-grandchildren. A few of the photos looked to be Mrs. Warren and the late Mr. Warren smiling together by different scenery, including standing in a studio, posing in front of a pretty brick house in front of a lake, and dressed in their Sunday best while holding hands. A shelf in the corner held a collection of plush teddy bears and cats.

From what Lindsay could surmise through the photos and the basket full of daisies on the windowsill, Mrs. Warren had a large, loving family and had enjoyed a full life before she came to the nursing home.

Lindsay tapped on the door frame, but Mrs. Warren didn't break her trance from the television set, which blared a black and white movie on the classic movie channel. Lindsay stepped into the room and moved to the bed.

Mrs. Warren looked up at Lindsay and a smile broke out across her lips. "Hello. How are you, dear?" she asked, her voice loud and raspy.

"I'm doing well, Mrs. Warren," Lindsay answered in an equally booming voice in order to be heard over the television. "Would you like me to read to you today?"

Mrs. Warren nodded, her gray curls bobbing in response to the moment.

After turning off the television, Lindsay lifted the Bible from the small table and lowered herself into a plastic chair next to the bed. "Do you have any particular chapter you'd like to hear?"

"No," Mrs. Warren said, closing her dark brown eyes. "Please just read."

Lindsay flipped to the book of Romans and began reading. After several minutes, she heard a grumbling sound. Glancing up, she found Mrs. Warren snoring. She gingerly closed the Bible and placed it on the table behind her. She then stood and straightened the pink blanket around Mrs. Warren's tiny body.

Lindsay walked into the hallway and nodded to a nurse who smiled while rushing past her. She glanced down the hallway and decided to go visit a nice elderly man who liked to do puzzles. Last Saturday she'd sat with him for nearly an hour, helping him with a five-hundred-piece puzzle of an underwater scene, complete with sea creatures and plants.

As Lindsay made her way through the knot of wheelchairs, she heard a crash and a loud moan coming from a nearby room. She changed direction and followed the moans, coming to the room occupied by two elderly ladies.

The lady by the door was asleep in her bed; however, the woman near the window was on the floor, mumbling words that were like music to Lindsay's ears. The woman was clad in a plain green dress and wearing a prayer covering that was slightly different from the heart-shaped ones worn in Lindsay's district. Lindsay had wanted to speak to her last Saturday, but the woman was sleeping during Lindsay's shift.

A nurse stood over the moaning woman and frowned as

she spoke. "I can't understand you, Mrs. Ephraim. Would you please speak slower?"

"*Ich hap schmatza,*" the woman repeated. "*Ich hap schmatza.*"

"*Dietsch,*" Lindsay whispered. It had been so long since she'd heard Pennsylvania Dutch that she couldn't stop a smile from forming on her lips. She'd wondered if the woman was Mennonite or Amish, and now she had her answer. She'd found a little piece of Pennsylvania in Virginia.

"Please calm down and try to speak in English." The nurse tried to calm the elderly woman by stroking her hair and moving it out of the woman's eyes, and Lindsay caught a glimpse of her name tag, reading "Gina."

"No!" Mrs. Ephraim said. "*Ich hap schmatza.*" She continued her moaning, and her eyes filled with tears.

Lindsay stepped into the room and cleared her throat. "Mrs. Ephraim," she began. "*Was iss letz?*"

As if on cue, both the nurse and Mrs. Ephraim widened their eyes.

"You understand her?" Gina asked.

"*Kannscht du Pennsilfaanisch Dietsch schwetze?*" Mrs. Ephraim asked.

"*Ya,*" Lindsay answered them both with a nod.

"What is she saying?" Gina asked. "Since her stroke a few months ago, when she is very upset or, as in this case, in pain, she can't get the words out in English."

"She's speaking Pennsylvania Dutch," Lindsay explained. "It's the language the Amish speak." She turned to Mrs. Ephraim. "*Was iss letz?*"

"*Mei beh,*" Mrs. Ephraim said.

"She says her leg hurts," Lindsay told Gina before turning back to Mrs. Ephraim. "Did you hurt it when you fell?" she asked in *Dietsch*.

Mrs. Ephraim nodded.

Lindsay looked at Gina. "She said she hurt her leg when she fell. I think she's afraid to move it."

Gina popped up from the floor and touched Lindsay's arm. "Thank you." She hit the button on the wall, and a buzzer sounded, telling the main desk that help was needed in the room. "I'll be right back. Would you sit and talk to her?"

"Of course." Lindsay sank onto the floor next to Mrs. Ephraim and her brain clicked to her language lessons from Kathryn. "She's getting help," she said in *Dietsch* while taking the elderly lady's hand in an effort to comfort her.

"You're Amish?" Mrs. Ephraim asked in *Dietsch* while rubbing her leg.

Lindsay smiled. "My *aenti* is Amish."

Soon Gina returned with another female and two large male nurses in tow.

Gina motioned toward the blonde nurse. "Lindsay, this is Cheryl. Would you please tell Mrs. Ephraim that Cheryl is going to examine her before we help her up?"

"Of course," Lindsay said before she turned to Mrs. Ephraim and explained what Gina had said.

Mrs. Ephraim nodded and Cheryl proceeded with her exam. She then turned to Gina and the other nurses. "I think she may have injured her leg. I believe it's safe to move her and I'll order x-rays. I don't think her leg is broken, but we need to find out for certain." She looked at Lindsay. "Would you please tell Mrs. Ephraim that the guys here are going to help her up? Thank you for your help."

"I'm glad I can help," Lindsay told Cheryl. She then repeated everything to Mrs. Ephraim before the male nurses lifted Mrs. Ephraim and gently placed her in bed.

"Thank you for your help, Lindsay," Gina repeated.

While Gina helped Mrs. Ephraim get situated in the bed, Lindsay couldn't help but grin. The nurses had needed Lindsay's help with a patient, and the feeling was like nothing she'd ever experienced. Despite what Jessica frequently said about Lindsay needing an education, Lindsay knew she had something to offer to the modern world, and she had "made something of herself" without going to college. She was making a difference in someone's life. And the education she'd received in order to help Mrs. Ephraim had come from Kathryn's informal lessons in the bakery, along with the practice she received at home with Rebecca and Daniel.

Lindsay couldn't wait to share the excitement of her day with Jessica and also with Rebecca and Katie. Wouldn't they all be surprised?

Gina wrote on a clipboard and then looked up at Lindsay. "Would you like to visit with her until we're ready to do the x-ray?"

"I would be happy to," Lindsay said.

Gina touched Lindsay's arm. "I'm so glad you were here to help. We've been trying to communicate with Mrs. Ephraim for quite some time. We could tell that she was speaking a German dialect, but no one could determine exactly what she was saying."

"I'm thrilled that I was able to help you and Mrs. Ephraim." Lindsay perched herself on a chair next to Mrs. Ephraim's bed while Gina disappeared through the door.

"What did she say?" Mrs. Ephraim asked in Pennsylvania *Dietsch*.

"She's getting ready to take you for your x-ray," Lindsay explained. "How are you feeling?"

Mrs. Ephraim frowned. "*Mei beh schmatze.*" She then nodded toward Lindsay. "You aren't Amish. How do you know *Dietsch?*"

Lindsay explained that her parents had died, and she'd been living with her aunt for four years. She also told Mrs. Ephraim that she was visiting for the summer.

"I'm also from Pennsylvania," Mrs. Ephraim began in a tired voice. "I remember Bird-in-Hand. I visited friends there often."

"What brought you to Virginia?" Lindsay asked while moving her chair closer to the bed and taking the elderly lady's hand again.

"I moved to Virginia to be with *mei dochder* ten years ago after my husband died," she said softly. "She didn't want to be Amish, but I wanted to be closer to her. When I became ill, *mei dochder* put me here and moved to California."

"I'm so sorry," Lindsay said. "You must miss her."

"I used to spend my days reading," Mrs. Ephraim continued, seeming to avoid the subject of her daughter. "However, since my stroke, I can't read or write."

"I would be happy to read to you," Lindsay offered.

"No," Mrs. Ephraim said. "Tell me about your life in Bird-in-Hand."

"Okay," Lindsay said. She was in the midst of sharing a story about the bakery when Gina arrived with a gurney.

"We're going to take Mrs. Ephraim for a few x-rays, but we'll be back soon," Gina said.

"*Kumm*," Mrs. Ephraim told Lindsay, reaching for her.

Lindsay turned to Gina. "She wants me to go with her. Is that okay?"

"I guess so," Gina said. "You can't go into the x-ray room, but maybe it would give her some comfort to have you wait outside."

Gina pushed the gurney down the hallway, and Lindsay followed. As they made their way to the x-ray room, Lindsay prayed that she could bring Mrs. Ephraim some comfort.

Later on that afternoon, Lindsay nearly ran out the door and hopped into the Suburban at full speed. She was bursting with excitement about her day at the nursing home.

"Well, well, well," Frank said with a grin. "You look like you had a good day."

"You won't believe this!" Lindsay buckled her belt and took a deep breath. "The most incredible thing happened to me today."

"All right," Frank said, steering out onto the main road. "Lay it on me, Lindsay-girl."

"I met a woman who speaks Pennsylvania *Dietsch*!" She gestured wildly with her hands as she shared the story of meeting Mrs. Ephraim and helping her by translating what she said for Gina.

"That is incredible," Frank said. "I bet it's a great feeling to be able to help someone in need."

"Oh yes," Lindsay said, clasping her hands together. "It's the best feeling in the world. I went with her when she had her leg x-rayed and then I sat with her for hours discussing Lancaster County."

"How is her leg?" he asked.

"Oh yeah!" Lindsay laughed. "I almost forgot to tell you. It's bruised up, but it's not broken."

"That's good," Frank said. "I bet she'll look forward to seeing you next Saturday."

"I know," Lindsay said. "I can't wait to see her again either. I think I'm going to call Jessica tonight and tell her all about it. I haven't talked to her in a few days. Oh, and I need to write a letter to Katie too. I've been so focused on studying that I haven't written her in almost a week. I bet she's worried I ran off to Mexico or something."

Frank pulled into the driveway, and Lindsay jumped from the truck, bolting into a run as she hit the stairs to the second floor. She found Trisha sitting in her recliner, and she dropped onto the sofa across from her.

"Why, hello there." Trisha smiled. "You look like you're about to burst."

"I have to tell you about my day," Lindsay said.

Frank came through the door and stepped over to the recliner. "Lindsay is very excited."

Lindsay smiled at him. "I'll make dinner after I tell my story, okay?"

"Don't be silly," Frank said, heading toward the kitchen. "I'll take care of it."

"What?" Trisha looked surprised. "You'll cook?"

"I didn't say that," he called from the kitchen. "I'll order pizza."

Trisha rolled her eyes. "Typical." She then folded her hands and studied Lindsay. "Tell me what happened today. I'm all ears."

Lindsay shared her story about Mrs. Ephraim. By the time she finished with all of the details, the pizza had arrived. Frank served them pizza on paper plates and cans of Coke, and they ate in the family room in front of the television set.

After they ate, Lindsay cleaned up the dishes and then started toward her room.

"Lindsay," Trisha called after her. "When was the last time you spoke to your sister?"

Lindsay faced her. "I think it's been about a week."

"You should call her," Trisha said. "See how she's doing and if she's staying out of trouble."

"Great idea. I was planning on it." Lindsay grabbed the phone from the kitchen wall and dialed as she walked to her room.

Jessica picked up on the second ring, and loud music and voices blared in the background. "Yeah?" she yelled into the phone.

"Jess," Lindsay said, almost yelling back. "How are you?"

"What?" Jessica called. "I can't hear you. I'm in a club."

"Jess," Lindsay said, louder this time. "It's me—Lindsay." She sank onto the edge of her bed.

The background noise faded slightly, and Lindsay wondered if Jessica had moved to another place in the club or if the DJ was taking a break. She hoped the DJ went for a long coffee break.

"Hey," Jessica said. "How are you?"

"I'm doing well," Lindsay said, flopping onto her back on the bed. "Where are you?"

"At a club with Kim and Eddie," Jessica said. "We're celebrating."

"Celebrating?" Lindsay asked. "What's the occasion?"

"You're not going to believe this," Jessica gushed. "They're engaged!"

"What?" Lindsay sat up straight. "Engaged? How long have they known each other—a month at the most?"

"I know!" Jessica exclaimed. "It's crazy, right? But they say it's true love."

"True love?" Lindsay said. "Are you kidding me?"

The music blared again, and Lindsay rolled her eyes. So much for the DJ's coffee break.

"I can't hear you very well," Jessica yelled into phone. "Can I call you later?"

"Sure," Lindsay said with a frown. "Tell Kim and Eddie I said congratulations."

"I will," Jessica said. "Love ya. Bye!"

Before Lindsay could respond, the line went dead. She shook her head and placed the phone on her dresser.

"So much for sharing my news," she mumbled with a sigh. As usual, Jessica seemed to be too wrapped up in her own life to take an interest in Lindsay's.

Her eyes moved to her study guide, and she knew she needed to hit the books again. The test was coming fast and she wanted to be prepared. Sitting on the bed, she pulled out the study guide and flipped to the marked page where she'd left off last night.

After a few minutes of studying, her eyes panned over to Katie's letter sitting on her desk. She felt wretched for not responding to Katie's letter or calling her during the past week.

Although she knew she needed to study, she wanted to let Katie know she was doing okay. Also, she'd been contemplating Katie's comments about Matthew for the past week, wondering if Katie was right about Matthew's feelings for her. She needed to write Katie and find out if Matthew had said anything about her.

Crossing the room, she snatched a pen, the letter, and her stationery from the desk and then sat with her legs crossed on the bed. Using the study guide as a lap desk, she began to write.

Dear Katie,

It was wunderbaar to hear from you. I apologize that it has taken me so long to write back. I've been so busy helping Trisha and taking care of the house that the days fly by too quickly.

How are you and your family? How's Aenti Rebecca? I spoke to her a few days ago, and she sounded gut. I was hoping that she was feeling better and more energetic and not putting on a show for me in order to quell my worries.

I'm surprised and excited that Samuel finally asked Lizzie Anne to ride home with him. I had a feeling that he liked her, but I didn't know how long it would take him to act on those feelings. I bet they both are very froh and excited to be together.

Please don't feel like the fifth wheel with Samuel and Lizzie Anne. They shouldn't be alone until they are officially courting when Lizzie Anne is member of the church. By then, I'll be back home, and we'll have each other at the youth gatherings. Besides, you're a schee and sweet maedel, and I'm certain you'll find a special bu soon too.

Lindsay studied the words Katie had written about Matthew and bit her bottom lip while debating how to respond. While she was excited to see that Matthew missed her, the idea of becoming more than friends with him scared her. She thought back to the day that they had strolled around the pasture, and he'd made her the special necklace.

She stood and pulled out her small jewelry box where she kept her special trinkets. Opening the top, she spotted necklaces and rings that her parents had given her and also a gold cross that had belonged to her mother. Lifting the top tray, she peeked into the bottom of the box, where she kept larger items, such as coins and broaches from her grandmother. She sifted through the items until she came to the little Ziploc bag that contained the dandelion necklace.

She carried the bag back to the bed, placed it on the pillow next to her, and then she continued writing.

I'm very touched to hear that Matthew misses me. Of course, I miss him too. Please tell him that I'll be home soon, and I look forward to seeing him again. And Katie, I'm not jealous that Matthew gave you a ride home. You both are my dear *freinden*, and I trust you to spend time with him. Besides, he and I aren't courting, and I understand that he is enjoying your company while I'm gone. I'm glad that you two can talk.

Please give Emma and Junior hugs and kisses from me. I miss them so much! I'm so froh that you are helping Aenti Rebecca while I'm gone. Danki for taking gut care of her and the kinner.

I must tell you what happened today at the nursing home!

Lindsay launched into a description of her day, writing nearly three pages before a tap sounded on her door frame. She glanced up, finding Frank watching her.

"Hi," she said, pushing a lock of hair behind her ear.

"Hi," he said, folding his arms over his chest. "Trisha would like to speak with you."

Kaffee Kuchen *(Coffee Cake)*

For the sponge:

1/2 cup yeast
1/3 cup lukewarm water
1 cup milk
1/4 tsp salt
2 cups sifted flour

Crumble and soak yeast 25 minutes in lukewarm water. Scald milk, add salt, and let cool. Add yeast to lukewarm milk and mix enough flour to make thick batter. Beat smooth. Cover and let rise in warm place overnight.

For dough:

1/2 cup milk
1/2 cup butter
1 cup sugar
3/4 tsp salt
2 eggs
4 cups flour

Scald and cook milk. Cream butter, salt, and sugar. Add beaten eggs. Mix sponge in lukewarm water milk, then add butter mixture and enough flour to make soft dough. Knead by hand. Let dough rise until doubled. When light, turn on floured board and roll out gently until 1/2-inch thick. Place in buttered pans. Brush top with melted butter. Let rise until double. Sprinkle with sugar or cinnamon and bake at 375 degrees for 20 minutes.

19

Lindsay stepped into the den and found Trisha eyeing her with a frown. "Yes?" she asked. "Am I in trouble?"

Trisha laughed. "No, silly. You're not in trouble, but you do work too hard."

"Excuse me?" Lindsay dropped onto the sofa. "I don't understand what you mean."

"You work here all day during the week, study all night, and volunteer at the nursing home all day Saturday," Trisha said. "You never have any fun."

Frank stood behind the recliner and touched Trisha's shoulders. "She's right."

"I do have fun." She looked between them. "I do have fun. I like writing letters to my family back in Pennsylvania, and I love walking on the beach and swimming when I'm not studying. That's fun to me. Plus, I only have a few more weeks before the GED test. I can't stop studying."

"You can take a break from studying for one night," Trisha said. "When was the last time you talked to your friends Vicki and Heather?"

Lindsay shrugged. "I don't know. It's been a few weeks."

"Call them," Trisha said. "See if they can go out to a movie with you or maybe go grab some ice cream."

Lindsay studied Trisha's smile. "You're serious."

"Serious as a heart attack." Trisha nodded with emphasis. "You need to enjoy your youth."

"You're only young once," Frank chimed in.

Lindsay blew out a sigh. "Fine. I'll go call Vicki." She retreated to her room and found Vicki's number on a piece of paper lying on her dresser. As she dialed, she sat on the chair next to her desk.

"Hello?" Vicki's voice sounded into the phone.

"Vicki?" Lindsay asked. "This is Lindsay Bedford."

"Oh, hey, Lindsay!" Vicki called. "How are you?"

"I'm doing fine." Lindsay studied the toes of her black sneakers while she spoke. "How about you?"

"Great," Vicki said as giggles and hoots sounded behind her. "We're camping at the Outer Banks this weekend. There's a group of us. I thought about calling you, but I knew you were tied up with your aunt. I'm sorry I didn't invite you, but I assumed you couldn't come."

"Oh," Lindsay said. "I understand. I hope you have fun."

"What did you need?" Vicki asked.

"I was just going to see if you wanted to catch a movie or something," Lindsay said, feeling stupid for calling.

"We'll be back Sunday night," Vicki said. "How about we get together next week?"

"Sure," Lindsay said with a shrug. "That would be fun."

"Cool," Vicki said. "I'll call you. Heather was just asking me if I'd heard from you. She'll be excited to hear that you called. We'll all catch a movie next week."

"Sounds good," Lindsay said.

"Take care," Vicki said.

"You too," Lindsay said. "Bye." She hung up and stared at the waves out the window. What made her think Vicki and Heather would be home on a Saturday night? Of course they were camping at the Outer Banks. They were all getting ready to leave for college, so it made sense that they were out having a great time before hitting the road for their new lives. But what would be Lindsay's new life?

"Do you need a lift somewhere?" Frank asked.

Lindsay found him standing in the doorway looking hopeful. How sad that Frank was counting on Lindsay's social life to perk up the evening.

"No," she said. "Vicki and her friends are camping at the Outer Banks this weekend."

"Oh." Frank looked disappointed. "I'm sorry."

"It's okay." Lindsay forced a smile. "I have studying to do anyway." She placed the phone on the desk. "Vicki said she'd call me next week, and we'd hit a movie or something."

He rubbed the stubble on his chin. "Sounds good."

Lindsay finished up her letter to Katie, and after addressing the envelope, she grabbed her study guide from the bed, sat on the desk chair, and tried to concentrate on the material on the page. However, she couldn't help but think about how her sister was dancing the night away in a club while Vicki and her friends were laughing and roasting marshmallows on a beach in the Outer Banks. Back home, her friends were probably at a youth gathering and also having a good time. Although she wasn't jealous or resentful, Lindsay couldn't help but think that she was missing out on something.

Lindsay pursed her lips and considered that thought. No, maybe the issue wasn't that she was missing out on something. Perhaps it was something more basic than that.

She was lonely.

She glanced down at the dandelion necklace. She wondered what Matthew was doing this evening. Was he at a youth gathering? Was he missing her too?

The phone rang and she grabbed it from the desk.

"Hello?" she asked.

"Hi," a male voice said. "Is Lindsay there, please?"

Lindsay's heart pounded in her chest. Was it Matthew? But it didn't sound like Matthew's voice.

"This is Lindsay," she said.

"Hey," he said. "This is Taylor Lane. How are you?"

"Taylor," she said, surprised to hear his voice. "I'm fine. How are you?"

"I'm doing well." Taylor hesitated. "I was wondering if you were busy tonight."

"Oh." She paused, surprised by the question. "No, not really."

"Would you like to go to a movie or something?" he asked. "I thought you might want to get together before you head back to Pennsylvania."

"Sure," she said. "What time?"

"I'll pick you up in twenty minutes," he said. "Sound good?"

"Yes," she said.

"See you then," he said. "Bye."

"Bye." Lindsay hung up the phone, and her heart raced. She was going out with Taylor Lane. Was it a date? But she hardly knew him!

She rushed to the mirror and brushed out her long hair and pulled it back in a ponytail. She then changed into a fresh blouse and jumper before heading to the den where Trisha and Frank were watching a movie.

"What's up?" Frank asked.

"Taylor Lane is picking me up for a movie," Lindsay said. She returned the phone to the base in the kitchen and then returned to the den, where Trisha stared at her, wide-eyed.

"You have a date with Taylor Lane?" Trisha asked. "How about that!"

"I don't think it's a date," Lindsay cautioned. "I think it's just a friendly outing."

"Nothing wrong with that," Frank said. "It's good for you to get out and away from that GED book for one night."

Lindsay fiddled with her skirt while standing by the

window. When a small pickup truck pulled into the driveway, she grabbed her purse from the coffee table and started toward the door. "Oh, Taylor's here. See you later," she said.

"Have fun," Trisha and Frank called in unison.

Lindsay rushed down the stairs and out to the driveway where Taylor stood by his truck.

"Hi," she said, pushing her long ponytail off her shoulder.

"Hi." He gestured toward the truck. "Let me get the door for you."

She followed him around the truck, and he opened the passenger door. "Thank you," she said as she climbed in.

He went around to the driver's side and jumped in. "Are you hungry?" he asked, buckling his seat belt.

She shook her head. "Not really, but thank you."

"Are you in the mood for a movie?" he asked.

She shrugged. "Sure. I haven't been to a movie in a long time."

"Great," he said. "We can head to the theater and see what's playing in the next hour or so."

While he drove, he talked about work and the weather. She nodded and smiled, but her thoughts moved to Lancaster County, wondering what her friends were doing and what they would say if they knew she was riding in a truck with a boy and heading to the movies. Although she was happy to be out with Taylor, she missed her friends back home.

Taylor steered into the parking lot of the theater located in Strawbridge Marketplace. After parking, they walked together to the ticket booth and studied the time listings.

"So, what are you in the mood for?" he asked. "Action, animation, chick flick, or a comedy?"

Lindsay tilted her head and twisted her lips while she considered the question. "How about a good comedy?"

"I don't know if it's good, but it's supposed to be a comedy." He fished his wallet from the back pocket of his jeans.

"Oh no," Lindsay said, pulling her wallet from her purse. "I have money."

"Don't be silly," he said. "I can buy a ticket for my friend."

"I'll pay for the popcorn," Lindsay said.

He smiled. "I'll go along with that. Far be it from me to argue with a pretty girl."

Lindsay felt her cheeks flush as Taylor paid for the tickets. He held the door for her and they stepped into the lobby. After purchasing a bucket of popcorn and two sodas, they headed into the theater and sat in the center of a row.

"How was your day?" he asked as he scooped a handful of popcorn from the overflowing bucket.

"It was great, actually," Lindsay said. "Something really exciting happened to me."

"Really?" He looked interested. "Tell me all about it."

She shared her story about Mrs. Ephraim and how she was able to help her. He listened with interest showing on his face.

"That's really special," he said when she was finished with her story.

"Thank you," she said before sipping her soda.

"I'm glad that you're enjoying our community project," he said. "It can be rewarding when you help someone else."

"That's very true," Lindsay said. "My sister has really cut me down with her lectures about getting an education, but I feel like I made a difference in someone's life and it didn't take a high school diploma or a bachelor's degree to do it."

He looked confused. "Jessica makes you feel bad because you're not going to college?"

She frowned. "That's an understatement."

"Why would she do that?" Taylor grabbed another handful of popcorn. "There's no rule that says everyone has to go to college."

Lindsay chewed a mouthful of hot, greasy popcorn before she responded. "Tell her that. She thinks I'm wasting my life living among the Amish and not pursuing a degree. I don't want to go to college, but I'm studying to get my GED. I'll take the test in a few weeks."

"That's fantastic." He touched her shoulder. "Good for you!"

"Thanks." She shook her head. "I just hope I don't flunk it. If I do, I'll never hear the end of it from Jessica."

He gave her a look of disbelief. "You won't flunk it. I think you're smarter than you give yourself credit for."

"Thanks, but the test is really hard," she insisted. "I've taken a few practice tests, and I've barely passed."

"But you passed, right?"

"Yes, I did."

"Well, there you go," he said, lifting his drink from the cup holder. "You can do it. Just have faith."

She chewed more popcorn and couldn't help savoring the taste. Boy had she missed movie popcorn! There was nothing like it. She wondered if Rebecca would let her buy some of the popcorn that she could make on the stove.

Lindsay turned her focus back to her friend. "Are you excited about college?"

He shrugged. "I guess so. I've never been a fan of school, but I know I don't want to work in retail for the rest of my life. I just don't know what I want to do."

"You'll figure it out," she said. "Are most of your friends going away to school?"

Sipping his drink, he shook his head. "I'd say a handful of them are going away, but there are a few who aren't going to school at all. So, your sister's rule that everyone must go to college in order to make a life isn't true. You can make a life without college, but it may not be as financially stable. It all depends on what path you choose."

Lindsay nodded. "Yeah, you're right. I know that she wants what's best for me, but I'm tired of her trying to make decisions for me. I think she feels like she has to take over for our mom, but she really doesn't."

"What do you like best about living with the Amish?" he asked.

"Family," she said without thinking twice. "I love being a part of my aunt's family and having the extended loving family in our church district."

She told him about the Kauffman cousins and also about Lizzie Anne and Matthew. She was about to share about the bakery when the lights dimmed and the previews began. Leaning back in the seat, Lindsay held the bucket of popcorn in her lap and lost herself in the movie.

"Did you like the movie?" Taylor asked from the driver's seat as the truck rumbled through the parking lot toward General Booth Boulevard.

"Yeah," Lindsay said with a nod. "It was really good. Very funny. It was nice to see a movie again."

"I guess movies aren't allowed in the Amish community, huh?" he asked.

"No," she said. "No movies. No television." Lindsay held onto her large soda, wondering why she thought she could finish a drink that big. She should've gotten the smaller size. "The Amish believe that movies and television can be a negative influence that takes the focus off important things, like God and family."

"Does that mean you'd be in trouble if your aunt found out you went to the movies?"

She shook her head. "No, she wouldn't be upset. I haven't joined the church yet, so I can pretty much do whatever I want, within certain limits."

He glanced over at her. "Once you join the church, then you're held to all of the rules?"

"That's right," she said.

"Are you planning to join the church?"

She sipped the drink. "I'm not ready yet, but I think I will someday."

"I'm glad that you like it there," he said. "I sometimes wondered how you were doing and if you were happy in Pennsylvania."

She studied his expression. "Really? You wondered about me?"

He nodded. "I did."

They drove in silence. Taylor negotiated the twists and turns of Sandbridge Road while they made their journey out to the beach house.

"Do you think you'd be up for another movie?" he asked.

"Sure," she said. "This was fun."

"Great." He steered onto Sandfiddler Road and into the driveway of the beach house. "Thanks for coming with me. Movies are no fun alone."

"Thank you," she said, gathering up her purse from the floorboard. "See you tomorrow in church."

"Have a good night," he said.

As she climbed the stairs to the second level of the house, Lindsay smiled, thankful that she'd made a good friend.

She found the family room empty, and on the way to her room, she heard the television sounding from Trisha's room. Glancing at her bed, she found her notepad Although she'd had fun with Taylor, she couldn't stop thinking about Matthew. She felt the urge to write him a letter but wasn't quite sure what to say.

While it was easy to write to Katie and Lizzie Anne, writing to Matthew was very different. She missed him but didn't want to sound too eager. Lifting her pen, she began to write:

Dear Matthew,

How are you? I'm enjoying my time here in Virginia Beach, but I do miss home.

Aunt Trisha is doing much better and is progressing with her therapy. I've gotten involved with the youth group at my former church and I'm volunteering at a nursing home. I'm very excited because I was able to help a patient who speaks Dietsch. She's from Pennsylvania too.

How's work? How are your sister and her family?

Katie mentioned that you've been going to singings. I've been able to see some of my old school friends, which is nice.

Aunt Trisha's house is on the beach, and every day I go for a walk and a swim. It's relaxing to be outside by the waves.

I hope you're doing well. Please write back when you can.

Sincerely,

Lindsay

As she sealed the envelope and addressed it, Lindsay hoped that he'd write back.

20

Three weeks later, Lindsay burst into the den holding the certificate high above her head like a balloon. "I did it!" she yelled to Trisha. "I passed! I got my GED!"

"Yay!" Trisha yelled. "I knew you could do it. Give me a hug."

Rushing over, Lindsay enveloped Trisha in a tight squeeze. "I'm so relieved. I was so certain I was going to flunk it."

"I told her that she doubts herself too much," Frank said, tossing his truck keys onto the coffee table. "I knew she could do it all along."

"I agree," Trisha said. "This calls for a celebration."

"I agree," Frank said with a grin. "Let's go to dinner."

"Dinner?" Lindsay said, studying Trisha. "But I thought you weren't thrilled about going out on crutches?"

Trisha waved off the thought. "Hopefully I'll get my walking cast on Monday. The doctor said that I should get good news at my next appointment. I can hobble around to celebrate this momentous occasion."

Lindsay smiled. "Great. Let's go!"

After a delicious dinner at Trisha's favorite Italian restaurant, Frank drove into a shopping center and parked in front of a cellular store.

"What are we doing here?" Lindsay asked.

"We wanted to get you a nice gift since you worked so hard to get your GED," Trisha explained. "Go in with Frank and pick out a phone."

"What?" Lindsay asked. "You're getting me a cell phone?"

"Yes," Trisha said. "Go in the store and pick it out."

Lindsay shook her head. "You don't need to do that."

"Come on," Frank said, wrenching open his door. "If you don't come with me, I'll just pick one out for you."

Lindsay followed him into the store and stared at the sea of complicated looking phones. She felt as if she'd walked into another world, a world that was foreign and strange to her after living with the Amish for four years.

"What do you think?" Frank asked. "Do you want internet access or do you just want the ability to text?"

Lindsay shook her head. "I have no idea."

He pulled out his rugged-looking phone and flipped it open. "I don't use internet really, but I text pretty often. Here. Take a look at it." He handed it to her. "What do you think?"

"Honestly," she said, turning it over in her hands. "I don't have the need for a phone, and I hate to see you spend the money. My friends and family back in Pennsylvania don't use them, and I'm not sure how I could keep it charged when I go back."

"But you can use it while you're here with us," he said. "You can call your friends, like Taylor and Vicki."

Lindsay considered his suggestion. She'd gone to the movies with Vicki and Heather last week, and Taylor took her out for ice cream. She could call them to make plans, but she could also use the house phone for that.

She looked up and saw the excitement in Frank's eyes. She knew she had to let him get her the phone, but she felt as if she would disappoint Rebecca and Daniel if they found out she had one. Cellular phones were a gray area in some Amish districts, but the bishop in the Kauffmans' district didn't allow them except for business or special circumstances. What would she tell Daniel and Rebecca if they found out she'd gotten a cell phone?

However, on the other hand, she couldn't bear the idea of hurting Frank and Trisha either.

"Okay," she finally said, moving over to a display of phones. "Which one do you think is best for me?"

Twenty minutes later, they walked to the Suburban with a phone that included a keyboard, complete with a hot pink cover. Lindsay climbed into the back and fastened her seat belt.

"What did you get?" Trisha asked from the passenger seat.

Lindsay handed her the pink phone. "The salesman said it's the best for texting."

"Great!" Trisha said, examining it and then handing it back to her. "Good choice."

"Thank you," Lindsay said, slipping it into her purse.

Frank discussed work on the way back to the house, and Lindsay stared out the window, contemplating her time in Virginia and wondering how everyone was back in Bird-in-Hand. She wished that she could go back soon. Although she enjoyed being with Frank and Trisha, she couldn't stop the feeling that she didn't belong here. The cell phone seemed to be a symbol of how much she didn't fit in.

The Suburban bounced into the driveway at the beach house, and Lindsay hopped out. She yanked open Trisha's door and held out her hand, which Trisha grasped.

"You need to call Jessica," Trisha said as Lindsay helped her climb down to the driveway. "She'll be so proud of you when she finds out you got your GED. You can call her from your new cell phone."

"Good idea." Lindsay nodded. "I will."

Frank appeared with the crutches and assisted Trisha on her journey to the door. Once they were inside, Frank hoisted Trisha up in his arms and carried her up the stairs while Lindsay followed behind them with the crutches.

Frank carried Trisha into their room to help her change into her pajamas, and Lindsay slipped into her own room and sat on the bed. She pulled the phone from her purse and studied it.

She then kicked off her shoes and headed outside through the kitchen to the deck. She descended the stairs and crossed to her favorite spot on the sand. Staring across at the waves she couldn't help but think that the beach calmed her. Sitting on the sand was relaxing for her, much like sitting in the porch swing back home at Daniel's house.

Lindsay dialed Jessica's cell phone number and waited for her to answer.

"Hello?" Jessica asked, sounding confused.

"Jess," Lindsay said. "It's Lindsay."

"Lindsay?" Jessica asked. "Where are you calling from? I don't recognize this number."

"It's my new cell phone," Lindsay said, crossing her legs at her ankles.

"Your new cell?" Jessica exclaimed. "You, my Amish wannabe sister, got a cell phone? How'd that happen?"

Lindsay rolled her eyes at the sarcastic comment. "It was a gift from Trisha and Frank to congratulate me on getting my GED today."

"What?" Jessica said. "You got your GED today?"

"Yes," Lindsay said with a smile. "I did it."

"I'm so proud of you! That's fantastic. Mom and Dad are smiling down on you."

Lindsay looked out at the waves. "I hope so."

"You must be flying high," Jessica said. "I wish I were there to celebrate with you. Did Trisha and Frank take you out to eat or anything?"

"Yeah," Lindsay said. "We ate at Little Italy and then went to get the phone. I'm so glad that all of that studying paid off. I really worked hard for more than a month."

"See? You're good at school," Jessica said. "You just don't

give yourself enough credit, and you used to give up too easily. Now you can start looking into college. Maybe you can come to Richmond and go to school with me. I could set up an interview for you with the admissions person, since I know her personally."

Lindsay bit her bottom lip and took a deep breath to calm her frayed nerves. Her sister was doing just what Lindsay had feared—taking her GED achievement and turning it into a reason to nag her more about college.

"Jessica," she said, fighting to keep her voice calm. "I don't want to go to college, and I want you to drop the subject now."

"Why don't you want to go?" Jessica asked, sounding annoyed. "You just proved to yourself that you can set a goal and achieve it. College is the exact same way. Is it the money? You know Mom and Dad set up a trust for us."

"But not everyone wants to go to college." Lindsay sat up and mustered all of her confidence from the pit of her stomach. "It's like Taylor told me—he has friends who went away to school, and he has friends who decided to get a job and work. Taylor is going to go to TCC because he's not sure what he wants to do. Not everyone is going to follow your path, and I'm really sick and tired of you pressuring me."

Jessica blew out a loud and dramatic sigh. "Lindsay, your whole problem is that you don't see your own worth."

"No, that's not my problem," Lindsay fired back. "I miss my family and friends back in Pennsylvania. I don't want to go to Richmond with you."

"So then go to community college back near Lancaster," Jessica said simply. "You could go to school during the day and still live with Aunt Rebecca. She'd never kick you out. You can still have the family and the friends but also get an education. I want to see you succeed. It's my job to look out for you. I care about you."

"Jessica, you just don't get it. Or maybe you're not listening to me yet again." Lindsay held her breath for a moment and then she shook her head and let the truth seep through her. "Jessica, the truth is that I want to be Amish. That's why I don't want to go college. I'm happy and I'm content with the life I've built with Aunt Rebecca and Uncle Daniel. I want to be Amish, so you can just drop the college lecture."

Jessica was silent for a moment, and Lindsay's heart pounded in her chest. The revelation and saying the words out loud made her feel a little light-headed. She'd finally figured out where she belonged, and the knowledge seemed to set her free from the burden of her anxiety.

"Well, I have to go," Jessica finally said. "Kim is ready to head out. We're having dinner with Eddie and some of his friends. We can continue this conversation later."

"Fine," Lindsay said standing up and brushing the sand off her jumper. "I don't think there's anything else to say. I'll never be like you, and I'm tired of you trying to change me. As I've said before, if you can't respect me, then we have nothing to talk about."

"Lindsay, don't take it that way," Jessica said. "You know I only want what's best for you."

"Look, I gotta go too," Lindsay said. "Have fun with your friends." She disconnected the call and climbed the stairs leading back into the kitchen, where she found Frank scooping vanilla ice cream into a bowl.

He faced her and gave her a concerned expression. "You okay?"

"Yeah, I think so," Lindsay said, pulling the sliding glass door closed with a whoosh.

Frank held up the scoop. "Would you like some?"

"Sure," Lindsay said, placing the cell phone onto the table. She opened the cabinet and pulled out a white bowl. She contemplated her conversation with Jessica and her revelation while Frank filled the bowls with ice cream and then smothered it with chocolate sauce.

"I hope you like a lot of chocolate," he said, carrying the bowls to the table.

Lindsay fetched two spoons from the drawer and sat across from him. "Thank you."

"Did you call Jessica?" he asked, nodding toward her phone.

"Yeah," Lindsay said, frowning despite the delicious dessert.

Frank gave her a suspicious expression. "You don't look happy. Did Jessica give you a hard time about your GED?"

Lindsay shook her head and studied her bowl of ice cream. "She told me she was proud of me and then she started nagging me about college again. I've had enough of her constant criticism. It's time she stopped hassling me about it."

Frank scooped more ice cream into his mouth and then swiped his sprouting goatee with a paper napkin. "I've never told you this, but my older brother is a lot like Jessica."

"Really?" Lindsay placed her spoon in the bowl and studied Frank with surprise. "I had no idea."

"That's part of the reason why he and I don't talk much," he explained. "Dean had ideas about what I should do with my life, and I had my own ideas. He never understood why I didn't join the family business and stay in Roanoke or have children like he did. But Trisha and I wanted different things. It was our choice not to have children, and it was our choice to build a house here at the beach. I got to the point where I couldn't stand his comments and I stopped answering the phone when I saw his number come up. I also avoided visiting my parents' place when I knew he was there."

Lindsay frowned. "So you think I should stop talking to Jessica."

He shook his head. "I didn't say that. But I do think that you should trust your own judgment and not let Jessica's words get to you."

Lindsay shook her head. "I know I should, but she seems to always upset me."

"I know." He folded his arms across his chest. "My brother's words used to cut me like a knife, but one morning I woke up and realized that I was my own person. We may have the same parents, but we are different people. You and Jessica are siblings, and you share the same DNA. But you're Lindsay, and she's Jessica. You'll never be the same. Don't let her push you into something you don't want. Your happiness is what matters."

She felt some of the tension ease in her shoulders. "Thank you."

"When you feel yourself getting frustrated by her words, pray about it." He lifted his spoon. "I believe in the power of prayer. It's helped me a lot over the years."

"It's helped me too," Lindsay said softly.

"You're a very special girl," he said. "Don't let Jessica's words damage your spirit. Promise me that you won't give Jessica the power to ruin the things that matter most to you."

"I promise." She smiled.

They talked and laughed about different subjects before finishing their ice cream and heading to bed. After changing into her nightclothes, Lindsay stared at the ceiling and tried to stop Jessica's words from echoing through her mind. Her sister had managed to take the joy out of her accomplishment.

Closing her eyes, she sent a prayer up to God, asking Him to give her a sign of where she belonged and what she was meant to do with her life.

Both Frank's words and Lindsay's decision to be Amish echoed through Lindsay's mind as she made her way past the line of wheelchairs in the nursing home the following morning. She'd fallen asleep thinking of Frank and Dean and the way that Frank managed to ignore and disregard Dean's criticism. She wished she had that strength. She hoped that she could squelch the anger and frustration Jessica gave her every time she harassed Lindsay about furthering her education.

"Lindsay!" a voice hollered. "Lindsay!"

Spinning, Lindsay found Gina rushing toward her.

"It's so good to see you," Gina said, sidling up to her. "I think Mrs. Ephraim has been asking about you. She'll be very excited to visit with you again."

"Good," Lindsay said. "How is she doing?"

Gina gave a halfhearted nod. "I think she's okay. She seems to have a bit of congestion and a cough, but I think she'll be just fine."

Lindsay and Gina walked to Mrs. Ephraim's room.

"Thank you for spending time with her," Gina said. "Mrs. Ephraim hasn't had a visitor in a very long time, and I think you're a blessing in her life." She patted Lindsay's arm before heading down the hallway.

Lindsay smiled. *I'm a blessing in her life.*

She again thought of Frank's words from last night. No, she wouldn't give Jessica the power to make her feel worthless. Bringing joy to a woman like Mrs. Ephraim was just as worthy, if not more worthy, than pursuing a bachelor's degree.

Lindsay greeted Mrs. Ephraim's roommate, who was eating a piece of toast and watching television, and then crossed to Mrs. Ephraim's side of the room.

Mrs. Ephraim looked up from her dish of scrambled eggs and toast.

"*Wie geht's,*" Lindsay said, sitting in the plastic chair next to her.

"*Gut,*" Mrs. Ephraim said. "It's *gut* to see you."

"You too," Lindsay responded in *Dietsch*. "How are you feeling?"

Mrs. Ephraim shook her head and pointed to her chest. "I have a bad cough, and my chest feels very tight."

"I'll tell Gina." Lindsay stood, and Mrs. Ephraim reached out and took her hand.

"Please stay and visit with me," Mrs. Ephraim said. "Tell me about your week."

Lindsay shared her news about passing the GED and also talked about going to the movies with Vicki and spending time with Taylor. While she was talking, Mrs. Ephraim listened and finished her breakfast.

While Lindsay watched Mrs. Ephraim straighten her prayer covering, she wondered how she felt about her daughter leaving the Amish community.

"Do you miss your *dochder*?" Lindsay asked while crossing her legs and smoothing the skirt of her jumper.

Mrs. Ephraim frowned. "Very much."

"Do you hear from her?"

The elderly lady shook her head. "I was not happy when she left our church district. I should've been more supportive of her when she married an English man, but my Mary never forgave me for telling her that she'd made a mistake by leaving the church. I never accepted her husband, and I wasn't a *gut mammi* to her *kinner*." She covered her mouth as a deep, rattling cough stole her breath and her words for a few moments.

Lindsay stood and poured a cup of water from the pitcher on Mrs. Ephraim's lunch table.

After drinking several sips, the elderly lady caught her breath and continued her story. "When I became *grank* after my husband died, Mary put me in this home instead of letting me live with her. I wish she would forgive me. She came to see me the day before she moved to California, but I was too proud to apologize. I wish I could take back my mistake and tell her how much I love and miss her."

Lindsay spotted a notepad on the dresser, and an idea burst into her mind. "Do you have Mary's address in California?"

"She sends me a Christmas card every year." Mrs. Ephraim

pointed toward the dresser. "I've kept every one, and they are in the top drawer over there."

Lindsay found the pile of envelopes and cards in the drawer and opened the one on top, finding a card with photos of two little boys inside. "They're *schee buwe*," she said, holding up the photo of the boys wearing matching red sweaters and smiling in front of a backdrop of a Christmas tree. "You must miss them."

A single tear trickled down Mrs. Ephraim's wrinkly cheek, and Lindsay handed her a tissue from the box on the windowsill. "I'm sorry," she said. "I didn't mean to upset you."

Mrs. Ephraim wiped her eyes and coughed. "I wish I could fix it." Her voice rattled. "I carry so much regret."

Lindsay plucked the notepad and a pen from the dresser. "I'll help you write a letter to Mary."

"Oh no," Mrs. Ephraim said. "I could never do it."

"*Ya*, you can." Lindsay's head bobbed up and down with conviction. "We'll make this right." She took the elderly lady's hand in hers. "We'll do this together. I'll write the letter and mail it on the way home."

Mrs. Ephraim coughed and then sniffed. "*Danki*."

Slowly, Mrs. Ephraim dictated a letter to her in *Dietsch*, and Lindsay translated it into English and wrote it down. The elderly lady expressed her sorrow and regret for losing her daughter and asked to be forgiven and accepted back into Mary's and her family's life.

After she finished dictating the letter, Mrs. Ephraim leaned back and closed her eyes. "I must sleep now. I'm very tired."

Lindsay folded up the letter and stood. "You rest." She leaned down and kissed Mrs. Ephraim's cheek. "I'll tell Gina you're not feeling well and I'll come back and check on you later."

"*Danki*," Mrs. Ephraim said, taking hold of Lindsay's hand. "*Ich liebe dich*."

Lindsay fought back tears as she repeated the sentiment. She then moved out to the hallway, holding the letter and an envelope with Mary's address. She found Gina sitting behind the desk at the nurse's station.

"Mrs. Ephraim is complaining of tightness in her chest," Lindsay said. "Her cough also sounds pretty bad."

Gina pulled out a chart and began flipping through it. "Thank you for telling me. I'll talk to Cheryl and tell her to order an x-ray." She wrote in the chart and then looked up at Lindsay. "Did you have a nice visit?"

Lindsay held up the letter. "She told me about how she'd lost touch with her daughter, and I had her dictate a letter to me. Once I find an envelope and a stamp, I'll mail this."

Gina gave a sad smile. "Lindsay, that is so wonderful. You truly are a very special girl." Gina rooted around in the desk and pulled out an envelope and stamp. "Here you go. Thank you for all you've done for Mrs. Ephraim. I've never seen her smile as much as she has this week."

"I'm happy that I can help." Lindsay put the letter in the envelope, sealed it, and then addressed it. "I'm going to check on Mrs. Warren. I'll see you later."

"Thank you again," Gina said.

"You're welcome." Lindsay moved through a knot of wheelchairs and stepped toward Mrs. Warren's door. When a hand touched her shoulder, she turned and found Andrea smiling at her.

"Hi," Andrea said. "How are you?"

"I'm doing fine," Lindsay said. "I didn't expect to see you here. I thought you volunteered on Tuesdays."

"My work schedule changed. I wanted to call you and tell you that I was coming today. You have to give me your number." Andrea pulled out her cell phone, and Lindsay recited her number, which Andrea programmed into her phone. Andrea pointed toward a break room located across the hall. "Want to go sit for a bit?"

"Sure." Lindsay followed Andrea into the room, where they

each purchased a bottle of water from the vending machine before sitting at a small table.

"What have you been doing today?" Andrea asked.

Lindsay held up the envelope from the pocket of her jumper and explained how she'd translated a letter for Mrs. Ephraim.

Andrea listened to the story with her eyes wide with surprise. "Lindsay, that is so amazing that you were able to help her. You have a gift."

Lindsay blanched. "You think so?"

"Are you kidding?" Andrea leaned forward. "You changed Mrs. Ephraim's life. You not only helped this woman communicate with the rest of the nurses, but you also helped her reconcile with her daughter after years of regret and sorrow. You're like a hero!"

Lindsay blushed. "Don't pin a medal on me yet. We're not sure how her daughter will react to the letter."

"If she wants to do the right thing, she'll forgive her mother and come visit. Maybe she'll even move her out to California so Mrs. Ephraim can be a part of her children's life."

Lindsay held up the bottle of water as if to toast the idea. "I'll definitely say a prayer for that."

"Me too." Andrea smiled. "You're amazing."

"Thank you," Lindsay said softly.

Later that evening, Lindsay found an envelope addressed to her sitting on her bed. Her heart thumped in her chest when she spotted the return address from Matthew Glick. Her fingers shook with excitement as she opened the envelope and unfolded the letter.

Dear Lindsay,

I was froh to receive your letter. I apologize for taking so much time to respond. Although I've sat down several times to write this letter, each time I've struggled to form the right words. I suppose I'm not much of a letter writer and I never know what to say.

That's wunderbaar you're enjoying your time in Virginia. I'm glad to hear that your aenti is doing better. I would imagine that the woman you're helping at the nursing home is very thankful to have you there. It's surprising that your knowledge of Dietsch has been helpful in Virginia.

I'm staying busy at the furniture store. It seems we can never get caught up on our projects, but we're happy that the Lord has blessed us with an abundance of work.

Youth gatherings aren't the same without you. Katie has most likely told you that Samuel and Lizzie Anne are spending a lot of time together. I knew that they would eventually start courting, but I didn't think Samuel would act this soon since Lizzie Anne isn't baptized yet.

Katie shared with me that she's been helping Rebecca and Daniel. Rebecca hasn't been feeling well, but I haven't heard what the doctor has said about her illness. I hope that she's doing better.

I've been working on a project at night in my barn. If you ever feel like calling and talking, you can find me out there in the evenings. I'll include the number to my barn phone at the bottom of this page.

I look forward to having more of your whoopie pies when you get home. My sister attempted to make them the other night, but they were nowhere near as good as yours.

Please respond and let me know when you'll be back in Bird-in-Hand.

Most sincerely,
Matthew

P.S. I've included a little gift for you. I hope it brings you happy memories and smiles when you open it.

Lindsay looked back in the envelope and found a smaller envelope stuffed inside. She ripped it open and pulled out a small necklace made of daisies. She laughed and put the chain over her head. Closing her eyes, she hoped that Matthew wouldn't think about making a flowery necklace for another girl. With a grin on a face and her cheeks heating with excitement, she pulled out a notepad and began to reply to him.

21

Rebecca sat at the kitchen table Tuesday morning while her children and husband ate. She couldn't even think of eating after the night she'd spent in the bathroom with an upset stomach. When a sudden overwhelming sick feeling rained down on her, she rose and rushed to the bathroom.

"*Was iss letz?*" Daniel called after her.

Entering the bathroom, Rebecca slammed the door behind her. She lowered herself to the floor in front of the commode and was sick. She then stood and washed her face with a cool washcloth. She wished she could escape this horrible sick feeling that continued to haunt her all day and night.

She then lowered herself onto the commode. After she was finished, she looked down and found blood.

"Oh no," she whispered, her heart racing. "No, no, no!" She cracked the door open. "Daniel! You must get me to the doctor. *Dummle*!"

Rebecca wiped her eyes while sitting next to Daniel in the van later that morning.

"Dr. Fitzgerald said everything will be okay," Daniel said softly, taking her hands in his. "You just have to stay on complete bed rest. You can't lift a finger. Katie and I will take care of everything. I'll talk to my *mamm* and she'll help us too. We just may have to let the community know that you're having complications so that everyone can pitch in and help us. You and the *boppli* will be fine."

Rebecca nodded, holding her breath in an attempt not to cry.

He lifted her chin with the tip of his finger, angling her face so that she looked into his blue eyes. *"Mei liewe, ich liebe dich,"* he whispered. "We'll be just fine. Hold on to your faith."

She nodded again, unable to speak due to the lump swelling in her throat.

"Let's go inside and tell Katie that you're all right," he said. "She was very worried when we rushed out the door."

Rebecca followed Daniel into the kitchen, where Katie sat at the table with the children, who were eating a snack.

Katie jumped up and ran over to them. "How are you?"

"She's going to be just fine." Daniel motioned toward the family room. "Let's talk in here."

Rebecca sat on the sofa while Katie and Daniel stood by the door.

"The doctor said that Rebecca needs to be on complete bed rest starting now," he explained. "She shouldn't get out of bed except to use the bathroom. I need to take her back to see him in a week."

Her face full of worry, Katie looked at Rebecca. "You go up and stay in bed, and I'll find a little bell you can ring whenever you need something. I'll take care of everything. I can stay at night and cook and clean up the kitchen too. Maybe I should just move in and sleep in Lindsay's room so that I can help at night if the *kinner* wake up."

Daniel pulled on his beard, considering the suggestion. "That may be a *wunderbaar* idea. I'll have to talk to your *dat.*"

Katie gave Rebecca a pleading look. "Don't you agree that I should stay? I'm really worried about you."

"*Ya,*" Rebecca whispered while fighting back her threatening tears. "Maybe you should."

Katie stepped over to her and took her arm. "Let me help you upstairs."

They climbed the stairs together, and Katie guided Rebecca into the master bedroom. She helped Rebecca change into her nightgown and then pulled back the covers for her.

"*Danki,*" Rebecca said, snuggling under the sheet. "You've been a tremendous help."

Katie patted Rebecca's arm. "You just take it easy. Don't get up at all. I'll be here as soon as you call for me."

Rebecca touched Katie's ivory cheek. "You're a *gut maedel.* Please do me one favor, *ya?*"

"What's that, *aenti?*"

"Please don't tell Lindsay that I'm not doing well. I don't want her to worry." Rebecca rolled onto her side. "I'm going to sleep now."

"Okay," Katie whispered.

Later that afternoon, Katie peeked into Emma's room and found her snoring on her belly in her crib. She moved to Junior's room and spotted him asleep on his side while sucking his thumb and hugging his favorite teddy bear. Tiptoeing down the hallway she looked in on Rebecca, who was also asleep.

She made her way down the stairs to the kitchen, where she poured herself a glass of tea and sat at the table. Flipping through an Amish furniture catalog, she pondered Rebecca. While she knew her brother had been right about keeping secrets and obeying their elders, Katie couldn't stop feeling like Rebecca's request to keep her pregnancy complications from Lindsay was wrong.

Katie knew Lindsay like she knew her sisters, and she believed with her whole heart that Lindsay would want to be here to help Rebecca. She also believed that Lindsay would be upset and very hurt if she found out that this information had been deliberately kept from her.

Closing her eyes, Katie sent up a prayer asking God if she should disobey Rebecca and write a letter to Lindsay, telling her everything about Rebecca's condition.

She opened her eyes, and the thought of writing the letter continued to poke at her. She moved to the counter and found a notepad and pen in a drawer.

Sitting down at the table, she took a deep breath.

"I hope Rebecca will forgive me someday," she whispered as she opened to a blank page. Then she began to write.

Kleina Kaffee Kuchen *(Little Coffee Cakes)*

1/2 cup shortening, half butter
3 cups flour, sifted
2 whole eggs
2 egg yolks
3 – 1/4 Tbsp sugar
3/4 cup cream
1/4 cup milk
1 yeast cake

Dissolve yeast cake in 1/4 cup of warm milk; add 2 Tbsp of flour and let stand in warm place to rise. Cream butter and sugar; add salt and eggs, beaten in one at a time. Add the sponge containing the yeast, the lukewarm cream, and sifted flour. Grease muffin pans with flour sifted over them. Fill pans to 2/3 full with batter. Set in warm place until dough rises to top of pans. Bake at 400 degrees for 30 minutes.

22

Friday night, Lindsay stood at the sink washing dishes from the fried chicken she'd made for supper. She couldn't stop her smile. She'd answered Matthew's letter last Saturday and already received another response from him this morning. This time, he didn't wait a few weeks to respond; he must've written her reply the day he'd received the letter. She planned to respond to him as soon as she'd finished her chores.

Trisha walked over to the sink, her walking cast thumping on the floor with each step, and deposited dirty utensils into the soapy water.

"You really shouldn't be helping me," Lindsay scolded. "You need to keep taking it easy."

"Are you kidding me?" Trisha said. "I've been taking it easy for too long. The doctor told me that I need to get up and walk with this cast, and I intend to do it. I'm just glad to get my rear out of the chair. In fact, you should take it easy. You've been my indentured servant for almost two months now. Go out with your friends tonight and have some fun."

Lindsay paused, considering the suggestion. She had the urge to write Matthew, but perhaps she could respond to his letter when she got home.

"What?" Trisha asked, leaning against the counter and studying Lindsay's expression. "What's on your mind?"

Lindsay wiped her hands on a dishtowel. "Vicki called me earlier and said that one of her friends is having a party out at Back Bay. And I was thinking that maybe—"

"You should go," Trisha said, gesturing toward the door. "Go freshen up. Frank can drop you off."

Lindsay hesitated. "I don't really know these people."

"You know Vicki." Trisha nudged her toward the door. "Get out of here and have some fun."

Lindsay changed into a fresh jumper and blouse and then styled her hair in a long braid that fell almost to the middle of her back. She reappeared in the den and found Frank sitting on the sofa.

"Would you mind dropping me off at a party over off Back Bay Crescent?"

"Sure," he said, standing. "Let me just find my keys."

Lindsay stepped over to the kitchen, where Trisha was wiping off the table. "How's your leg?"

"Fine," Trisha said. "I don't even care that it's throbbing. It's good to be upright." She smiled. "You look pretty. Have fun tonight."

"Thanks," Lindsay said. "I won't be too late."

"Don't rush," Trisha said. "Just enjoy yourself."

"I'm ready if you are," Frank said, holding up his keys.

Lindsay followed Frank to the truck, and they motored down Sandfiddler Road with the waves crashing out on the beach parallel to the road. Lindsay knew that she would miss the sound of the waves when she returned to Pennsylvania, but she also missed the sound of the hooves clip-clopping up the rock driveway, announcing the arrival of family or friends who were coming to visit. She missed baking with her aunts and cousins, and she missed the simplicity of her life there. She missed worshiping the Amish way with her family. She missed so much.

Frank steered down Rock Lane to Sand Bend Road, and then

negotiated the turn onto Little Island Road, heading toward Back Bay Crescent.

"Who lives out here?" he asked.

"I think it's a friend of Vicki's boyfriend," Lindsay said. "I've never been out here."

"Do you know if the parents will be home tonight?" he asked.

Lindsay shrugged. "I honestly don't know for sure."

Frank paused and she noticed that he looked concerned.

She directed him to a large, four-story beach house sitting on the bay. Cars, SUVs, and pick-up trucks were parked in the driveway and then lined up down the block. Frank stopped the Suburban parallel to the row of vehicles in the street, and rock music blared from inside the house.

"The Johnsons live here. Trisha and I know Derrick and Brenda and their son seems like a good kid," he said. "They're a nice couple. I'm sure that they're aware of the party."

"Okay." Lindsay turned to Frank and forced a smile despite the uneasy feeling creeping into her gut. "Thank you for the ride."

"Do you have your cell phone?" he asked.

She tapped her purse. "Yes, I do."

"Call me when you're ready to come home," he said. "You can stay as late as you want. I'll be up working on some reports tonight."

"Thank you," she said, grabbing the door handle. "Make sure Aunt Trisha doesn't overdo it."

He chuckled. "I doubt she'll listen to me. She's so happy to be up and walking that she may repaint the bedroom tonight."

Lindsay laughed as she climbed from the truck. Her smile faded as she approached the house. The music was even louder than she'd experienced at Vicki's pool party. She rapped on the door and waited for a response.

After knocking again, she pushed the door open and stepped into the foyer, finding scantily clad young people dancing in the middle of the den while others stood around talking, laughing, and drinking from bottles of beer. Another couple sat in the corner kissing and groping each other. The sight caused her to doubt Derrick and Brenda Johnson were aware of the party.

Feeling queasy, Lindsay turned to go. A strong hand grabbed her arm and spun her around.

"Lindsay," Heather said. "You made it!"

"Hi," Lindsay said, pushing a stray hair that had escaped her braid back from her shoulder. "I was looking for Vicki."

"She's out there." Heather jerked her thumb toward the back door leading to a large deck. "Come join us."

Lindsay glanced back at the front door, wishing she could leave, but she didn't want to disappoint Vicki. "Sure."

She reluctantly followed Heather to the back door, wincing at the booming rock music and dodging couples that were slow dancing and kissing. She couldn't help but think that Uncle Daniel would be appalled if he knew she was here with these wild young people.

She approached the door and felt a hand run down her back and stop at her rear. Gasping, she turned and found a young man grinning at her.

"You're cute in a parochial schoolgirl sort of way," he said, slurring the words.

"Don't touch me!" Lindsay shouted, swatting his hand away.

The boy laughed and moved away.

With her hands shaking, Lindsay stepped through the doorway to the large deck overlooking Back Bay. A crowd of young people stood in small groups talking, laughing, and drinking. Bottles of beer and wine coolers peppered the railing of the deck, and Lindsay's stomach twisted. She was certain that not all of the partygoers were twenty-one, and she didn't want to be a part of this. She needed to leave, especially after being groped by a drunk.

Vicki emerged from the crowd, her arms outstretched. "Lindsay!" She pulled Lindsay into a tight squeeze. "It's good to see you. I'm so glad you made it. Tonight is our last hurrah. I'm leaving for college on Monday."

"It's good to see you too." Lindsay attempted to force a smile, but it felt like a grimace.

Marci and Robin, the girls from the last party, joined the group and nodded hello to Lindsay before sipping wine coolers.

Brandon appeared behind Vicki and hooked his arm around her shoulder. "How are you, Lindsay? Can I get you something to drink?" He held up his beer. "How about a cold one?"

Lindsay hesitated. She suddenly remembered an excuse her mother once told her she would give at parties with her father's business associates. "Alcohol gives me bad headaches. What else do you have?"

He looked unconvinced. "Don't you want to live a little?"

"Yeah," Robin chimed in. "You don't have to be such a prude."

Marci snickered and they shared a private exchange of smiles.

Lindsay felt angry tears fill her eyes. "I'm not a prude," she said, her voice shaking with her growing embarrassment.

"That isn't nice," Vicki snapped, glaring at Marci and Robin. "She doesn't have to drink if she doesn't want to."

"Of course not," Marci said with a smirk. "Nerds don't drink."

"I'm not a nerd," Lindsay said. "It's my choice not to drink."

"Why don't you just go back to your Amish friends?" Marci asked, her words slurred.

"Yeah," Robin added, swaying slightly. "Then you can be a prude and nerd with your own kind."

Lindsay blanched at the sting of their hateful words but then suddenly felt a surge of confidence bubble from within her. "If not wanting to drink and/or wear skimpy clothes means I am a prude, then yes, I am!"

Marci's and Robin's mouths both gaped with surprise.

"You may call me a nerd, but I don't agree," Lindsay continued, her voice strong and unshaken as she spoke. "My values may not be your values, but I stand up for what I believe in. I'm true to myself and my Christian faith. You may think that you're cool because you drink alcohol and make fun of people like me, but I won't stand here and let you amuse yourself by bashing what I believe in." She turned to Vicki, who gave her a sympathetic expression. "I'm going to head home. Thank you for inviting me, but it's obvious I don't belong here."

Still feeling confident, Lindsay turned and headed for the door.

"Wait!" Vicki called. "Hang on a minute."

Lindsay rushed into the house and pushed through the crowd in the den on her way to the front door. She wrenched open the door and marched down the stairs.

"Wait!" Vicki called out again, yelling over the blare of the music. "Don't go! I want you to stay."

Lindsay reached the street and then stopped and faced Vicki, who stood on the stairs. "I don't feel welcome here. I'm going to head home now."

"Don't go," Vicki said, making her way down the stairs. "You're my friend. I wanted my friends to spend some time with me before I leave."

"It's obvious that this isn't the right place for me," Lindsay said, gesturing toward the house. "Your friends are so fixated on how I dress and the fact that I won't drink that they can't have a pleasant conversation with me. I'm tired of being judged by people who can't respect who I am."

"I'm sorry they treat you like that," Vicki said, touching Lindsay's arm. "You're my friend no matter how you dress or what you drink. You don't have to be like them. They're nasty and mean."

Lindsay shook her head. "I appreciate that, but I really don't belong here. In one way, your friends are right. I should go back to my Amish community. That's where I want to be."

"But you don't have to leave this second. I want to spend

time with you before I leave on Monday." Vicki frowned. "Please don't listen to them. I want you to stay. You can drink Coke and hang out with me and Brandon."

Lindsay's cell phone began to ring in her purse. She pulled it out and found Andrea's cell phone number on the display. She glanced up at Vicki. "I need to take this call."

"Will you come back in when you finish?" Vicki asked, looking hopeful.

Lindsay sighed. "Maybe."

"Okay." Vicki walked backward toward the front stairs. "I'm sorry that they were nasty to you."

Lindsay nodded. "Yeah. Me too."

"I'll see ya." Vicki jogged up the front steps, opened the front door, and disappeared into the house.

Lindsay pushed the send button and held the phone up to her ear. "Hello?"

"Lindsay?" Andrea asked, her voice sounding thick. "It's Andrea."

"Hi," Lindsay said, walking slowly down the street. "What's wrong?"

"I have bad news," Andrea said. "My aunt works at the nursing home and she just called me."

"Oh?" Lindsay's heart thumped in her chest. "What happened?"

"Mrs. Ephraim passed away earlier," Andrea said. "She had pneumonia."

Lindsay gasped. "No," she whispered as tears streamed down her hot cheeks. "Oh no."

"I'm so sorry," Andrea said. "I thought you'd want to know."

Lindsay couldn't stop the sobs from racking her body. She took a deep breath. "I have to go," she said before disconnecting the call.

Standing in the street, she wiped her tears while she stared back toward the house where the party continued on, the music blaring, and the loud voices carrying out over the water. She couldn't go back in there and face those people who judged her without knowing her.

She looked up toward the sky and thought of sweet Mrs. Ephraim, her friend who depended on her to bridge the language barrier between her and her caregivers. She wondered if her precious letter had made it into the hands of her daughter, Mary, and if Mary had considered responding. Perhaps Mary was so moved that she had planned to come visit her mother and mend the broken fences between them.

But now those fences would never be mended. Mrs. Ephraim was gone and so was Lindsay's purpose for volunteering at the nursing home. The joy Lindsay had found in Virginia Beach had died along with Mrs. Ephraim.

With fresh tears pouring from her eyes, Lindsay started down the street, heading back to Trisha's house. Her mind returned to thoughts of the party. Robin and Marci had made it clear—Lindsay should go back to Pennsylvania, and she knew they were right. Trisha was back on her feet, and Mrs. Ephraim was gone. She had nothing holding her here.

Crossing to Sandfiddler Road, Lindsay gazed out over to the waves crashing on the beach. She inhaled the salty air and thought of Katie's letter asking if she'd walked on the sand. She pulled off her sneakers and stepped onto the beach, enjoying the feel of the warm grains of sand seeping through her toes. She continued her journey toward Trisha's while walking along the water and inhaling the air. She found the loud cadence of the waves so much more refreshing than the obnoxious rock music she'd had to endure.

By the time she reached Trisha's house, she'd made up her mind—it was time for her to go home to her true joy, her life in Lancaster County.

She wiped the remainder of her tears from her cheeks as she climbed the stairs to the main level of Trisha's house. She found Frank and Trisha watching a movie in the den, sitting next to each other on the sofa. They both gave Lindsay a confused expression.

"What are you doing home so early?" Trisha's expression transformed from confusion to worry. "Have you been crying?"

Lindsay nodded as a lump swelled in her throat. "I left the party."

"Why?" Trisha asked. "What happened?"

"I didn't belong there." She let her sneakers drop to the floor.

"Did you walk home?" Frank asked.

"Yes. I wanted to walk to clear my head." Lindsay started toward her room.

"Lindsay, what happened?" Trisha called after her.

"I don't want to talk about it," Lindsay said as fresh tears trickled from her eyes.

"Wait a minute," Trisha called, hobbling toward her room. "Let's discuss this."

"Not now," Lindsay said, closing her door. "Please, I need some time alone."

"Wait a minute." Trisha pushed the door open. "I want to know what happened. You never should've left that party without calling us. That's why we got you the cell phone—to keep you safe."

"I'm fine, okay?" Lindsay said, sitting on the bed and wiping her tears. "Just leave me alone."

"No, I won't leave you alone," Trisha said, wagging a finger with emphasis. "I want to know what happened to you. It's my responsibility to take care of you while you're here, and I have a right to know what happened."

Lindsay felt her anger bubble up inside of herself again. "The party was awful," she began, almost spitting out the words. "They were all drinking and there were couples making out in front of everyone. Some drunk boy tried to grab my rear end, and I smacked his hand away."

Tricia gasped. "Oh no!"

"I was so appalled and uncomfortable," Lindsay continued. "When I refused to drink, two of Vicki's friends called me a nerd and a prude and told me to go back to my Amish family."

Trisha grimaced and stepped toward her. "I'm so sorry."

"I gave them a piece of my mind and told them that I stand up for what I believe in, and I don't consider myself a prude or a nerd. After I defended myself, I went outside because I knew I didn't belong there," Lindsay continued. "Vicki followed me and tried to get me to stay, but I just wanted to leave."

Trisha gingerly lowered herself onto the bed next to Lindsay and put her arm around her neck. "I'm sorry that they did that to you, but you never should've walked home."

"I felt like I had no choice," Lindsay said, staring down at her lap while her tears flowed. "I had to walk and clear my head."

"You should've called Frank. Do you know how dangerous it is to walk these narrow streets at night?" Trisha asked. "You could've been hit by a car."

"I only walked a block to the beach and then walked the rest of the way on the sand," Lindsay said.

"Still, it's not safe to walk alone at night. You never know if you might run into someone who likes to prey on pretty young girls," Trisha insisted.

Lindsay cleared her throat and looked Trisha. "Anyway, I haven't even told you the worst of it."

"What else?" Trisha pushed a stray lock of Lindsay's hair back behind her shoulder.

"My friend Andrea from church called my cell phone," Lindsay said. "She's the one who also volunteers at the nursing home."

"Oh?" Trisha asked.

"Mrs. Ephraim died today," Lindsay said, her voice breaking on the last word. She dissolved into uncontrollable sobs, and Trisha pulled her into her arms and rubbed her back while she cried.

"I'm so sorry, honey," Trisha said. "But you were there for her in her last days. You helped her contact her daughter, which means she died knowing that she'd made things right with her. You were a blessing to her, Lindsay. You should be proud that you helped make her last days here happy."

Lindsay held onto Trisha and closed her eyes, praying that Mrs. Ephraim was out of pain and resting in peace with Jesus.

"Would you like a drink?" Trisha asked, standing. "I'll get you some iced tea. I just brewed it." She headed for the door.

"Thanks." Lindsay snatched a tissue from the box by her bed and wiped her nose.

Trisha returned with a glass of iced tea. "Here you go. Would you like to come out to the family room and watch a movie with Frank and me?"

Lindsay shook her head. "No, thank you. I think I'm going to go to bed. I'm exhausted."

Trisha squeezed her hand. "Feel free to come join us if you change your mind."

"Thanks." Lindsay watched Trisha leave and then changed into her bedclothes. She watched the dark waves out the window for a few minutes and considered writing to Matthew. However, she was too emotionally distraught to form the words she wanted to express to him about her day. Instead, she curled up on her bed. Within a few minutes, she was asleep.

23

Late next morning, a knock sounded on Lindsay's door. She looked up from her Bible. "Come in," she said.

"Hi," Frank said while standing in the doorway and holding an envelope. "How are you doing?"

"I'm okay." Lindsay leaned back against the headboard. "I've been reading the Bible and thinking about Mrs. Ephraim."

He gave her a sympathetic expression. "I bet you are. I'm sorry you had a horrible time at the party and then you got the news about your friend."

"Thank you," she said, pushing back a lock of hair that fell into her face.

"Do you feel like going to the nursing home today?" he asked while leaning on the door frame.

"No," she said, running her fingers over the cover for her Bible. "I think it would be better just to stay home instead of looking into her empty room, you know?"

"Yeah." Frank nodded. "I can understand that." He held up the letter. "The mailman came early today. This is for you." He handed it to her.

"Thank you," Lindsay said.

"I'll give you some time alone, sweetie. Let me know if you need anything." Frank disappeared through the door, gently closing it behind him.

Lindsay opened the envelope, finding a letter from Katie.

Dear Lindsay,

I have to tell you some important news that may upset you. I feel that it's your right to know, even though I've been asked specifically not to tell you.

Aenti Rebecca is having complications with her pregnancy, and she could possibly lose the boppli. The doctor has put her on complete bed rest, and I'm going to get my parents' permission to move in with her in order to help her with the kinner and make certain she stays in bed.

Aenti Rebecca doesn't look well at all. She's very tired and pale. It breaks my heart to see her this way. The kinner also don't understand why their mamm can't play with them or hold them.

Aenti Rebecca asked me not to tell you how ill she is because she's worried you'll come home early out of obligation to her. She wants you to enjoy your time in Virginia and help Trisha as much as you can. I know we're supposed to obey our elders and respect their wishes. However, in this situation, I felt you would want to know.

Lindsay, I'm not suggesting that you should cut your trip short and come home, but I wanted you to know what's going on. Follow your heart and trust God to lead you in your decision about whether to stay in Virginia Beach or come home to Bird-in-Hand.

You're like a sister to me, and it breaks my heart to have to share this news with you. I know how much you love Aenti Rebecca and the kinner.

I'm thinking of you and praying for you.

In His Name,
Katie

A wave of panic washed over Lindsay as she finished reading the letter. She stood, jammed the letter in the pocket of her jumper, rushed from her room, and crossed the den to her shoes.

"Where are you going?" Trisha called from the kitchen.

"Out for a walk," Lindsay said, pulling on her sneakers. "I need some time alone."

"But where are you going?" Trisha asked, making her way into the den.

"I'm just going out to the water," Lindsay said, yanking the door open. "I'll be back soon."

She hurried through the door and ran down the stairs, not stopping until she hit the beach, which was like quicksand under her feet. She tried to run, but she was stuck, forced to move in slow motion.

She dropped to her knees in front of Trisha's deck, which overlooked the vast Atlantic Ocean. Lindsay pulled Katie's letter from her pocket and reread it, memorizing each word as fresh tears filled her eyes.

Rebecca needed Lindsay but was afraid to tell her. Reading between the lines, Lindsay knew what Katie was trying to say: It was time for Lindsay to come home.

Her work in Virginia was done.

Bird-in-Hand was where she belonged.

Lindsay jumped up and ran back to the house, hugging her arms to her chest.

Once in the house, Lindsay stood before Trisha and Frank in the den. "I have something important to tell you."

Frank flipped off the television, and Trisha looked concerned.

"I've made a decision." Lindsay took a deep breath. "It's time for me to go home." She held up the letter. "Katie wrote to tell me that *Aenti* Rebecca is having complications with her pregnancy and could possibly lose her baby. She's been restricted to complete bed rest."

"Oh no." Trisha cupped her hand to her mouth. "I'm so sorry to hear that."

"I feel like I'm needed back at home." Lindsay pointed toward Trisha's leg. "I think you're doing better now, and you can get around okay without much assistance."

"Oh yes," Trisha said. "I was going to tell you that you're welcome to stay, or you can leave as soon as you'd like."

"Thank you," Lindsay said. "I really appreciate all you've done for me. Thank you for helping me get my GED and for giving me the cell phone."

Trisha stood and hugged Lindsay. "Don't be silly, Lindsay. You don't need to thank us. You and your sister are the daughters we never had."

Frank stood and also hugged her. "And you got that GED all on your own."

"I enjoyed my time here," Lindsay said. "But I know that Rebecca needs me now. And I've realized that Lancaster is where I need to be and where I want to be. It's where I belong. I want to be Amish."

"I understand and I respect that decision," Trisha said. "Frank and I will also support you, no matter what you want to do. We love you."

"Thank you." Lindsay looked at Frank. "Could you see if there's a bus that leaves tomorrow morning?"

He sat on the sofa and opened his laptop. "Have a seat, and we'll check out the schedules."

Lindsay sat with him and they booked a ticket for her to leave in the early afternoon the next day.

Trisha stood over Frank and Lindsay while they confirmed the ticket. "Are you going to call Rebecca and let her know that you'll be home early on Monday?"

Lindsay considered the question. "No, I think I'll surprise her." She walked toward the kitchen. "I'm going to go arrange for a ride from the bus station and pack." She grabbed the phone from the cradle and then started down the hall toward her room.

"Do you need any help?" Trisha called.

"No, thank you." Lindsay pulled out Matthew's first letter from her dresser and glanced at his phone number written at the bottom. She wondered if Matthew would schedule a driver to pick her up at the bus station. It would be an added plus if he would come to the station to meet her as well.

She dialed the number, and after four rings, voicemail picked up.

"This is Matthew Glick," his voice said. "Please leave me a message."

Once the beep sounded, Lindsay took a deep breath. "Hi, Matthew," she said, her cheeks flushing with embarrassment. "This is Lindsay. I hope you're doing well. I need to talk to you as soon as possible. Please call me back." She rattled off her phone number and then hung up, hoping he would get the message soon.

She returned the phone to the cradle in the kitchen and then began packing her clothes. While she worked, she thought of Rebecca and sent up prayers for her. Although she was tempted to call and check on her, she didn't want to get Katie in trouble for sharing the news of Rebecca's condition. She would have to hold onto her faith that Rebecca would be just fine.

A little while later, a knock on the door frame drew her attention to the doorway, where Trisha stood grinning and holding up the phone.

"It's for you," Trisha said, handing her the phone. "It's a boy." She then leaned in close. "He sounds awfully cute."

Lindsay raised her eyebrows with curiosity as she lifted the phone. "Hello?"

"Lindsay?" A voice asked. "It's Matthew."

"Matthew," she said, sinking onto her desk chair. "Hi."

"*Wie geht's?*" he asked.

"I'm doing well," she said. "How are you?"

"Doing fine," he said. "I've enjoyed your letters."

"Yeah," she said. "Me too." She wished she wasn't so tongue-tied.

There was so much she wanted to say. An awkward silence passed between them for a few moments.

"I sort of got the impression from your message that you wanted to talk," he said. "It sounded urgent."

"Yes," Lindsay said, leaning back on the chair. "Do you have plans Monday morning?"

"I don't think so, other than work," he said, sounding confused. "Why do you ask?"

Lindsay smiled. It was so good to hear his warm, smooth voice. "Would you arrange for a ride and come to pick me up at the bus station in Lancaster around eight on Monday morning?"

"You're coming home?" His excitement emanated through the phone.

"Yes," she said.

"I can definitely have a car there for you," he said. "Is there a reason why you're coming home now? I had thought you were staying longer. Not that I want you to stay longer, but I'm kind of surprised."

"Trisha is doing much better," Lindsay said. "She's using a walking cast now, so I'm not really needed."

"That's *gut* to hear. I'm glad she's doing better."

Lindsay's eyes moved to Katie's letter sitting on her dresser. She wanted to tell him the truth, the whole truth, and she knew she could trust him. "There's more, though. I got a letter from Katie that made me realize I'm needed at home," she said, fighting back tears. "Katie told me that *Aenti* Rebecca's condition is getting worse, and I want to be there to help her."

"I didn't know that," he said. "I hope she's going to be okay." He paused for a minute. "That must be why Daniel has seemed so upset at work. He hasn't talked much to anyone, and he seems very preoccupied and stressed. He must be very worried."

"I'm worried too," she said, wiping a tear.

"Is she gravely ill?"

"She's pregnant and having complications," Lindsay said. "Katie mentioned that she could even lose the *boppli*."

"Oh no," he said.

"The doctor has put her on complete bed rest, and Katie is staying overnight at their house to help out. I should be the one caring for her and the *kinner*." Lindsay grabbed a tissue from the box next to her bed and wiped her nose and eyes.

"You'll be home Monday morning, *ya*? And then you can help out and take *gut* care of her and the *kinner*."

Lindsay smiled. "That's right." She gave him the details of her itinerary. "Now remember, it's a secret that I'm coming home. Don't tell Katie or anyone else, okay? And we have to keep Rebecca's condition a secret too."

"I promise I'll keep it all a secret—everything you've shared with me," he said. "And I'm glad that you told me."

She asked him how his sister and her family were doing, and he updated her on his family and the rest of their friends.

"I guess I should let you go," she said. "Are you doing chores this afternoon?"

"*Ya*," he said with a sigh. "I just came out here to feed the animals. I better get back to work. You have a safe trip."

"I will," she said. "I can't wait to see you and tell you about my adventures here."

"I look forward to it," he said. "Good-bye, *mei friend*."

"Good-bye, *mei friend*," she echoed before hanging up.

The following afternoon, Lindsay hugged Trisha and then hugged Frank while they stood in the parking lot at the bus station.

"Thank you for all you did to take care of me," Trisha said. "I couldn't have gotten through the past couple of months without you."

Lindsay kissed her cheek. "I enjoyed being here for you. Maybe my friends and I can come for a visit sometime."

"I would love that." Trisha hugged Lindsay again and then wiped a tear from her cheek. "I love you, Lindsay-girl."

"Love you too," Lindsay said. She turned to Frank. "You take good care of her."

He grinned and hugged her again. "Thank you. We enjoyed having you with us. Come back any time and bring your friends. We'll have a good time."

Lindsay nodded. "I know someone who would love to see the beach."

"You better go," Trisha said. "The bus is boarding."

Lindsay hugged them once more and then hoisted her purse and tote bag onto her shoulder. She climbed onto the bus and took a seat near the back.

Settling into her seat, she smoothed the skirt of her plain purple frock. She then checked her tote bag and found her prayer covering. Once she got closer to Lancaster, she would fix her bun and then put her covering back on her head, where it belonged.

She leaned back and took a deep cleansing breath. Closing her eyes, she said a prayer for Rebecca, the one she'd recited over and over last night before she fell asleep.

The bus engine rumbled and came to life and more passengers took their seats.

Glancing out the window, Lindsay smiled. It was good to visit the place of her birth for a short while, but it wasn't where she belonged. Tomorrow morning, she would return to her true home and the future waiting for her.

Zimmet Waffles *(Cinnamon Waffles)*

1/2 lb butter
3/4 cup sugar
2–1/2 tsp cinnamon
3 eggs
1 cup flour

Cream the butter and sugar; beat in eggs one at a time and add cinnamon. Work in flour making soft dough. Form into small balls. Place several in hot waffle iron, press down top, and bake until golden brown.

Discussion Questions

1. Throughout the book, Lindsay feels the pull of two worlds—her life in Lancaster County and her former life in Virginia Beach. By the end of the story, she decides that she belongs in Pennsylvania. If you were in her situation, which life would you have picked? Share with the group.
2. Rebecca is heartbroken when Lindsay decides to go to Virginia Beach to help Trisha heal from her accident. Although she wants Lindsay to stay in Bird-in-Hand, she lets her go, telling her to follow her heart. Take a walk in Rebecca's shoes. Would you have encouraged Lindsay to go to Virginia Beach? Why or why not?
3. Throughout the story, characters quote Psalm 41:3 (print out the verse). What does this verse mean to you?
4. Lindsay is frustrated by her sister's constant criticism of the choice she's made to not continue her education beyond eighth grade. Have you ever been criticized by a close family member for a choice you've made? If so, how did you handle the criticism? Share this with the group.
5. When Lindsay first arrives in Virginia Beach, she feels like a misfit. She notices people staring at her clothing and she can't relate to her former school friends who are excited to leave for college. Think of a time when you felt lost and alone. Where did you find your strength? What Bible verses would help with this?
6. Katie breaks a promise to Rebecca when she writes Lindsay and shares that Rebecca is suffering from complications

in her pregnancy. Have you ever felt obligated to break a promise even though you knew there could be negative repercussions for your actions? How did you handle this situation? Did it turn out as you'd hoped?

7. Elizabeth Kauffman recites Romans 5:3–4 (print out the verse). What does this verse mean to you? Share your thoughts with the group.
8. Which character can you identify with the most? Which character seemed to carry the most emotional stake in the story? Was it Lindsay, Rebecca, Katie, or even Jessica?
9. Print out the verse Hebrews 12:1–2. Discuss with the group what this verse means to you.
10. What did you know about the Amish before reading this book? What did you learn?

Acknowledgments

I'm so thankful for the people who shower me with their unending love and support, especially my mother, Lola Goebelbecker; my husband, Joe; my sons, Zac and Matt; my mother-in-law, Sharon; and my precious aunts, Trudy Janitz and Debbie Floyd.

I'm more grateful than words can express to my patient friends who critique for me—Sue McKlveen and Lauran Rodriguez. Thank you for always editing and proofing my books and offering your suggestions to improve the stories. Stacey Barbalace was integral in helping with the authentic Amish details in the story. Thank you for your help and your wonderful friendship!

Special thanks to my dear friend Kim Moity, who helped with the medical details in the book. I wish you much luck and success in your nursing career.

I'm very grateful to my special Amish friend who patiently answers my endless stream of questions. You're a blessing in my life.

Thank you to my wonderful church family at Morning Star Lutheran in Matthews, North Carolina, for your encouragement, prayers, love, and friendship. You all mean so much to my family and me.

To my agent, Mary Sue Seymour—I am grateful for your friendship, support, and guidance in my writing career. Thank you for all you do!

Thank you to my amazing editors—Sue Brower and Becky Philpott. I appreciate your guidance and friendship. I also would like to thank Alicia Mey for tirelessly working to promote my books. I'm grateful to each and every person at Zondervan who helped make this book a reality. I'm so blessed to be a part of the Zondervan family.

To my readers—thank you for choosing my books. As always, I appreciate the wonderful emails and your prayers for my family.

Thank You most of all to God for giving me the inspiration and the words to glorify You. I'm so grateful and humbled You've chosen this path for me.

Special thanks to Cathy and Dennis Zimmermann for their hospitality and research assistance in Lancaster County, Pennsylvania.

Cathy & Dennis Zimmermann, Innkeepers
The Creekside Inn
44 Leacock Road — PO Box 435
Paradise, PA 17562
Toll Free: (866) 604 – 2574
Local Phone: (717) 687 – 0333

The author and publisher gratefully acknowledge the following resource that was used to research information for this book:

C. Richard Beam, *Revised Pennsylvania German Dictionary* (Lancaster: Brooksire Publications, Inc., 1991).

Kauffman Amish Bakery Series

A Gift of Grace

A Novel

Amy Clipston

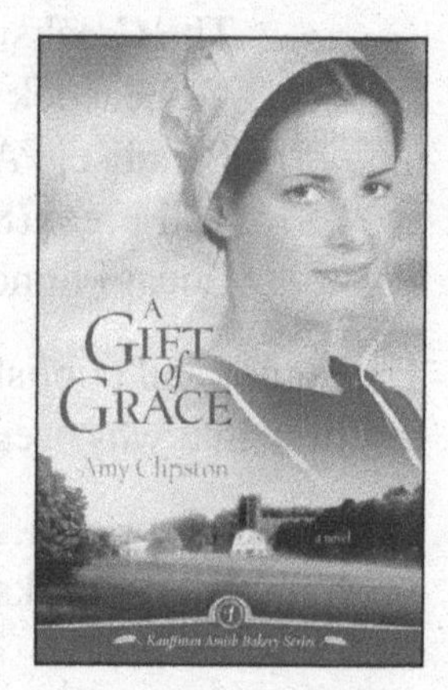

Rebecca Kauffman's tranquil Old Order Amish life is transformed when she suddenly has custody of her two teenage nieces after her English sister and brother-in-law are killed in an automobile accident. Instant motherhood, after years of unsuccessful attempts to conceive a child of her own, is both a joy and a heartache. Rebecca struggles to give the teenage girls the guidance they need as well as fulfill her duties to Daniel as an Amish wife.

Rebellious Jessica is resistant to Amish ways and constantly in trouble with the community. Younger sister Lindsay is caught in the middle, and the strain between Rebecca and Daniel mounts as Jessica's rebellion escalates. Instead of the beautiful family life she dreamed of creating for her nieces, Rebecca feels as if her world is being torn apart by two different cultures, leaving her to question her place in the Amish community, her marriage, and her faith in God.

Kauffman Amish Bakery Series
A Promise of Hope

A Novel

Amy Clipston

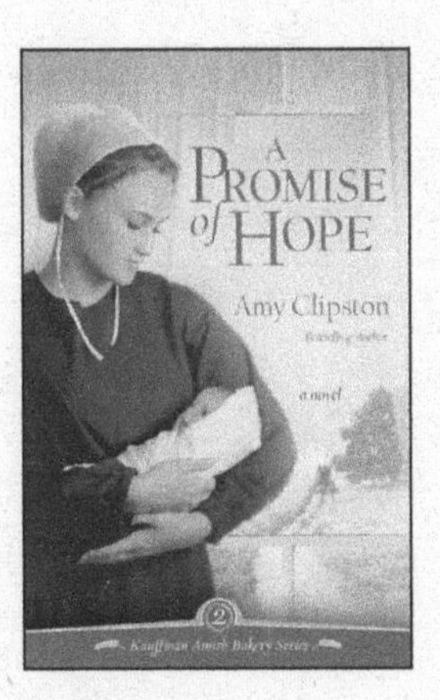

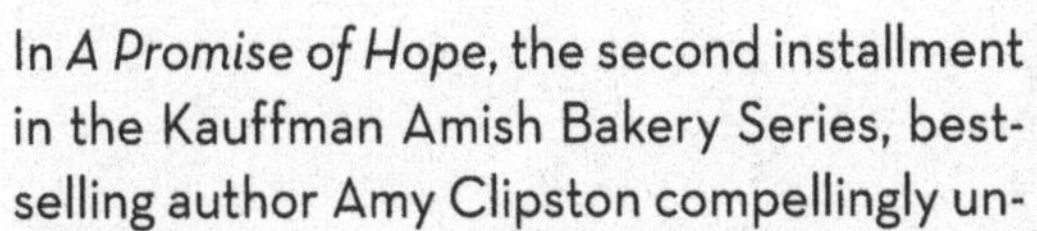

In *A Promise of Hope*, the second installment in the Kauffman Amish Bakery Series, bestselling author Amy Clipston compellingly unfolds the tensions, loves, and faith of the inhabitants of an Amish community and the family bakery that serves as an anchor point for the series.

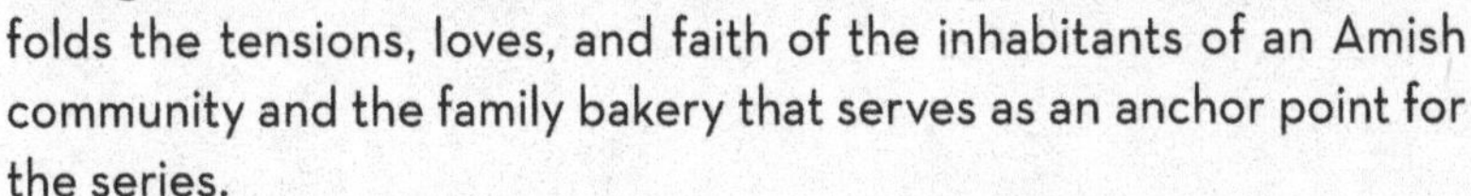

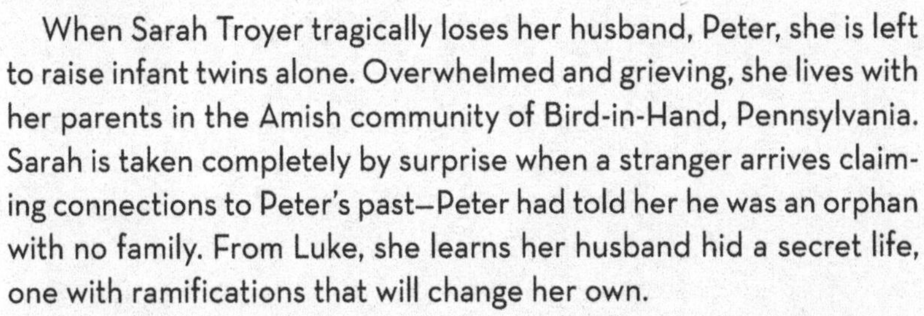

When Sarah Troyer tragically loses her husband, Peter, she is left to raise infant twins alone. Overwhelmed and grieving, she lives with her parents in the Amish community of Bird-in-Hand, Pennsylvania. Sarah is taken completely by surprise when a stranger arrives claiming connections to Peter's past—Peter had told her he was an orphan with no family. From Luke, she learns her husband hid a secret life, one with ramifications that will change her own.

Sarah's family, concerned for her and the future of her twins, encourages her to marry again. It should make sense ... but Sarah's heart says no. She feels trapped. Should she marry a man she doesn't love? Or discover if her growing interest in Luke can be trusted?

A Promise of Hope is filled with surprising twists that will grip you to the very last words.

Available in stores and online!

A Place of Peace

A Plain and Simple Christmas

Naomi's Gift

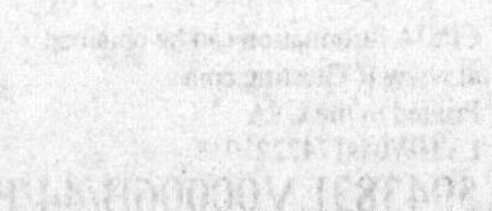

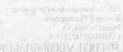

CPSIA information can be obtained
at www.ICGtesting.com
Printed in the USA
LVHW04s1742221018
594383LV00006B/44/P

9 780310 319962